A broken hallelujah

An Australian collection of heart stories

LINDA RUTH BROOKS

A copy of this book can be found in the National Library of Australia

ISBN: 978-0-9808161-5-0

Fiction/Short stories/Nursing/Romance/Humour/Drama

Author's website address:
http://www.lindaruthbrooks.com/

This book, and others by Linda Brooks, can be found at www.amazon.com, online retailers and bookstores.

A broken hallelujah is a work of fiction. Any similarity between the characters in this book and real people, living or dead, is coincidental.

I love thee to the level of everyday's
Most quiet need, by sun and candlelight.

I love thee with the passion put to use
In my old griefs, and with my childhood's faith.

'Sonnet 43'—Elizabeth Barrett Browning

Index

A broken hallelujah

Sue groaned inwardly. It would never do to groan aloud. The head sister might hear, and then she would make sure that whatever had caused your misery would be increased tenfold. Sue had seen her eat one of the new nurses, alive for mumbling about the patient allocation.

Sister Brandon had pounced on her with, 'Something wrong here, Nurse Janice Broadbent?'

Janice tended to take everything literally, and had mistaken this question to contain a caring sentiment. Wrong. She received a tirade worthy of a Roman emperor, and was then given the same difficult patient for five days in a row until he was discharged.

Mr John Lambton's name was on Sue's patient list. Drat. It wasn't that he was difficult. He was impossible. And he got away with it. He'd been in hospital for six weeks after being in a horrific car crash that killed his wife. John Lambton had every reason for the cloak of misery he carried, which made his care even harder.

He'd just been to surgery to have the pin and plate in his leg removed and returned with a cast. The head sister had attempted to deal with him, but her usual ferocity quailed. She retreated from the sheer power of the agony in his eyes.

Every day he refused to get up until after morning tea and then slumped in the chair. Nothing could induce him to leave his room. He systematically rejected television, radio and sympathy. With his leaden gaze fixed somewhere on the floor he spent the day in misery.

Sue's wasn't impressed. As the designated softie, she wondered what to do with this towering pillar of despair. She started out coaxing and explaining about moving his legs and avoiding thrombosis, then stopped when he crossed his arms rebelliously, his lips a thin tense line.

'That's just what you want, isn't it, you contrary man,' said Sue, 'that would settle things for you wouldn't it - a nice DVT that could break away, run into your head and kill you stone dead. Well....' She turned away, throwing his toiletries together and whipping the towel off the rail with a snap. 'It might not work, you know, you might end up only half dead, and then you would be a dense old vegetable of a thing, and your granddaughter will come and wipe the custard you dribble off your face.'

'When you go home you can kill yourself properly, but right here, right now, you are going to help me help you, you great lumbering obelisk of misery.'

'You're a strange little thing aren't you,' he said.

'Well, stop being selfish. You have three daughters, a son and a granddaughter. You've just been sitting here as if you have already departed this world and isolated them with your wallowing distance. You aren't the only one suffering - your oldest daughter is pregnant, and she doesn't need two babies. Your family doesn't need you to leave them too. Your wife would be ashamed of you.'

John's face crumpled. Long overdue tears fell in a cleansing torrent as his shoulders shook. Sue knelt in front of him, touched his arm, and handed him a handkerchief.

'Come on then, Lucretia Borgia, lead the way.'

'I was going to get you some pain relief first.'

'Good girl! Dope me up. I was wondering when you lot would

offer me some drugs. A man shouldn't have to have his body torn as well as his heart.'

So firm friends they became. He didn't stop talking all through the shower and the journey into the day room where he sat apart in a corner. Sue bargained with him for a few hours in the public lounge. He grumbled, but it was a paltry effort.

'You're a dreadful bossy boots, Lucretia,' he said.

The battle was over.

'That I am, but you're not alone.'

'Yeah, I know, I'm not bloody Robinson Crusoe.'

After three days off, Sue returned to the Orthopaedic Ward on an afternoon shift. She was eager to visit with John and see his progress. She'd only seen him briefly on arriving on duty. The hectic pace of the afternoon had been replaced with the calm of late evening as the staff finally finished discharging five post-op patients. Because it was Friday night there had been no new admissions for routine surgery. There would only be a new admission if there was an emergency.

Sue went cheerily into John's private room and was surprised to find his son Elliot lying on the bed with ankles crossed and hands folded indulgently behind his head. He turned his cool assessing gaze on her. Elliot was a senior nurse with a reputation for sharp-minded efficiency, and an irrepressible sense of fun. Most rumours about partying involved him, and he was never short of female company. She hated that she had noticed that, but Elliot Lambton was hard to ignore, and gave every indication that he knew it.

His slate grey eyes followed Sue around the room. The shower was running and Sue busied herself tidying up while she waited for John.

'So, you're Lucretia Borgia, shall I call you Lucy?'

'Not unless you want me to tyrannise you.'

'Are you always this prickly?'

'No, I'm making a special effort today.'

'For me?'

'Not really, I'm being democratically prickly to anyone rude enough to call me Lucretia Borgia.'

'My father does.'

'He has a license to be rude that expires at the end of the week. You don't.'

'So you're the Minister for Rude Licensing are you?'

'But of course, I thought you knew that.'

'Are you always this accommodating?'

'Only on days I'm not being prickly.'

'But you're being both today.'

'I have a license to change my mind, I'm a woman.'

'I noticed.'

Sue blushed with anger. Elliot unfolded his long legs and stood by the bed with his hands plunged deep into his faded jean pockets, as she snapped the crisp white sheets. He came to the other side of the bed and they worked in unison, making mitred corners and tucking rhythmically. Sue thanked him. Looking into his crinkled mocking eyes she saw warmth.

'I've offended you, I'm sorry. My sisters say I'm a shocking torment. It's just that you're so easy to tease.'

'Regular windup toy, that's me.'

He rumbled a spontaneous chuckle. 'At least you give as good as you get, that's rare.'

'Why thank you, kind sir, never serve a meal you won't sit down to yourself,' Sue mocked, giving him a fake curtsy.

Sue turned to hide a rush of colour. His intent gaze and soft attitude was melting her resistance. She didn't need attention from someone who clearly specialised in casual relationships. It was taking all her time to concentrate on work, much less embark on word plays with a handsome man. Oh dear, where had that thought come from.

A trolley clattered by in the hall outside.

The door swung open to reveal Maisie, the resident geriatric patient, who was using the linen trolley as a walker. Tiny and birdlike in her frailty, she entered the room just as John was coming out of the shower. The two eyed each other suspiciously.

Maisie stood her ground courageously. Straightening herself up to her full four feet ten inches she demanded, 'What's that man doing in my room! Mum will have our guts for garters!'

Just weeks shy of her one hundredth birthday; Maisie had a liberal dose of dementia. Normally she would have been on the Geriatric Ward, but she'd recently suffered a fractured shaft of the femur after a fall at home. Her equally ancient cat had wound itself around her legs when Maisie went to the toilet in the middle of the night. A pin and plate had been inserted surgically ten days ago, and she was beginning to become restless, wandering in and out of other patient's rooms.

Clad only in a thin pale blue nightie that was delicately embroidered, she regally eyed John.

'I'm waiting for an explanation,' she said.

Then she turned to Sue.

'Celia, I would like to see you outside. What are you doing in my room with a strange man? Mum and Dad have only just gone on holiday, and here you are. While the cat's away the mice will play, dreadful state of affairs.'

Stifling a smile, Sue went to Maisie's side.

'This isn't your room, Maisie. You're lost again. Where have you left your walking frame?'

'It's here,' Maisie said, thumping the linen trolley with a rheumy, blue-veined hand.

'Oh dear, Maisie.'

Maisie looked down at the overflowing linen trolley.

'Good grief, what have I done now? Oh bother!' Her pixie face collapsed into silent tears. Her mood was quick to change. Sue put her arm through hers as they teetered back to the hallway, and went in search of her walking frame.

'I am such a silly billy,' Maisie moaned.

'Nonsense. You've just had difficult surgery and you're doing well. You'll be back to normal in no time.'

'That's a load of rubbish you know, but thanks for trying to cheer up an old lady,' she said, as a smile lit up her face.

'*Oh Maisie*, where have you left your teeth?'

Twinkling a wicked eye, she tilted her head, 'Don't ask me. I've just had a difficult operation and I'm not normal yet.'

A flustered Janice arrived on the scene and remonstrated with Maisie about 'going missing'. Maisie began the story of her parents going on holiday. This story started Janice on her usual 'let's be rational' mode, 'Now Maisie, if you are 99, how old would your parents be?'

Maisie gave Janice a pitying glance, 'In my day it was rude to ask questions like that.'

Sue returned to John's room and apologised for Maisie's intrusion.

'She seems a bright old bird,' he said with a chuckle. So, he was noticing the world outside of himself. A good sign. They could hear Maisie's cackle as she remonstrated with Janice that she preferred to go back to 'that nice gentleman's room'.

'Not half bad looking was he?' She sighed. 'If only I was ten years younger.'

'I think you need to lose a bit more than ten years,' said Janice.

'What sort of a party pooper are you, anyway? You girls don't know how to live—don't wait until you are my age, Celia.'

'I'm not Celia,' said Janice, 'Celia's your dead sister.'

'Negative Nancy, you're a real wet blanket, that's what you are Celia.'

Janice groaned. Their voices became a murmur as they entered Maisie's room three doors down the hall.

John's eyes twinkled. 'Well, how about that, I have a centurion girlfriend, or is it a centogenarian? She's a great old broad isn't she? Made me feel life could be normal again for a few minutes.'

'Good grief, Dad, if you think that's normal you've been in here too long!'

'About that,' said John, 'I've been thinking.'

'Here we go,' moaned Elliot.

Sue left them to chat after inquiring if John was ready for his night time pain relief. Clearly he had something on his mind he wanted to discuss with his son.

When Sue returned to the nurses' station from admitting a 15 year old boy with a fractured ankle, Elliot was leaning on the nurses' station.

Janice came and threw herself dramatically into a chair.

'How can a 99 year old have more energy than a toddler!' she said, swiping Sue's pen out of her pocket.

'Use your own pen Janice, why are you nicking mine?'

'I don't have mine - Maisie decided that she has to write to Celia, to tell her there's a vicious rumour going around that she's dead. The only way I could get out of there was to set her up with writing paper in bed and let her go.'

'Yeah well, it's your own fault for trying to rationalise with a dementia patient,' said Sue.

Elliot reached into his pocket and handed Sue a pen.

'I want to ask you if you'd accompany Dad and me to the cemetery. The admin won't let him go without a nurse escort.'

'But you're senior to me.'

'You know what admin is like. It has to be official. Anyway, I have to drive. And Dad has asked for you.'

'Well, of course. I'll come.'

'We can't thank you enough for that. He will be more comfortable with you than any of the other nurses, sorry Janice, don't mean to offend.' He threw an apologetic glance at Janice.

'No offence taken Elliot,' she said, 'our Miss Softie saves us all the grief of the difficult ones. We love her for it - why hell, we use and abuse her dreadfully!'

Elliot helped his father into the large black car with careful regard for his father's leg. There was a huge basket of cut flowers in the back seat. Around each bunch was a roughly wrapped bundle of wet newspaper. Sue wondered if Elliot was responsible. She sat in the back with John who stared absently out of the tinted window.

They glided through the lunchtime traffic. The car purred; a negligible sound. John's hand absently sought the roses at his side. He caressed the petals of a white rose that was tinged with pink. Sue stilled the automatic response to stop him when his grip on the rose tightened, and blood trickled down his finger, as a thorn dug into his tender flesh. A solitary tear mirrored its path on his cheek.

When he brushed it aside, Sue took the handkerchief out of his shirt pocket, pressed it to the wound and left her hand grasping his. Elliot's eyes caught hers in the rear vision mirror. They shone with gratitude.

They left John to his silent musing as they drove through the outer suburban delis and furniture stores. The gentle thrum of the engine lulled Sue's thoughts. She only realised they had arrived at the cemetery when the tyres crunched on the gravel circular driveway.

Sue surfaced into alertness and assisted John into the wheelchair Elliot had waiting at the door. She carried the basket of flowers with its abundance of fragrance and colour. Elliot pushed the wheelchair, leading the way. His purposeful stride showed he'd visited often.

Judging by the car, John was obviously a man of some wealth. Sue expected to head to the area of the cemetery where the elaborate headstones stretched mutely to the sky, but Elliot headed towards the lawn section. He stopped at a simple white wooden cross that was surrounded by cut glass vases of all sizes, each of them overflowing with flowers in various degrees of decay. At the sight of these, John's head slumped and silent tears ran down the grooves of his cheeks.

Sue took the vases to the nearest garden tap and began to replenish the faded blooms in the vases after rinsing them. This gave father and son time together at the graveside.

After a while, she returned and placed the vases on the cement path near the grave. Elliot placed his hand under Sue's arm, including her as he pushed the chair towards the outdoor chapel, then gestured to a nearby bench. Sue nodded approval.

Elliot and Sue retreated to the fragrant arbour and sat on the lace wrought iron bench. John's lips moved as he bade farewell to the woman who had shared his life for three decades.

Mum always said...

Mum always said I acted before thinking. Oh crap! What had I done?

The man at my feet still had a pulse. Thank God for that! I felt sorry for a brief moment, then remembered the breaking of glass and the clunk of the lock when the front door had swung wide open several long minutes ago. Long enough for me to be out of bed, fully alert.

I had been sleep deprived, I reasoned. Working 24 hour shifts in the Beauville Lodge for handicapped boys will do that to you. It wasn't my fault. We were often wakened to some crisis or other and sprang into action, 'feet to the floor', ready to protect our charges.

Why was *I* feeling bad for goodness sake, I chastised myself. I'd just had a home invasion. The guy who ran through the door had brandished a crowbar, was wearing a balaclava and carrying a sack. It was just a shame I hadn't hit *him*, but had given the fellow that followed him a swift uppercut. My brother had shown me how.

'Smack your fist upwards into your attacker's jaw as if you're aiming for the ceiling, Emma. They'll be out like a light,' he said.

It had worked like a treat. The man at my feet was testament to that. However, I was experiencing strong doubts that my victim had anything to do with the lowlife who'd broken in, and taken off like greased lighting when I screamed.

For one thing the man on the floor was barefoot, and I was pretty sure no self-respecting burglar would go on a crime spree minus footwear.

My suspicions of his innocence were increased by the fact that he was bare-chested. It was also worrying that his thick head of mahogany hair was unruly, as if, like me, he had been wakened suddenly. He was wearing grey track pants and hadn't been carrying anything that I could see.

I quickly dialled 000, then wondered whether to say ambulance or police. I chose ambulance.

There was a soft murmur from the man. I approached him tentatively and knelt by his head again. He must be regaining consciousness. His pulse was regular. I looked at his broad chest. His breathing was steady. At least he hadn't hit the tile floor too hard. He'd slumped against the wrought iron baker's stand on the way down.

I would never forget the look of shocked surprise on his face; he'd probably never been hit by a woman. Come to think of it, I'd never hit a man. I was beginning to wish I hadn't hit this one. His masculine face was tanned by the sun, but there was nothing to hint at a criminal career. In his unconscious state he looked a little vulnerable, even with a 5 o'clock shadow. There were no ominous tattoos or piercings. In fact, he wouldn't have looked out of place in an advertisement for men's cologne.

Damn, where was that ambulance? There was still no movement from the man. Then the front room was flooded with light from the ambulance headlights. Thank God, they were here. They wasted no time assessing the man; I gave them a brief, slightly sanitised version of the home invasion.

'I didn't phone the police, though,' I muttered, feeling uncomfortable.

'So this guy broke into your house?' inquired the slim efficient ambulance officer, his pen poised.

'Well, not exactly,' I murmured. 'There was another guy who broke the lock and came in, then this man here came rushing in after him.'

The ambulance man flashed me a confused look. I squirmed.

'So you think they were working together?'

I shrugged, feeling less sure of myself by the second.

'Never mind, love, the police will sort it out. They'll be here in a jiffy.' A frisson of panic gripped me. I had visions of being hauled off in handcuffs. He flashed me a reassuring smile. I was not reassured. 'You work at that group home for teens don't you? Haven't we seen you there? We ambos get called out there a bit.'

His companion nodded.

'Yes, I do six 24 hour shifts a fortnight,' I said, relieved. At least they knew me, and weren't looking at me as if I was a violent maniac.

'So, you don't know this guy at all?'

'Nope. I've lived here for years and I don't think I've ever seen him,' I said. Then a memory stirred of a removal van in the street a few doors up on the other side.' Oh dear,' I added, suddenly feeling sick to my stomach.

The ambos lightly bandaged his head, taking care with his jaw that was fast swelling and where dark bruising was appearing. They applied a neck brace, then transferred him deftly onto the trolley using a spinal board.

'Well, we're ready to take him to Southwest General.'

'I'm coming with you.'

So just like that, I walked out the door in my hot pink pyjamas, grabbing my mobile phone as I went and my new snakeskin handbag. As I said, Mum always said I acted before I thought.

As they pushed the trolley up into the ambulance, the man fluttered charcoal eyelashes, opening his eyes briefly to reveal deep chocolate eyes that registered pure terror when he saw me, before passing out again.

'He was conscious for a second,' I informed the ambo who was driving, as I settled into the front seat. I didn't mention my casual observation that Mr Unconscious was heart-stoppingly handsome. That was hardly a relevant medical detail. Only *my* pulse was affected by that knowledge.

By the time they had begun assessing the mystery man in the Accident & Emergency Ward, I had woken my best friend, Victoria.

'Oh, for God's sake, Emma, it's 3 am! What have you done this time?' shrieked Victoria.

'I can't help it if trouble finds me. I've had an attempted burglary. They must have thought the house was empty. My car was at the mechanics being serviced. Never mind the whole story. Just tell me what you know about the new people who moved into the house opposite. It's an emergency.'

'It wasn't one of our properties, but I'll get hold of Lance from Banker Realty and get back to you.' Victoria was a real estate agent, as well as a miracle worker.

The attending Accident & Emergency doctor was Dr Jean Blake. I knew her well. She was a passionate fundraiser for the Home. We'd also met many times when I escorted teens for assessments, or stayed with them during hospital visits.

By the time Doctor Jean returned, I had the mystery man's name and a few sketchy details. He was Jake Melville, the CEO of *Computer Solutions*, and I had broken his jaw in two places. What I hadn't been able to find out was anything about his family. Victoria's friend Lance knew nothing about any possible next of kin.

'Well, Emma, they have to operate now,' Jean said, looking over her glasses and tapping her clipboard.

Two theatre attendants arrived with a trolley.

I burst into tears.

'It's all my fault,' I bawled miserably.

'Don't feel too bad. It's a mistake anyone could make.'

'Thanks for letting me stay with him, Jean.'

'Well you've been the only one able to find out his identity. And anyway ...' her eye twinkled, 'you're hardly a threat to society. You've got enough credibility here. Mind you, you'll never live down the 'right hook' jokes from the staff. Oh...' She turned to leave. '...*and the hot pink PJ's!*'

'Crap, I forgot.'

Jake likes to play Scrabble and is astonishingly good at it for a computer geek. He hates it when I call him that, but I've discovered that a man with a wired jaw has a greatly compromised ability to argue.

Yes, we're on a first name basis now.

The newspaper lapped up the story and I've become used to being the butt of jokes. 'Vigilante Homeowner Hits Wrong Guy', 'Crazed Martial Arts Homeowner Packs a Punch', 'Good Samaritan Out Cold', and my personal favourite 'CEO of Computer Solutions Hospitalised over Home Invasion Gone Wrong'. I liked this one as it almost made Jake sound as though he was in the wrong. Which, technically, he was—sort of anyway. I was most put out by being accused of having martial arts experience. I only went to a meeting once. I couldn't even twist myself into the starting position, and was told my 'war cry' wouldn't scare a mouse.

For a man who can't talk, Jake can certainly get his point across. Scribbles instructions like a Major General. Must drive his secretary nuts. Come to think of it, he did— drive her nuts, that is. She came to sit and take notes, but couldn't stand the ward and its smells because she's in the first trimester of pregnancy. So she left. Which is how I ended up doing his letters, making his business phone calls and rearranging his diary. Naturally.

Well, I was there anyway. Driven by deep compassion to help, and *not* by guilt, as Jake uncharitably claims. I was already feeding and shaving him, so what was a bit of extra work? The nurses were grateful as they were terminally busy. I didn't mind helping them out. When Jake was offered a bed at a ritzy private hospital with around-the-clock nurses to special him—the pigheaded man refused to go. I think he did it to punish me.

He addresses me as Ms New Sance, at the top of his notes to me.

'Ha ha, funny man,' I said. 'I'll give *you* nuisance.'

YOU ALREADY DID, he scribbled.

'I don't think capital letters are necessary. No wonder your secretary left,' I accused, muttering 'pompous prat' under my breath.

I HEARD THAT!

'If you keep using capital letters to intimidate me, I'm leaving too,' I threatened.

I'VE NEVER BEEN ASSAULTED, AND THEN INSULTED BY THE SAME WOMAN, scribbled His Royal Pain in the Arse.

'Oh, you usually keep those two separate, do you Sweet Cheeks? Clever you!'

I'VE SACKED PEOPLE FOR LESS THAN THIS.

'Really, so there's just you and Ms Morning Sickness left in the company then?' He got a triple word score then—on my word! 'You can't sack someone you don't pay, you cheapskate,' I retorted.

No-one pays someone who regularly threatens the boss.

'Well, good for you, you're beginning to learn not to use capitals. There might be hope for you yet, you ungrateful man. Now, about my wages. How about I threaten you *ir*regularly?'

You always have an answer for everything? He wrote.

Just then he reached out to grab my hand to stop me sneaking one of his scrabble tiles. I would have answered, but my fingers were having a strange reaction - neurologically speaking, of course, but the tingling stopped my brain, and inevitably my mouth. He grinned.

Bother, he knows he's affecting me and he's enjoying it, I

thought. If I blush now, I'll have to pretend to pick something off the floor. If only he'd let my hand go I'd be able to think.

This "helping him out deal" was getting complicated. I began to wonder why I was here, my motives were getting fuzzy. My hand was still buzzing after I left.

I might need a doctor myself. I told myself not to be daft; I was only there for completely innocent charitable reasons. But just in case, I cleaned the whole house so I wouldn't think about him, I mean the buzzing thing.

It's just lucky for him that my supervisor at the group home forced me to take stress leave, or I wouldn't have become so bored that I'd decided to take care of him at all. Just to make things clear I told him the next day he should pay me. That should get things back in the right direction.

You're on stress leave, you can't get paid twice! he scribbled.

'You should be nicer to someone on stress leave.'

They put you on stress leave because YOU WERE STRESSING THEM! he wrote furiously.

'Arrggh! *Again with the capitals!* It's the equivalent of yelling, you know. This is workplace harassment. And I was *not* 'stressing them'. They just got sick of the television camera crews in the front yard of the Home. Let's not lose sight of who's the victim here.'

Jake just rolled his eyes (did I mention gorgeous chocolate brown) and threw down the pen, after writing, *I give up.*

'So I win?' I crowed with glee, starting to pick up the Scrabble tiles.

NO!!!!! My score is double yours!

'Exclamation marks now—I should call a lawyer. Did I tell you I hate Scrabble?'

Only a thousand times already!

We were interrupted by Jake's specialist, who was a gentle Pakistani and also the surgeon who operated on him.

'So, Mr Melville, you are okay to go home. This pleases you, yes?'

Jake's beaming grin said it all.

'Your wife ... she is taking good care of you, no?' asked Dr Nahoo, smiling shyly at me.

'I'm not...' I began, but Jake's hand snaked out and trapped mine, stopping me mid-sentence. I looked down at our hands intertwined. I think I blushed, but I wouldn't admit that, not even under torture.

We're getting married as soon as I recover. Jake wrote.

Dr Nahoo read the note aloud. He was all gleaming smiles and congratulations. Enthusiastically shaking our hands, he called the staff in. They became excited, saying how wonderful it was. Fate, they'd seen it coming. I hadn't, or had I?

'So, Jake Melville, does this mean I'm relegated to playing Scrabble for the rest of my life?' I asked, when the staff had left.

Unless you can think of more interesting games.

'Anyone could think of more interesting things to do than Scrabble,' I said, as he pulled me towards him.

I wondered briefly how a man could melt you with a kiss when his jaw was wired.

They didn't find the burglar, which is just as well. It would be highly inappropriate to thank someone who had intended to rob you blind.

Fear is a diligent master

The hospital looked like a monument to a bygone era. Northside Private nestled in bush land in a quiet outer suburb of the city. It resembled the gracious stately homes of the Deep South in America. Built early in the 20th Century it possessed the grandeur and elegance reminiscent of the classic style portrayed in *'The Great Gatsby'* and *'Gone with the Wind'*.

An essence of charm permeated the three-storey building, from the corridors, where white veiled sisters sailed serenely past, with heels clicking efficiently on the highly polished oak floors, to the vast verandas that faced north. The large windows captured the sun's warm rays from pale rosy dawn until vermillion sunsets ruled the sky. The ornate cornices reflected the philosophy of tranquillity and restoration, because this hospital was not only for those ailing physically, but for those wearied from the burdens of life.

It was long before Government health-funded scrutiny demanded a better diagnosis other than 'rest'. The hospital was also a sanitarium where holistic health and preventative medicine were espoused.

On our arrival at the hospital we were given shapeless blue uniforms, and like all the hospital novices before us, we were called 'blue bags'. We were to wear these uniforms for the first three months, perhaps to warn the world of our ignorant status.

To add to this humiliation, after we had been fastidiously measured for them, by some strange intervention of fate our uniforms arrived a few sizes too big. At least all the girls' uniforms, that is. By some equally mysterious quirk, the boys' uniforms fitted perfectly.

One of the girls left in the first few days. Her uniforms were smaller than mine so I managed to swap mine with hers. She handed my misfits in when she left. Even though I wasn't into the trend of hair-teasing and heavy make-up that was popular in the Seventies, I was extremely self-conscious when it came to clothing. I'd been making my own clothes for years and was appalled by anything remotely ill-fitting. We looked tragic enough announcing our initiate state in our blue uniforms when everyone else wore white, without walking around in something that could have fitted another whole person in it.

Our first six weeks would consist of Study Block. We would be kept away from the action, until we had learned a thing or two. Along with my packed suitcase and my books, I brought a heavy dose of compulsion, but it didn't feel like a burden. It was the fire and the light that drove me. The passion that enchanted me. I was terrified to be in a new place, but thrilled to be facing new horizons of learning.

Until I began. And then it was *'oh dear God this'* and *'oh dear God that'*. I had no idea of what I was taking on. Not long after arriving I discovered, contrary to the old idiom, ignorance was definitely not bliss. The lofty idealism of my new calling lagged in the dust.

I should have been prepared for life in Science class. However, our effusive and outgoing science teacher mysteriously ran out of time, and the Biology curriculum was covered with a hasty 'Just read the text book'. The poor man slumped into his chair with his head down. His fingers raked his long black beard while the tension slowly drained from his lanky frame. I am sure he muttered grateful thanks to the Almighty that he had survived another plague of rambunctious teenagers, and bypassed the Anatomy curriculum with its inherent snorts, giggles and questions.

Mum espoused the philosophy we would learn all things in life, by any means other than her taking on the difficult task of explaining anything more difficult than how much salt to add to scones. This set me up for the most embarrassing experiences of my young life.

It had been bad enough when I had been naïve and innocent at high school, when I was invited into the inner sanctum of the 'cool kids' to eat lunch. Much of the conversation went over my head and there was much sniggering over my innocence. So, along with walking away, I learned to bluff. This talent would be most useful in my new life. Unfortunately, bluffing involved quite a deal of 'shutting up', which was never one of my strong suits. My ignorance was sure to be exposed. After all, nurse training was a long way from high school bench conversations that could be avoided.

Anatomy classes were confronting enough, but then we began studying Surgical Procedures. We girls began fainting. One after another, down we went. One of the male nurses sang, 'Another One Bites the Dust', as some poor girl was dragged out into the hall. There was usually the added humiliation of the "blue bag" ending up around her waist, leaving her knickers showing. We fought hard, but we fell. Determined not to succumb, when I felt lightheaded I posed a pensive face, and put my fingers in my ears. I hoped this action would go undetected under my long thick hair.

I remember an exuberant doctor telling us about operating in bush theatres in rat-infested, poverty-ridden countries. They didn't have suction equipment to remove blood, and had to scoop it out with their hands and throw it on the dirt floor.

If I had known any chants I would have used them, but I just kept repeating a panicked '*I can't hear you, I can't hear you!*' in my head to keep from going down. I'd chosen to sit by the window. While gulping great gasps of air, I thought how far I was from the door. If I fainted over there, by the time they dragged me out, my 'blue bag' would be wrapped around my head like a turban. Our Surgery doctor seemed to delight in his ability to terrify us into fainting. He hadn't done his job unless at least one of us was out cold by the time he finished class.

'Simple syncope,' he diagnosed concisely as someone went down.

It was the end of January and the Australian sun was at its zenith. The cloying heat oppressed us and sank into our skulls. The afternoon sun in the west glared mercilessly through row upon row of windows into our classroom and drenched us with fatigue. Two of the boys were asleep; one with his head on the desk snoring. We had been in our first study block for two weeks and the shine had gone off the original excitement of our new lives.

Our nervous anticipation had dwindled into monotonous dullness. There was no fainting or diversion on that day. We were in the middle of anatomy class and instead of revelling in the novelty of our new careers, we were enduring the seemingly endless afternoon in the stultifying heat.

Summer was retreating in a triumphant blaze. Too tired for restlessness, the only movement among us was the occasional desultory glance at the clock on the wall. A plain, no nonsense clock, suitable for classrooms of bored students; and on that day it was an extremely slow clock.

We sighed collectively. Our vigorous lecturer gave up his enthusiastic slapping of the anatomy chart, where he was showing the various muscle groups, to eye us all with resigned frustration. His mouth turned down with reluctant exasperation. He walked to the desk of the boy who was snoring, opened his mouth to utter some reproof, and then closed it.

The dull whirr of the overhead fans broke the silence. There

would be no tirade. This wasn't high school. We wanted to be here—
we had hoped and dreamed to come. We wrote applications, sent
essays on our heart's desires. We added references, and then waited
for the post to bring us the good news. We were the chosen. But
we'd had enough.

'Go on outside, the lot of you. Drink lots of water, walk around
the building. *And Mr Williams, you can stop snoring,* and pull the
shades down! If you're not back in fifteen minutes I'll take ten
marks off your next assignment. Now get moving, and come back
here looking alive, instead of like occupants of the morgue!'

'It'd be cooler in the morgue, sir,' said Mr Williams, staring
certain death in the teeth.

The initiate & the tyrant

Why did I ever think I could be a nurse? What maggot did I have in my brain that had made me think I could do this? What new miseries would face me day after day? How would I endure? Would I ever lose this feeling of terror?

I am standing in the Nurses Station on Surgical II and I have managed to appear to be very industrious on my first day on the ward. I've spent several hours bustling and tweaking things without actually having any contact with a real live patient. But my time is up.

The Ward Nurse, Jean, who is a seasoned second year and a lovely human being, is standing in front of me and requesting me to answer a bell. My agony is evident to her; any bluff I used in high school has been left behind

The 'real world' I hungered for is just beyond me down the corridor where a buzzer has heralded that someone needs me to be what I came here to become. I can procrastinate no longer. I am a nurse.

I am a nervous wreck.

I opened the door and stepped wide eyed and trembling into the room. The elderly woman in the room grasped the monkey bar firmly in front of her. She had a quiet, firm voice that reassured me this was an everyday event in an everyday world and not the catastrophe I feared. Her request was simple; a bedpan. Surely I could handle this.

I headed anxiously to the pan room. Jean smiled indulgently at my nervousness, perhaps remembering her own first day on the ward.

I grabbed a metal pan and scuttled triumphantly back to 3A, only to have the elderly rotund patient, Mrs Clyde, inform me that I'd brought the wrong type of pan. She required the blue plastic 'slipper' pan, thank you very much. My already fragile confidence plummeted. I should have asked. I am useless. I returned with the slipper pan and gingerly lifted the sheet back to help her onto it.

Oh dear God, she had a leg missing! Trying to hide my horror, I attempted to position the pan and was quickly dismissed quietly and tolerantly as Mrs Clyde grabbed the pan herself and, raising her stump and ample buttocks, shoved the pan expertly into position with a harrumph of satisfaction.

'You're new, aren't you? Blue bag are ya? You look twelve years old. You girls get younger every year. Skin like an angel,' she said gently as she touched my face with a rueful soft expression. 'You're too pretty to be a nurse. Hard life for a young girl. Never mind, love, you'll get used to it. You'll do alright, you will.' Apparently she had no need for my responses because she ended this ramble with, 'I'll be ok love, I'll give you a tingle when I'm done. Might need a while. Number two, you know.'

There were three of us on that ward who were 'blue bags'. Joy was the chirrupy mainstay of our trio. Ruth and I were terrified at every turn. It didn't help our anxiety that our ward sister was the notorious sister Melody Reid. She was renowned for her ability to reduce the hardiest nurse to a wobbling crying mess. Ruth and I were no exceptions in our dread of incurring her ire. Joy was entirely different. 'Barks worse than her bite, but for God's sake don't let anyone hear you say it.' The rest of us were unconvinced.

After I had finished with Mrs Clyde, I went in search of Ruth. I hardly had any triumph to share with her as Mrs Clyde had dismissed me.

'Just hand me the loo paper love, I can do for m'self. It's a sad day when ya can't wipe yer own bum.' She chuckled. 'I'll find me bum for a few years yet I reckon. Just leave the roll near me so I can reach it m'self next time.' she saw my crestfallen anxious face. 'Never mind, love, you'll feel like you've been doing it all your life in no time at all.'

I found Ruth in the Dirty Utility Room in precisely the same state of panic that I was. She was conducting the weekly inventory of the Dirty Utility Room and was half way through counting the stock in the large steel cupboard. I recognised the look of alarm in her brown expressive eyes instantly as it mirrored my own trepidation. She had a sweet and delightful nature and had applied herself to this new task with terrified zeal.

I stopped to help, or at least join the panic. I didn't know any more than her and was just as daunted by the task but felt I could at least supply moral support. In truth I was little help at all. We were counting the metal bowls and kidney dishes, pans, enema trays and other instruments. The only problem we had was the fact that we had no idea which name applied to some of the utensils.

We bungled along but were completely stymied when we came to the item on the list titled Galley Pots. We couldn't begin to imagine just what galley pots were and searched high and low. We decided that galley sounded like something large and we stuck our heads in every shelf of the large cupboard and pulled everything out and discussed and speculated on it.

We fastidiously ploughed our way through our dog eared pocket sized Baileys Nurses Dictionaries. None of us were ever without our Baileys as Sister Reid was fond of cornering unsuspecting trainees at any time or place and firing a barrage of complicated questions regardless of whether they related to your applicable knowledge level or that of a seasoned consultant surgeon. This particular book proved of no help as it had few illustrations, and they only depicted the more hideous diseases and nothing as mundane as a metal bowl.

Ruth began to cry and I was on the verge of joining her when Joy came to our rescue. Joy was no more enlightened than either of us about the nature of galley pots but she had the 'devil may care' attitude that was lacking in us.

'Oh, s'alright, just tick it off. Sister Reid will never check the thing. She isn't going to come in here and spend her precious time checking every bally thing on that stupid list. Just tick it and say 'Yes sister' to anything she asks.'

She finished her bold speech and saw our eyes widen in astonishment.

'Oh, give it here,' she said confidently as she took the Masonite clipboard that held the list and proceeded to tick the remaining ten items with a 'Yes, of course we have those, yes, that's there, yes, yes, all accounted for, all done.'

Ruth and I looked at her with awe; never had we witnessed such courage. Never had we faced such certain doom. With ill-concealed dread and faces as guilty as sin itself, we followed her confident steps out of the Utility Room for the usual interrogation with Sister Reid. Ruth and I stood behind Joy as she gave Sister Reid the most convincing 'Yes, Sister, No, Sister, all finished sister' while our hearts stood still. Sister Reid dismissed us to go home and we escaped her clutches giddy with success. We later learned that galley pots were the smallest bloody things in the cupboard and were tiny metal bowls only about two inches across. To this day I can't look at one without wanting to hurl it across the room.

As we left the ward Ruth and I began to breathe normally again. Joy had given us the crucial life-lesson that there were more important things to lose your appetite over than a few metal bowls.

Some of the older, more experienced nurses sailed serenely

around Sister Reid and calmly dealt with her tyranny, but there were none that achieved it with the accidental panache Joy did.

Sister Reid often kept us late.

'For no other reason than to show us who's boss,' said Joy.

One day when we were well overdue to leave work, Sister Reid told Joy and me that we were not leaving the ward until we had arranged all the flowers into vases. The nurses' station desk seemed covered in flowers. I was appalled and saw a tense hour of perfectionist floral-arrangement ahead of us.

Joy had no such plans. She picked up the large bunches of flowers and plonked them unceremoniously into two crystal vases that Sister Reid had positioned on the desk.

'I didn't come here to learn to arrange flowers, Sister. If I'd wanted to arrange flowers I would have applied at the florist downstairs, but I doubt if they would have me because I don't have the first idea.'

Having said that, Joy turned on her heel and headed for the Fire Stair Exit. I would have followed her into heaven or hell after that. I stole one fleeting glance at Sister Reid as I slunk after Joy and was amazed to see the trace of a smile lurking at the corner of her usually severe thin lips.

I learned to lose my fear of her. She was a marvellous sister, fastidious and exacting. Even though she was not free with praise for even the best of us, she gave us taciturn, but genuine respect when we earned it. I found a place of comfort with her because she had a routine of firing questions at us before the morning report. She was fast, furious and relentless. Always one to enjoy reading any encyclopaedia I relished the challenge of this exercise. Even though she had many reasons to roll her eyes over me she never caught me out with her rapid-fire questions.

We nurses were like warring compatriots with her. Circling and sparring. Only on the same side of the war - the war she was waging to make the best of us.

One day I arrived late for work with my hat in its usual slightly tilted status - for no effort of mine would produce the pristine elegance of the other girls. But Sister Reid's glare conveyed that something else was amiss. With an economy of movement she made a simple gesture at my uniform. Oh dear, it was a cardinal sin to carry a meal tray wearing a cleaning gown. I hastily removed the gown with a truly penitent, 'Oh dear, sorry Sister. Won't happen again, Sister.'

The corners of her mouth twitched. She was exercising great self-control. She again gestured at the front of my uniform. I saw she was in danger of breaking into the side-splitting laughter of which we knew she was occasionally capable. I looked where she was pointing.

I had my name badge perfectly placed. Upside down.

She walked away, a tell-tale shudder shaking her shoulders. She could never again muster full-blown ire to bring down fire on me. That was the day I knew I had won her over.

A dish best served cold

Sometimes life sends a moment that seems so perfect that even the most hardened sceptic could begin to believe in fate. Anna had one such day soon after transferring to General Surgical in her second year of nurse training.

One languid afternoon she arrived to a casual atmosphere on the ward for the evening shift. The regular morning Charge Sister was ill, and even though her replacement was a little frayed around the edges, she was efficient and the ward was running well when the afternoon staff arrived. It boded well for a good shift.

Anna checked the bed list and began to write the relevant patient information for the shift. Then her eyes fell on a familiar name on the afternoon admission list.

Miss Avery Cuttingham. It couldn't be! Not the teacher - the torturer of her middle Primary School days. *Surely not.* But it was an unusual name.

The evening shift was shaping up to be unusually slow. There were very few admissions. Evening shifts were usually more relaxed as showering and theatre preparations were routinely attended in the mornings.

Most of the nurses' time would be taken up with medications, taking observations, attending to toileting and settling patients for the night. Alice, the Ward Nurse was dedicated but panicked easily, and buzzed around the ward in a constant flurry of activity. She wouldn't trouble the nurses. They'd been working together for some weeks and were accustomed to working harmoniously in a fairly informal way, so were confident of a good shift, with little supervision needed.

Anna had to know if it was her old teacher. She went to the room. It was a luxurious, private room with an ensuite. There was a small, grey-haired woman staring out of the high clear windows at a cloudless sky. She turned as Anna entered the room. Her voice was quiet, placatory, and respectful, but this was definitely the teacher who had constantly rapped the steel ruler across Anna's tender knuckles just over a decade ago.

The pupils used to claim her feet actually left the ground as she raised the dreaded steel ruler high in the air, and brought it down on her unsuspecting victims. She was a stealthy as a sniper.

Miss Cuttingham made them balance on small chairs on tip-toes with their heads jammed in the corner of the room. She tore unsatisfactory pages out of workbooks as she rampaged up and down the kingdom of her classroom. She made students go without lunch. She called the class's attention to the 'dummies', the 'lazy' and the 'indifferent'.

She was without a doubt the cruellest teacher Anna had ever known.

But now as she faced Anna, she was all genteel charm. She was transparently eager to please. She was 'lost in this place'. She deferred to Anna. A smile that was false, but determined was pasted on her face. She was in Anna's world now. It was 'Nurse Dear this' and 'Nurse Dear that'. She looked precisely as Anna last remembered her, even down to the nylon full-skirted dress. With a shock, Anna realised the old woman hadn't recognised her.

Oh well, it has been ten years, she thought.

Miss Cuttingham stood quietly, her hands delicately folded together in front of her in hesitant submission.

'Just what do you need me to do, Nurse Dear? I am at your *complete* disposal. This is all new to me, you see. I have seldom been ill. I have had a very fortunate life, you know.' A condescending smile followed, triggering a long lost memory. 'You wouldn't think it to see me now, but I was once quite a physically strong woman.'

'You don't say,' Anna muttered, teeth clenched.

'What is your name, dear?' the old woman enquired politely, 'Although I can't promise to remember it. I am a little forgetful these days. I'm sorry to ask dear, but I can't read your badge without my classes.'

'My name is Sarah,' Anna said sweetly, 'Sarah Bernhardt.' She turned and unobtrusively removed her name badge, slipping it into her top pocket.

'What a lovely name, dear,' Miss Cuttingham purred. 'Now, what can I do to make your job easier? I don't want to be any trouble. I have *never* been one to cause any fuss.' The words tripped over her lying tongue.

Anna was at the point of mercy or revenge.

She chatted about the layout of the room, the admission process and showed Miss Cuttingham where everything was and how to use it. Anna told her about taking her observations; blood pressure, pulse, temperature and collecting a urine sample for testing. Miss Cuttingham would need to be weighed on the large set of scales in the main bathroom.

Miss Cuttingham followed like a lamb. On arriving at the bathroom, Anna showed her the huge scales and told her to stand on them very carefully, explaining the importance of an accurate measurement, and for that she would need to be naked. The anaesthetists were very fussy about these things.

Anna told her the scales were finely tuned, and electronically sensitive, so she must stand perfectly still. Because of their delicate calibration it might take a little while to get an accurate reading. Anna would pop out for a minute to collect some paperwork.

Anna left.

She didn't go back.

She had no idea how long the old woman stood on those dodgy old scales, but later the Head Nurse was heard to comment at handover to the next shift that the new lady was as 'batty as a fruit cake', because she'd been found after lights out in the main patient bathroom at the wrong end of the ward, standing naked on the scales. She had informed them that 'Sarah Bernhardt had told her to stay there.'

'Good grief,' Anna said, 'Silly old bat!'

And that was how the rather proper, but only slightly forgetful, Miss Cuttingham earned the reputation for an alarming, although entirely undeserved state of dementia.

But that is just between you and me.

The curious incident of the dyed dog

Even in the tiny rural haven of Crawley Creek, far from the evils of the city, the townsfolk were not free from racial tension. Although, it could hardly be rated as tension. It revolved around the only dark-skinned man in the neighbourhood, in a rather apathetic and detached manner.

It was one-sided tension, because the recipient was so mild mannered and good natured he never knew he was the object of pitying glances, and whispers traded behind dish washer hands.

It hardly even seemed to be the colour of his skin that was an irritant to the neighbours. The pious concern seemed to exist because he 'refused' to act like a black man. Or more correctly, how the neighbours thought a black man should act.

He was more the colour of warm caramel and had laughing friendly eyes. Of Indian descent, he had no more affiliation to his country of genetic origin, than Mrs McClare had for Scotland, from where her ancestors hailed.

Perhaps the townsfolk would have liked him to be more exotic, but he was blandly Australian. He had no accent at all, and no concept of himself other than being Australian. He was nonplussed when people asked where he was from. 'Here, of course,' he said.

His colour was incidental and afforded him neither creed nor discomfort. He simply shrugged his shoulders when anyone called him a 'pakky'.

Mrs McClare lived with her husband and two daughters three doors down from the Sinta family. Her youngest daughter Sheila, who consistently favoured the underdog, and one summer caused more ructions trying to get to the bottom of any prejudices about him, than if she'd left well enough alone.

It all happened when Sheila was eleven, and her older sister, Lucy, was thirteen.

Sheila was always going through stages. And not just the usual tantrum throwing, or curious stage, or believing in Santa phase, although she tackled these with breathless abandon.

She also embraced the kind of phases where she lived and breathed another reality. She was hopelessly affected by any new book she was reading, and immersed herself in the times and dialogue of the characters. Her family and friends teased her mercilessly when she mimicked the language of her favourite author, or babbled for weeks in the vein of her latest political allegiance.

When she read Charles Dickens, life became dreary, every task was drudgery, and she waffled on about filial devotion and soul-scarring humbug. The rest of the family alternated between being her social inferiors, and her better selves, but they were never bored. Her brother David, wound his finger around his ear in the way children did to signify madness in others, and escaped her loving clutches.

When she read Animal Farm, her mother and father were 'fascists'. But it was when she described her parents' argument at breakfast as an 'uneasy alliance' that even Jim McClare was compelled to say, 'Oh, do shut up, Sheila!'

Sheila was always embarrassing herself, and never more so than when she developed a Scottish accent. Her class had a Scotsman who was the relieving Maths teacher. She caused great offence with her 'ochs' 'noos' and 'ayes' - offense the poor man was quick to point out before sending her to the headmaster.

It was only when she was subjected to a heated meeting with the Headmaster that Sheila realised what she was doing. She hadn't intended any harm, and was mortified when the Scotsman accused her of being 'a heartless lassie with a waspish tongue'.

Like all the women in the neighbourhood, Mrs McClare was fond of leaning over the back fence to chat. Not to gossip mind you, she couldn't tolerate *that kind of thing*. But, with her apron tied sensibly around her ample girth -announcing her work ethic, and her hair in metal butterfly-clips, she felt morally obligated to keep up good relations with the neighbours.

On a blistering summer day in January she was at her insightful best, as she and Mrs Rudge picked the dry bones of the other residents in the street, while she fended off the ever-present flies with a frond of bracken fern she'd plucked from the edge of the fence line.

'Can you believe that man,' she said as she kept a desultory eye on the nearly dry clothes flapping on the Hills hoist. 'Bad enough to be cursed with black skin, but to carry on like that! Really, I ask you!'

Sheila and Lucy were in the precarious tree house David had built in the flourishing mulberry tree. Their mother's voice carried stridently up to the girls who were lying back eating plump mulberries.

Lucy jabbed Sheila in the ribs.

'Don't listen, Sheila. It's eavesdropping. Mum will have our guts for garters.'

Lucy was seized with panic, but not because of being caught out eavesdropping. She justly feared she'd be unable to save Sheila from herself. Sheila had a look in her eye that usually meant rouble.

Mrs McClare warmed to her subject. Her bosomy neighbour was

held in Mrs McClare's considerable thrall, eager to hear the latest news with some impatience. Mrs Rudge licked her lips in anticipation. Sensing her power, Mrs McClare hesitated to savour the moment before continuing.

'He's gone and got another job!' She let all the air out of her lungs in one victorious whistling asthmatic wheeze, and folded her arms.

'No!' was the gratifying response. Mrs Rudge gazed at Mrs McClare with awe that bordered on worship.

'Yes indeed! The baker saw Mr Sinta when he arrived to start baking at five o'clock in the morning.' She allowed this to sink in, 'He *already* works at the printing press, *as you know*.' Mrs McClare thrust her hands deep into her apron pockets. 'And there *he* was with his Ute.'

Mrs Rudge held her breath.

'Delivering newspapers if you please. *Two* jobs! Two *Australian* jobs!' said Mrs McClare.

Oblivious to the presence of the girls in the tree house above them, the two women sifted through every detail of their coloured neighbours' lives. Escape was impossible for Sheila and Lucy. They would be soundly whacked for their intrusion. Lucy sat in a mire of anxiety.

Sheila lay on her stomach and peered at the women through the gaps in the wooden slats of the crooked timber floor. She placed a careful line of mulberries in front of her, tilted her head speculatively, and continued to listen unashamedly as she devoured the succulent berries.

Licking her fingers with a sated kiss, she turned purple-berried lips to her sister, 'Lucy, have some, they're delish!'

Lucy chewed her nails nervously.

'We shouldn't be here, Sheila. Mum will kill us if she knows we're eavesdropping.'

'Don't be silly Lucy! Of course we should be here. It's our tree house for crying out loud! What are we supposed to do? You worry too much. Here, have a mulberry.'

Not for the first time, Lucy was forced to hear a lecture from her little sister on how she let things 'go to her stomach' after she refused the berry.

'You're too skinny, Lucy. There isn't an ounce of fat on your bones.' She mimicked their mother's voice to a tee.

Lucy laughed a forgiving laugh, 'I can't help it if my stomach goes on strike when I stress.'

'Don't worry Lucy, I wish I was like you. When I'm anxious, the fridge is my best friend. Soon I'll look like a fridge.' Sheila rolled theatrically around on the rickety timber floor puffing out her rosy cheeks.

'You don't have anything to worry about Sheila. That's just a bit of baby fat; your brain will use it up in no time.'

The women leaned comfortably on the fence, their Indian neighbour remained the focus of the conversation. With the washing forgotten, the exchange degraded into a discussion that centred on, of all things, the man's dog.

Sheila, an inveterate animal lover, pricked up her ears. She caught the end of the sentence. Mrs Rudge was gearing up.

'....black man with a white dog, how bizarre is that?' said the bosomy neighbour, as she swatted at flies half-heartedly with a lace trimmed handkerchief.

'Not the kind of dog you'd expect at all. Bad enough he should have a blonde, blue-eyed white wife, but two jobs *and* a dainty white poodle, what is he thinking?'

Lucy saw the wheels turning in Sheila's head. 'Don't go there, Sheila!'

A loud 'Shush!' was her only reply.

Lucy had no idea what her sister was thinking, but knowing Sheila it would involve impulsive action. Passivity was not in her dictionary.

The women went on a little longer about the man with the effrontery to sit on his front veranda, work too hard, marry an Australian woman, watch the sunset and pat his little blond dog.

Then, tiring of the subject, they moved on to other neighbours, finally coming full circle - back to the latest moan about their husbands. This material was so old and tired, they soon lost momentum and turned to bring in the washing.

Lucy knew Sheila would not leave well enough alone.

She discovered what Sheila had done when Mrs Cavendish came over that evening, and related the sorry tale of the neighbour's dog being mysteriously dyed brown. Sheila had taken her mother's semi-permanent rinse and dyed Empress, Ray's dog, 'California Brunette'.

This faux pas was seen as a racial slur of the highest order. Mrs Cavendish said Ray's wife had sworn never to leave the house again, and told the children to stay inside.

The police were called. They came and took notes, harrumphing and making half-hearted attempts to hide their amusement.

Sheila had taken great care to avoid Empress's eyes with the dye, so the poor animal looked like a kind of reverse bandit with white fur still around her eyes.

The crisis was solved very quickly. Sheila was always one to face the music. As soon as she heard about the fuss she'd created, she climbed out of the bedroom window in her baby-doll pyjamas and pink chenille dressing gown, and presented herself at the Sinta's. She offered grand and eloquent apologies saying she'd mistaken it for shampoo and hadn't meant to offend in any way.

She diplomatically omitted the conversation the girls had overheard that day.

This dubious explanation was gratefully accepted, probably because Mrs Sinta was relieved that Sheila was the culprit, and not some racist protagonist.

Sheila arrived home an hour later with a dozen lamingtons. A relieved Mrs Sinta bestowed them on her because she confessed so beautifully, and also offered to come back the next day to wash the dog 'thousands of times if that is what it takes to make things right.'

Sheila didn't explain she was attempting to right a wrong—that she was unable to change the colour of the man to make him more acceptable in the bigoted eyes of two women, so she had tried to equalize the world by changing the colour of his dog.

She climbed triumphantly back through the window, producing a cold can of their mother's beloved lemonade from the voluminous pockets of her dressing gown.

Although Lucy thought the lamingtons came under the category of 'ill-gotten gain', she demurred and helped eat them, but only to destroy the evidence. To make doubly sure they left no clues, they let Brandy, the cat, in to lick up all the crumbs.

Then, terrified their mother would catch them with the cat inside, Lucy dropped Brandy out of the window into the cool night air. The cat took off with an indignant *riaow*, and hissed at Alphonso, their mother's Afghan hound, as he enjoyed a late night snack from the rubbish bin.

A Nurses Revenge

The night nurse was sullen and bug-eyed with exhaustion as the nurses scraped their chairs in the large staffroom and waited for handover to begin. Sister Giselle arrived, bristling with efficiency. She was short and stout, with close cropped dark frizzy permed hair. An ancient spinster, she ruled with an iron fist.

'Gizzards would like us to think she was a nun,' Duncan muttered, as he threw his large frame into the nearest plastic chair with a theatrical sigh.

Duncan was a second year trainee. With a magnificent operatic voice he often sang at functions. A sandy haired giant of a man, he exuded charm and poise, and was never heard swearing. His cultured manner was mistaken for arrogance, even though he was a conscientious tireless nurse and never thought himself above anyone. Arrogance was viewed very poorly by the nurses, and no one knew how to get revenge like a fellow trainee. Pranking was a sport.

'Duncan is so up himself,' Janice said out of the side of her mouth after the nurses left handover.

'"Thou protesteth too much", Janice,' Ella said.

'Don't quote the Bible to me, Ella.'

'It's Shakespeare, you twit. You fancy him rotten.'

'I will make you sorry you ever said that, you shrew.' Janice slapped Ella's arm.

'Ouch, I'm sorry already,' howled Ella.

Duncan brushed past and muttered, 'Now girls, don't fight until you can find some mud to roll around in.'

'I'll give him mud, pompous prat!' snapped Janice.

Just after morning tea, a drama was being played out in the foyer of the ward.

Duncan's booming voice could be heard down the corridor. Sister Giselle had attempted to corner him without success. He was wearing a theatre gown on backward over his nurse's uniform and making a getaway to the lifts. Sister Giselle had all the fury of a terrier guarding her prey as she stood between Duncan and the lifts. He ignored her and strode off the ward.

'Where do you think you are going, *Mr Woods?*' she demanded.

'Home, dear sister' he replied politely, looking as if no-one on the earth was particularly dear to him at that moment.

Sister Giselle sputtered and ranted, 'Just what do you think you are going to do, *Mr Woods?*'

In his grandest voice Duncan replied, 'Change my trousers, sister. You see I have shit myself and I would thank you to let me go and get on with it.'

Not missing a beat Gizzards enquired, 'Are you coming back *Mr Woods?*'

'Certainly sister,' said Duncan, giving her an imperious nod, 'just as soon as I can arrange a *nappy*, then find and kill the sonofabitch who put Agarol in my hot chocolate.'

The lift arrived. Theatre gown swirling around him, Duncan entered with all the flair and style of a fashion icon, ignoring the fact that the theatre gown covered a brown stain on the back of his white trousers. Someone else went into the lift. By the look on Duncan's face he'd failed to consider the inevitable stench.

'Oh shit!' he said, running out of the lift and down the fire stairs.

A day in a nurse's life...

'But...but...the doctor said she had three weeks,' I said, clenching and unclenching my hands. I had returned to the ward to find that Mrs Partridge had died on my days off.

'At best, they're only ever guessing about how long anyone has,' said Jean, the ward nurse, touching my arm gently. She came around the nurses' station and put her arm around me. I'd only been training for a few weeks and become fond of Jessie Partridge who suffered from liver cancer. 'She looked quite beautiful, you know. We did her face and hair, then put a single red rose in her hands.'

My inner eye could not bring the vision of beauty to my memory of Jessie, with her yellowed eyes, grey skin and swollen belly.

I swallowed back tears.

'It gets easier,' said Jean. 'You can go and see her in the morgue if you like.'

I shook my head. She was gone. From this world; from me and my words of comfort and hope - the reach of my straining heart. Did she take any of my words with her? Or had they been gentling sounds like the laps of ocean on seashore. Did she hear my last words, 'I'll see you in the morning'?

Shaking these thoughts from my mind, I asked Jean what she

wanted next.

'Why don't you and Kathy read to Mrs Stanford? There's a letter for her in her room.'

'But isn't she unconscious?' I asked.

'Not fully, she fades in and out. Anyway, hearing is the last sense to go and it's important. You never know.'

Kathy and I looked fearful. We were both 'newbies' - in the same class, and good friends. We still wore 'blue bags' - the uniform of the nurse in their first three months. The shapeless pale blue shift-dresses announced our ignorance to the unsuspecting world of the hospital.

'It's really irrational to fear the most helpless patients. We tackle the belligerent with less trepidation,' I said, as we walked to Mrs Stanford's private room.

Kathy groaned. 'Don't start your philosophising now, Brooks. I don't know how you fit all that in your head. We'd better get started or we'll be here 'til midnight and I'm leaving on time today!'

I took the letter from the bedside table and opened it.

'It's six blooming pages!' I moaned.

'Here, give me that,' said Kathy, snatching it. 'Oh well, at least the writing is neat. If we were reading your scribble I'd give up now.'

I snatched the letter back. 'I'll do it. You've cast enough aspersions on me for one day.'

'Stop with the big words already. What is it with you? If it isn't tumultuous, it's exuberant, now it's nasturtiums.'

'It's not nasturtiums...'

'Oh, give it a rest and read the thing.'

The writing was an elegant, but firm cursive.

'Jeez! I bet this old bird got an A+ for writing,' I said.

'Mind your language, Brooks! Hearing is the last to go - remember?'

I glared, and began.

'Dear Adelaide,

Spring has come early this year. The garden is flourishing, except of course, for my favourite pale pink Azaleas.'

'Bit flowery... sure she's not related to you, Brooks... OUCH, don't hit me!'

I continued, *'Mavis says it's because there has been too much rain, but what would she know, she couldn't grow weeds. John Forbes died last week. He was found in the duck pond at the end of the retirement village. Such a tragedy, with him losing his wife only six months ago. Really, they're dropping like flies around here.'*

Kathy muffled a snort of laughter.

'Don't start,' I said, 'you'll set me off.'

'Ethel Croudace thinks he killed himself over the grief, but I told her that was rubbish. No man so full of his own self-importance would drown himself in a duck pond.'

We both choked on irrepressible mirth.

'People have nothing better to do around here than gossip. They've got the wrong end of the stick with this. I know for a fact that John was already stepping out with Grace McKinley of Number Six - you know the one with the Pekinese and too much makeup. Not that I'm spying, mind you, but one can't help but notice these things.'

Kathy and I broke out in a fit of giggles.

'What sort of letter is this to send to a friend in hospital?' said Kathy, between chortles. 'Has the woman no sense. What are we going to do? We're only on page one. I hope this gets better. Here, give it to me - you're making it sound hilarious.'

'Anyway, he was always dodgy on his pins - couldn't cross the path without veering from left to right. It's MY belief, not that my opinion matters much around here, but I think he was taking Gracie's dog, Sparkles, out for a tinkle and fell in. They never found the dog.'

This mental image started us both off again. We were no giggling uncontrollably, but appalled with ourselves. I went to look out of the window to try and compose myself.

Kathy continued. *'Well, of course, it had to be more than that - I know they had a mug of sherry every night - together. Not that I'm a nosy parker like some around here, but one can't help what one sees on an evening stroll around the village. Well, Gracie always did leave the blinds up. Showing off, if you ask me- she's been after every man in the village since she arrived - and not just the single ones, if you get my meaning. Of course, my Bert wasn't taken in by her - not him. Called her a trumped up piece - mutton dressed up as lamb.'*

By now there were tears streaming down our faces as we held our aching stomach muscles - our sensibilities for the unconscious Mrs Stanford all but forgotten.

'Who would write this stuff to a dying woman? It would make you want to jump off a cliff,' I gurgled. Kathy handed me the letter.

'I can't read any more. You read it.'

'Well, be quiet and don't look at me if I have any chance of getting this done,' I said. 'Surely there's some good news in here somewhere.'

I cleared my throat.

'Sheila Davis has gone to the nursing home. She fell down the back ramp and broke her hip. I told her she should use the railing - that's what it's there for, after all. At least they had a bed in the home - Eloise Franks died in her sleep. Great way to go, I say. Gracie made a cake of herself at John's funeral. Cried over everyone and begged the administration for a police enquiry. Silly woman. When a constable actually came and talked to her, she screamed and slapped his face. Apparently he was cranky for being called out to investigate an incident on someone who was 94. Mavis Burns made things worse by asking if Gracie had ever been on the stage, but I held my tongue. It isn't seemly for a lady to run her mouth off the way Mavis does.'

'This is straight out of a Jane Austen novel,' laughed Kathy. 'It's hysterical!

I ignored this remark with great effort. *'Of course, Mavis is my best friend, next to you, of course, my dear. I will never hear a word against her, but she does have a tendency to put her foot in it.'*

'I can't do this anymore,' I said, leaning on the wall. 'We're not even past the third page and there's been two deaths, an assault on the police, a missing dog called Sparkles, midnight liaisons. I thought the elderly lived out their lives in boredom, sleeping in front of the telly. Who knew? Well, I'm just reading the last paragraph, that's it.'

'Well, my dear Adelaide, I must say goodbye for the moment. I have to go to Eloise's funeral. It's at the crematorium on the other side of town, but the village is taking the bus and we're stopping at the Rose Gardens for morning tea on the way home. Of course I couldn't let Mavis go alone – she's in a walking frame now.

I do hope I've cheered you up, my dear, and you are soon back among our happy little group. Your friend always, Jessie.'

'Good grief,' said Kathy, 'and I thought my life was hard.'

Wiping our eyes and returning the letter to its envelope we sauntered back to the desk.

'How did you get on, girls?' asked Jean. 'Did that make you feel better?'

'Yes, Nurse Jean. I feel that it put the precarious nature of life back into perspective,' said Kathy, with a remarkably straight face. Turning to me she said, 'You're not the only one who knows a few big words, Brooks.' She winked.

He's mine now

Father O'Brien removed his glasses and rubbed the bridge of his nose in agitation. A headache was scuttling around his skull, deciding whether it would stay.

It had been a tough week. He had spent most of it in a London hospital at the bedside of a dying woman, Charlotte Medhurst.

He sat quietly in the priory kitchen in Dunnstown, glad to be home. His sister Elaine had been busy while he was away. The timber floors shone with polish. He watched her bustle around the kitchen and was deeply grateful for her company. She had come to live with him in Dunnstown five years ago after her beloved husband died.

His thoughts returned to the hospital. It had been strange meeting Eve and David Medhurst after all those years. He remembered when David brought Eve home from the city to meet his mother and sister, and plan for their wedding. David had just finished a degree in architecture at Oxford and was returning to his hometown to work for a local building company.

Father O'Brien would never forget the first time he met Eve.

'I'll have that verse,' said Eve, rather more forcibly than she intended.

Father O'Brien looked up from reading his Bible in astonishment. Eve threw him her most sparkling smile. Oh dear, she couldn't afford to offend the priest as well. It was bad enough keeping on her toes in David's new family. They were starting to treat her as if she were a control freak. She was sure she'd overheard David's teenage sister Kym call her The Bride From Hell on the phone to her friends. Time to backpedal. She leaned forward in the pew, bridging the gap with the young priest.

'I think it has such a lovely sentiment,' she said. Her voice was softer, almost compliant. 'How did that go? Something about leaving his parents and cleaving to his wife?' Another dazzling smile followed.

Father O'Brien opened his mouth, then shut it again.

'I've heard that some of the Bible is praised as poetry,' Eve continued hastily, desperate to please the parish priest that David's family clearly adored. She didn't understand their sentiments. He seemed a bit thick really. Maybe he was hard of hearing.

Father O'Brien stared at the bright young thing in front of him and sighed. He'd had quite enough of this brash young woman. She had spent most of her time yawning, rolling her eyes or tapping her foot against the pew. The future Mrs Medhurst was obviously bored out of her tiny mind, and making no effort to disguise it.

What was it with people these days? Only turning to the church to make a splashy show at a wedding. He'd bet good money Eve hadn't put her head inside any book vaguely religious before today. Eve seemed shocked earlier in their meeting when he told her she was expected to participate in pre-marital counselling. 'Good grief, is that really necessary?' she asked. He had stood firm. Only an hour later he was almost sorry. This young woman was testing his considerable patience. She was so different from quiet, calm David.

Only in his twenties, it had been a weighty decision for the young priest to embrace a celibate life. He gave Eve a slow assessing gaze. The priesthood was looking better by the minute.

He included the text against his better judgment. His parishioners looked confused when it was read out, and he groaned inwardly. How could he explain that the woman was a steamroller?

The night sky peeked blackly through the window over the sink. The kettle whistle brought Father O'Brien back to the present.

'Have you a headache, Frank?' asked Elaine, watching him rub his temples. She placed a steaming cup of coffee in front of him, and sat down at the vast oak table to join him. When her brother had first entered the priesthood she continued to call him Frank, rather than Francis. At the tender age of 21, she protested that she was far too old to call him something else, especially as he had been the torment of her life. It bothered him at the time, but he was nearing sixty now, and couldn't give a toss what anyone called him.

Everyone turned to the priest in times of trouble, never thinking about what a priest might need when he was troubled. Thank God for Elaine.

'It's only mild,' he said, touched by her concern.

'It's that dreadful Eve woman isn't it?' asked Elaine, rolling her eyes.

'She hasn't changed a bit,' said Francis.

'That type never do, you should know that by now Frank.'

'No, that would be a miracle right up there with raising the dead,' muttered Francis.

Elaine's eyes widened.

Francis wished priests could swear out loud. He was sure it would ease his headache. It had rapidly become a dull roar.

'So, how did the trip to the city go?' Elaine smiled. '...as if I couldn't tell.'

'Well, thankfully I was able to conduct Charlotte's last rites without Eve there.'

'A minor miracle then.'

Francis threw her a scornful look.

'She is just so ... grating. She wouldn't leave David alone with his mother apart from that short time. And her absence from that was accidental. She showed up and complained that she hadn't received David's message.'

'Or maybe David sent it late,' said Elaine. Francis mulled over this. David must have learned a few things if he had outmanoeuvred Eve.

'That's a cheering thought,' he said, smiling.

'At least you could be with Charlotte in the end.'

'Yes, I'm always glad when I can see them through to their last breath.'

'Did David spend much time with Charlotte?'

'Yes, I was surprised really. His visits home have been sporadic to say the least, but he was inconsolable when she passed.'

'Guilt.'

'You're probably right. The number of times Eve spouted, 'David has nothing to feel guilty about, he's been a good son' made me suspicious.'

'Methinks the lady doth protest too much.'

'Wise man, Shakespeare.'

They sat in silence sipping their coffee, each to their own thoughts.

'I worked with her, you know,' said Elaine. 'Eve, I mean.'

'Really? I didn't know that.' Francis turned incredulous eyes to his sister. She was always surprising him.

'Yes, we both worked at Plimstone & Bridgeworth soon after they moved to London. She was a secretary there too. She was very efficient.'

'I can imagine,' said Francis.

'But cold as ice,' continued Elaine. 'One day when we were all talking in the staffroom, Eve admitted she had engineered their move to London to get her husband away from his 'needy family'. Apparently she had contacted various architecture firms, and one of them made David an offer. Eve swore the firm to secrecy, and David thought he'd been headhunted.'

'Oh my. How did she justify that?'

'Oh, we asked her, don't worry about that! She stared at us as if we were imbeciles.'

'What did she say?'

"He's mine now'. That's all she said. As if nothing, and no-one else mattered.'

'That says it all.' Francis resisted a shiver. Charlotte was a lovely woman who raised the children on her own when their father had run off with another woman.

'She'll get her own one day. What comes around goes around,' said Elaine.

Francis jolted in his chair. 'Speaking of which....'

'What?' asked Elaine, intrigued.

'Oh my. I met their son, Robert, while I was there.'

'Really? Do tell.'

'He introduced me to his girlfriend. She was an exuberant little thing, real stunner too. They were such a refreshing young couple. Now that I think of it, he introduced her as his fiancée.'

'Oh, what did Eve say?'

'Nothing. She just opened and shut her mouth. I think it was the first she'd heard of it. But from the look of things she didn't like the girl. She had a mouth likes a cat's bum, and I'm sure I heard the sound of teeth grinding.'

Elaine snorted. 'I wonder if they'll have the same wedding verse.' They had joked over the years at Eve's appalling insensitivity.

'Not likely,' said Francis, laughing for the first time in over a week.

'I wonder what David will decide about Charlotte's house? It will be such a shame if his sister has to leave. Those two fatherless boys of hers have only ever known one home. They'll be devastated if they lose that as well as their Nana. They adored her.'

51

'Oh dear,' moaned Francis. 'I'd forgotten about that.'

'Would you like a nip of Brandy in your coffee?'

'I thought you'd never ask.'

Elaine tipped the brandy straight into her mug, and then his, giving him a generous amount.

'To Karma,' she said, grinning wickedly.

'To Karma,' Francis responded, clinking his mug against Elaine's.

'So you know about Karma?' she asked.

'I'm Catholic. We invented Karma,' said Francis recklessly. 'We just call it something else.' He couldn't remember what, and concentrated on his medicinally enhanced coffee.

The subject of their conversation was not thinking about Karma. Eve Medhurst was unsuccessfully willing herself to sleep in the luxurious king-sized bed she shared with David. She was separated from him by only inches, but the gulf between them felt enormous.

David's grief was deeper than she had expected. She thought he would turn to her for consolation; instead he was shutting her out. This was new to Eve and she was terrified. He had never rebuffed her before. She tried to console him; then resorted to begging him, and finally berating him for not considering her feelings.

'For God's sake Eve, give it a rest!' he said. And then nothing.

This will pass, she told herself sternly. David has a difficult conversation ahead of him. Discussing the sale of the house with Kym won't be easy for him. Kym should be happy about leaving the ramshackle old house with its constant need for maintenance.

Father O'Brien would have been sinfully pleased about Eve's state of mind, if he had known it. However, he was seeking inner calm as he prepared the eulogy for Charlotte's funeral. It was midnight. He was tired. Thirty minutes later he read quickly through what he had written, let out a satisfied sigh, and folded the page into his well-worn Prayer Book.

The service went well the next day. Eve made an attempt to join in with the cheerful modern hymns Kimberly had chosen. Perhaps she would remain gracious for the rest of this difficult day.

Then he'd blanched at her rudeness when she confided to the local gossip, Mrs Snodgrass, 'It was a 'novel' way to run a funeral, but what could you expect from that scatterbrain sister of David's.' Gracious? Perhaps not. David's usually calm face became tense.

Mingling later at the wake David seemed relaxed. The house was full of Charlotte and Kym's friends. Eve took over the kitchen and busied herself cleaning up. She appeared to be relishing her role as martyred in-law. Several of the women praised her efforts, but Father O'Brien suspected that Eve had used domesticity to escape. As she gazed out of the window she exuded quiet confidence, as if an unpleasant episode was behind her.

Up in the attic, David sat in the bay window seat opening an old suitcase covered with decoupage roses. Kym had waved a generous hand in his direction and said, 'go up to the attic and take what you like of Mum's things.'

Father O'Brien saw Eve's smug smile as David mounted the staircase to the attic.

David remembered Eve's words when they'd left home.

'At least the house should sell quickly. It's not our fault Kym has to move in winter. Nothing can be done about that. We all need to move on with our lives. I'm sorry you have that difficult conversation ahead of you.'

She had stroked his arm sympathetically. He knew what Eve wanted. Paris, Italy, the Greek Islands. He had seen the travel brochures laid out on the coffee table.

Seeing Kym and her twelve year old twin boys overwhelmed with grief had pulled at his heart in an unwelcome tide of emotion. The boys had started high school only a month ago. Was there another way?

He reached into the battered suitcase and pulled out a pile of yellowed butchers' paper.

Nearly every page he picked up and turned over was in childish writing, promising undying love. One jerked an unexpected groan from deep in his chest. He hadn't seen this, surely, for over fifty years. But he knew it to be his with the recognition of his soul, that strange sense beyond the knowing of the eyes, and belongs to the knowing of the heart. The message was simple—

Your beudiful arndt you

The page was crinkled with age. It was embellished with stick figure drawings of a woman with masses of hair, and a boy and girl.

Then he saw the photographs. A laughing girl and a solemn little boy, wrapped in the arms of a slim woman with tawny hair cascading down her back. Others were of two children, their golden heads together, playing. Every one was different to the childhood photos in shining chrome frames in the house he and Eve shared. There were no pictures of his original family there, only him, alone. It was as if those photos fitted a different reality, a forgotten story.

Halfway through the suitcase he found some artwork. There were watercolours of flowers in pots, watering cans, an ancient pet; everyday life. He remembered sitting at his mother's feet in the garden, while she lost herself painting. The lines were sweet and clean; the colours pure and translucent.

Underneath the watercolours was an oil painting. Its beauty took his breath away. The ethereal quality of the others had been replaced with a boldness of colour. This one had substance, texture and emotion. It was the tender touching of cherub lips to mother's soft cheek. It was a picture of undiluted joy. It was he and his mother. It bore the title, 'Butterfly Kisses'.

Tears ran down his cheeks, unchecked. Long forgotten memories stirred. He remembered tumbling in the grass with his laughing mother and vying with his sister to give her 'butterfly kisses' with their eyelashes.

David looked up. Through the slanted window, the pale blue sky was clear. He heard footsteps on the stairs, then Kimberley sat down beside him. She seemed surprised by the peaceful expression on his face. Placing a loving arm around him, she leant her head on his shoulder.

He looked into the eyes of his grieving sister. Suddenly everything was clear. His eyes shifted wordlessly to the garden they had shared as children. Her eyes followed his.

'It will be pretty in Spring,' she said sadly.

'It's yours Sis, this house, your home. I'm signing it over to you and the boys.'

Tears flowed gently from Kimberley's eyes.

'You're sure David?'

'Absolutely sure.'

He felt lighter. The world had shifted.

The 'difficult conversation' was still ahead of him. But with someone else. No doubt it would occur in the car on the way home. Smiling to himself he realised he didn't care. David returned to his search in the suitcase, lost in the past.

He felt a soft caress on his cheek. Turning to respond to his sister, he found she'd left the room. Mystified, he looked back at the painting. His mother's face smiled warmly at him. Reverently he touched his cheek. A butterfly kiss.

'Good-bye, Mum,' he whispered.

The guests were beginning to leave. Father O'Brien waited at the bottom of the stairs. He reminded himself to remain detached. This was family business. Shaking David's hand by the car as they were leaving he noticed the oil painting. David lifted it to show him.

'Wow. That's beautiful David.'

'It is that.'

I Want to Go Home Now

'At exactly what time did you find the victim?' asked Detective James.

His voice was calm and precise—almost indifferent, but Amanda did not miss the sharp intensity in his eyes. She sighed extravagantly.

'Precisely how many times are you going to ask me the same question?' she countered, fanning herself with the official statement forms that had been placed in front of her over an hour ago.

'It's police procedure Miss Sleight, you know that,' he said, quelling a desire to grind his teeth.

'You presume too much, George,' said Amanda. 'How on earth would I know anything of police procedure?—being, as you so clearly pointed out to the Sergeant, I'm 'nothing but a gossipy florist'.'

She pinned him with clear blue eyes. If the paper she was using as a fan created an unwelcome breeze in his face, Detective James did not show it.

She was deliberately ruffling his feathers, but she didn't care. She saw his jaw tense and almost felt sorry for him. She had found Harry Campbell dead inside her florist shop at opening time, then consoled the man's distraught widow. All the while, trying to hide a large overdue account run up by that woman's unfaithful husband for extravagant floral arrangements for other women. An account which the poor delicate thing would never see.

After all that, and the ensuing questions, Amanda Sleight was well and truly sick of the sight of pompous Det. George James.

She knew it was grossly inappropriate to use his first name, but if she hadn't overheard his disdainful remarks to the duty Sergeant, she wouldn't have been goaded beyond endurance.

Detective George James loosened his tie, perhaps indicating that this was going to take a while.

'Amanda, you don't have to make this harder than it already is. I'm sorry for what I said. I was out of line. You're not gossipy, you're just friendly. Please accept my apology.'

He smiled.

Amanda ceased her fanning movements just long enough to give him a sharp look of disgust. Det. James began again, his voice tight.

'I'm know you watch enough late night crime shows to realise that I'm only doing my job,' he said.

The fact that he knew her evening occupations only pushed Amanda further towards the brink of losing her temper completely. The only reason he knew about her life was because they had shared those evenings with an intimacy that died as quickly as Harry Campbell, the victim. Amanda snapped the papers onto the desk.

'That's low, George!' she said, barely controlling the pain in her voice. 'Bringing our private times into the conversation.'

'Well, it's common knowledge that the very married Harry Campbell spent a lot of time in your presence.'

A tense silence followed, while Amanda pursued her tired thoughts. She saw the past months and George's changing demeanour in a new light. Her mind began to race. So that was it. The wretch! How could he think it of her? Fury gnawed at her stomach. She slipped into icy calm.

'Scumbag cheating husbands with many 'interests' tend to find themselves in frequent need of expensive floral arrangements.'

She paused. 'Let's see - there's the 'understated thank you' arrangement, the 'shy enticement bouquet', the 'initial seduction arrangement' ... oh, and—the rushed after-hours visit to my home to order the 'guilt extravaganza for the suspicious wife'.'

She let the information sink in, watching George's Adam's apple dance in his throat. Then she saw enlightenment in his eyes.

Picking up her handbag, and pushing the papers towards George, she stood.

'I will answer no more questions. I did not kill Harry Campbell. I am, however, experiencing a strong desire to kill *you*, George James. Put that in your stinking report. I want to go home now.'

Amanda Sleight smoothed her short charcoal skirt, retrieved her red clutch, and left. She would have been most gratified to see Det. George James banging his head on the desk, if only she'd turned to look. But she had walked briskly down the corridor, her footsteps echoing.

George James silently flicked through his Teledex. Where on earth would he find another florist as good as Amanda? He could hardly make arrangements for an 'apology bouquet' from Amanda's store.

Ancient Love

She is gentle of spirit and fiercely loving. She touches his face as she asks each question. His hungry eyes follow her every move. It is the day of the Christmas Party at the nursing home.

I am a bystander in so many ways to this ancient love. This meshing and joining of two souls. This joyous reunion, this daily miracle. They are old, these two; old and frail. He sits in his chair, propped up by the pillow I made him in an attempt to do something for him, to ease the desperate sense of helplessness I feel towards them both.

His mouth is momentarily soft, not presently twisted from the stroke he suffered 12 years ago. He is relaxed as he sits in the billowy chair that cushions his ancient bones.

He is quiet now, rapt in the music of the Christmas carollers as they warble energetically. He is no longer articulate of speech. The phrases he speaks are basic and simple since the stroke claimed so many of his faculties but not his indomitable spirit.

In some indefinable way he is different from the others, this man.

In essence, he is happy. A conundrum in this place of disability and death—the nursing home. His capacity to enjoy seems oddly to have increased instead of diminished. I don't know what part of the brain controls enthusiasm, but for him this area is strangely enlarged, childlike even. He laughs at many things these days, something I don't remember him doing a lot before.

As the daily sister on his ward I know him well. Living in the same village, I have known him a much longer time than these, his helpless days.

His wife has also noticed the change. She laughs a tinkling laugh as she tells me that it is quite strange that he can now sing in tune, whereas before he had no sense of pitch or tone. We joke together about some deep part of his brain having been mysteriously switched on to make up for the loss of the rest of his grey matter.

I often wonder what is going on in his mind. For wondering is often all you are left with after a stroke robs the power of speech. You fill in the gaps somehow or are just left guessing; and right or wrong that is the best you can do.

I have listened so many times to his wife tell me of conversations that she claims to have had with him. And I have said nothing; God knows she must need a little denial to get through the day. She believes the best, not because she is a coward. Quite simply, for her he is still the man she married, the love of her life. She threads her fingers through his, touching his face with reverent grace.

The dining room, bedrooms and corridors are lined with dedicated carers; encouraging a few extra haltering steps, another reluctant mouthful of food. Some carers are subtly pained, with listless empty eyes as they tend their loved ones. Some mourn the lost spirit of the living physical body, and others the mind when their loved one no longer knows who they are.

Not so for Alice, as she combs his few stray strands of hair with careful hand, watched by his alert and knowing eyes. I realize that for her he is still husband; friend. However, she is also a realist, a nurse like me, and she faces each day with a mixture of pleasure and grief in his company when he has good days and bad days.

But here today, watching them side by side, I see something new, something wonderful. Gently he caresses her hand with his good left hand. The hand that is not clawed and useless. He looks into her eyes and communicates a lifetime together. Now I understand why it is so hard for her to let go, to 'take a night off'.

He is still here.

He looks at his watch often. At the time the concert is due to finish he becomes a little agitated and gestures to a passing nurse. His chair had been hastily put in the hallway to cram the residents in for the concert. It is nearly time to leave and he doesn't want to be in anyone's way. Then I remember him as a man who always thought of others.

Vigilantly watching those around him, he acknowledges old friends with a 'yes, too long'. He does not shrink in embarrassment at his obvious disabilities but freely offers his good left hand for others to shake. He answers their awkward questions of 'How are you?' with an emphatic 'good'. He listens to their woes and responds with a measured 'Oh dear, too bad'.

Now I understand his language; their language. I understand why Alice always asks him what he wants rather than talks about him as if he isn't there. She is a genius. A gifted, compassionate genius.

The conversation is not stimulating or riveting but it has a charm of its own. It is a tango, the dance of words, of love.

She poses the same question she asks every day, 'Do you want me to come back tonight?'

I have to stop myself from rushing in to tell her not to ask him. I feel she needs a break, a free night. But he says the predictable *'my word'* and she holds his hand against her face and sighs with contentment. It is a game of love they play. I have a lot to learn about love, and I am in awe.

I may work in a nursing home, but I nurse the living not just the dying.

An Angel's tears

'Oh, Fleur, I don't know if I can do this.'

'But you asked for this assignment, Andriella.'

'I know. But it's so much harder than I thought - especially knowing she can't see me - doesn't even know I'm there. And that's heartbreaking when she's alone.' Andriella let her head sink into her hands.

'But you love her, don't you?' Fleur's question was gentle.

'Oh yes! So much. So very much. That's precisely what makes it harder. The love.'

'So you don't want to be reassigned?'

Andriella smiled. If a smile could be described as sad, then her smile was sad.

'Of course, not. She's mine now.'

'And you'll see her all the way?'

'Yes. After all, even though I'm a novice - I am her guardian angel.'

'So she's never alone, you'll understand that one day. As she will. Well, then...' Fleur said, but her voice was lost in the flutter of snowy gossamer wings. She sighed. It was never easy with the new ones.

The tiny blonde head was bowed over a worn toy monkey. A soft baby voice sang softly as little hands made the monkeys hands clap together. Little Bridget tilted her head, as if listening to the soft floppy monkey. The tot's hair was fine and gently curled. The nurse had just brushed it, but it looked the same. Like the child, it had a mind of its own. The curls had resisted the nurse's gentle attempts at tidiness, just as the little girl was resisting the world around her.

Andriella's heart ached as she hovered in the corner. What was the use of being a guardian angel when she felt useless most of the time? She must stop thinking this way. That was exactly the distorted thinking of the mother of this tiny sick tot. Every day the mother came, looked through the small ward glass window and watched Bridget for a few minutes, before leaving again. There were no familiar arms to hold the vulnerable child, little more than a baby.

Bridget had been very sick on her arrival three months ago. Her body was healed now from the infection that raged as an aftermath of measles. But the little toddler had shut down; her spirit waning. She would only talk to the monkey, who she called Mung Mung. She answered the nurses through him. Mung Mung had the voice she'd lost. The nurses were saddened and tried everything. They often said that the children who cried and fought them were easier than this little pet, who showed every sign of accepting her lot as separate from the world. Sometimes the aunt came and there seemed to be some difference for a while, but Bridget soon withdrew again.

'I don't understand,' said the aunt, 'she's such a lively little cricket. Chatters like a little bird. Has the sunniest temperament.'

No, you wouldn't understand, thought Andriella. You don't know her like I do. Haven't seen what I've seen. Oh dear, my stomach's in knots now. Fleur said that wouldn't happen when I learned a little. I can't wait. This is agony. The parents are due soon. The last time they tried to take Bridget home, the little dot screamed blue murder and the parents had to bring her back to the hospital. To Mung Mung, and home. For that's how she thinks of the hospital ward now.

The father hadn't understood at all. They lived an hour and a half away and he worked long hours. The mother had spoken of visiting, but only the nurses knew that the child hadn't laid eyes on the woman who gave birth to her. The mother was confused too, for the wiring of her mind didn't allow understanding of a child who once clung to her, but now treated her like a stranger. They had tried to connect with the little girl, but failed.

Andriella knew they adored the child. There was no question of that, but humans seemed to have so little understanding of the heart, and its connection with the mind. And as for soul, well forget it. So very few understood anything about that. 'Discouraging,' Andriella sighed.

The ward door swung open. Andriella held her breath, then remembered to breathe, for an angel's breath is magic. The parents had arrived. Hope and love shone in their eyes. The mother's held an extra dose of fear. Her confusion was evident, but she was a tireless woman and she was ready to try anything to connect with her tiny daughter.

They both knelt by the cot.

Bridget didn't look at them and continued to talk to Mung Mung.

The Head Sister stood at the end of the cot, ever watchful. She had her own opinions on this situation, and they were not kindly disposed towards the mother. Why she even had the papers on her desk to refer the case to Family Services.

The mother reached for the worn monkey. The child gave her a brief fierce look as she clutched the toy tighter.

'Wouldn't she listen better without that ugly monkey?' asked the mother, annoyed that the Sister had to be witness to this, her failure as a mother.

'No,' said the Head, 'the child has attached to the toy. It would be cruel to remove it. You'll have to try to get through to her. You'll have to be patient. She has been here a long time. Alone.'

The father's confused eyes met the Sister's.

He put the cot-side down and sat near the child. The little girl didn't react. He sighed heavily. 'Bubby, it's Daddy,' he said, bringing a tiny doll from his large overcoat pocket. He handed it towards the tot.

Looking up briefly, Bridget said, 'Not Bubby's. Yours.' She pushed it back towards him and turned her attention to Mung Mung.

The father's eyes filled with tears.

The Sister moved closer to the cot end. 'She looked at you, at least. Keep talking to her.'

His questioning gaze was desperate. 'Okay. Bubby, that's a lovely monkey.'

Tiny hands held it up for him to see. 'Mung Mung.'

'Hello, Mung Mung. Is he a good Mung Mung?'

'Ess, good Mung Mung. Berry good Mung Mung. No smacks for Mung Mung.'

'Is Mung Mung happy?'

Bridget made the monkey dance. 'Happy Mung Mung.'

'Is Bridget happy?'

The tot considered this. 'Ess, Bidge happy.' She hugged the monkey. Then her face crumpled. 'No. Bidge not happy.'

The child hung her head. Two huge tears hovered, before being wiped away quickly by chubby fingers. Her father's heart ached. 'Does Mung Mung make Bidge happy?'

'Ess.' The child looked into her father's eyes. Her grip on the monkey loosened a little as she regarded him.

He smiled.

The child titled her head.

'Bidge play a game with Daddy?'

Bridget slipped the monkey under one arm. 'Ess.'

'What else makes Bubby happy?'

'Mine Bidge.'

'What else makes Bidge happy?'

The child shrugged.

'Do you remember Swing Swing?'

Bridget shook her head vigorously.

'Do you remember kitties?'

Her head shook again.

The father continued his gentle questions, and Bridget's mother's eyes filled with something near hope. She crouched down by the little girl and asked some questions of her own. The child's gaze never wavered. With both her parents at eye level she regarded them with a neutral assessing eye. They looked at each other as if to prompt some other memory. The mother's face glowed as a sudden thought hit her. Bridget's brother was three years older. Perhaps...

'Do you remember Den Den Boy,' said the mother, anxiously holding her breath.

'Den Den Boy! Den Den Boy! Where Den Den Boy?' the tot asked as she peeked around her parents, as if by some trick her beloved brother might be hiding there.

The child reached out one small hand and gripped her father's finger, then carefully did the same to her mother. Mung Mung slipped to the side of the cot.

'*Where* Den Den Boy?'

'Den Den Boy is at home. With Mummy and Daddy.'

Andriella cried a crystal tear. It fell on the child. The child looked up and smiled. Pushing the hospital cot sheet aside she reached for her father. 'Den Den Boy,' she whispered as she rested her golden head on her father's shoulder, 'Den Den Boy. Home.'

Never too late for a hero

Wesley stood outside the office of Goodwin Investigations & Recovery Agency. It was an old stone building in an upmarket area of the city. He was early for an interview as personal assistant. The Goodwin Agency was prestigious. The hours were flexible and the pay rate was more than generous. He loved being an artist, but even though his paintings sold well, the money was irregular.

Taking a moment to check his appearance in the large glass windows, he realised he should have had a haircut. He put a hand up to tidy his hair and saw a daub of paint on his hand. So much for a good first impression.

While the Estefan's Café & Restaurant opposite was enjoying brisk trade, there was no-one on the Agency side of the street. Wesley wondered how many other applicants would be attending. Squaring his shoulders, he pushed open the ancient timber and glass door. A bell tinkled in the back room. He looked around. The office resembled something out of the Forties with its antique furniture.

A tall elegant woman was shuffling papers on a mahogany desk that dominated the room. 'Drat,' she said, as a sheaf of papers hit the ground and slid across the floor.

Wesley stooped to retrieve them.

'Don't worry, young man. I'll do it later. I need to pick them up in a particular order.' The woman tucked a stray strand of coal black hair into an off kilter bun that was held in place with a pencil. 'I'm Veronica Goodwin, owner, investigator, dogsbody, you name it. And you are Wesley Brent.' She twisted around, eyes scanning the room. 'Now where are those ... darn, can't find a thing. Nice to meet you.' With a wide smile she reached out and shook his hand. 'Well, Wesley Brent, you can see my drastic need for a personal assistant.' She gestured at the shambles of paperwork on her desk. 'Please take a seat.'

Wesley folded his lanky frame onto the chair. He opened his mouth to begin the spiel he'd been rehearsing for days, but Veronica had flipped open the laptop computer and was tapping random keys.

'Wretched thing. I hope you understand it,' she said. The computer beeped into life. Veronica squeaked in surprise. She shuffled the papers on her desk. 'Oh there they are,' she said, placing a dark rimmed pair of glasses on her face with a satisfied sigh. 'I hope you'll like it here, Wesley. The job is yours.'

'Oh? I thought this was an interview. The employment agency told me to bring these.' Wesley held up a black folder.

'Daft lot, those agency people. I have all your information on file.'

Wesley's eyebrows flew up. 'You do?'

'Naturally. Um, cyberspace, internet, you know.' She pointed at the computer, eyeing it suspiciously.

'Ah, the agency sent my information. Of course.'

Veronica frowned, then seemed relieved. 'Ah yes, that must be it.' The computer pinged. Veronica shut the lid down. 'I see you're quite the artist.'

'How did you know that?' Wesley squirmed in the chair.

'I've seen you painting the mural for the Estefans café opposite.'

'Oh, of course.'

Veronica leaned back. 'I believe you are perfect for the job

Wesley. You have a good reputation for confidentiality.'

'But I haven't worked as a personal assistant before.'

'You're much too humble Wesley Brent. Always have been. Why that fiasco back at University, with the student newspaper—you only wanted to protect Sara, of course, sorting the petty cash theft by replacing the money yourself. Wouldn't have worked the second time though.'

'Say again.' Wesley sat bolt upright. 'How can you possibly know any of this? *Were you there?* This is bizarre.' Wesley mopped his forehead with a handkerchief that had seen better days.

'Oh Wesley, the world is never quite what it seems.' Veronica smiled. 'I'll start from the beginning...'

Wesley slumped in the chair. Veronica brought him a glass of water.

'I'm a time traveller Wesley, you know—travelling to different...' Wesley choked on the sip of water. When the coughing fit ceased, he viewed the woman opposite him with watery eyes and a shocked expression.

'Oh dear. You look like you want to run out the door. Please stay and hear me out, Wesley.'

'Don't think I could stand if I tried.'

'I'll give you time to take it all in. I can almost see the cogs in your head turning. You were like that back then too.'

'So you *were* there. I don't remember seeing you. Were you invisible?'

Veronica laughed. 'One Superpower at a time please!'

'Wait a minute—you said something about the *second* time. There wasn't a second theft.'

'Ah Wesley, but there so very nearly was.'

Wesley leaned forward, alert. 'Ah. I know. A week after the money went missing I was working late on the artwork for the paper. There was an almighty noise, but there was nothing out of place. I would've searched longer but Sara phoned me from the hospital. Her father had broken his leg.'

Regret flashed across Veronica's face. 'Were you alone in the building, Wesley?'

'Well yes. Everyone had gone home. Wait on, there was just a janitor, some new woman. Said she hadn't seen anything, kept her head down. Funny sort of a...Oh my god, *that was you!*'

Veronica nodded. 'There was a reason you were protecting Sara. Apart from the massive crush you had on her. You thought she knew something.'

Wesley flushed.

'Oh, you poor dear. You're still carrying a flame for the girl. After ten years. It was a noble thing to do—replacing the money. Ill advised, but noble.'

'Sara was the only other one with the keys to the office. But I knew it wasn't her.'

'And you were right. She didn't. It was her father.'

Wesley's face turned white. 'Her father? *Bill took it!*'

The phone jangled. Veronica picked it up, and in perfect diction spoke into the mouthpiece. 'You have reached the office of Goodwin Investigations & Recovery Agency. This is an automated message. We apologise for not being available, but your call is important to us. Please leave a message and we will return your call.'

Wesley's mouth dropped open. 'You're very good, you think quickly. Guess you've been doing it for centuries.' He held up a hand. 'Don't tell me. I don't want to know. But, how did Bill take the money?'

'Simple really. Crime often is. He only had to stay hidden in the staff toilets in the main administration block at closing time, then slip out the fire exit afterwards. Security wasn't great in those days, as you'll remember. He was disappointed to find less than $50 the first time so he decided to make another attempt.'

'Oh dear, this is starting to make sense. Bill was always short of cash. He would borrow from Sara. I'm pretty sure he had a gambling problem. But I never thought he'd do something like that. Sara can't possibly know. It would break her heart.' Wesley ran tense fingers through his hair. 'I was just returning from the toilets when I heard the ruckus. What on earth did you do to stop him?'

'Simple. I came rattling past with the cleaning trolley. Bill got a shock, lost his balance, then ran off.'

'But his broken leg?' Wesley rested his elbows on the desk, watching Veronica intently.

'Bill's, er, shall we say *loan officer*, was waiting for the money in the car park with a couple of thugs.'

'Bill claimed he'd stopped to help a homeless man and been attacked. My God, the lies he told.'

'Bill was trouble. I think that's why Sara has that bad boy attraction thing going on. It's often the way, it's why nice guys like you finish last.'

'Just for once I'd like to finish first, with Sara. Do you think...?'

A loud knock at the door deferred any words of wisdom Veronica may have offered. It was Estella Estefan with two pizza boxes. The aroma filled the room. Wesley's stomach growled.

'Estella, how kind,' said Wesley, ushering the woman inside with a grin, 'but where is Veronica's pizza? She'll be hungry too.'

Estella slapped his arm. 'You tease an old woman too much, Wesley. One is for your new boss. You have the job? Yes?'

Veronica nodded and laughed.

'Good,' said Estella. 'Don't you be letting this one have your pizza, Senora. Like a horse he eats and yet he stays thin and handsome. It's enough to make a woman cry.'

After they had eaten, Veronica became crisp and businesslike, filling Wesley in on his duties. She swept around the room, filling the air with exotic perfume as she detailed his role and explained the filing system and client records.

Wesley's eyes widened when Veronica told him that her previous assistant, Evan, was still back in time. 'He's lost, somewhere,' she said, quickly wiping a tear aside. 'So you see, you really must be very particular.'

Veronica handed Wesley a handwritten list.

Stay close.

Follow instructions immediately without question.

Don't act on any other matter except the case in hand.

Don't interact with anyone you know unless it's unavoidable.

If you speak to anyone, say nothing to affect their destiny.

Worry lines creased Wesley's forehead as he contemplated the last line. He held it up. 'I hope you don't expect me to eat this Veronica, because I don't think I could fit it in after all that pizza.'

'You've been watching too many movies.' Veronica laughed. 'And they said you were boring.'

'Who said that?' Wesley shrugged. 'Never mind, I don't want to know.'

'Precisely why I hired you, Wesley Brent. Tomorrow we begin...'

As soon as Wesley walked through the door the next morning he saw Veronica buzzing around the room. She retrieved a small card from the file with a photograph attached.

'This one will do today, Wesley.' She tapped the client card with a red nailed finger. 'Are you ready?'

The first mission wasn't what he had anticipated. He'd expected to be involved in preventing some terrible event in history—a bombing or a plane crash at the very least. But that first assignment had been a tense waiting game in a seedy downtown bar, late on a wintry night a mere ten years in the past.

A middle aged socialite had paid an exorbitant fee for Veronica to intercept her husband, an ageing Don Juan, from meeting his current mistress. Because the wife had no way of knowing the exact moment her husband had met the dazzling creature who'd become his latest lover, Veronica and Wesley endured a long wait.

The prospective mistress was in an upstairs room singing a

collection of sultry ballads. The cheating husband didn't arrive for hours. Finally, he swept through the door bringing an icy blast.

Veronica flicked a cigarette lighter near the fire sensor. A narrow flame rose and flickered unnoticed. The alarm shrieked. Chaos reigned. Patrons screamed and shoved, desperate to escape. Wesley seized the man's arm and ushered him into a waiting taxi. The would-be lover was on his way in a matter of minutes, none the wiser.

Over the next few months Veronica relaxed. Wesley was sure she had grown to trust him. She didn't comment any further about Evan. Perhaps he had failed to stay near her when they were on a mission or broken one of the other rules.

They slipped into an easy routine. Veronica gave him a brief outline of the mission ahead along with concise instructions. Then they entered the creaky lift at the rear of the building; their conduit to another time. Veronica used an ornate fob watch to select the parameters of their destination. When they stepped out of the lift they were at the precise location and time she'd programmed.

It was Wesley's job to arrange incidentals. Detours and meals were often necessary and it was also his role to source the correct money and maps. Wesley hadn't imagined these necessities, but it made sense that even supernatural powers needed organisation. Once they were on assignment, Veronica had bigger things to worry about.

When the mission was accomplished, Veronica would signal to Wesley. Taking the small black mobile he'd been given, he pressed #. That summoned the lumbering George with their taxi. The taxi was different according to the era, but it was always George who collected them. When they were in the taxi Veronica tapped the watch. They were instantly back in the lift at the office.

To Wesley's disappointment, the assignments continued to be mundane. They stopped Mrs Damson's Labrador wandering from home. They travelled back to the day Mrs Wiltshire decided to dye her hair a fiery red. One assignment had involved showing up at a ritzy hotel to remind a young bride-to-be to pick up her handbag containing a ridiculously expensive engagement ring. They sent Mrs Beverly home early from the supermarket the day the decorators were due, forestalling a 'truly hideous colour choice' by her husband who was taking revenge on his wife for inviting her mother to stay.

Wesley consoled himself with the thought that his new life was the closest he'd ever come to being a hero. Anyway, he had plenty to keep him busy. There was research in the library building to ascertain whether the client was attempting to use their services for criminal purposes. 'Better safe than sorry,' Veronica said. And there was always the weather to check.

Winter slipped into spring. Wesley finished painting the mural for the Estefans and had arranged to meet Sara at the café after work. The mural was a vibrant portrayal of life in Italy. Wesley had painted all the Estefan family members from their village, sitting at tables and dancing in the square.

The last rays of the sun slanted onto the rooftops. Wesley whistled as he walked. He was looking forward to spending the evening with Sara. The café was their favourite eatery. It was full of the aromas of Italy and throbbed with the hum of friendship and life. Inside, the stucco walls were painted a muted crimson. The floor was covered with black and white harlequin tiles that shone and sparkled all day. Estella achieved this by rolling out the ancient metal bucket and mop at least half a dozen times a day.

Wesley greeted them and sat with Dimitri.

'Oi, that woman, she makes me tired,' Dimitri said. 'She will wash away the tiles and we will have just concrete left.'

Estella swished the mop in the direction of her husband. 'Why are you sitting old man?' she asked. The men exchanged sly looks and grinned. 'Oh, you have finish our mural Wesley? May I see?

Dimitri does not let me have even one peek.'

'Come woman, and stop your bellyaching at me.' Dimitri led the way outside.

Estella wiped her apron across watery eyes. 'Bellissimo Wesley! Where did you learn such things? It is just like home.' Her voice was rich and caressing. She embraced Wesley. 'Why did you not wait for Sara? Oh see, here she is now.'

Wesley turned. Sara had left her corporate image behind. Her long chestnut hair was loose and she wore a casual sundress. She looked like sunshine, young and free. The image of her in the twilight reminded him of the first time he'd seen her at their University orientation event. He found it hard to breathe and hoped she didn't notice.

Estella bounded up to meet Sara and swept her aside. 'Ciao bella. Is not the mural Wesley painted bellisimo? He is wonderful. And so are you, coming to help an old man with his accounts. Grazie, molte grazie.'

Estella cleared the tables while Wesley swept the floor.

Dimitri sat at the corner table with Sara. He leant over the old ledger stained with sauces from the kitchen. The old man watched the earnest young woman tally the accounts; her eyes alight with enthusiasm.

'How can you love numbers on a page?' Dimitri said, 'when there is so much more.' He placed his hand on his heart.

Sara looked up. 'Are you all right, Dimitri?'

'Of course, cara. It is *your* heart I think about. It is for you time to fall in love.'

Sara laughed. 'I have had too much love, Dimitri.'

'You have had too much something, I think. But it is not too much love.'

'I keep getting love wrong, Dimitri.'

'It's not the love you get wrong cara, I think you maybe get the wrong man.' Dimitri removed his glasses and wiped them on his red handkerchief. 'Don't listen to me. I'm just an old man who wishes everyone happy.' He glanced across at Wesley who was emptying bins while Estella sang to the pigeons crooning on the beams under the awnings. 'Come, enough work. Wesley, join us and celebrate.'

Dimitri brought two bottles of red wine, dragging Estella from her cleaning on the way.

As the chill of the evening fell, Estella lit the candles and coaxed Dimitri to dance with her.

Wesley took Sara's hands and led her to a space between the tables. He pulled her close. 'This will have to be a very slow dance Sara, there's not much room.'

'The mural is wonderful, Wesley,' said Sara. 'I don't know how you've had time for it. You've been helping me set up my new office on top of your own work. It's a big step for me, starting an accountancy practice on my own. I couldn't have done it without you, you know. You're my best friend.' She gave a nervous laugh. 'I don't know how you've put up with me. All those tears I've cried on your shoulder over some stupid man.'

Wesley struggled to find words, but couldn't. Instead, he kissed the top of her head. Just one tear for me, Sara. I'd give anything for you to cry one tear for me, he thought.

Sara put down her glass and took Wesley's hand. 'I have something I want to ask you.'

Wesley's eyes searched hers.

'I would really like you to be my partner in the business. We're a great team.'

Disappointment formed a lump in Wesley's throat. 'I'm sorry, Sara. I have a job,' he said, his voice thin. 'It's, well it's important. I help Veronica find things and people, make a difference.' He spun her around, forcing a smile and cursing his cowardice for not revealing the real reason—that it would be unbearable to see her all the time, loving her as he did. Friendship would have to do.

'I'm sorry. I shouldn't have asked,' she said.

He blanched at the pain in her eyes. He smiled to soften the words. They continued to dance, but the mood between them had changed. Estella chided the grandchildren for peeking when they should have been in bed. Wesley heard the deep rumble of Dimitri's words of love to his wife and her laughing response. He experienced a sharp pang of longing and drew Sara closer.

The next morning Wesley woke early and ran a hasty hand through his hair. His mind was annoyingly foggy. He must have had too much red wine. While Sara was in his arms he had almost hoped ... but now he had to focus on the day and the next mission. When he arrived at the office Veronica briefed him. Derby Day, Kentucky, 1974. A father had gambled away his daughter's college fund on a 20-1 horse named Patience.

At the races they recognised their target from the photo his daughter had provided. The man was waiting for the betting booth to open. He paced, patting a fat wallet. Veronica tipped a glass of wine on him and began a long-winded argument with him. He missed the queue.

'That's great,' said Wesley. 'All over quickly.'

'I wish it was that simple. There are three more days of the racing carnival.'

'Oh. He's still going to blow his money, isn't he?'

Veronica sighed. 'If he gets the chance. We'll have to stay. Tramping around a soggy racetrack isn't my idea of fun but we have to see this through.'

Wesley wondered if Veronica ever tired of time travel. Being a Superhero wasn't all it was cracked up to be as far as he could see. He booked them into a small Bed & Breakfast near the racecourse.

Their man was a vain and superficial creature who seemed to care only for fancy clothes, inane conversation and copious quantities of whisky, and survived on a few hours' sleep at night.

Wesley could quietly murder him. God only knows what *that* would do to the cosmos. Veronica was in fine form. She managed to prevent the man from placing a single bet. After the final race was run, the two time travellers sat exhausted in the refreshments marquee.

'The last three days have been the most terminally boring of my entire life,' said Wesley, resting his head on the back of the chair.

Veronica dropped her wine glass.

Wesley touched her arm. 'Veronica! You're as white as a ghost!'

Veronica's hands shook. Her eyes were fixed on some point in the straggling crowd that was streaming towards the exit gates. All at once she was off, throwing herself into the jubilant arms of a well-built man with a thatch of blonde hair. Spinning her around, the man rained kisses on her neck.

Wesley froze.

'What the...? Veronica! You'll mess with the time space continuum thingy.'

Veronica turned to face him, her arm firmly around the man beside her. 'It's all right, Wesley.'

'No it's not! This can't be good, it's dangerous. It's against the rules—*your* rules.' He reached for his notebook. It wasn't in his pocket. 'This can't be happening. We'll never get home.'

'Wesley, stop. This is ... my assistant, the one I lost, remember?'

Wesley gaped at them. 'Evan?'

'Yes, Evan. Evan *Goodwin*.' Veronica placed a gloved hand on Wesley's arm. 'Everything is as it should be, Wesley.' She peeled the glove from her hand, revealing a wedding ring. 'This is where I belong. Here with Evan; in the past.'

'Oh! I see,' he said, scratching his head. 'Actually, I don't see at all.'

Veronica smiled a soft smile of regret. 'Think about it, dear man.'

'Oh, my! So, I'm from the future.'

'Yes, Wesley dear.'

It was quiet in the taxi with George. Wesley watched the outside world blur by the darkened taxi window.

'What happens now, George?'

'Whatever you choose, Wesley.' George handed him the fob watch; the key to going home.

Wesley looked down at the watch. The legacy of time travel was now his to accept or reject. He could be the next Superhero if he wished.

Wesley handed the watch back. 'You tap it George. I'm going home. For Good.'

He ran from the lift. The office didn't even warrant a sideways glance. He needed Sara, wanted her. He would accept the partnership. She might come to love him. It was worth the chance.

Sara stared out into the darkness. The city lights blinked mutely. Where on earth was Wesley? He'd been gone for days. She wound her hair around tense fingers, wavering between anxiety about his safety and anger that he hadn't called. Now and then, she wiped salty wetness from her face.

She thought of everything they'd been through together. All the times he had been her calm and stable rock. She thought of the weeks she had spent with him after his parents died, when he hadn't been able to face the world. She'd made him get up and keep going, forced him to eat, gone through every corner of the cottage he grew up in, sorting all the possessions of his parents' lives. She remembered all the times they'd helped each other shift. When had her feelings turned to love? How had she ever been content with friendship with this wonderful man? The one who never let her down. She wept bitter tears. Tears for Wesley.

Finally, as the pink dust of dawn intruded she curled into a ball on the sofa and fell asleep.

There was a loud rap on the door.

She flung it open.

'Sara, you really must remember to check who's at the door before you ... Oh no, you've been crying.'

She crushed him to her.

'Who hurt you this time?' Wesley murmured against her ear. 'I'll kill him.'

'Then you will have to kill yourself, you idiot! Where have you been? I've been worried out of my mind!' She rained salty kisses on him.

'I haven't been gone that long,' he said. 'What do you mean? I'm the one who hurt you?'

'Do I have to spell it out for you Wesley?' Sara's eyes sparkled.

'Yes, please.' Wesley drew her closer and manoeuvred them to the couch where he pulled her into his lap. 'Spelling would be great. I've always liked spelling. Did I tell you I once won a spell...'

Sara silenced him with a lingering kiss.

'I think you misspelled that. You may have to do it again.'

Sara laughed. 'I love you.'

'It's about time. I've loved you for ages.' Wesley smiled. 'Now *do* stop interrupting a perfectly good spelling lesson.' He returned her kisses with all the passion of those hungry years.

Ancient grief

Her eyes are shiny bright with unshed tears. Like hardened diamonds, unseeing but not unknowing. But what these eyes know now, they cannot share. Cannot tell. Cannot face. She sits amidst the crowd in this place for which she has no name. She lives here with the other 39, or perhaps she exists. Her progress notes call her a resident so perhaps she resides.

Bending over the dining table, clutching her walking stick, she still manages to appear erect, although she has not been straight-of-back these many years. She is 89, and for all those around her she is essentially alone, surrounded by people; but isolated by grief.

Her son has died. He was 71, so in the eyes of many, an old man. But not to her, never to her—she who is older than him by the years of her motherhood. She measures all the years of her days by her children, her three sons, now two. She rose early the day after he died, putting two curlers in her hair as she usually did. Then took them out again before going to the dining room for breakfast. As she always did.

She put her make-up on as she usually did, but today with trembling hand, a little heavier handed than usual. She walks a little slower. Stays a little longer at the table as if to avoid being alone in her room.

These little signs are the only indication of her breaking heart.

She will get up at the same time she always does tomorrow. She will sigh over the ritual of the bed-making. She will thank the nurses. And we who nurse her do not know how to go to her, in this world of her devastation. For she is from the generation where emotions have 'their place'.

Not like we nurses who vent and share and cry without shame. But we must leave her there. In the memorial of her own choosing.

We talk of how we would throw ourselves out with the rubbish, go to bed for weeks, cry all day if we were in her shoes, but we leave her to grieve, seemingly without comfort. And if, while she stares out of her window, she is remembering bright sunny days when children played at her feet, tugging on her apron with their incessant demands, we leave her then too.

She brushes the crumbs from her skirt with an absent gaze that glances, but never connects with her fellow residents. She has kept her distance from other people all these years. Even when she was a young mother, with white sheets flapping and snapping in the rhythm of summer days near the paling fence, she gathered her own to her. Even then, she was reserved, inwardly nurturing - serenity mistaken for solemnity.

Reaching out with guarded hand, she gently touches her son's face in the photograph by her bedside, when she thinks we are not watching. The tears struggle down her wrinkled cheeks. She hears a door open. She is so afraid to be seen exposed and vulnerable that she flees to the bathroom, to the shower, and the comfort of silent grieving.

She lives her life like this every day for the next two weeks. Clinging desperately to the routine of her days. But like a shaken leaf on an autumn tree, she falls. Unable to fall into her grief, she falls in the shower. The nurses find her naked and bleeding, broken and alone.

This is the one thing she is afraid of, helplessness and exposure.

The ambulance comes and she is stoic still, looking past the concerned eyes of the nurses and the ambulance officers.

When she comes back, she seems the same, but there are subtle differences. We watch her carefully, thinking she is a little more stooped, a little more fragile.

Then she begins to get up earlier in the mornings, and she sits in the foyer where she has never sat before. When we ask her why she is there early in the morning and late at night she focuses us with clear, direct eyes.

'I am waiting for the school bus.'

She has wandered to a place that is safe; a place where everything dear and everyone precious still exists.

Leaving our reality, she has found her own. Her grieving and memories have combined in this new world. She lets us lead her. She doesn't ask us to take her back to her 'room' the way she used to.

'Take me home,' she whispers.

I'm not crazy

'I'm not meant to be here,' she said in a deceptively light whisper, 'I don't need this wheelchair, you know.'

Abbie smiled. Soon to graduate from nursing she'd been appointed to admit June Stein and had read the notes. Over a decade had passed since June Stein had walked. Abbie knew the elderly woman suffered from dementia, but Abbie had a special touch with the dementia patients and admired the old girl's sass. She was enthusiastically, gloriously mad.

While others cringed and crept into dementia, June Stein had gone boldly and fearlessly. There was no tremulous footfall on the doorstep to the house of Alzheimer's.

Her thick grey hair was swept into a meticulous top knot. She wore a tailored dress with a matching jacket. The old girl had style. Her clothes screamed designer fashion.

'Oh, well then,' said Abbie. 'We'll put it away. It will give you more room.'

She was rewarded with a look of respect from the man wheeling June.

'Oh, but you can't walk, Mrs Stein,' said Tiffany, a second year nurse, known for her 'ditz factor'.

Mrs Stein pinned Tiffany with clear bright eyes, like an ancient bird of prey. The man wheeling her chair wiped a tired hand across his dark handsome brow. He had seen his aunt in this mode before. June had chosen her next victim.

Tiffany shifted her gaze from June to the man behind her and Abbie saw the shock of attraction in her eyes. Tiffany preened and began the spiel about the admission process, all the while openly admiring the man. Normally keen to avoid anything remotely resembling work, Tiffany was in her element. Her usual sulky attitude evaporated as she pulled out all the stops to impress. June's eyes narrowed and exhaled a loud harrumph of disgust.

'Tiffany don't you have something else to do?' asked Abbie. She wanted to get out of the crowded corridor and on with the job of admitting June Stein.

'Yes, Tiffany, don't you have something else to do?' the woman repeated. Turning to Abbie she said, 'You can call me June, dear.'

'My aunt is a tyrant,' said the man as he raised both hands in an elegant gesture of defeat, a rueful smile lighting up his handsome face.

'Don't listen to him. He's trying to steal my house and put me in one of those atrocious homes for *old* people.' June whispered behind an arthritic hand laden with large showy rings.

'Now Aunt June, do be fair, darling. You are living in *my* house with *me*,' said the tall newcomer as he expertly wheeled June through the door of Room 5. 'I am James Stein, by the way,' he said with a bemused smile.

God, but the man was gorgeous, thought Abbie.

A fact not lost on Tiffany who was positively glowing.

'I'm Tiffany, I mean Nurse Barrett.'

'And you are?' he queried, pinning Abbie with eyes as black as ebony.

'I am Nurse Banks, otherwise known as persona non gratis,' she said. She threw a sideways glance at Tiffany who had systematically pawned her work off on everyone else all shift.

'Tiffany!' the word was like a gunshot.

Sister Renshaw had entered the room and after a formal nod to James Stein, she beckoned Tiffany to the doorway.

'I thought you had diarrhoea and were going home, Nurse Barrett. I asked Nurse Banks to admit this patient. Would you like to tell me why you are here drooling over some patient's relative, when not ten minutes ago you were moaning about feeling sick?'

Tiffany stuttered and Sister Renshaw held up a warning hand, 'I have made an appointment with Dr Broadside. He will require a stool sample. Get going. Now!'

Flushed with humiliation, Tiffany offered a meek, 'Very well, Sister, if you wish, I was just trying to soldier on.'

For the first time since Abbie had met Tiffany her naturally glowing cheeks outshone her strawberry blonde hair.

Sister Renshaw came back into the room where Abbie was putting June's suitcase into the wardrobe. 'Are you alright, Nurse Banks?' she questioned with a sharp look. 'Certainly sister, no mystery illnesses, no hideous diseases,' Abbie said.

'That's enough, Banks. You have to watch this one,' said Sister Renshaw with a warning finger pointed at Abbie. 'You never know what is going to come out of her mouth next.'

'She'll be a match for this one then,' June said, with hand waved casually in James' direction.

With a small smile of respect for another grand dame, Sister Renshaw left the room with the simple injunction to Abbie, 'Watch what you say to him, Nurse Banks, he's a lawyer and my godson.'

'Yes, Sister.'

'*I'm* saying nothing. I know when I am beaten,' said James.

'Don't let that fool you; he's more dangerous when he is quiet.' June rummaged through her tapestry bag.

'My aunt oversells me, I'm afraid,' he said as he moved closer to the bed, 'What are you looking for, Aunt?'

'My pills, James, where did you put them?'

He deftly removed a plastic bag and handed it to Abbie. While June fussed over her cosmetics and toiletries James answered Abbie's questions. She was surprised. He gave all the details of her medications and private health insurance by memory, even though he held the paperwork loosely at his side.

His eyes never left Abbie. Draped casually in the chair one minute, then leaning forward, gaze intent the next. He must be one hell of a lawyer. As a man he was even more formidable. Abbie couldn't deny she was impressed. Her last boyfriend had been just that – a boy, but there was no immaturity in this man's demeanour. There was a smattering of grey hair beginning to show in his sideburns. Abbie could imagine him serious and aloof in a courtroom, but at that moment his playfulness unnerved her. Giving herself a mental shake, she continued to ask the usual questions about allergies and aids.

'He's just showing off to a pretty young thing,' muttered June, finished with her organizing and bored with the conversation. 'He's a lawyer; he gets paid to remember things. He doesn't care about me.'

She eyed him with a petulant stare. James didn't rise to the bait, merely patting her on the head fondly.

'That won't curry you any favour, James. Why can't you let me talk for myself? I'm not stupid you know.'

'I'm sorry aunt, you may have the floor.' James made a gracious gesture that was pure theatrics.

June gave him a look that she obviously intended to be menacing, but it came over as a reluctant smile. 'I dare say you got it right, you always do,' she acquiesced. 'I just don't like it when nobody is talking to me.'

'Ah, my dear Aunt June. We are talking *about* you, and there is so much to discuss that I fear Nurse Banks and I will need to meet after work so that I can fill her in on all my crimes. I stand accused of many, you see,' he said, watching Abbie intently. 'Of course they are nothing compared to those committed *to me.*' He paused, his gaze on June, and was gratified to hear a spirited snort from her. 'Abuses of a heinous nature; slander, bribery and corruption, not to mention denial of freedom. And then there was that rather unfortunate episode last week of attempted poisoning when you laced my omelette with disinfectant.'

June let out an indignant chuckle. 'That wasn't my fault. It was that darned Jeanette you call a housekeeper who rearranged the pantry.'

James threw his head back and laughed with joyous abandon. The two of them tripped over each other telling the story of how James had let his housekeeper have the night off and June had refused to eat food that was 'delivered'. She'd insisted on hobbling around the kitchen attempting to cook tea. Where his arrogant practiced routine had failed to impress, his self-deprecating humour and his warmth to his aunt enchanted Abbie.

They heard the clink and rumble of the tea trolley. After a gentle tap, the door opened to reveal Abbie's sister, Jem, who was serving as a pink lady in her school holidays. James looked from one to the other, confused until he noticed Jem's name badge.

'Good grief, there are two of you,' he exclaimed.

The two girls laughed. Only one year apart, with dark, wavy long hair they were often mistaken for twins.

'Wow,' said James, 'and both gorgeous!'

'And single,' chirped Jem, hamming it up with her hand behind her head, imitating a Hollywood siren. 'I'm Jemima, and this is my sister, Abbie.'

James eyebrows rose. 'Abbie. So the raven-haired sprite has a name, it suits you.'

Abbie blushed.

'Bugger!' said a deep male voice from behind Jem. 'Flaming trolleys, why don't you watch where you put them girlie?'

Jem stepped aside to reveal Reverend O'Brien with his crisp white collar askew. He was wearing his immaculately tailored vest under his faded brown cardigan. His thin grey hair was combed over his bald pate and he gazed sternly over his horn rimmed glasses. The dressing on his head had come undone on one side and the blood soaked pad hung down over his left ear.

He held them with a gaze that must have terrified many from the pulpit in the cathedral where he had been a reverend for decades. He had his King James Version of the Bible under his arm.

Unfortunately, he was naked from the waist down.

Jem squealed.

'What the hell!' said June.

An elegant rising of the eyebrows and a quizzical stare was the only reaction from James.

Reverend Chapman had been a patient on the general surgical ward for six weeks now. He had originally come in for a resection of the prostate gland, but his dementia increased, and he had suffered several falls since his operation.

'Oh dear! Reverend, you can't roam around like that!' said Abbie, calmly threading his arm through hers and leading him to the door.

'Don't drag me around girlie, that woman requested a Bible study from 2nd Corinthians. Don't stand in the way of the Lord's work!'

'Reverend! You have no pants on; you can't go into other rooms half-naked.'

He interrupted his stumbling gait to look down.

'Stone the crows!'

Abbie snatched the towel the tea lady handed her, threw it around Reverend Chapman and steered him out of the room. She had great difficulty holding the towel in place, as well as the old reverend's arm as they navigated an unsteady progress down the corridor.

'Here, Reverend, you hold the towel so I can guide you.'

He looked down at the towel, then at his Bible where one long finger was keeping his place.

'But I will lose my place,' he moaned, cagily eyeing Abbie as one fallen from grace who'd lost all sense of the importance of Bible studies.

With a harrumph he let the towel drop.

Corinthians II had won out.

With his pious head held high he proceeded half-naked to his room with Abbie desperately trying to cover him with the towel in front.

The tea lady smiled and shook her head at the sight of his sagging ancient buttocks.

When Abbie returned to June's room to finish the admission by taking her routine observations—Jem was calmly ensconced on the bed chatting. All three were still chuckling over the old reverend's antics. It seemed the whole 'debacle' had cheered June no end.

'Well handled, Nurse Abbie, I will have you on my law team any day,' said James.

'Oh dear! I hope you don't have much need for assistance with half-dressed dementia sufferers!'

'Oh, she specializes in difficult people, our Abbie,' Jem added with a cheeky grin.

'Shouldn't you be somewhere *else* putting flowers in vases, Jem?' said Abbie.

The hint was lost on Jem who calmly announced, 'James is taking us both for coffee seeing as we've both finished our shift. Isn't that sweet of him, Abbie?'

Jem threw Abbie a defiant look.

'Oh yeah, he's about as sweet as the 'grandma' in Little Red Riding Hood.'

James put his hand on his heart—'You wound me,

mademoiselle.'

Abbie hesitated. 'Well...'

'I promise to behave. I'll put it in writing if you like.'

June snorted.

'Oh go with him, girl. He hasn't shown this much interest in years. He's become a boring workaholic. Do me a favour, and put some life back into him.'

June gave a dismissive wave, but her eyes were warm with affection.

'I suppose you're going to get rid of me now?' Jem pouted.

'My aunt's cooking will take care of that,' said James, steering Abbie quickly towards the door.

Sonnet 116

Rebecca smiled as she watched a father and son at the water's edge. The man was teaching the boy how to skim pebbles across the smooth surface of the lake. The pain in her side stabbed as if to remind her that her allotted time for enjoying the vistas of life was short now. Idly checking her watch, she breathed in slowly – the pain relief would work better if she was calm. The doctor would be here soon with the news. There hadn't been much hope, other than that surgery might buy her a little time. She was ready.

The boy squealed with glee as his stone skipped twice. The father lifted him up and swung him around in triumph, while the little boy clung tightly, nestling his head into his father's neck. The child was breathless when the father put him back on his feet. The man turned an anxious gaze to a woman sitting on the grass shielding her eyes from the early afternoon sun. The woman waved briefly and the man carried the boy back to her. The woman turned to look at the hospice courtyard and Rebecca's heart constricted. For a moment she had thought the woman was her daughter Candace. The young woman who had walked away so many years ago.

A tiny girl ran to the woman and grabbed her from behind with a joyful, 'Mummy, Mummy, look what I found.'

The woman swung the girl around to wrap her in her arms in a gesture that brought memories tripping back to Rebecca. Of sun-bright days, of playful times so full of love that she had felt so much happiness couldn't possibly be hers. Couldn't possibly last.

Adopted herself as an infant to an unprepared couple in the later years, Rebecca had always struggled with a sense of belonging and Candace, her only child, had been her first experience of unconditional love.

However, it was a love that later found conditions, reasons, limits. 'Love is not love which alters when it alteration finds, or bends with the remover to remove,' she whispered.

She clutched the battered book of sonnets, vainly hoping that repeating lines from Shakespeare's sonnet 116 would bring a long hungered for release. None came. Rebecca sighed as she wrapped the delicately crocheted shawl over her legs - a gift from a friend. The afternoon chill was creeping along the headland, but she wasn't ready to go inside yet. Anyway she had to wait for the nurses.

While she waited she allowed herself to drift into those memories that she had denied for so many years. As she did, she watched the mother and daughter. They were walking towards the hospice, and as they came closer Rebecca recognised them. The little boy was a patient. The father adjusted the child's beanie as tiny wisps of hair escaped. Leukaemia. How would the parents cope? The loss of a child was unthinkable. The errant thought that twisted her nights crept into Rebecca's consciousness, 'Would it be easier to lose a child who wasn't leaving of their own will, but would fight to stay—stay with love?'

It was harder to shake those thoughts these days. It wasn't as bad as the early days when she had pled with Candace, begged for understanding and soaked her lumpy pillow with a hurricane of tears. Every explanation, every apology was met with the same tense silence. Candace's body language should have been enough - her eyes averted, her movements stiff and cold. With every attempt to breach the gap, it widened. There would be no forgiveness. No forgiveness for a marriage gone wrong – a chasm between a broken-hearted child and a mother bowed down with the guilt of failure, but too generous to taint the child with details, deeds or a mother's personal consequences. Deep in her heart, Rebecca knew it wouldn't have made any difference.

How much she had been tempted to answer her friends with hopeful phrases, but the words would have been lies. What was done was done, and half a bridge is no bridge. There was much she had left out in the telling. Of how she had paid for Candace's degree, with no expectation of reward or gratitude. It had galled Candace to accept help, and her rancour increased through the years of her study. Her attitude had soured so much towards her mother that Rebecca had thought twice about attending her daughter's graduation. Though uninvited, in the end she had gone, gliding quietly into the back of the Great Hall, as the grandly robed academics filed past, followed by the proud graduates.

Later, she had seen Candace outside embracing her friends. Their eyes met briefly and that look told Rebecca what her heart dreaded. Rebecca placed a small exquisitely wrapped gift into Candace's hand. Candace flushed, nodded and accepted it with a swift gesture, then turned away.

Glad that she hadn't told her friends what she'd done, Rebecca disappeared into the crowd of strangers. There wasn't one person there who knew her identity. She had denied that reality before, but now it gripped her heart with icy fingers. How foolish her friends would have thought her; to keep reaching out, striving, accepting the label of unforgiven, unwelcome.

A bustle at the doors to the courtyard told her the doctor had arrived. She tensed, then relaxed. It was okay. Inevitable.

The loved the soft murmur of the doctor's voice. She'd been lucky with him - he'd become a friend. The words swirled around her, but she felt detached from them - wondering how bad news could come with such lyric. Then the word 'remission' startled her.

'Reprieve...?' Turning her gaze to him she saw the broad beam of his smile.

'We got it all,' he said. 'Rare indeed.'

The nurse hugged her. There was talk of discharge when the pain was under control. Then the word that stunned her the most, *home*.

Joy filled her like a song. 'Oh,' she said.

'Do remember to breathe, Rebecca,' laughed Dr Miles, stooping down to pick up the tattered pad that had been keeping her place in the book. Narrowing his eyes, he looked at it. 'Goodness me, Rebecca, what are you doing with a cheque book? Bribing the nurses?'

He left briskly with a chuckle to the sister, who called a nurse to 'bring Mrs Bentley inside now'. Rebecca looked down at the cheque book. She hadn't used it in over twenty years. It fell open to where it usually did - the stub dated the day of Candace's graduation. She closed the book and placed it on the coffee table.

'Are you ready, Rebecca?' said a young nurse manoeuvring a wheelchair.

Rebecca slid into the chair with the girl's help. As the passed through the Activity Room Rebecca asked the nurse to stop while she slipped the book into the hospice library, and then flung the unfinished cheque book into the rubbish bin. Reprieved.

'I'm not sure if anyone is going to read a book of Shakespeare's sonnets,' laughed the nurse.

'Well, I've no further use for it. You never know... someone might...' said Rebecca. 'It's the second copy I've given away...'

The nurse just nodded as she tucked Rebecca into the bed efficiently. When the girl left, Rebecca smiled. For the first time she was glad Candace had thrown out the gift of her love, the book she'd given her on that distant graduation day. For if her daughter had found the hefty cheque next to Sonnet 116 Rebecca would never have known if she was loved for love's sake alone, or if love had found alteration.

My Fair Lady

The old woman shivered on the park bench, causing several of the petals of the decaying rose on her lap to fall to the ground. 'Ah, 'tis a bitter wind that it is,' she said, 'I'll be sellin' no flow'rs today, I feah.'

Strangers walking past bent to ask soft questions, but she continued to talk to herself while she delicately arranged her faded long skirts.

'Are you alright, Madam?' asked a woman. A bright eyed child ran to join the newcomer and knocked the bench.

'Nah then, Freddy: look wheah y'gowin, deah.' The old woman's voice had changed to a course Cockney accent.

'Who's that, Mummy?' asked a boyish voice.

'Eliza Doolittle,' breathed the woman, shocked as memories of reading George Bernard Shaw's 'Pygmalion' surfaced.

'Y'know me then, luvvy?'

The young mother was silent.

'Fancy some flow'rs, deah? Wot's y'name, pet?'

'Hope...ah Benton,' said the woman, sitting and reaching into her handbag and taking out a mobile phone. '...er...this is my son...'

The boy tilted his head to look at the old woman. 'My name isn't Freddy, it's Damien,' he said.

'Oh, never you pay me no mind, my deah. I calls everyone Freddy. S'easier y'see.'

While the old woman and the boy chatted Hope phoned the police. The woman began to cough, a hacking, rasping sound.

'Nah, Freddy, ev'ry winter I gets the chills.'

The police arrived and the gentle nature of the old woman changed. 'Leave me be, y'feckless Bobbies. I aint doin' a liv'n soul no 'arm.'

Hope turned questioning eyes towards the police officer.

'Thanks, ma'am. She lives in a nursing home nearby and every now and then she escapes.' The officer shrugged.

'Who is she? She was talking normally then started sprouting lines from... well... My Fair Lady... you know the...'

'Yes, love. She's what we call a regular. Name's Beatrice Ormiston—an actress at one time. Only minor roles mind you, but apparently her 'crowning achievement' was being understudy as Eliza Doolittle. I don't know why she chooses the first Act.'

'So, you've seen...'

'Yeah, well, you know the wife dragged me along...'

'Right.' Hope laughed. 'Will she be okay?'

'Sure, the nurses will sort her out...'

'I outlived him, you know.' The old woman spoke in clipped upper class tones.

Hope's forehead creased.

'Yes, Beatrice, you won,' said the officer, shaking his head.

'Wha...' muttered Hope.

'Look, I shouldn't...you're not a journalist are you?' asked the burly policeman. He hesitated, but the young woman had been so kind. It had been days before anyone had found Beatrice the last time.

'Do I look like a journalist?' asked Hope, holding one handle of the child's stroller and struggling to keep a large carry bag from dragging on the ground.

'Sorry. We have to be careful.'

'...I won out in the end. That I did. Philandering waster that he was...I stayed with that beastly man, never complaining, biding my time. Waiting for freedom. Waiting and waiting.'

'Who is she now? Another part in a play?'

'No, she's herself at the moment. Won't last long though. Then she'll go back to Eliza... always Eliza. She hated her husband you see, but was too proud to leave him. Was always polite to his face, but pure venom behind his back. He suffered from gas poisoning in the war and wasn't expected to live...so she waited...'

'Oh. What happened to him?'

'He struggled with his lungs, but lasted remarkably well. Only died last year. They owned a mansion, but by the time he died she'd lost her memory and didn't even know where she lived, couldn't even find her way home from the street corner. Turned out, he'd been holding her together.'

'So she got dementia...around the same time...?

'Hard to say, really. She wasn't a great actor, but she was a good one. She would ignore him, then chuckle to her friends that she was Dame Vague and say how much she was looking forward to living alone in the mansion. Whenever something was unpleasant, she acted as though she hadn't caught on... So no-one really noticed how far she'd slipped. Of course she couldn't hide it when she began to regress to 'Eliza'. At first everyone thought it was a joke, her husband humoured her in it. I guess the act became real.'

'So did she ever get to live alone in the mansion?'

The policeman laughed. 'Not for day. The husband had to put her into care years before he died. He hired a nurse and domestic staff and died at home. Well, I'd better...'

'Oh, sorry to keep you. She seemed so...lost. What a story?'

'That's life, truth's stranger than fiction they say.'

'Ah-ah-ah-ow-ow-ow-oo, get orf with yer, Freddy,' the old woman shouted, 'This 'ere taxi won't drive its flamin' self.'

Mother's Day

The church was filled with ruffled chrysanthemums, vibrant dahlias and the low murmur of cheerful chatter. Slanted rays of the early afternoon sun seeped through stained glass windows. The pulpit had been replaced by a row of flower arrangements that spoke of an informal mood of celebration. Many of the women still proudly wore the tiny bouquets that had been pinned to their dresses at the morning Mother's Day service.

Penny smiled softly at eighteen month old Dylan who was carefully turning the pages of his favourite book. Her eyes wandered to the large window nearest her, and stayed looking beyond, drinking in the beauty of the park across the road. Wishing she was there. Her husband patted her knee in consolation of her respect for his desire to attend. She sighed. She wanted to drag her eyes back to the meeting, but couldn't. At least there would be no standing, kneeling or sitting routines to get wrong. Inattention wouldn't be noticed today.

Pages crackled, voices rose and fell, someone sang; but for Penny it was all happening so far away. There were several speakers, men and women. Words of 'joy', 'courage', 'sacrifice' and 'happiness' filtered through. Someone's voice caught Penny's attention, or was it the words? She couldn't tell. The 'oldest mother' was announced and an elderly woman walked quickly to the front to be presented with one of the large bouquets by the beaming main speaker. The audience applauded. Dear old Mrs Rankin, how sweet, thought Penny. She was about to return her gaze to the park when her heart began to race, thundering in her throat. What had he said? The 'newest mother'. Oh no. He was holding one of the bouquets as the panel and the congregation suggested a few names.

Then stunned silence. The man at the front had turned pained eyes on Penny, his face pale. Others turned to look, their gaze a mirror of his. Penny's hands trembled. The man stood in momentary confusion, and then with a soft smile walked from the front of the church down the long aisle to Penny. Wordlessly, he handed her the bouquet. By now, embarrassed tears were streaming down her face. Everyone held their breath, uncertain, awkward.

Penny stood and clutched the bouquet, mouthing grateful thanks to the man. From somewhere deep inside a tentative smile surfaced. The audience applauded. It was her first smile in several weeks. It was also the first bouquet since that day when the ground was covered with flowers beside a tiny white coffin.

Eyes like the Ocean

Oh dear God! '*Be still my beating heart*', thought Kayla as she gunned her Ute out of the car park, spewing gravel. *The man was gorgeous.*

Of course it was her luck to see him in the middle of a frantic early morning dash to the local hardware store. It also had to be on a day when she had tied a cleaning rag around her hair. Tearing out of the door she had thrown a faded denim shirt over a lacy singlet top.

'*Kayla*, your underwear is showing!' her shocked mother declared.

Underwear my eye. Her mother was such a dinosaur. The strappy top cost a fortune and was a soft grey with fuchsia lace edging. It was a rare celebration of her femininity. Just because she renovated houses didn't mean she had to look like a complete fashion tragic.

On any other day she might have attempted to saunter casually past the gorgeous man and engineer a 'chance' meeting. She could have dropped her keys or exercised some other female ploy that she'd read about. Naturally, she couldn't try any of those tricks because she was driving her car, making all those things completely useless. She could hardly drive back round to the car park after her manic exit and coolly pretend to 'bump' into him. None of the romantic movies or stories of her experience had ever begun by mowing down the object of your desire.

The plastic buckets she had bought to mix her next batch of milk paint leaned perilously towards her from their place in the passenger seat. She was in a complete strop as she roared past him. Their eyes connected. He turned his head to watch her tire-squealing exit. She could have sworn his eyes held a mixture of awe and attraction. But what would she know? It had been a long time since a man had caused such an instant reaction to the pit of her stomach. It was purely physical. She shouldn't have skipped breakfast.

Anyway, it didn't matter. She would never see him again. He didn't look as if he was from around here. It was a small community where everyone knew everyone; at least in a tacit head nodding way. Truth be told, he didn't look as if he was from anywhere she'd ever been. He belonged in Hollywood but he looked a little rugged.

Dark, negligently waving hair contrasted with dreamy blue eyes. She just loved the combination of dark hair and blue eyes. Why *was that?* Was she genetically programmed? He was wearing a chambray blue shirt, a bold manly blue that matched his eyes. One hand was casually thrust into the pocket of chocolate chinos. Oh damn, now she would think of him every time she saw chocolate.

If she hadn't been in such a snarly mood she might have still been strolling the car park casually and walked into him instead of nearly running over him. Mind you, his eyes had lit up and a beautiful smile creased his fabulous face. Perhaps he had a preference for maniacal stroppy women who drove beat up Ute's. It was probably better that she had missed the opportunity for conversation. Her hair was still a disaster from her early morning swim in the pool. She could have tried out her new eye batting techniques but her eyes looked crap without gobs of mascara.

The snarly mood had started yesterday when the timber for the skirting board failed to arrive. This morning things had only gotten worse. Much worse. Her frantic dash to the hardware included not one, but two lengthy stops for road works. She only wanted a strip of muslin to strain the milk paint and two plastic buckets.

'All this for a piece of fabric,' she muttered in frustration. Great, now she was talking to herself.

She could have spit nails when the helpful guy in the paint section said they had no muslin and that he had used his wife's pantyhose to strain paint the last time he made milk paint. This was a trick she remembered, but she had thrown all her pantyhose in the trash when she'd sworn off men. She was glad at the time. Take Jeff. Never mind, nobody needed to take Jeff because he had taken himself off and out of her life. She was well rid of him.

But that was months ago—22 to be exact. Not that she was counting.

In the rear vision mirror she could see the tall man watching her drive off. He was certainly breaking her man drought. She developed a serious thumping of the heart and jelly legs. Just as well she was sitting down. Sadly, she was driving away from the liberator of her lost libido. She moaned out loud.

She momentarily considered driving back and pretending to have forgotten something. She did that often enough lately. If she had made a list before going to the hardware store yesterday she could have saved herself grief today. As it was, she had been there three times yesterday. Honestly, where was her head? She vowed never to get in a strop again. She'd even argued with the television yesterday so she was definitely losing it.

The handsome stranger stirred her. She would have to put herself 'out there' again. All she had to do was discover the mystery location of 'out there'. Never mind. All was not lost; she would make good use of the buzz the gorgeous man brought to life.

However, before she put herself 'out there' she had to go to the supermarket and buy a pair of pantyhose - for the paint. As she turned into the supermarket car park she was stopped by yet another road worker. The Ute was half in and half out of the entrance, blocking the traffic from both directions. She saw a huge pile of sand. No-one would be going in there for a while.

All her intentions of never having a bad mood for the rest of her life went out the window. She reversed quickly back into the stream of the traffic and roared off down the street, leaving early morning shoppers open mouthed in shock.

Then she remembered another option. The craft shop would have muslin. Turning into the parking lot near the shop she sighed and wondered if she would ever see Mr Gorgeous again. Oh dear, I am being very Jane Austen, how desperate. It wasn't likely that he would be in a craft shop. He was too well dressed for a delivery man and he would hardly be buying a few yards of fabric to whip up another stunning blue shirt to match his 'get lost in the ocean' eyes.

The fantasy died quickly. The only other shop in that whole street was the Op Shop. He was too up-market for there either. He was too tanned and virile to be doing good works inside a dusty charity shop.

He looked more like a sales rep. She laughed out loud as she thought of the improbability of a sales rep of any kind going to the Op Shop—'Would you care to see our latest line of second hand tea towels, Madam?' As if! Her mood lifted.

The craft shop was mercifully quiet and she chatted with Georgina, the elderly owner who also ran the quilting classes. Georgina gave her one metre of muslin free of charge as Kayla was contracted to paint the store. She had already rendered the brick walls and would start painting in earnest the following week. Jauntily stepping out of the craft shop, she looked down to avoid the dodgy top step that usually had a gaggle of old ladies gathered around it moaning about its potential for causing an accident.

She walked straight into Mr Gorgeous and looked into the blue of the Mediterranean ocean and every other ocean of her dreams. His eyes were even more incredible up close. He was holding her with both arms to steady her. Which she very much needed now that she was so near him. But not because of the dodgy step.

Her usual motor mouth lost its batteries. She was gawping like a guppy.

'You have quite a driving style,' he said with a cheeky grin that was reflected in the ocean eyes. So he remembered her; interesting.

'Yes, I was Peter Brock in a past life,' she riposted.

Damn, was that the best she could do?

'You look a bit old for Peter Brock's reincarnation; didn't he 'pass over' not long ago? I may be a sceptic but that seems a very dubious claim.' he said. She was grateful that he was still steadying her with his arms.

I could still fall any minute, she thought.

'No offense intended,' he added, with another heart stopping smile.

'None taken,' she said generously.

She leaned closer and adopted a conspiratorial whisper. 'There is a new fast track process for reincarnation, 21st Century stuff; Top Secret technology. It's very *hush hush*. So you see, I really *am* Peter Brock.'

'You know, I always wanted to meet Peter Brock.'

This was the perfect time for a flirty response that would overwhelm him with wit and intelligence. Unfortunately, the battery for her mouth died again.

It didn't seem to matter. Her face was an open book; he seemed to be reading everything he wanted to know in her eyes. The smile on his face told her he liked what he was seeing.

'And here you are,' he finished.

Her bones were melting.

'And here I am.'

Lame, lame. She mentally kicked herself.

Amused by her loss of speech but not bothered by it, he let her go gently. He extended a warm brown hand.

'I'm Kieran Stern, by the way.'

She accepted the handshake. The rest of her traitorous body

wanted to join in the shaking. Pressing her legs together to support each other, she willed herself to stay upright.

I must look like a constipated chook, she thought. Say something, say anything. 'And I'm Kayla Watkins,' she murmured, 'and I'm not usually a deaf mute.'

'I'll bet you're not,' he roared laughing, 'If your driving is anything to go by!'

A light switched on in her brain. She remembered Georgina talking about her only son who had been helping rebuild housing in Indonesia after the Boxing Day Tsunami. She knew he was returning to live near Georgina after her recent cancer treatment. Kayla had heard so much about him as she sanded and prepared the ancient walls of the craft shop. She had come to know Georgina well.

'Oh, you must be Georgina's son, the one who went overseas to rebuild the orphanage!'

'The very same, although I must say I didn't rebuild the whole orphanage by myself. It's very boring to be thought a saint.' Self-deprecation in a man was *so* attractive.

His eyes sparkled.

'I guess it would be,' she responded, 'I haven't had much experience of sainthood but I've heard it can be a real downer.'

He tilted his head to the side and regarded her with humorous eyes. He was enchanted. 'I can believe that,' he said drily.

Kayla tried to frown in mock fury but she had to repress a smile. It was impossible to be offended when the man in front of her was looking at her as if he didn't want to let her go.

'I'm helping my mother refurbish the shop,' he said, still holding her hand. She was glad they were away from the main street with the inevitable hustle and bustle of the shopping crowds. She repented for every time she had cursed the shop's 'off the beaten track' locale as she lost herself in his eyes.

'Oh really,' she said, trying to dampen her excitement. 'I'm doing the painting.'

'Ah, I was wondering why you had a chisel in your pocket. It's a relief to know that you're not a chisel murderer on the loose.' He was laughing at her.

'I hope you are going to fix that dodgy step,' was all she could muster.

'I'm not sure I should if it delivers beautiful girls into my arms,' he murmured.

She blushed. If this was flirting, she could definitely get used to it.

'So, it looks like we will be working together,' he gently prompted, leaning towards Kayla.

'Looks like.' She couldn't remember a single clever line from any of her trawling of magazine articles. She should have tried harder after the disastrous result when she did the 'Rate Your Flirting Skills' questionnaire in her latest magazine. Apparently a score of two meant you should just give up and join a crochet group.

He handed her down the last of the steps. Her skin tingled and her head began to buzz in an alarming fashion.

'That means I have a little time to get to know you before I pluck up the courage to ask you out.' His smile was totally disarming. The battery to her mouth flickered and died again. She just looked up at him like a mute idiot. He looked down at his hand. Oh dear, she was gripping his hand.

'Or not,' he said, drawing closer. 'We could have a coffee and consolidate our mutual refurbishing plans.' His eyes simmered with hidden meaning.

'I just love a man with a plan,' she said, her eyes bright and teasing. 'I could murder a coffee!'

'If you don't slow down, you'll murder more than a coffee!' he said.

'In that case I will leave my chisel behind. Since you're new in town I know a great little coffee shop,' she said, thinking of the coffee shop attached to the local art gallery. It was even more remote than the craft shop.

'Shall we take my car?' he offered with mock fear in his incredible eyes. 'I'd like to be alive for our next date.'

Over a simple lunch of warm Turkish bread and spicy pumpkin soup they discovered they shared a love of antiques and flea markets. Kayla wondered why she hadn't read in any of the magazines that it was possible to fall in love on a 'bad hair day'.

Kieran found her to be was natural, warm and funny. He discovered it was possible to fall in love with someone who had run out of the house without seeing a great daub of white paint on their cheek.

The first thing Kayla was going to do when she got home was to throw out that flirting test. She didn't need to redo it after all.

'Iss goot'

Katya was Russian. She had just started nursing, and her English - wasn't 'verry goot right yett'. But her dedication and nursing care was excellent. She worked like a Trojan. She wanted to be like the rest of the nurses, to be 'Propper Orstrarlian'. The staff tried to tell her that to be a genuine Aussie she would need to be a little laid back.

'Vat iss dis laying bakk?' she asked.

This was going to be harder than they thought.

'You work too hard. You can't keep that pace up, you'll burn out,' said Jenny, the NUM (Nurse Unit Manager) of the Low Care Unit.

'*Dis iss haard vurk?* In my Kountry dis iss nutting. Vat iss dis pace meaning? Vat iss burning? How iss fire anyting to do with all dis? I will neffer be propper Orstrarlian.' Katya sighed.

'Oh yes, you will. You will be a beaut Aussie.'

'Goot, I vant only to be beaut Orsie.'

She made the beds to perfection. She never sat down. She wrote everyone's notes. She never stayed a minute longer at break times. She was relentless.

The staff shook their heads, knowing the harder she worked; the harder she'd hit the inevitable brick wall when it came.

It arrived on the day Sister Careless had given two people the wrong morning medications. Swapped them in fact. Both of them were on about 7 pills and had very different diseases.

Mr Hypochondriac was already a problem when his illnesses were under control. When his diabetes was out of control because his relatives had bought him bags of lollies, he became very confused, anxious and downright demanding. Suffering from mild dementia in the first place didn't help, but when his sugar levels went through the roof he was manic. He wandered at a fast and erratic pace around the ward, to find a nurse to tell them he couldn't walk, and was terrified he'd never walk again.

'But you're walking now,' the nurses would say.

'No, I'm not. Don't you listen to me? I can't walk. I'll never walk again. You must get the doctor. *Immediately!*'

Sadly, Mr Hypochondriac had low blood pressure as well as his diabetes and Mrs Fluffyminded had high blood pressure and arrhythmia. So there was Mr Hypochondriac feeling faint, tearing around like a demented greyhound with high sugar levels. Mrs Fluffyminded's blood pressure was through the roof, she had a headache that would split bricks and low blood sugar because she'd been given Mr Hypochondriac's diabetic medication. Her heart was galloping like Phar Lap, and Mr Hypochondriac was hell on wheels - literally.

None of this was easy to explain to Katya, whose single minded purpose was to be a 'goot nurse' and get the patients moving. Disaster loomed.

Now, Katya had given special attention to all her patients, and this included both Mrs Fluffyminded and Mr Hypochondriac.

Their expectations were elevated by her constant ministrations. This situation was bad at the best of times but with the medication error, disaster loomed. No matter what Sister Jenny said, Katya didn't understand that the treatment of both her favourites must change, and dramatically. They both needed monitoring and bedrest. This did not suit Katya's well trained routine.

'Dat Mrs Fluffymindt von't get outa da bett. She is being difficoolt tooday. I tell her she *must*, but she just moan and refuse to do any ting. Nutting iss what she does. Nutting at all. She iss lazy. You must speak to her, Sister.'

'Katya, she has been given the wrong tablets and she needs to rest.'

'Vat iss dis giving wrong tablets? Too many pills in dis place. Why in my Kountry, eek. You don't get pills for nutting. They come to my Kountry. Den day know dey alive. Here spoilt, all da time spoilt, spoilt.'

'Just leave her today Katya, and I need her blood pressure taken every hour. Just give her a wash in bed,' Sister Jenny said.

'Oh vash in bett now it iss! Of course, I be goot Orsie. I give vash in bett to woman who is lazy. Sure, dat's vat I do.'

Now sweet little Katya had been plumping Mr Hypochondriac's pillows, fixing his blinds, putting his Polka records on and helping him with long walks.

All this worked well when he was in his blissful, grateful 'I'm not going to die today phase'. But Katya hadn't seen him cranky and confused, and was incensed at the change in him. He was in the hall, loudly proclaiming, 'I'm going to faint, help me nurse. I'm going to faint.'

'Why iss dat you iss stanting up if you iss going to faint? You iss hypochondriac.'

Jenny shuddered.

Of course, the one word Katya pronounced perfectly, was the word Jenny would rather she hadn't said at all. Jenny moaned. Perhaps she'd failed to say that hypochondriac wasn't actually a medical diagnosis.

'I'm going to faint, I tell you. Why doesn't anyone ever believe me?' he blustered, standing straight-as-a-die and pink-cheeked. Sharp eyed and intent.

'Vy you tell me dees lies? If you going to faint, you faint alreddy. But no, you stanting here ten minutes now telling me, telling me, you faint. But still you don't faint.'

Hiding smirks, Edwina and Jenny exchanged knowing looks. That brick wall was looming.

'I'm going to lie down. You are useless!' said Mr Hypochondriac.

Vat iss dat you say? You going to lie down on MY nice tidy bett I just make? No! You just stant here and faint. Vat iss matter wit you? You tink I made bett five minutes before you lie down agen! If you can stant here talk rubbish wit me, you can go to your room and sit on da chair. Dat's all.'

Katya was confused and offended by the sudden change in the happy, singing, dancing man. The man who sang her praises to all. Who danced around the dining room with her in therapy time.

Sister Jenny got on with the job of phoning the doctor to tell him of Ms Careless's mistake and took instructions on which medications to give to counter the effects.

It was only later that the staff experienced the full extent of Katya's ire. They were sitting down together for lunch when Katya 'spat the dummy' - the way she did everything - thoroughly.

'Dis man I cood kill. If I wass in my Kountry I vood scworsh him like cockroach.' She squeezed her fingers together on the table to demonstrate just how she would achieve this. Everyone was in awe. 'In my Kountry ve are heppy to haf bett to die on in horspital. Most people die on floor. No pills, no dancing, no fixing dis, fixing dat, opening blindts, shutting blindts, fluffing up da pillows, make smooth the bett. Spoilt, spoilt, stupid man. No more weel I care for him like King. In my Kountry I vood scworsh him like cockroach.' Katya repeated the squashing motion. It was hysterical.

Jenny choked on her laughter, and then giggled uncontrollably. Katya was magnificent.

'Vat iss laughing for?' she asked, confused. 'Dis iss not funny, *truly* I scworsh him. I neffer be propper Orsie.'

'Oh yes,' Jenny said, 'you are a truly proper Aussie. They should *not* be spoilt; they must do what they can for themselves. It's important for them, AND for you.'

The rest of the shift Katya's irritation didn't abate.

'Don't be speaking to me! Tell me you faint one more time I stant you on your hedd,' she ranted at Mr Hypochondriac. To Jenny's shock he became as meek as a lamb, something the rest of the staff had never achieved, and Jenny was dubious about any of them ever pulling it off.

Sister Jenny retold the story to every staff member, who then walked by to see the 'new' Katya. 'I told you she'd make a damn good nurse.'

It was a few weeks before anyone could bring the subject up with Katya, without her repeating her desire to squash him 'like cockroach'.

Then she calmed down, had reasonable expectations of the patients and taught them to help themselves.

'Now I see vat you mean, Sister,' she said to Jenny one day, 'dis iss vat you try to tell me. I understart now. Now I am propper Orsie.'

'Oh, I think you are better than the rest of us Katya,' Jenny said smiling.

'Iss goot.'

113

Eric Sinclair's dirty little secret

Edith Sinclair had often been heard to say that the worst thing about her husband Eric, was not the mistakes he made, but the fact that he never learned from them.

Felicity had been for an early morning jog and stopped to collect a message from Sister Margaret, when she saw Eric Sinclair standing before the notice board in the main nurses' home lounge. His presence surprised her, so she sat in a quiet corner of the lounge room to watch him without being seen. Not that he knew her, or would be bothered by her presence. But she knew Eric Sinclair.

He methodically unfolded a piece of clean white paper from his sports jacket and stood reading it. Satisfied with its contents he took four thumbtacks and pressed them purposefully into the corners of the sheet of paper, fixing it in the centre of the notice board. He rested back on his heels with arms crossed. He was a handsome man, accustomed to getting what he wanted.

Just nudging forty he was seasoned in life. Felicity knew just what kind of spice this man liked to season his life with, and suspected this was the purpose of his visit to the boarding house. With a smorgasbord of young, naïve girls, this was just the sort of place he would frequent.

Felicity had met Eric a year ago - although 'met' would hardly be the correct word. Right when his life had fallen apart. Eric was never one to do things by halves, and when his world unravelled it did so in spectacular style.

Felicity had been babysitting the couple's two children when Edith underwent a breast biopsy. It was an anxious time for the family. The results of the frozen section could change their lives. Edith's mother had died of breast cancer in her early forties. Edith was 38 with a recently discovered lump the size of a pea. Eric had been a perfect picture of the concerned spouse. But the only thing that concerned Eric Sinclair was Eric Sinclair.

In the hospital room he had been distracted and restless, running his long elegant fingers through his dark thinning hair.

'Don't do that Eric, your hair will fall out,' Edith said as he paced her room, wishing him to be still and comfort her instead of making this his drama. Felicity had thought Edith hard on him until she overheard him say that it was just as well they had life insurance as he could never raise the children without a paid nanny. When he saw the shocked looks of the staff he made a quick recovery.

'You're irreplaceable darling, it would take a king's ransom to cover the half you do for us. I'm just so worried for you.'

But funny things happen when life makes your stop and think - and Edith had stopped and thought. Maybe it was lying in a bed for the long despairing night bargaining with God, or perhaps it was seeing the reaction of the nurses to her husband; the shy giggle in response to his friendly wink. No, she had always seen that. Eric was an attractive charismatic man. His job in advertising combined with his dark exotic looks meant that Eric would always be noticed. No, it was the more subtle things. The way he was impatient with the children.

The older sisters were immune to Eric's charm. Sister Margaret had given him a right serve. 'Do sit down, Mr Sinclair. Stop worrying your wife. Anyone would think it was your breast getting the knife.'

This simple statement from the nun stunned him into silence, and he sat in the corner quietly for a whole five minutes. Then he stormed from the room declaring he was not going to be told what to do by a nun who was a waste to the male race and had never satisfied a man in her life. It wasn't even that outburst that unsettled Edith because she was used to his chauvinism.

It was the fact that she felt so responsible, so blameworthy, for his mood and sudden departure. It wasn't the first time he had stormed off. She'd become accustomed to him leaving, welcoming the relief of avoiding a long argument.

However, there in that bed, she had no laundry to attend, no homework with the children to distract. His absence was a glaring, grinding sign of the distance in their marriage. And for the first time in living memory Edith Sinclair did not blame herself. All the other times she had accepted that his job needed his attention, or any one of the many areas intrinsic to his happiness. But now, for the first time, she needed him. And the children needed him.

Edith desperately needed someone to talk to, and she chose Sister Margaret. An irony that would not have amused Eric, but Edith had chosen well.

She apologized to Sister Margaret for Eric's departure.

'Being married to God is a lot easier than living with most men,' Sister Margaret said.

This down to earth humanity opened the floodgate. Felicity in her youthful naiveté had been stunned by the avalanche of emotion from Edith. Not that she heard the sad tale, but all the nurses were witness to her tearful distress.

When Eric returned that night he was aloof and distracted and left early when a client paged him, leaving Edith to face the surgeon's preoperative consultation alone.

Eric regretted not being there for his wife. But his angst hinged on the fact that he regretted his other "appointment" more. Having their regular babysitter pregnant with his child was a bigger problem. It had been hard work to talk a good Catholic girl into an abortion, but he had managed just that. He told Teresa that her timing was appalling.

She had cried and crumpled under his tirade. She remonstrated that she'd taken the Pill every night, and didn't know that a bout of gastric flu would make the Pill ineffective.

He relented towards her, after all he didn't want a scandal, and anger would achieve nothing. But, honestly no-one understood how provocative some teenage girls could be. A man would have to be made of steel to resist. And Eric Sinclair was not made of steel.

The night he'd left his wife early Teresa had a late night consultation at the nearby Medical Centre with a gynaecologist. The Centre was actually a part of the hospital system. Even though it was on the hospital grounds it was quite a distance from the hospital, and not everyone knew of the connection. Eric Sinclair didn't, and that wasn't the only gap in his knowledge. He hadn't been unaware that Teresa was 17.

Thinking she could keep a pregnancy and abortion quiet, Teresa turned to a doctor she could trust. Her faith in Dr Peter Hampton was not misplaced, although not in the way she expected, because he went to the only car in the patient parking lot to speak to Eric.

'I will take it from here. Just where I take it depends on you and how fast you leave here now.'

Felicity was the nurse on duty at the medical centre that evening and saw the duty sister writing up a theatre booking for a 'therapeutic D & C' for Teresa Bernstein.

It might be the Age of Aquarius in the secular world, but moral decay was not tolerated inside the hallowed walls of St Ellen's. Teresa was gently counselled and Dr Hampton contacted her parents immediately. Eric Sinclair would not cause Teresa any more grief.

Felicity mused on this as she sat in the huge soft lounge chair. Eric was calmly chatting to one of the first year nurses who came to enquire if he needed help with anything. Bethany was 18 and a gentle girl, slim as a reed. As she stood in front of Eric, her laughter tinkling at something he said, Tiffany walked over and read the notice. Eric Sinclair needed a regular babysitter.

Indeed he did. Two years had passed since the Medical Centre episode. After her surgery, Edith had left him and taken the children, selling the house her father had given them as a wedding present.

But her 'coup de gras' had been to die. She was overseas on a speed boat in the Greek Islands when tragedy struck. The boat collided with a fishing vessel and Edith had died saving the children. Eric flew over to get the children, paid to bring her body home, and then found Edith had changed her life insurance.

His phase of playing 'good time dad' was over in earnest. Being sole parent was altogether different than holidays in Disneyland. Without their mother his children despised him. His eleven year old son was silent and bitter, and when his daughter deigned to speak to him she burst into tears and said, 'I hate you, you pig!'

Trust Edith to be dramatic and up and die on him. She probably planned it. He pictured her laughing up her sleeve in some paradise or other now. After all, she'd left him in such a farcical way he'd been too embarrassed to tell any of their friends about it.

A few short years ago he thought he was home free. Edith hadn't found out about Teresa. Weak with relief he plied her with flowers and promises of blissful times together. He'd even been so thoughtful that he made an appointment with a cosmetic surgeon for her. She often lamented that her breasts weren't the same after the children. With her rich, dark humour she joked that she had to fetch her breasts from the floor before she went out. It wasn't his fault that she had taken it the wrong way when he had left her a pair of silicone implants, and an appointment card beside her breakfast that last morning, with a note saying he loved her and wanted to 'do something special for her'.

He would never understand as long as he lived why she put two forks, one in each implant and left them there. When he arrived home that night he found a note, 'Get forked yourself, Eric' written on the back of his message in her flamboyant scrawl.

Obviously, she had gone off the deep end. He suggested that she needed help, she was suffering from stress. Edith agreed, and went to Greece. Eric hoped she would come to her senses over there. She had. She prepared divorce papers and took back every atom of her life. The money from the house was left in trust for the children.

Eric Sinclair had nothing.

Felicity watched the animated conversation between Bethany and Eric. When she saw his hand slowly move to the delicate curve in Bethany's arm, and her reaction of confused attraction Felicity froze.

Eric shifted the baseball cap forward and looked into Bethany's eyes. Felicity noticed the rows of tiny wounds at the back of his head, evidence of recent hair transplant surgery. Bethany couldn't take her eyes off him.

Felicity had seen enough. With alarm bells ringing in her ears she quietly retreated to the reception desk whispered to Sister Margaret.

'A word, Mr Sinclair, if you will,' said Sister Margaret, unpinning the notice and crushing it in her hand.

How to lose a guy in 10 seconds

Edwina pushed back a stray strand of hair, while the morning sunlight fell like brittle shards in the corner of the courtyard. She strained to listen to Di, her neighbour, whose soft lilting voice was mixed with birdsong. Di was talking to their cat, Bear, this morning. Telling him to leave the food alone that she left out for the birds.

'You already turned your nose up at that food, Bear. I'll have to put you on a diet. I'm sure George feeds you too much.'

In her mind Edwina could see the huge grey and white Persian wind himself around Di, nuzzling her for early morning comfort.

'Come on now, Proud Mary,' Di warned a fat Magpie with strutting gait and head held high, 'don't eat all the food, you greedy bird. Leave some for Slim. Come on Slim, have your share.'

Edwina sighed. There was no early morning comfort for her. Ever since Dave had died in the mining accident, life had been a constant struggle. Unlucky Dave, his mates called him. When he had been alive, and death had been no different. The only casualty in the collapse of the section of the mine where he was working, he'd proved it to the end. And now she seem to have been donated his mantle.

Without life insurance, or mortgage insurance, her happy go lucky husband could never have foreseen the legacy he had left.

Other men would have, but not Dave.

Shading her eyes against the sun, Edwina realised that morning would have been less of a shock if she'd had a few hours of sleep. Common sense told her that the sun was no brighter than it had been yesterday, but her eyes disagreed.

She pulled the fluffy robe around her legs - a Christmas present from her son. A son who was worth diamonds, but was too far away to help with this latest problem. She decided not to tell him. After all, she'd been sorting things for years, even before Dave died. His practicality in life was limited to turning up to work and coming home. And that was perfectly fine with Edwina. She knew what some women had to deal with, and being a born organiser, she'd never felt that Dave fell short in any way. It was hard work and long hours, more than most men could do, and Dave had been working there for twenty years.

Bear wandered through the fence to claim his chair at Edwina's, and stopped with an air of disgust to find Edwina occupying it.

'Sorry old boy, but I need my chair at the moment,' said Edwina.

'Are you up, Edwina?' asked Di, 'come on over and I'll get the "hired help" to make us coffee.' She was referring to George, her husband of 40 years.

'I'll be right over,' said Edwina. 'Poor Bear, you are going to be really put out when you find me sitting in your chair on your own patio.' Picking up her cup of tea, Edwina laughed to see Bear's dismissive flick of the tail as he headed home through the fence.

'Cats don't need to talk, do they. Even their tails communicate elegantly,' she said to Di.

'He's been 'communicating' with the guest bed again,' said Di, 'made himself a lovely spot by clawing out a hole in the mattress.'

'Oh no!' laughed Edwina.

'Oh yes. And it had to be the queen size bed, of course. The old single in the other room isn't good enough for His Royal Highness.'

'You rang?' said George, carrying two coffees to the glass outdoor table.

'Ha ha. In your dreams, George. I'm talking about the cat.'

George shrugged and went back inside.

'How's the new boarder?' asked Di.

'Don't ask,' said Edwina. 'Everything's different now that the new development put in short term units. The mines have an arrangement with the owners and most of the contracted men go there now. Which leaves me the ones who don't want the scrutiny of close living. Guess I'm a soft target as a single woman.'

'Rotten shame. You've had seven years of boarding people work out well. What's this guy's deal?'

'Can't put my finger on it yet, Di.'

'And to think I once thought I'd like to run an English Country Boarding house. Huh!' said Edwina. She took the coffee cup inside and went home.

'Good luck,' said Di.

Mark was an older guy and he seemed the perfect boarder. Paid on time. Was away a lot. Ate at work. Kept to himself. Had the occasional conversation. He thought Edwina should be on television – she'd be a great comedienne. Apparently, she didn't just do the usual female blah about manhating and child raising, she had substance.

'You're different,' he said, 'I can't quite work you out.'

'Why bother,' said Edwina.

Mark was an electrician with a cause. He obsessed about global energy and all manner of conservation issues. Edwina used the dryer. This annoyed him.

'People are dying in South American countries because trees are being cut down for energy,' he preached.

Mark smoked like a nuclear chimney. This annoyed Edwina

Mark was a "relocated Pomme", he refused the term immigrant. He ranted about Aussies living in the land of milk and honey and living off welfare – obviously targeting Edwina on a part pension. Edwina didn't like his aggressive tone. She decided he was pushing his toe over the line and it was time to push back.

Mark found her standing in front of the dryer. Staring at it. He wanted to move around her to the freezer. He had his own fridge, but used some of Edwina's freezer space. She pretended not to notice him and kept staring. He sighed. Loudly. Still nothing.

'Are you alright?' he asked.

'I don't know what to do,' Edwina said in her best 'lost' voice.

'About what?' He was getting terse. She could hear it in his voice.

'About the dryer.'

'Is there something wrong with it?'

'No.'

'Then what the bloody hell are you worried about?'

'Well – since you told me that people are dying in the Congo because of Western greed over electricity, I feel like I'm offering up a human sacrifice every time I turn the dryer on. It's killing me.'

Mark took off in a huff. He must have forgotten what he wanted.

Edwina found out just how eccentric he thought her when she dropped him at the RSL club to watch the footy and have a Sunday lunch and beer. He offered to buy her a drink as thanks so she slowly nursed a West Coast. He became loquacious as his pre-lunch drinks kicked in.

Being eternally fascinated with people Edwina listened. He didn't seem to notice that she was sipping a 3% drink very slowly. He talked about his travels.

'Been all over Europe and it was the best time I ever had. Don't remember any of it though.'

'Really? Shame.'

'Well, I was high on everything I could get my hands on and I had money to burn, so I could get my hand on everything. I only smoke pot now.' His eyes were glazing a bit. Edwina's weren't, they were alert, but hooded. Mark went on to talk more about his drug use.

When he came to the part of his life where he'd worked at Heathrow Airport and smuggled heroin into the UK, Edwina heard all kinds of warning bells, but she hadn't had acting lessons at high school, and worked in a nursing home for 20 years to show any reaction.

'I can't think why you're telling me all this.' Edwina calmly took another sip and leaned back in her chair.

'Well, you're ripped sometimes.'

'Ah ... ripped?'

'Yeah, you know.'

'Actually, I'm not.'

'What do you mean 'you're not'? You talk ninety to the dozen and your mind is fast and furious.'

'That's just me.'

'What? What are those tablets then?'

'My mother's. She's in hospital at the moment.'

'Well, I'll be...'

Edwina left when the conversation had turned and he wouldn't assess how freaked out she was about his disclosure. She had to get him out. But how? Not the way a man could, that was for sure.

She had noticed on one occasion when I was watching television program about nursing homes that he bolted out of the seat in a sweat with a frantic, 'Jeez, I can't watch that.'

Because he'd been getting a little aggressive in his conversations about 'welfare', Edwina had fixed him with a sharp eye and said, 'So you can't watch something for two minutes that I've done for nearly twenty years?'

This memory triggered a hasty plan. Edwina bought a huge lounge/commode chair for a few dollars at St Vinnies. Then she bought a huge pile of extra-large incontinence pads.

When Mark came 'home' the next day Edwina was cleaning the living area from top to bottom – always a good way to discomfort a male. They want it to happen, but they don't want to have to see it.

'Oh sorry about the disruption,' she said.

'What the hell's that thing?' He was pointing at the huge chair.

'Oh, that's a recliner. My mother is leaving hospital. She's going to be living with me. But don't worry, she won't bother you. She's a bit deaf, but rarely wanders at night.'

Mark blanched. Pointing at the huge bags of pads he squeaked, 'What are those?'

'Incontinence pads.'

'F*&K!'

Edwina was washing her mother's clothes at the time. That proved helpful. She put a nappy bucket beside the fridge with some huge frayed old-lady undies with a suitable brown 'drag stripe' on them.

Mark arrived home. He went to the freezer for ice.

'Shit!' he said, blanching at the bucket contents.

Mark was very grateful when Edwina 'reluctantly' let him move out with one day's notice. She expressed that was so sorry he needed to move on to be closer to the job. He was in advance by $300, but that was the last thing on his mind as he revved up the road.

Edwina donated the props to the Salvos.

Except the undies, of course.

Waiting

Emily Brand sat and waited for sons to come home from war. In a small country town her vigilance did not go unnoticed.

'Doesn't she know the war is long over?' asked Mrs Pinkerton.

'I believe she does,' said Harold Wharton, pulling his hat down over his eyes. He glanced at his grandson playing in the corner of the family hardware store. The boy's father hadn't come home either.

'I want an outdoor setting, Harold. A long grand table,' said Mrs Pinkerton.

Harold's eyes narrowed. He reached under the counter and handed her a catalogue. 'I think you'll find something to suit your particular taste, Mrs Pinkerton,' he said.

Emily Brand had a white-slatted reclining chair under the May bush in her front yard. She painted it carefully every year. Beside it, she kept an ancient toolbox with gardening bibs and bobs. A circular garden held price of place nearby. It was said to have been quite grand, once. Emily had torn everything out the day the last telegram came.

She watched busy neighbours coming and going, living. Deliveries came. Wishes were granted. New things arrived, especially when houses sold and bright new people came with shiny hopes. Emily toiled over the circular garden, but it didn't come to much.

'What are you growing?' asked a passer-by.

'Oh, this and that.'

John Brand came to visit his sister, years before.

'People are talking, Emily,' He stood poised, hat in hand.

'Of course,' she said, 'it's their way.'

They found her in the white-slatted chair, with her gardening gloves still on, lips blue, body soft and breathless. The funeral was a small, discrete, simple affair. A FOR SALE sign appeared.

'Oh my,' said a new wife, with babe in arms. 'What a gorgeous cottage, let's buy it Eddie.'

Her fresh faced husband smiled and shrugged at the realtor, who grinned like a Cheshire cat.

'The garden is lovely,' he said.

There, where Emily Brand sat waiting for sons to come home from war, Flanders poppies grew.

Parlez vous francais?

I survived the first month on the Female Medical Ward and the domination of Sister Renshaw. Just. While not actually succumbing to complacence, I was feeling a little more comfortable. My next roster rotation was on Surgical I, which was devoted to general surgery patients. I was beginning to feel like a nurse and would soon shed the dreaded 'Blue Bags' that signified our newness to the world. I was even beginning to feel a little pride in myself. And we all know what they say about *that*.

I arrived on the ward for the am shift early; feeling bright-eyed, bushy-tailed and at peace with the world. I showered and prepared a gentle little woman for a radical mastectomy and attended several other patients. When we were at morning tea in the staff room the charge sister approached us and asked if anyone spoke French.

My tiny bosom swelled with self-importance. I had done five years of high school French and enjoyed it passionately. I had read Parisian Magazines, read Albert Camus' novel *L'Etranger*, watched French films on excursions to Metropolitan theatres and visited with my French teacher and his garrulous family, joining in their conversations.

I was up for this task. There was a French speaking Mauritian woman who was post-operative and deeply distressed and there was no family member present to interpret for her. Off I went to save the day.

She was a tiny woman with the vocal capacity of an opera singer. Her tightly curled black hair stood on end and gave her a surprised look. She was brandishing the nurse call bell, shaking it as if it was a weapon. I responded with my best French, interspersed with English whenever I lost the plot. Which was a little more often than I expected.

'Oui, um Madame, vous desirez, um, a nurse, um, et je suis ici, um, to, um vous aidez.' I sighed with some satisfaction.

Grossly *unfounded* satisfaction as it transpired.

I immediately discovered that people who are *not* helping you learn the language, have a lot less patience with you than those hired to teach it to you. They also speak at the speed of light. Only the accent resonated; not one single word sounded familiar.

The only phrases that seemed to have stuck in my swelled head were simple ones of greeting or asking directions to regions in Paris.

It was at this point that I realised the formality of asking 'comment ca va?' (How are things going?) was not only completely inadequate it appeared to be a downright insult. 'Things' were obviously *not* going well and the woman conveyed with eloquent gestures that I was an idiot for asking thank you very much.

She continued to shake the call bell menacingly.

The next phrases that came to mind were how to ask for directions to the railway station and enquire 'mon frère, ou est la plume de ma tante' (my brother, where is my aunt's pen?) I also uselessly remembered how to request the location of the local 'gendarmerie' (police station).

Apparently the school curriculum was designed for students with artistic and cultural leanings and would only ever need travel vocabulary. None of our French classes even vaguely covered the possibility that one might need to enquire about constipation, difficulty with urination, levels of pain or any other conditions that might relate to physical symptoms or disease processes.

Trying to remember the marvellous essays I had written in French and thought magnificent at the time only hurt my head. My silent agony caused the woman in the bed to repeat frantically whatever it was that she wanted; still waving the call bell, with an increasingly strident voice.

In the true style of the obsessive perfectionist, I would not give up. So I started a mime sequence that would have done credit to Marcel Marceux.

Unfortunately, I then faced the problem that some of the things I might want to ascertain could possibly look a little obscene to the uninformed and were sure to insult this poor woman if I was off the mark.

Which I apparently was. Repeatedly.

When her level of distress rose to fever pitch, I thought it wise to leave the room as graciously as possible, because it began to dawn on me that I was actually increasing her frustration and ire.

As I left the room, she threw the water jug at my retreating back, and then spoke the only French I understood that day.

'Imbecile!'

The first cut is the deepest

The low dulcet murmur of early morning voices echoed along the high empty corridors that connected the operating theatres. Even the air smelt bracingly clean. In the silence before the usual hectic pace of the day commenced it was easy to feel confident.

Jane was nearing the end of her second year of nurse training, and beginning her second stint in the operating theatres. Knowing her way around meant she wouldn't be considered a novice, and provide a target for pranks from any of the senior nurses. Many a new nurse is sent to the stock room or to Central Sterilising to search for fallopian tubing, or some other quest that inevitably ends in tears for the victim and loud guffaws from the perpetrators.

Jane enjoyed the calm, letting it seep in while breathing deeply.

This was the day she would assist one of the surgeons in a minor operation, have her competence assessed and marked complete. Each nurse was required to assist and attend instrumentation for two appendectomies, two tonsillectomies, two D & C's (Dilatation and Curettage of the uterus) and whatever other theatre experience they could wrangle.

All six theatres were running. Jane scanned the allocation sheet taped to the wall beside the administrator's office and saw she was rostered in Theatre 1 with Dr Stokes, an ENT specialist with a weekly theatre list. It would be her first tonsillectomy.

Sister Reilly would assess Jane, and Jane was thrilled. Sister Reilly was a favourite with the nurses. Competent and cheerful, she made sure they had adequate preparation and observation. Calm and focused she boosted the nurses' confidence, then broke any tension with her lilting Irish humour. A true professional, she could switch from cracking a joke to solemn instrument-snapping efficiency instantly.

Some of the sisters favoured letting the nurses stew while they strained to remember the correct gauge needle, the right catgut or nylon sutures, while the doctor fretted, fumed and occasionally threw instruments. But not Sister Reilly – she would be right on hand to remind nurses on their first attempts, then step back when they were more proficient.

None of the usual male nurse practical jokes worked with her.

'What regular eijits you boys are, for sure and for certain your mothers dropped you on your heads at birth!'

It was all brisk business while the theatres were running. But calm efficiency did not always reign unchallenged. There were times when it seemed like an alternate world where the title 'theatre' of the Broadway kind was more applicable. Apart from 'wild goose chases' for the naïve, the surgeons sometimes had their own flair for the dramatic.

One surgeon liked to make an extravagant entrance, with the huge theatre light on him as he came into the theatre from the scrub room to perform a shimmy and sing a show tune.

Then he would be all business and replace a hip.

There were some prima donnas. Even though the doctors often took second place on the wards to an experienced sister who considered that particular ward her kingdom, this was not always the case in the operating theatres. Many surgeons reigned supreme and lorded it over everyone in fine fashion.

Often the biggest enemy was boredom. In movies and television the atmosphere is charged with tension and drama as silence reigns and nurses snap instruments swiftly into busy surgeons' hands.

In reality the radio blared with the surgeon's choice, usually cricket, Mozart or parliament. Some surgeons talked non-stop to their assistants, the anaesthetist or even lesser beings—the nursing staff. Many of the surgeons had the casual abandon more common to someone perusing the aisles of a supermarket. A few were prone to punctuate their conversation with grand hand gestures, waving various shiny instruments as they recounted anecdotes or jokes.

Sister Reilly walked Jane through the steps of the surgery before the doctors and the patient arrived. She revised the instruments, their use and order. Apparently this particular surgeon favoured the use of a Struder's Snare to remove the tonsils.

Jane knew the proper and practiced routine. Apart from Sister Reilly there would be a scout nurse, whose job it was to source any stock, or relay messages. Officially Jane was 'scrub nurse'. The scrub nurse was so named because they underwent rigorous scrubbing and hand washing before they would 'gown and glove' in sterile theatre garb to assist the surgeon.

The scrub nurse would have scrubbed her hands meticulously and dried them on the sterile towel that was in the pre-packed paper parcel the scout nurse had torn open. Then the scrub nurse would put the sterile theatre gown on with the scout nurse tying the gown at the back, then wait for the surgeon. A little extra time hand-drying ensured the gloves went on smoothly. Wet hands and surgical gloves did not mix.

The surgeon would enter with water dripping from pink scrubbed hands held high while the scrub nurse handed him a sterile towel from the crisp white paper packages prepared by the Central Sterilising Department, and then they would hold the operating theatre gown up for him to walk into and glove him with deft hands, taking great care to maintain sterility.

Done well, the process had all the beauty of a perfectly executed pirouette from an acclaimed ballet recital. It was all about timing; a synchronized flow of efficient control in an acutely controlled environment.

That was the theory. And it worked well. Most of the time. And this process was the immaculate flow of events Jane was anticipating.

Before the surgeon arrived she made sure everything was lined up to perfection. The patient was a seven year old boy and the anaesthetist had quickly and quietly induced 'sleep' with the mask with Nitrous Oxide and intubated him with the Guedel's airway that would provide oxygenation during surgery.

Jane scrubbed her hands thoroughly for the obligatory three minutes and went into the operating room from the scrub room. She headed towards the pack that had been opened by Betty, the scout nurse for the day. Betty was a tall thin intense girl who had just commenced her first roster in OT. Her dark hair tied back randomly and her lanky awkward limbs had earned her the name of Olive Oyl by Sister Reilly due to her resemblance to Popeye's girlfriend. Betty was as large hearted as she was tall and hovered anxiously to assist. Her large doleful eyes looked huge behind black rimmed spectacles that she adjusted constantly.

So far, so good. Jane sighed.

Before she could grab the towel opened for her the surgeon entered and snatched it, and wiped his hands. Then he wandered around the theatre gabbing full throttle to the anaesthetist.

Jane gave Sister Reilly a panicked glance. There was no towel to dry her dripping hands.

Then Dr Stokes grabbed Jane's gown as well, leaving her standing gobsmacked by the instrument table. She moaned softly. She had no sterile gown. Her hands were too wet for the gloves, but protocol demanded she wear them.

Betty's eyes grew alarmingly larger. Sister Reilly sighed theatrically and pulled her mask on, gesturing for Betty to do the same. Dr Stokes sat casually at the instrument table with the gown hanging crookedly. It was untied and hung off his shoulders. He hadn't put sterile gloves on. He perused the instruments with the casual concern of one surveying a buffet table, picking instruments up and putting them down again.

This action alone would have had any nurse evicted from the theatre with a smart dressing down in store. Dr Stokes still maintained his rambling conversation with the anaesthetist. Jane looked wildly around for Betty to open another pack with a sterile towel and gown, but there was no time.

The anaesthetist began wandering around the theatre and walked into the theatre light, which was carefully trained on the open mouth of the boy, with a loud whack. The huge orb tilted awkwardly, steering the light beam uselessly to the empty wall. He continued on his way leaving Sister Reilly to adjust the light.

Betty's glasses steamed up.

Dr Stokes began prodding the tonsils.

Betty fainted.

Dr Stokes turned once more to the instruments.

Oh help, he's starting without me, thought Jane.

She turned to the open gloves and desperately tried to drag them on wet hands.

Oh no, I'm going to fail this assessment.

Sister Reilly went to the theatre door and called for an orderly.

'Olive Oyl's hit the deck, one of you boys get in here and help.'

The gloves refused to go on, and to make it worse they wouldn't come off either.

The anaesthetist hit the light again, swinging it off to another wall. Sister Reilly adjusted it and helped the orderly drag Betty into the corridor amid loud guffaws from the male nurses.

Dr Stokes was waiting for the instruments and even though Jane still had half an inch of glove extending from all ten fingers she grabbed the Struder's snare, with its wire retractable circle and handed it to him. The protruding glove hanging from her right forefinger got caught in the snare. Dr Stokes attempted to put the snare in the boy's mouth, but it was still attached to Jane's glove.

Bang, the punch drunk anaesthetist whacked into the light yet again.

Jane's glove stretched and broke off in the wire circle of the snare. Dr Stokes removed the torn remnant and flicked it on the floor. Jane's right hand now had four stretched glove fingers and one bare, unsterile finger.

Dr Stokes proceeded to snare the tonsils one by one, with not a break in the conversation with the anaesthetist. Jane struggled to follow procedure, feeling as if she was supposed to be in a marathon and had ended up in a hundred yard dash.

When the operation was over the nurses began the usual flurry to clean up for the next operation. Jane rolled her eyes at Sister Reilly.

'Unbelievable! It's just my luck to be in the theatre with 'Laurel and Hardy'. Those two galahs performed a slapstick routine straight out of some ancient comedy archive. I don't think I'll ever recover. I won't pass the assessment today.'

'Rubbish, you did fine.'

Jane passed. The patient survived.

And every rule in the book had been broken.

Don't wake me, I'm working

'I've had the shift from hell,' said Brendon.

'What! It's only an hour since handover,' said Chloe.

'I'm not talking about this shift. I'm talking about my day job - specialling James Dent. He's a quad - motorbike accident.'

'Oh, you guys and your double lives. I don't know how you do it.'

'Most times we get to sleep during the shift, while the patients are having therapy or physio. It's part of the deal.'

'And you didn't get a nap today?'

'No, his physio called in sick, so I had to fill in and do the exercises myself. An hour in the pool and an hour of passive exercises, well, *passive for him.*'

'Yes, but that's hard work for the therapist.'

'You can say that again.'

'Why do you do it? Most of you guys with two jobs work at least three days a week with your day clients.'

'It's fine when we get sleep.'

'Well, you'd better get some matchsticks to keep your eyes open because we've got 'Hitler's Apprentice' tonight.'

'Oh no, not Sister Dart.'

'The one and only.'

Sister Dart was a tall bitter blonde in the middle of a nasty divorce. She was as hard as nails and reigned with absolute power. The Magna Carta had outlawed The Divine Right of Kings, but Sister Dart had no equal. The nurses called her 'Hitler's Apprentice', but truth be told she could have taught Hitler himself a few lessons.

The male nurses were notorious for winding her up, increasing her ire against the world in general, and men in particular.

On night duty the rules were relaxed, but only because there were less sisters to enforce them. The sisters who worked night duty seemed to fall into one of two categories; those who wanted military efficiency, and those who believed that night duty was hard enough and gave the staff a little leeway.

The former made the nurses scrub pans, every minute must be filled. Just because it was night was no excuse to be idle. But the latter sat down and asked about the nurses knitting. There was something repetitive and soothing about knitting, but mostly it served to keep an exhausted nurse awake.

There were two sisters on night duty, each had three wards. The Charge Sister had the three lower floors, and was rarely summoned to the upper wards, and then only if the other sister had an emergency. Each ward had a senior nurse, often a third year trainee, experienced enough to handle most dramas.

The male nurses called Sister Dart to their wards for the slightest problem, engaging her in lengthy discussions about broken toenails or collapsed air beds. She was such a control freak that she couldn't let them know verbally how much this aggravated her, merely expressing tension in her rigid stance. She never seemed to be able to work out if their need of her presence was genuine or not, so she was drawn into all manner of nonsense at their behest.

The nurses had early decided that Sister Dart took great pleasure in making their lives difficult. But she certainly made them interesting.

Chloe had felt the lash of her tongue many times for the most minor infractions, like forgetting to close the curtains at night in an empty room, or supposedly taking too long to answer a call bell. Sister Dart never deigned to help, even on the busiest nights, unlike the other sisters.

Sister Dart was ruthless with regard to anyone sleeping on duty. She was known to thump files down in front of nurses who merely closed their eyes. There couldn't even be a moment's relief for bloodshot, scratchy eyes when she was hovering near.

Chloe and Brendan began the first ward round. It was Sunday night on the general surgical ward, so most of the patients were at least two days post-op.

'We shouldn't have any dramas, Brendon. Should be a quiet night.'

'Yeah, that's not quite the good news it should be. Keeping busy also keeps you awake.'

Brendon was normally a tireless dynamo of raw energy, but that cold September night he was exhausted. He was professional efficiency for the first ward round, changing IV fluids and answering patient enquiries with meticulous concern, but at midnight as they sat at the nurses' station desk he began to flag. His head jerked as he fought sleep.

He sat with his black plastic chair tilted precariously back, and every time he dozed off, his knee hit the desk where Chloe was writing. Fifteen minutes of this was enough.

'Brendon, I can't write a word. You're bumping the desk. For goodness sake go somewhere and take a nap. Go down to one of the wards where Dart won't find you.'

'No, I can't leave you here on your own. If there's an emergency you'll cop it. I don't care about Dart. I'm going into one of the empty rooms to sleep for a few hours.'

'You're sure? You know what Hitler's Apprentice is like with bed-checks. She doesn't take our word for a thing, and has to check every patient. Drives me mad. Half the time she wakes them up with that great lumbering torch of hers. Don't know why she doesn't get a little pencil number like everyone else,' said Chloe.

'And shining the bloody thing in their faces isn't exactly helpful.' Brendon grinned. Then yawned.

'Come on then. I'll help you. But don't snore or I'll be in trouble for aiding and abetting. Room 1 is empty. Mrs Collins was discharged late in the afternoon. I'll tell Sister Dart the room's empty, and hope she misses it.'

The long corridor was dimly lit and eerily empty after the chaotic pace of the day. Tiny pearl globes behind louvered slats just above the skirting lit up the hallway with pinpricks of light. Brendan's shambling walk showed his fatigue as Chloe walked with him to the newly vacated room. Assuming he would climb on top of the bed she brought a sheet to cover the hospital quilt, but Brendan wound the bed up and rolled underneath it.

'I won't risk Hitler's Apprentice finding me and dragging me off to Matron. I'll be fine under here.'

'I'll come and wake you if Dart arrives and needs you. Maybe she'll just make a quick visit.'

Just after 1.00 am Sister Dart bustled importantly onto the ward in high energy mode and demanded Chloe accompany her on a ward round. The large industrial torch bobbed briskly at her side, as her hard-soled heels clipped on the industrial linoleum, echoing ominously down the hall. Chloe's steps were silent. Her nursing shoes were practical and standard issue.

The nervous drumming of Chloe's heartbeat seemed in time with the tattoo of their footsteps.

I wonder how much coffee she's had, Chloe thought. I don't have time to warn Brendan. Everything should be fine. She doesn't always check the empty rooms. Anyway, Brendan is out of sight under the bed.

Chloe matched Dart step for step into every room. She winced as the overly vigilant sister shone the torch beam in the sleep slackened faces of the patients. As usual, Dart felt compelled to check on every patient.

Between rooms, Chloe quietly informed her of the patients' diagnoses and their current status. She left Room 1 until last, and told her breezily that the room was empty and kept walking. Praying a silent prayer she hoped Dart would follow. Not a chance. Chloe felt a frisson of fear as she saw Dart's grip on the door handle.

As she opened the heavy creaking door a narrow slit of light illumined the room. She walked right into the room and Chloe followed with a sinking heart.

Don't snore Brendan. Please!

The room was still and silent.

'What is this bed doing raised?' asked Dart.

The beds were supposed to be left at their lowest level when unoccupied. No one else would have cared during the day, much less in the wee hours of the night, but Sister Dart was in full Hitler's Apprentice mode.

She's drunk a truck load of coffee, thought Chloe. This will end badly.

Her heart sunk even further when Dart walked purposefully to the bottom of the bed and rhythmically wound the bed back down to its rightful place. There was a dull clunk as the bed reached its lowest point.

Chloe couldn't breathe, sure Brendan was crushed. With sweaty palms she escorted Sister Dart off the ward. As the glass doors to the ward clanged shut she raced back to rescue Brendan, imagining broken bones and mayhem.

She looked under the bed. He was sleeping like a baby with his mouth open in angelic repose, his nose mere millimetres from the bed above him, snoring softly.

I can't believe it, she thought. I let him be now, but I'll give him hell when he wakes.

Chloe was upset on Brendon's behalf, but she also had her own score to settle with Hitler's Apprentice. She tried to cause trouble for Chloe one night when she made buns at work in the staff oven. Chloe's oven at home died just as the dough was rising for hot cross buns with gourmet dried fruit, seasoned with cinnamon.

Sister Dart was infuriated and contacted the Charge Night Sister to report Chloe. Sister Evangeline arrived and sought Chloe out in the kitchenette.

Sister Dart was appalled when she arrived minutes later eager to witness the 'dressing down', only to discover that Sister Evangeline had brought marmalade jam and was sitting there with the nurses enjoying steaming fruit buns and slices of butter.

All the staff loved Sister Evangeline. She was humane and kind. She was also quietly competent, even though she was prone to apologise to walls when she walked into them.

Brendan sauntered out refreshed at 2.30 am in search of a baked dinner. Chloe was incredulous.

'You scared me half to death! Oh, what's the use. I can't believe you can face a baked dinner at this hour.'

Brendon shrugged.

Chloe watched him go on in search of sustenance. She vowed she'd never be so whacky and disorientated by night duty to wish for baked vegetables and heavy meals in the middle of the night.

Brendon returned with Peter and Jeff. They'd been on a rampage to the kitchen. All three carried baked dinners. The smell wafted towards Chloe.

'Oh, that smells good. I could kill for a baked dinner,' she said.

Peter offered her a piece of gravy-soaked, baked, potato on his fork. It was delicious.

Brendan, now alert and playful, regaled them with his bravery and cunning.

'He slept through it,' said Chloe, accepting another mouthful of food.

Brendan splayed his hand millimetres in front of his nose to demonstrate his lucky escape. The boys roared loudly.

'Took ten years off my life,' said Chloe.

Jeff went to pat her nurses' cap and found the huge dent she'd put there when she'd leaned on the wall.

'Hey Chloe, you have a crater back here!'

'Buzz off, Jeff, I'm not a prissy perfectionist, I'm a minimalist!'

'Don't stress; I'll fix it for you,' he said.

Chloe doubted this very much, but Jeff had already removed the boxed cap and was showing it to the other guys. He and Brendan turned it over and pronounced it DOA (Dead On Arrival).

'How do you girls work these things, anyway?' asked Jeff. He'd managed to remove the dent, but the cap was now scarily crooked.

'Obviously, we don't! You're no better Jeff; you've made it look like the Leaning Tower of Pisa.'

'Well, you learn something every day,' said Brendan, taking the cap and eyeing it suspiciously, 'women are tireless at making their lives difficult.'

'And ours!' said Jeff, '*That's* what I've learned!'

A buzzer broke their comradeship. Brendan groaned.

'Room 16; that'll be Mr Ellis wanting to go the toilet. It doesn't matter how many times I tell him he has a catheter in, he still insists he 'needs to go'. What is it with TUR patients?'

'Mess with a man's crown jewels and his brain dies,' said Jeff.

Mr Ellis had pulled his catheter out. Jeff stayed to help Brendan re-catheterise the old man and settle him.

Sister Dart held a double standard. In spite of her rampage against sleeping nurses, she regularly went to sleep at her desk in the Nurses' Station. She could nod off with coffee cup in hand mid-air, while holding a magazine. Sometimes she snored, and on one occasion was 'out for the count' for half an hour.

The medication room was a recessed cubicle in the Nurses' Station right next to the Sister's Desk.

Chloe smiled a secret smile. Revenge would be hers at last. Most of the Nurses' Station was carpeted, except for the medication area, which was tiled due to the possibility of medication spills. Chloe waited for Sister Dart to sink deep into the realms of slumber.

Then, she quietly brought a heavy metal bowl into the medication room. Holding it above her head for maximum benefit, she let it drop to the floor. The clang was like a sonic boom in the early morning quiet.

Chloe heard a loud snort. The coffee cup fell with a crash, spilling sticky liquid all over the patient notes.

'Bother,' said Chloe, picking up the bowl.

Keeping her back to Sister Dart, she headed calmly down the hall to Brendan.

'Jeez, Chloe. Why didn't you let me in on it?'

'Sometimes in life Brendan, you just have to seize the moment.' Chloe smiled.

Her debt to Hitler's Apprentice was paid in full.

Heartbreak Hotel

'I'm going to have to dump her.' Matt Williams pulled a distracted hand through his gleaming hair. He took a step back as his friend Dan brushed past him on the way to the hand basin.

'She's gorgeous,' said Dan, a tense edge to his voice. He had seen his charismatic school friend go through women like a greedy toddler in a toy store. He often wondered why Matt still bothered with him, but as he'd just put in a couple of hours fine-tuning his latest acquisition, a BMW sports car, Dan realised that Matt was using him as much as all his women.

'Yes, she's certainly easy on the eye,' said Matt, looking at Lisa with pride. 'I can sure pull the hotties.'

Dan threw the towel onto the basin, hoping Matt would leave so that he wouldn't have to watch yet another beautiful girl have her heart broken. Usually he didn't care much. The types that hung off Dan were usually empty-headed vain models who couldn't stand to be around the workshop. Why would he care about this one? He thought she seemed different to the others. Ah, but what would he know? Flicking his cleaning rag into his back pocket he made a great show of gathering his tools, hoping Matt would take the hint and leave.

'You can leave the car with me, you know Matt. I have to wait for the part for a few hours yet.'

'I would mate,' said Matt, eyeing his watch. 'But Lisa wanted to wander around the yard for a while.'

Dan turned surprised eyes to Matt.

'She doesn't exactly look dressed for the occasion. I reckon those designer clothes won't last long in this place.'

'Yeah, beats me why she'd want to be here.'

They both looked at Lisa, who seemed to be in another world. With her sunglasses pushed back onto her head, she was standing with eyes closed, blissfully enjoying the sun on her face. To Dan she looked like a goddess. Her caramel hair fell in careless abandon half way down her back. She opened her eyes, saw them looking and threw them an artless dazzling smile. She turned to open the black bag she'd been carrying.

'Probably getting her make up out of her purse. Better tell her there's no mirror in the 'bathroom facilities',' said Dan, his voice edged with sarcasm.

He didn't want to like this girl. He was sick of Matt parading his conquests around him. Looking down at his grimy overalls Dan realised he didn't stand a chance with any of the women who fawned all over Matt.

'No, she doesn't wear make-up. She could improve herself a bit if she did. Her hair would look great with blonde streaks too. I've given her the hint - tried to push her towards my stylist, but she says she likes her hair 'wild'. Oh no! She's getting her bloody camera out. She'll be ages. Never leaves home without the thing. She could make a fortune as a model, but no, she's into 'art photography'.' Matt's voice took on a bitter edge. 'I'll be stuck here now. Bloody high maintenance women; don't know how I keep finding them.'

'I've got to get back to work, mate,' said Dan, fast losing patience.

He stole another look at Lisa as she took shots of the outside of the garage. This was a change anyway, one of Matt's women more at home behind the camera rather than playing up to it.

'I mean, they want their own way all the time,' continued Matt.

Dan gave in and leaned negligently against the doorway to the workshop. It seemed Matt wanted a moan, and knowing Matt as he did, Dan knew there was no way out. Might as well get it over with and listen to his narcissistic friend blow off steam. They sooner he'd finished, the sooner Dan could get on with things.

'So, you're chucking her because she's high maintenance?' he asked. Not much in the way of conversation but Dan was bored stiff.

Matt turned fiery eyes to Dan. 'No mate,' he began. 'It's much worse than that. She's been holding out on me.'

'Oh, I see, she won't sleep with you?' Dan grinned. This was a turn up for the books. He could seriously enjoy hearing about a woman impervious to Matt's charms.

'Well, no, it's not that. I mean we haven't slept together. Of course she wants to, but she's been busy.'

Dan's imagination was fired. Deliberately showing his poker face he waited for Matt to continue.

'No she's holding out on me about a kid.' Matt looked into Dan's eyes. 'That's as low as it gets, right mate? Having an ankle biter and acting like a single woman.'

Dan's eyes narrowed. He was the proud uncle to his sister's children. Chelsea was a single mother with three children.

'I was looking around in her handbag and found baby wipes. And there was this photo of some baby with hair the same colour as hers.' Matt waited for Dan's response.

Dan saw Matt look around for a chair and decided to take action. He'd had enough.

'I tell you what mate. I'll get Damien to take you back to the car dealership, so you don't lost a sale on one of your prestige cars. Ms Sneaky here can roam around and get a few pics. You'll be on your way and she'll be happy. You can book that fancy restaurant that you usually break up in...'

Matt leered. 'Yeah, 'Heartbreak Hotel'...'

'...and it will all be good,' said Dan. If he had to hear another cheesy rendition of the Elvis hit, he would have to strangle his friend.

'Sweet mate, I owe you. I'll just go and explain to Lisa.'

Lisa hardly seemed to notice Matt and waved him away airily. Funny, thought Dan, I think Mr Ego has missed his mark with this one. She doesn't seem that into him.

An hour later, Dan decided that he was definitely into Lisa. From the time she slipped effortlessly into a spare pair of overalls, wound her luxurious hair into a spiral and fixed it with one of his carpenter's pencils, he was sold.

'I'll give you that back,' she said. 'I know how you guys are about your pencils.'

Dan roared laughing and Lisa blushed.

'Oh, I didn't mean, oh bother. I'm always doing that. You'd think with three brothers I would have learned by now.'

'So what's the fascination out here with the camera? Most of these cars are junk. I only use them for parts.'

'You'd be surprised. It's all about the angle and the perspective.'

'So, you don't photograph models?'

'Oh *puleease!* I've got better things to do with my time. Models are Matt's thing,' said Lisa. There was a glint in her eye. 'Although I do know a few.'

Dan raised a quizzical eyebrow. This was one intriguing woman. He opened his mouth to ask her to explain, but she moved beside him to show him the photographs she'd taken. Dan was amazed. She'd caught the shine of the mirror reflecting the combination of green paint and orange rust on the old truck at the back of the lot.

'Wow, you have quite an eye. That would look really good on a poster at the front.'

'It's yours,' she said, smiling.

'Well...' said Dan, losing the power of speech, '...stay as long as you like. You're welcome to take as many as you like.'

'Thanks, I'd like that...' Her mobile phone beeped.

'That'll be Matt.'

Dan's heart plummeted.

'Yeah, sure. I'd love to, Matt.' Her face lit up.

For the first time, Dan actually hated his friend. '...so, another perfect date with the wonderful Matt then?'

Lisa laughed.

'Oh, it will be perfect, all right,' she said, 'but not for the "wonderful" Matt.'

'Really?' Dan's voice squeaked. A kernel of hope rose.

Lisa leaned towards him. 'Can you keep a secret, Dan? I mean...are you a really good friend of Dan's?'

'No...well we were at school...but...Oh go on, spill. I'm dying here!'

'Okay. That was the phone call for the 'let me down gently' date at 'Heartbreak Hotel'.'

'You know about that?'

'Oh yeah. Word gets around, especially when your sister was the last one to get the Matt treatment. She was hurt—badly. At least she never mentioned her son, my nephew Damien. Otherwise she'd have thought it was because she was a single mother and blamed herself.'

'You're mighty cheerful for someone who's about to be dumped,' said Dan.

'Oh, dear Dan. *He thinks* he's dumping me, but the girls will all be there.'

'The girls?'

'Yes, all the girls he's used and thrown aside for the last year or so. Most of them are models, like my sister. I met the others at Yoga. They asked me to set him up. I told them I wasn't his type and he wouldn't go for it, but he did. Of course, they had to load me up with make-up the first time and coach me about him. I never thought I'd have to go through with it, but he took to me like a duck to water. I guess I *am* his type. *Female.*'

'Oh, I think you have a bit more going for you than that,' said Dan, leaning towards her.

'You're too kind,' said Lisa, dropping a curtsy, which looked a bit awkward in Dan's overalls. 'The hardest thing has been pretending to be into him. I don't know what anyone sees in him.'

'Really? You know, I think I like you more and more. So Matt isn't your type. Will wonders never cease,' said Dan. 'Well then, what is your type, Miss Conniving Lisa?'

'Oh, I'm beginning to think overalls might come into the equation.' Her smile was shy, but flirty. 'Not prison issue, of course.'

Dan laughed. 'The only 'time' I'd like to do is with you, lovely lady. I would give anything to be a fly on the wall tonight.'

'Then come,' said Lisa, grabbing his forearm.

'Don't you have to stay for the 'break-up'?'

'I don't think breaking up will be on Matt's mind when the other girls walk in, and I walk out.'

Dan laughed. 'So you won't be staying for the main course?'

'Not likely!'

'You'll be famished then...'

'I will.'

'Terrific. I know this great little place...'

'This is NOT the time...'

Every family has a raconteur, a storyteller. An aunt or perhaps a grandfather would could gather and spin a tale that held, enchanted and entertained.

Georgia's paternal grandmother was their family storyteller. Between cousins and friends there was no dispute that she could weave an ordinary day, and imbue it with magic. One often hears of a person universally loved and we wonder if time has erased their faults. But Anna O'Day deserved the description, and no-one loved her as much as her grandchildren.

She had a favourite knee rug. It was mohair and tickly, pale lemon-and-brown check. Her name was sewn in the corner. It was soft and fluffy. Georgia would tuck Nana into a lounge chair and sit at her feet, in much the same way as her many grandchildren, who were proud to share her. There was plenty of Anna O'Day to go around. Though poor all her life, she loved with extravagant grace, and believed with unshakeable faith.

She was unique.

Georgia awaited her visits with a hungry heart, racing through her chores, applying a thoroughness that was usually lacking, looking forward to the time when Nana would be hers alone. Running with the mohair blanket, and tucking it firmly around

Nana, Georgia would sit on the floor. Even on the warmest of summer days Nana O'Day allowed this awkward tenderness.

'Which story would you like to hear?' she asked, her warm dulcet voice already weaving its spell.

'The one about the man who fell from the roof when he was shingling and broke his leg, then had to be taken to the doctor in a bumpy sulky, behind a black horse with a shimmering mane.'

'Oh, Georgia,' laughed Nana. 'You've nearly told the story yourself. What is left for me to tell?'

'Oh lots! Lots, lots more.'

So Nana O'Day would tell it again and again. Georgia never tired of any of her stories. They were always surprising and funny.

Her eyes would mist over when Georgia invariably asked, 'Tell me about my grandfather.'

'His name was Charles. He was a very dapper gentleman.'

'What's 'dapper'?'

'Smartly dressed. He always wore a vest with his suit, and his tiepin was perfectly placed.'

'Was that why you fell in love with him?'

'Oh no. He was a gentle man, kind and true. Not all gentlemen of fine birth and breeding are gentle.'

'Oh.'

'And he always smelt wonderful.'

Georgia giggled. 'Did he wear aftershave like Daddy?'

'Well, I didn't know the secret for a long time.' Nana paused. Georgia's eyes were wide. 'Oh, do go on.'

'He used to keep a sprig of lavender in his suit pocket.'

'Oh, that's wonderful. I hope I meet a wonderful man who carries flowers in his pocket,' sighed Georgia. 'Tell me about when you got a job on the railroad.'

Nana O'Day laughed. 'It wasn't exactly on the railroad. It began like this... I went for an interview... 'Oh, my...' the rail inspector said when I walked in dressed in coat and gloves, 'we're not accustomed to having women apply for positions as fettlers'.'

'The inspector looked me up and down. He was nonplussed. It wasn't as if the position called for great strength, but it did require making sure the rail gates were open on time - come what may. Women tended to be involved with child rearing back then. It was uncommon for a woman to work outside the home, much less with a 'man's job'. Many women took in laundry and cleaned for the wealthier homes in town. Clearing his throat, the man viewed we prospective employees. Quite a few had turned out, all of them men apart from me, so he would have someone employed by the end of the day. He smiled. There were nearly 30 in the community hall. He must have thought it wouldn't do any harm for me to sit the test along with the men. I was so quiet and polite with my hands folded in my lap, hoping that he couldn't bring himself to say anything. Leaning into a large box he took out dozens of balls of string. The task required each person to unroll the ball of string and then rewind it by hand. Patience and focus was crucial to the position – an unopened gate could cost a rail disaster, and left open it would cause chaos with wandering cattle. There was no written test as some of the best men couldn't read or write other than sign their names. One by one the men left in various states of frustration. I was the only one who completed the task. With small children at home and a sick husband, I was delighted to become a fettler for the New South Wales State Rail.'

Nana O'Day usually only visited for a day at a time, never overnight. She stayed longer with her daughters and her other sons. Georgia longed for her to stay with their family. She knew Nana stayed for weeks at a time with the country cousins.

Georgia began to suspect this oversight had something to do with her mother, Valerie. For weeks before Nana's visit her mother would become tense and terse. The house was turned upside down and the words, 'spotless', 'tidy', 'perfect' were thrown into every conversation.

'My family are a lot less fuss and bother,' she said.

Georgia said nothing. In her opinion anyone entering the sacred domain of Valerie Scote, automatically stepped into the category of 'fuss and bother'.

One day, Georgia's joy was complete when she learned that Nana O'Day was coming to stay. The little room at the front was made ready. A lounge chair was put in there for Nana's comfort. The usual contents of the 'spare room'; the cleaning things were stored carefully out of the way. Nana O'Day was going to stay for a week. Georgia was over the moon, offering to scrub the house with a toothbrush if it would help her mother calm down.

The first three days were bliss for granddaughter and grandmother. The same could not be said for Valerie. She was becoming tenser by the day. The cleaning rituals grew noisier. She snapped at the children and was with short with her husband. Georgia went into overdrive to keep the peace, to no avail. Valerie could not be made comfortable.

Valerie's ritual for the washing involved hanging it out, and then bringing to Georgia for her to sprinkle it with water and roll every item, ready for ironing. Valerie had very strict routines. She always rose early to hang out the washing, usually bringing it in just before lunch.

One particularly frantic day she was a little later than usual, and a little more frustrated. She left the basket of clean clothes in the doorway to Nana O'Day's room. When she returned she found the basket on its side.

'Georgia, come here! What were you doing to knock the wash basket over? I've had enough of you.'

Valerie grabbed a switch and sliced at Georgia's legs. In her anger she'd forgotten Nana, who was sitting only a few feet away in the corner of her room.

'Oh Valerie, I'm sorry. It was my fault. I knocked it over,' said Nana.

Georgia held back tears. Nana would pay for this interference, and so would she.

'Say nothing, say nothing. Let her beat me every day of my life rather than lose you. Say nothing,' she thought.

All three knew Nana hadn't knocked it over. Georgia hadn't even been inside, so how it came to be on its side was a mystery. Georgia bit her lip, wondering why it was such a big deal to have clean clothes on a clean carpet. The only thing she did know was that Nana O'Day's intervention would bring an end to her visits.

Georgia stood mute. With stiff formality Valerie sought to regain her dignity, but there was fire in her eyes. Nana O'Day left that afternoon. She was 'needed elsewhere'.

How stupid do they think I am? Georgia thought.

When Georgia was older, Nana O'Day left her home in the country to live with a family nearby. Georgia could visit as she pleased, thrilled to feel that they could never be parted. She longed for the day when she could repay her Nana's love, her audacious championing of a little girl. Primary school ended and high school passed in a flurry.

Georgia's wedding day dawned clear and bright. The January sun was fierce, the sky cloudless. The church was fragrant with Frangipanis, as they lay on the crimson carpet as far as the eye could see.

Valerie was in her glory. Her daughter was marrying 'up'. Valerie even tolerated Georgia's impertinent attitude when she was making decisions about the decorations, layout and place cards, and her recalcitrant daughter said, 'Would you like to say 'I do' for me as well, Mum?'

The wedding was declared a triumph. The food was abundant, the guests sated.

Georgia's glorious bouquet sat in front of her at the bridal table. Nana O'Day lay in a nursing home across the road. It was deemed 'too much' for her to attend.

Someone gathered the single women, the maidens, for the traditional throwing of the bouquet. The MC, a prestigious uncle of the groom, approached Georgia.

'We're ready for you to throw the bridal bouquet now, Georgia?' he said. He seemed secretly pleased the whole affair had come this far without Georgia being 'eccentric'.

'I'm not throwing the bouquet,' she said.

Valerie stiffened.

'Georgia! For goodness sake, the bride always throws the bouquet! I paid a fortune for those flowers! This is NOT the time for your...'

'Then you'll be pleased that I'm not going to throw them across the room, to a group of women who don't need a pagan custom to tell them if they'll ever get a man.'

Georgia rose, looped her bridal train over her arm and began to leave the reception hall.

'Where are you going? Honestly Georgia! You can't leave your own wedding!' Valerie said, shrinking in embarrassment.

Georgia didn't answer. Out of the corner of her eye she saw consternation in the faces of her new in-laws.

Her new husband, Geoff, stood. At over 6 foot, he towered over his petite bride. Looking deeply into her eyes, he wound his fingers through hers and let her lead.

They walked across the road. A walk that had none of the measured elegance of her arrival, but just as much purpose. They walked through the doors of the nursing home and were welcomed by the squeals and glee of the nurses. Georgia asked for a vase, and bride and groom went to the familiarity of Nana O'Day's room. Laying the flowers on the over bed table they sat on her bed to tell her everything about the day.

They stayed longer than they intended—Nana O'Day's smile was irresistible. The nurses insisted on putting 'Anna' in a wheelchair and taking a tour of the whole ward. Nana O'Day was radiant.

Georgia removed her pinching high heels. Then the bride and groom walked hand in hand back to the hall, with Georgia barefoot, and Geoff carrying her shoes. After all, a girl can only take so much for tradition, and the arbitrary rules of society.

Then, and not before, she told Valerie where she had been, and who she had chosen to honour.

'Hummph,' said Valerie.

Then Georgia mingled graciously with their guests, all two hundred of them - three quarters of whom she'd never met and who couldn't remember her name.

The lemon and brown check knee rug grew pale and prickly with age, but still held pride of place in Georgia's home, long after Nana O'Day had need for it.

It's there now, if one cared to look.

Wordless

The comforting whirr of the ceiling fan soothed the silence that was also punctuated by the deep rhythmic breathing of the pale girl in the bed.

Reality retreated as the fragile moments passed. Tense, tight words had been spoken. Truces had been offered and rejected. And still they sat. Estranged, but united. In sorrow.

Heath was isolated in grief for his broken wife, and the tall, clenched woman in the other chair was a torn witness to his pain, his loss. A loss he would not let her join, a bond she had forfeited when she disdained his choice of bride. Recriminations had given way to remorse, but it was insufficient.

Tamara Jayne Gainsford was eighteen, rosy cheeked, her face in gentle repose. She looked like a vulnerable Sleepy Beauty. But she was in a coma. A coma that had extinguished the radiant light of her youth; her exuberant folly. She was an ethereal earth child and Heath, her new husband, was the calm, deliberate man who loved her with passion and devotion.

Her senior by only two years, he was the rock that anchored her. But he had not been enough to save her.

Deirdre leaned forward in the chair, desperate to breach the distance from her only son, if only by inches. He held up a large, square hand that commanded silence. She sighed and retreated.

Tamara was angelic in sleep, a tousled curl fluttered in the inadequate breeze the fan created in the stifling heat. She did not yet know of her loss, but Heath's heart ached for both of them. Distracted with anxiety, he tolerated his mother's presence, but his anger simmered. His calloused fingers worried the tapestry of the ancient armchair he'd slept in overnight during his desperate vigil, his anguished guardianship.

He and his mother were on opposite sides of the bed. The intravenous drip slowly delivered blood into Tamara's vein. Her helplessness tore at his impotent misery. He couldn't even donate blood to her.

All the family had rallied. Stepfather, uncles, aunts and, yes, even his mother. Deirdre had sent desperate prayers heavenward that her blood would be a match, so that part of her life could flow into her daughter-in-law's veins, bringing healing to a ravaged girl and forgiveness to a family estranged by the scandal of the creation of a child, and then a hasty wedding two weeks ago.

A nurse entered and took Tamara's observations: BP, pulse, respirations and temperature. As she looked up from writing in the notes, two anguished sets of eyes held her gaze.

'Tamara's doing fine. There's no fever, no sign of rejecting the blood transfusion,' she said.

Heath's voice caught, fear holding the words captive. He cleared his throat.

'Will she be able to have more children? We really wanted this baby. A family. She'll be so heartbroken over the loss of this one, when she wakes up.'

'You'll have to talk to the doctor. He'll be finished his theatre list soon. He will come and talk to you all.'

The nurse left. The taut silence returned.

Time dragged, the fan whirred, the outside world of the ward was distant. A world away.

With an efficient bustle of movement the surgeon entered the room. His voice was brisk, confident, calming. Mother and son strained towards him.

'The surgery went well. Tamara has had an ectopic pregnancy. This means that the baby was developing in the fallopian tube, instead of the uterus. When the pregnancy advanced the tube ruptured. We were not able to repair the tube, but she still has one healthy tube. Although her chances are lessened a little for falling pregnant – there shouldn't be a problem having more children. She must have fainted from the pain and fallen down the stairs.'

'So the fall didn't...'

'The fall didn't cause her to lose the baby. There is always a chance that a pregnancy will occur in the tubes. It happens. There is no rhyme or reason, except that the fertilised egg settles in the tube, rather than travel to the uterus to embed safely.'

Deirdre Gainsford wept openly, her face buried in her hands. Heath flinched.

'But the coma...?'

'You'll have to wait for the neurologist's report, but all her vital signs are good.'

'Thank you, doctor,' said Heath, offering his hand.

'You're welcome, son. I hope to see you both again and be able to deliver a healthy baby for you. All the best.'

The room emptied of words once more.

Heath and his mother were replaying the same previous conversation in their minds. The one that had burned bridges.

Heath had phoned in tense agony.

'Tamara's in hospital. We've lost the baby.'

Any hope of understanding or reconciliation was shattered by Deirdre's next statement. 'So, you didn't have to marry her after all.'

'That's not...Forget it...'

The phone went dead.

It had taken word of mouth for the rest of the tragic news to be conveyed. And then they had all arrived, all those who had condemned their union and refused to attend the wedding.

Tamara had a rare blood type, and Heath was distraught. One of the male nurses immediately donated when he heard of their dilemma. He waved Heath's words of thanks aside, claiming no hero status - he gave blood regularly, anyway.

Heath was glad a caring stranger's blood had saved his wife. There would be no words of gratitude owed, no lingering sense of obligation to a family who had caused so much pain.

Heath paced the floor. He could take no more of his mother's cloying presence.

'Please leave, mother.'

Head bowed, she fled.

A quietly spoken man entered the room and introduced himself as Dr Eager.

'I'm your wife's neurologist, Mr Gainsford. I'm pleased to report that your wife came to just before the operation. She isn't fully aware of her condition, but I have every confidence that she will make a full recovery. Her MRI scan was clear, so there has been no brain damage, no sign of intracranial haemorrhage. I think that fairly soon after the anaesthetic wears off, she will wake up and be able to take all this in. I would think she'll only need to be in hospital a day or two after that.'

'Oh God. Thank you. Thank you,' said Heath, pumping the doctor's hand.

'All she needs now is some rest and TLC.'

Compass of the heart

She snarled through bared teeth, like a rabid dog in the dense, dark night. To hear such guttural sounds from a human throat sent chills down the night nurse's spines.

Evelyn Spector had dementia, but this seemed a paltry diagnosis in the small hours of the night, before the tendrils of morning glow broke the gloom. She was mad, crazy.

One of the nurses muffled a scream. Julia was the registered nurse on night duty for a 70 bed nursing home and had two nurses working with her. It would be more correct to say that Julia was working with them, because they were the 'regulars' on night duty, and she was only doing a week relieving the regular night sister, then returning to day shifts.

'Does she do that in the daytime?' asked Rhonda, grimacing.

'No, but she's not exactly a picture of bliss. Come to think of it, I've never seen her smile,' said Julia.

'She's demon possessed,' pronounced Ellen, known for 'getting to the point'.

'Rubbish,' Julia said, turning on the night lights.

'So there's no reason, then?' asked Rhonda.

'Of course there's a reason, we just don't always know it. We can guess, but the brain is a complex thing. It could have been some trauma in her life that's surfacing now, or maybe that part of her brain has been affected by a stroke.' Julia shrugged.

'So,' began Rhonda, 'does personality change with a stroke? Or do they just lose their inhibitions?'

'If I had three PhD's I still couldn't tell you that, but it fascinates me,' Julia replied.

The nurses ministered to the patients in the four bed ward; washing, changing and turning them.

Fascinated with this new view of Evelyn, Julia watched her carefully when she was back on day duty in her regular role as Nurse Manager. She told the story of Evelyn's night-time habits to the day nurses. 'Have you girls noticed any behaviour like that?' she asked during one of the patient care meetings.

'She never speaks to us, but I've heard her mutter to herself,' volunteered Jean, adding intrigue to the tale.

'She never eats when we're in the room,' said Karen.

They sat silently in the staff room. Through the window they could see the patient lounge room.

Julia studied Evelyn. She refused the lounge chair with a view to the garden, choosing to face the one blank wall in the room. Her eyes were cold and narrowed, hard as black diamonds, her lips were a tense thin line.

Who had she been? Where had life taken her? Julia wondered about her family. It was in the time before it was common practice to take family histories to better know and understand patients. This has proved particularly important when they sink into dementia; for knowing their family, fears and lifestyle helps immeasurably in respecting their world.

The answers to Evelyn, at least in part, came one wet and windblown December. Her daughter came to visit, carrying a huge bunch of red roses, garlanded with Christmas bush, and a gift wrapped with obvious care.

Oh well, Evelyn must have been a wonderful mother to inspire such devotion, Julia mused as she went about her nursing routines.

After a short time Julia walked into the main dining room, now empty, except for Evelyn's daughter. The woman's eyes were full to the brim with all the emotions missing from her mother, her anguish palpable. She didn't speak, but her gaze held Julia with such intensity that she went to her, hands outstretched. Evelyn's daughter gripped Julia's hands.

'I can't get through to her,' she wailed. 'Sorry, I'm Caroline. Oh dear, I'm so sorry.'

'Don't be. Never apologise for tears or grief,' Julia said, tasting the words as they left her mouth. Words that she herself so often longed to hear. 'Sometimes this happens with dementia—the change in people.'

Caroline raised shocked eyes, and emitted a moan that tore Julia's heart.

'Change! *Change!* I've waited fifty years for change. A change from the heartless treatment of my childhood. The cruelties of a woman with no time or love for children. A woman who kept my brother and I in a cupboard under the sink ... like dogs.' Her voice faltered as she ended an outburst that she clearly never intended.

Her tears flowed. Julia folded Caroline in her arms, and Caroline clung desperately to the embrace offered.

'I'm sorr...'

'Don't say it,' Julia said.

They sat at a corner table. The world faded into the background as Caroline poured out the tale of a lifetime of reaching for the love of a woman who had brought her into the world, and then abused her, systematically and thoroughly. She spoke of a brother who vowed never to lay eyes on that woman again, unless in a coffin.

'I can't move past it. I can't give up. Surely the time will come when she appreciates me, loves me... I don't know... responds...

something, *anything.'*

Julia grasped her hand.

'She still has you imprisoned, as surely as she did when you were a child. She had the key then to free you—but didn't. She doesn't have it now; through choice, or the arbitrary losing of her mind, *but you do.* You, and only you.' Julia willed the words to cut through the fog of a mind tormented for decades.

Caroline left, in the same torn, rent, frame of mind that she came. Julia looked out after her, through the large front windows of the nursing home. Caroline found her car keys with trembling hands, fleeing this place of torment, this broken dream.

The spray snow on the window, of Christmas joy, glittered and softened Julia's view of her, as she watched - helplessness to ease the pain of a woman who had lived a good life, loving the children of her own body in a way she had never been shown. And still begging, yearning for a mother's love.

Then, as the silver car flashed past the window, Julia saw her own reflection and drew in a ragged breath. Julia wondered why Caroline had never confronted her mother when she had the chance.

In that moment of clarity, Julia realised she had never asked her own mother why she was relegated behind the dining room door for hours, until the anxiety tore at her and she chewed her tongue to soothe the angst.

Caroline was twenty years her senior. Would Julia be Caroline in twenty years? Still standing in those painful shoes, trying to shrug off inadequacy and self-blame; waiting?

The car raced out of sight—the image gone. Julia hoped she'd helped Caroline. But she had gained a new insight. As she stroked the palm of her hand she pictured a key there. Her key; her liberation and peace.

'I am the key,' she whispered. 'I am the adult daughter desperate for affection and approval, for the wounded child I have been.'

During the following nursing report Julia told the nurses about the exchange with Caroline. They listened in silent dismay, but not in shock. For there, in the nursing home, daily stories of angst and pain were told.

'God, Julia! How will we treat Evelyn now? Knowing this?' asked Ellen.

'The same way we always have. We're nurses, not judges, juries or instruments of punishment. We're nurses. I cannot measure the sum of what I know, what I have learned, but this I know—the measure of our character is who we are to the mute, the helpless and the fallen—not who we are to our betters or peers. To honour the silent, is evidence of the true North of the compass of our hearts.'

I'll be waiting

'Hey Rembrandt!'

Jenna groaned. It was Mike again. Her new neighbour was paying far too much attention to her comings and goings, or at this moment, her backyard activities. She was quietly weeding around the Camellias with her auburn hair tied up. She wiped the sweat that trickled down her neck with the back of her hand – her very grubby hand. She couldn't see him. The man was positively panther-like. Perhaps he'd been a spy in a past life. Maybe if she ignored him, he'd go away.

'Oh, very attractive Jenna,' he purred, his eyes mocking.

Jenna jumped a foot as Mike appeared over the fence. She looked down, and froze as she realised she'd trailed stripes of soil between her breasts.

Why did I wear a bikini top? She wondered. Arrggh. Because I was in the privacy of my own backyard, which has become decidedly less private since Mr Perennial Bachelor moved in next door. I won't let him faze me.

'Thanks for noticing,' Jenna said between gritted teeth.

'You're welcome.'

Jenna continued to pull weeds and turn the soil. He'd soon tire of this.

'You had such a faraway look on your face, Jenna. Were you in another place? Or just wishing?' He leaned negligently on the fence.

Thank God for the fence or he'd probably wander on over, she thought. Maybe I could make it higher.

'I did have a faraway look didn't I? I wasn't wishing, but I am now—for peace and quiet.'

'Ah cruel lips, how dost thy heart beat?' he rambled, throwing himself elegantly on the ground and folding his arms behind his head.

'Shakespeare is rolling over in his grave.'

'I'm not quoting Shakespeare.'

'That's why he's rolling over - crimes against the English language.'

'I'm being original.' Mike smiled.

The man was impossible. He never gave up. He must have an ego the size of the Sahara. The constant parade of gorgeous women to his door had convinced Jenna early on that Mike Nelson was a player. How dare he flirt with her? Bored, that was obviously it. He had introduced himself when he first arrived and given her his business card. The card displayed his profession as a Design Photographer, whatever the hell that was. He certainly seemed to have 'designs' on a lot of leggy, glamorous women.

As much as Jenna wanted to run inside like a sulky teenager, she was determined not to let him get under her skin, or let him know how much he annoyed her. She thrust the fork between the wild violets wondering if she could possibly manage to flick dirt on his pristine white T shirt. That would be easy enough, but making it look accidental would be quite different. Instead she changed the subject.

'You still haven't told me why you call me Rembrandt,' she said.

'Haven't I? Oh, that's easy. I saw your studio.'

'You what? When?'

'The real estate agent showed me through.'

'Where?' she squeaked.

'Oh, everywhere. He must be new. He thought it was your house for sale instead of this place.'

'I'll kill him,' said Jenna straightening up, 'they only have the keys to show tenants the granny flat.'

'Hmm. Oh well, no harm, no foul.'

'That's easy for you to say! It's unprofessional.' She paused. 'You saw my paintings?'

Jenna felt colour rise up her neck to her face. How she hated that. She'd always struggled to hide her emotions, but there they were, written all over her face. Her mother said she could read her like a book.

'They are very good, you know.'

'You shouldn't have seen them. I just...I don't...'

'They are good enough to exhibit. I've been around, you know.'

'Thank you,' said Jenna, biting back the temptation to say 'I'll bet'.

'You really love flowers, don't you? It shows. The colours are vibrant.'

'Oh. Well, I work at a nursery, so I suppose it's true.'

'And you bring your work home with you,' he said, eyeing her mud-spattered neck.

'Just like you,' she snapped, then felt regret at the withdrawal in his eyes. It was none of her business what he did. He was just being neighbourly.

'Well, then. I'll let you get on with it.'

Mike turned and walked to the house. He didn't know why his new neighbour was so prickly. According to their sparse conversation, usually one-sided, it seemed part of the problem was that she despised his work, which was a bit unreasonable really. A guy had to make a living. And if that living meant glamorous women turning up at his door day and night, why should he explain to Ms Prickly next door. How dare she judge him? He shouldn't care, but he did. Gliding to the kitchen window where he could watch Jenna without her seeing him, he was highly amused to see her banging the shovel against her head.

He laughed. She was human, after all.

One day they might actually have a conversation where he could tell her of his career in journalistic photography. His assignments in Afghanistan, his years of covering disasters, famine, flood and poverty. It irked him enough that his former mates ribbed him over his new career as a commercial photographer. It wasn't his fault that he had only attracted models wanting portfolios. He was stuck with it until his leg healed. In a few weeks he would have the pin and plate removed, where the bullet had shattered his tibia. Maybe then he could get back to serious work. But the specialists had told him not to get his hopes up. At best, his leg would be a long time healing.

The clicking of doggy toenails heralded the arrival of his pug, Nero, tongue hanging to one side. His owner in the kitchen meant one thing. Food. Scratching the mutt's head, Mike obliged.

'You're going to be a problem, Nero,' he said.

Nero wagged his tail, clearly excited to have a conversation with his beloved master.

'What am I going to do with you when I go to hospital? I guess I'll have to ask Debbie, again. I wouldn't dare bother Ms Prickly.'

If Nero heard Mike over the chomping of his meat, he didn't show it.

'Ms Prickly' was well and truly bothered. It was bad enough to miss the two darling neighbours who had become like family. Jean and Arthur Bainbridge moved interstate to be near their children. Jenna kicked herself for hoping for another retired couple, with time on their hands, where she would be welcome without expectation. People she could wander over for a cup of tea, a walk around the garden where she could give advice on their plants, and feel needed.

It was just her luck to get the Playboy of the Year. She groaned as a sleek silver car drove into Mike's driveway. And of course, a gorgeous blonde flew out of the car. How many women did this man have? Although this one was a bit different. No glamour make-up. And a bit frazzled. The woman opened the back door of the car and picked up a pink bundle of softness from the baby seat. Jenna's heart constricted. When would she stop reacting? She put her head down behind the rose bushes. It wouldn't do to appear to be spying on her new neighbour.

Any minute now Mike would wander outside with that ridiculous walking stick he used. She was sure he didn't need it. He was too bloody cheerful to be in pain. Or maybe one of his paramours had kicked him in the shins. Jenna's face creased in a smile at the thought.

'Excuse me.'

Oh no, she'd been spotted. She wasn't in the mood for conversation with any of Mike's women. She looked up and attempted a smile.

'Sorry to bother you,' said the woman, 'but my brother isn't home. He's usually reliable. I don't have time to wait. Oh sorry, I'm Debbie Waters, Mike's big sister. And don't believe him if he says I boss the life out of him. It's just that he's so annoying about accepting help.'

'Oh,' said Jenna.

'Oh dear, I'm prattling on, I'm sorry,' said Debbie. 'Shsh darling one, I know,' she murmured to the baby, stroking the soft downy head.

'Anyway. I wonder if you could give Mike a message. I seem to have everything in the baby's carry bag but a pen and paper. His appointment for the specialist who's going to remove the pin and plate is at 2.00 this afternoon. He'll need to phone our other sister, Jane, as soon as possible. Teagan has a temperature and I have to take her to the paediatrician. Oh dear, this is too much information. I just don't want him to miss the appointment, which he's likely to do, because he won't ask anyone for help. He can't afford to miss this one. We were worried enough when the bullet shattered his leg bone ... oh blast, I can't remember the name of it. Didn't pass Anatomy. Never mind. Could you just tell him when he gets in that Debbie can't take him and to ring Jane. Or else.'

'Um... er... of course. I've got it. His *non*-bossy sister, Debbie, demands his attendance at the specialist.'

'Ha Ha. I'm going to like you...'

'Jenna. Jenna Slater. I'll pass it on to Mike. I'd shake your hand, but...' Jenna held up grubby hands.

'Ta,' said Debbie, and she was gone.

Jenna smiled. What a lovely woman. Then she remembered that she'd agreed to go to Mike's. Darn.

Mike arrived about five minutes later. Jenna felt a pang of disappointment that she hadn't had time to clean up. Oh dear, what was she thinking? Just because the man was drop dead gorgeous and at least one of his female visitors was a lovely down to earth sister, didn't make Mike a saint.

In her attempt to head him off before he got to the front door, she fell headlong in the rose garden. Looking up, she saw Mike grinning.

'You all right?' he asked, ambling over to her.

Jenna noticed the slight wince in his face as he walked. That was something else she was wrong about. 'I'd help you up, but with this dodgy leg, I'd probably end up on top of you. Going somewhere?'

'Yes, actually,' she said, clambering up inelegantly. 'I was coming to give you a message from your sister, Debbie. She can't take you today because Teagan isn't well, so you have to ring Jane.'

'Good grief, regular blabbermouth, that Debbie. Did she tell you my shoe size?'

'Almost.'

'Blast. Oh well, I'll have to cancel. Debbie must have forgotten that Jane's gone away on business.'

'You can't do that!'

'Not you too!'

'She said it was important.'

'Did she now?'

'Yes, on account of the bullet, and the plates and screws ... and stuff...'

'I wear a size 10.'

'Pardon?'

'Well, it would be a shame to miss out the only detail about me you don't have.'

'You should talk. You prowled around my studio.'

'I did not *prowl*. I never prowl.'

'Well, you can't miss the appointment. I'll take you.' Jenna shocked herself.

She must have shocked Mike too, because he didn't answer.

'I'll come over at 1.00. That should give us time to get to the city. I'll just finish this lot, tidy up and come over and get you.'

Mike hesitated. He could walk to her place, but the thought of having her on his home turf was irresistible.

'Okay. I'll be waiting,' he said.

'Right,' said Jenna, with more conviction than she felt. He'd hesitated. She must have been too pushy.

The afternoon went smoothly. Mike gained a small victory when he talked Jenna into driving his Lexus, claiming he needed leg room. Jenna remembered the potting mix in her car and agreed. She didn't want to be surrounded by the smell of manure while she was with Mike.

To her surprise, conversation with Mike was easy and relaxed. He told her about his overseas tours as a photo journalist, and she talked about her job at the nursery. She even demurred when he suggested they 'grab a bite' and enjoyed the up-market café he chose. Pushing down the thought that he might take all his women there, she allowed herself to relax.

173

Several men slapped him on the back, and asked after him. It seemed to Jenna that they were observing her keenly, almost as if it was unusual for Mike to be out with a woman. That didn't seem right, but she couldn't dismiss the fact that his friends were protective towards him.

Over the next few days Jenna was introduced to several of Mike's clients, two who were very pregnant, and to his other sister, Jane. She was very much like Debbie in looks and personality. Working in Human Resources, she was a human dynamo.

Jenna managed to meet them all without going inside Mike's house. He invited her in, but she consistently declined. She resisted being drawn further into his life. Maybe she should spend less time in the garden. She'd never met so many people over the fence in her life.

Mike was nonplussed.

Jenna was friendly and compassionate, but she obviously had some invisible line drawn in the sand. Surely, by now the woman realised his job had integrity. He was becoming more attracted to her, but they were at an impasse. He realised he had his work cut out for him. Even though they conversed with ease, she hadn't ventured even into his back yard.

So it was with surprise and pleasure to find her at his back door, holding a basket of home-grown vegetables. Everything nearly fell apart when Nero licked her leg. She screamed, and would have dropped the basket if Mike hadn't caught it.

'Oh help. Sorry. I'm not fond of dogs.'

Nero, impervious to this indictment on his species, repeated the welcome.

'Erk! Why do they do that? That licking thing?'

'I think it's a doggie hello. I could be wrong, of course. You might just taste great.'

This remark earned him a sharp look. He shrugged.

'Who's going to feed him when you're in hospital?'

'I thought you didn't like dogs. Don't tell me you care!'

'Well, I wouldn't want him to starve. And those sisters of yours are busier than the Prime Minister.'

'And just as capable.'

'That too. I don't know how they do it.'

'Frankly, I don't want to know,' said Mike. 'I'm getting addicted to life in the slow lane. But hey, you can feed Nero for me, if you're offering.'

Of course that gave Mike the perfect opportunity to usher Jenna into the house and show her all of Nero's food and vitamin needs. And if he detoured to his photographic studio, who could blame him. A man had to do what he could.

Jenna was wide-eyed when she saw his work. There were very few glamour shots. And not one nude. Not that she was looking. There was a hint of his former life with a discreet portfolio of overseas photographs, but most of the pictures were of families, gently reposed pregnant women, children at play, and his sisters.

Mike felt unaccustomed warmth at her obvious interest.

'These are wonderful, Mike.'

He had no glib words. 'Thank you,' he said. He didn't take his eyes off her as she wandered around the room, totally at ease, admiration shining in her face. 'Your art is just as wonderful, you know, Rembrandt. I hope you go back to painting.'

Jenna smiled. She'd missed him calling her Rembrandt. 'You don't have any here of your models.'

'What?'

'You know - the glamour models that arrive with cosmetic bags the size of small aircraft.'

Mike laughed. 'You're very observant, Ms Slater.'

His lazy grin unnerved her.

'Well it's a bit hard not to notice when they sometimes trip trap to my door looking for you.'

'Oh I see,' he said. 'And there I was thinking you hadn't noticed my existence. So you thought they were models?'

'Well, aren't they?'

'Not many, as a matter of fact. They're mostly women wanting photos for dating sites.'

'Oh, big market for that is there?'

'Apparently.'

'How are you going to manage work after your op?' Jenna concentrated on one of the family snapshots.

Mike sighed. Rather dramatically, Jenna thought.

'I guess I'll have to hire an assistant for a while.'

'Would I do? I mean it must be hard to get someone short term. I learn fast.'

'Why not. You're not squeamish though, are you?'

'Why?'

'Well, I do videos as well.'

'Oh,' Jenna squeaked.

'Births, sometimes funerals, but labour ward mainly. Would you be okay with that?'

'Sure. Yes, I would.'

Jenna's hands trembled.

I'll be okay, she thought. It's time. It's past time.

Mike moaned. His heart raced. His leg was white hot with pain. There were popping noises, women screaming, men yelling and smoke, so much smoke.

'Oh my God. They're shooting. Get down. Get down. There's a child. The girl. Grab the girl. It's okay. I've got her. I've been hit.'

A damp cloth wiped his forehead. Gentle hands soothed his stubbled chin.

'It's okay, Mike. You're dreaming. It's over.'

Mike's eyes focused on Jenna. Then it came to him. He was in hospital. The operation must be over.

'How did it go? Is my leg okay?'

'Yes. It's just a matter of time now.'

'Debbie. Jane.'

'They've just gone for tea. They'll be back soon.'

Mike writhed, and made a useless attempt to sit.

'Hell. Where is the pain relief?'

'You just have to press this button.'

'I can't. You do it.'

'I don't think I'm ...'

'Just do it.'

'Alright Mr Bossy. Honestly Mike, you're a right sook. I thought you'd been in war zones.'

'Behind the camera, Ms Prickly. I'm not a soldier.'

Jenna smiled at being referred to as Ms Prickly. A few months ago that would have stung, but things had changed, subtly at first. And she was pretty sure he was partly affected by the anaesthetic and drugs. She carefully put the damp face cloth over his face.

'Oi, what'd y'do that for?'

'I plead the fifth. What you don't see won't hurt you.' Jenna pressed his pain relief button, then removed the face cloth. 'You'll have to learn to do this yourself, you know.'

'I've been doing it for hours. I just wanted to see if I could get you to do it.'

'You wretch! If you weren't lying in a hospital bed I'd...'

'What...'

'You'd be lying in a hospital bed.'

Mike chuckled.

The next few weeks passed quickly. Jenna learned that Mike's job entailed a lot more than pandering to vapid women in search of their elusive Romeos. She became so comfortable as his assistant that she began to anticipate his needs before he asked. She would miss this when her long service was up and it was time to return to her job at the nursery.

'Oh Nero! Stop that! Don't lick me. When, and if, I ever decide I want to be licked, you are the last one on my list, Slobber Chops.' Jenna scratched his head, and Nero growled in gratitude.

Mike kept his head down on the other side of the room so Jenna wouldn't see the grin wreathing his face.

The phone shrilled. Mike answered it.

Jenna tried to work things out from the patchy one-sided conversation.

'Oh, I'm so sorry... Of course... No. It's fine... No problem. I'll be there as soon as I can.'

He turned to Jenna.

'It's okay if you're not up for this, Jenna. It's a difficult one. I'll understand. I'll get Deb or Jane if it's too much.'

'If what's too much?'

'One of my clients that I was going to film the birth, is... well, the baby has died. She still has to go through labour. I won't be there for that, of course, but they want photos of them holding their baby. Just still shots.'

'Oh.'

Jenna thought she would faint, as the room swam.

'I've got time to get Deb, she's had kids. You don't have to do it.'

'I'll be fine. Truly.'

You can do it, Jenna thought. You can do this.

'What about you, Mike? You're using crutches. How will you manage?'

'I've got you.'

Jenna thought she'd never known such terror, faced such fear. Keeping busy helped. She made a supreme effort to mask her feelings. She had a job to do. Mike needed her.

Mike came into the birthing suite and spoke softly to the couple, who clung quietly to each other. They were waiting for the sister to bring the baby to them. Mike introduced Jenna. She busied herself, getting Mike's equipment ready and finding a stool for him to sit on. That was easy enough as the nurses gave him an adjustable one. Jenna wondered how the nurses could be so normal at a time like this. Compassionate, but competent.

I'll stand in the background, thought Jenna. *I'll be fine. I'll stay back. Way back.*

The sister brought the baby in and handed the tiny pink blanket to the mother. Mike snapped continuously as the mother, then the father lovingly cradled their baby. They seemed unaware of Mike's presence. The sister left the room. Gentle tears crept down the mother's face from eyes that were already red-rimmed. The father's shoulders shuddered from time to time. Mike handed him a large handkerchief. The man took it without noticing where it came from.

With an understanding gaze the husband and wife locked eyes. They were ready. Their goodbyes had ben said. The woman glanced at Jenna and held the baby out.

Jenna froze.

'I work in a nursery... oh dear... not that kind... It's okay. I've got her.' Jenna took the baby. Husband and wife melted into each other. Jenna looked around in panic for the nurse.

Then she looked down.

The baby was perfect. Warm and peaceful, her skin showing just a hint of dusky blue. The baby's fingers were curled around the edge of the blanket. Jenna couldn't take her eyes off the tiny infant. With feathery fingers she gentled the baby's cheek. Mike snapped the shutter again and again. Mike held his breath. He understood so much about Jenna now, and yet so little.

With infinite tenderness Jenna kissed the tiny forehead.

'Goodbye, Rose.'

'Her name is Belle,' said a nurse at her side.

'Of course,' said Jenna.

'Don't worry. Are you okay for me to take her now?'

'Yes, of course. I'm not... related...'

But the nurse was gone.

Something in Mike's chest pinged. Oh, he'd had zings and zaps before, but nothing like this. *I love her*, he thought. *I'm falling in love with the value of a woman. For the first time. For the last time. A woman as beautiful on the inside as the outside.*

They packed up the equipment and went to the car park in silence. A comfortable silence. Mike's Lexus was an automatic, so he drove.

'I had a stillborn baby,' Jenna said.

'Rose.'

Their eyes connected, with only the dashboard lights to illuminate the distance.

'You did well, you know?'

'I did, didn't I? They didn't allow that when it happened to me... to us. I wish they had. I thought it would be terrible, but it wasn't. Parents need to say goodbye, properly, you know?'

'I think I do. It was almost like having your own goodbye, wasn't it.'

'Yes. A forever goodbye, a proper one. How did you know?'

'I could read it on your face. I'll show you the photos I took when you were holding her.'

'Oh, thank you.'

'You're welcome. Jenna?'

'Yes, Mike.'

'When you're ready ...'

Jenna tilted her head quizzically.

'When you're ready for hello. A forever hello. I'll be waiting.'

Jenna slipped her hand into his, and smiled in the semi-darkness.

A fine romance

'When did you fall in love with Dad, Mum?' I asked one day as I stood on an orange box helping peg out the washing.

'For goodness sake, Linda. I don't know where you came from. You ask the daftest questions.'

It was true. I was a child of endless curiosity. And that day's 'bee in the bonnet' question demanding answers was how my parents had met and fallen in love. Mum looked at me as though I'd lost my marbles. That didn't bother me at all. Most of the neighbour children told me I was nuts. They found their parents to be terminally boring. Not I. I knew they had lived a life before me and I was fascinated.

'Well, when *did you?*'

'A long time after he did,' she said.

'Oh really?' I gasped. I was on to something.

'Don't 'oh really' me with your nonsense. You watch too much Disneyland. Go and bother your father.'

So I did.

'When did you fall in love with Mum, Dad?'

He smiled.

'I was fifteen.' His eyes twinkled.

'Good grief, Dad! That's a bit young. You said I couldn't go out with boys until I was 21.'

Dad laughed. A full bodied sound of joy.

'But Mum would only have been thirteen!'

'So she was,' said Dad.

This was a bit hard going, but I was making more progress than with Mum so I persisted.

'What did you do to show her how you felt?'

'I threw clods of dirt over the fence at her.' His face was deadpan.

'*You never did!*'

'I did.'

'But... but... that's awful. What did *she* do?'

'She threw them back at me, but she was a better shot.' He flinched at the memory. 'Anyway, I wasn't trying to hit her, just get her attention, but she was livid.'

I laughed. 'Livid' was one of Mum's favourite words. She was never 'a little put out'. That happened to people other than my mother.

'I guess you didn't do that again,' I said.

'Yes, I kept doing it. We lived next door to each other...'

'...I know that... So what happened next?' I was hungry for more now.

'Well, we met again when we went to College. We went out for a bit.'

'What does that mean?'

'Hand me the small spanner, Bubs. Might as well help out.'

Try as I might I couldn't get any more out of him.

So I did what children have done with their parents since the beginning of time. I went back and forth from one to the other. Most children do this in order to gain toys or permission. There was no use doing that with my parents because they were 'dirt poor instead of filthy rich'. This was one of Dad's favourite phrases, but it found no favour with Mum. We were *not* poor. In mum's book, we were not endowed with this world's riches. And they was no use arguing for any permissions because to me, no meant *no*. My brother avoided this whole scenario by never asking, just 'nicking off'. It never occurred to me to follow his lead.

'Dad said he fell in love with you when he was fifteen and you wouldn't go out with him until you went to College,' I said to Mum, hoping for more information. I climbed back on the orange box and put on my helpful face.

'I told you that!'

'But you didn't like him when you were kids...'

'Of course not. He was a gawky, stupid boy who teased me.'

'But you liked him when you went to College. Is that when you fell madly in love and married him?' I clasped my hands over my heart dramatically.

Mum rolled her eyes heavenward. 'Oh dear. I suppose you won't give up until I tell you.' There was a half-smile on her face as she settled onto the orange box beside me. I held my breath.

'We went out for a while at College. You know, to concerts, here and there. They had lots of things on. Of course we had to sit on different sides of the chapel...'

'What? Was that in the Dark Ages?'

Mum gave me a sharp look. 'Never mind,' I said, 'go on.'

'Well, I went to work in Warburton and that was that.'

'What? You mean ... you stopped liking him ... and left?'

'I didn't stop 'liking' him. We were still friends. I just thought he wasn't for me. Didn't have enough 'go' in him.'

By the time I had another question formed, Mum was gone, leaving me gaping after her, alone on the orange box.

I was deeply disappointed, and 'a bit put out'. I looked down at the orange box. 'Don't you laugh,' I told it, 'I'll cut you into kindling tomorrow.'

'Linda, for goodness sake! Come inside and stop talking to yourself!'

I grew tired of the instalment pace of the story, so the next time

I questioned Mum was when she was brushing my hair. She did this most evenings, 100 strokes. The rhythmic, nurturing was wonderful.

'So, what happened in Warburton, Mum? Did you forget Dad?'

'We kept in touch sometimes. I met a man there. Fell hard for him.'

'Oh!' This was a twist I hadn't expected. 'Did he have enough 'go' in him?' I asked, not sure what else to say.

'Ha!' she said, 'he sure did, but it was all in the wrong direction.'

I waited.

'He invited me up to his room.'

'And that's a bad thing?'

'Certainly was, a man only wanted one thing if he asked that. It was really disrespectful. Next thing he had his hands all over me. 'I'm not that sort of girl,' I said to him. So he said that I was the sort of girl who could walk home.'

'He left you in the street?'

'Yes, just before sunset. It was dark when I got back to the boarding house we stenographers shared. I was humiliated and heartbroken. I didn't talk about it though. I'd worked hard and was working for the top boss.'

'That guy was a jerk!' I said.

'You'll get no argument from me on that score.'

'Then what?'

'After I got over that man, I realised that your father was the only one for me. He was engaged to another woman. But I had to tell him. He'd always loved me. I wanted to at least let him know how I felt.'

'What did you do?'

'I gave up my job and was transferred back near him. Then I went to him.'

This narrative had me on the edge of my seat. Nothing of the story sounded like the practical, no-nonsense mother I knew. I was blown away by the risk she had taken.

'What did you say?'

'Oh nothing much. Just that I hadn't valued what I had in him. That I was his, if he wanted me.'

Dad hadn't needed any time to think. His heart's desire was granted. Like my mother I didn't appreciate the strength of their love, or the true romance of their lives, but the older I became the more I realised the beauty of their love story. They threw away their pride, risked so much, gave up what they had to be together.

The Legacy

Sinking back into the gentle rocking motion of the clattering, swaying train, Melissa closed her eyes and willed the tension of the day to seep away. She realised with a wry smile that she was enjoying the jarring to and fro long associated with travelling in old trains.

Perhaps it was the memories, she mused, memories of journeys homeward after she first left home; journeys of anticipation and delight.

She surrendered to the magic of the red-tipped eucalypts that crowded the tracks like expectant children at the seashore. The sonorous sounds of the hissing engine were oddly soothing. The rumbling symphony of grinding steel combined with the hypnotic haze of the lush scenery that passed in a rhythmic blur. The womb-like rhythm of the old carriages mesmerized Melissa into forgetting the cracked-brittle stained vinyl with its musty odour.

She drifted effortlessly back in time to long journeys home after she first left home for the city to study hospitality at the prestigious Susan Clarendon College.

Resisting the urge to lean her forehead on the sooty glass she placed one well-heeled boot either side of her briefcase. This was a habit of old to protect her things while she slept on the long journey home. She smiled a brief and humourless smile. On this trip she would not doze slack-jawed and exhausted as she had done long ago when returning home after a 14 hour day. This home-coming was different than the others.

Willing the knot in her stomach to subside, Melissa wedged her lamb's wool jacket behind her head in an effort to provide the comfort she sought.

Coming home at eighteen had meant slotting seamlessly back into family life. Running into her father's arms and having him pretend to be embarrassed as she ruffled his ever-thinning hair for 'signs of life'. Rifling through the fridge and listening to the endless list of 'you should' from her mother.

Her thoughts were interrupted by the intrusive conversation warming up in a nearby seat. A brash, buxom girl was loudly and brashly laying claim to possessing 'rather a weak stomach'.

Whereupon the girl launched into various descriptions of her country life experiences, one that involved killing her first pig, alone in the dark of night with a knife, no less. She went on to cheerfully declare how her boyfriend and his mates were *terribly* pleased with her and *allowed* her to come with them often.

Melissa rolled her eyes and sank further in her seat. In years of experience in hotel management she was constantly astounded by the willingness of people to confide enormous chunks of their life history to less-than-willing strangers. She'd heard enough secrets to curl her toes, and probably enough to write a Joan Collins novel on the elite of Sydney society. The Debutante convalescing after an abortion. The liaisons and the lies. The bedroom bargains and the boardroom blunders. And vice versa. Not much shocked her now.

Well, she had her own secret life anyway. Only the closest of her city friends knew that her job at The Grande was only a small part of her life now. Even though she still lived at the hotel, very few knew that since becoming owner she had very little involvement in the day to day management.

Her real job and her true passion was fulfilled in the running of a small AIDS clinic and hospice created from the renovation of an old boarding house overlooking the ocean at Coogee.

Melissa was appalled by overt acts of charity; having grown up in a religious environment where church attendance involved ticking the Good Deeds Box. Perhaps living with the hypocrisy of the self-confessed Kings Of Straight had prompted her to work for gays and other assorted unacceptables.

She did not define her role at the hospice as charity when her life was so blessed by the realness of so many wonderful people, patients and carers alike. In this new world when you sent love out— it arrived. You knew it had reached its destination by the response of those who winged it back to you like a swift whirring boomerang.

It had been like that with her father. Although not an overly affectionate man, her love for her father reached him and then returned; instant and whole. There would always be the flash of response in his eyes, so often accompanied by tears in the last years of his life when she had given up city life for a year to return home to nurse him. She could do no other; she did not count it as sacrifice. It would have hurt her too much *not* to be there with him. She couldn't bear the thought of missing the times when they choked with laughter over movies like 'Grumpy Old Men'.

Melissa had not been home since her father's funeral. She still remembered with a sharp physical pang the heated row that erupted with her mother.

It was the mother of all rows, or perhaps the child of all rows. It seemed to have ancestors and descendants. It had gone from the past and rocketed into the future at amazing speed. It seemed to have been born in her childhood and felt at the time as if it would last longer than life itself.

It would have been too prosaic to say that it was born of grief or stress or fear. The roots went deeper. It was a living breathing thing that would not die with one apology; and there had been many on her part.

Perhaps it was one 'should' too many from her mother. Perhaps it was the sense of injustice; Melissa had been the one to bathe and dress her father. To discuss euthanasia with him. To make a thousand little things with him that would make his life easier.

She lived in her old bedroom, never telling them of the hotel suite she had left behind. Every phone call to a friend was interrupted with a 'should' from her mother. Every task she started, every load of washing was too late or too early; for what she did not know. She listened to her mother's endless conversations to her friends about the burden of caring for an invalid husband and having to contend with Melissa being 'between jobs again'.

After the funeral, tension between the two women reached boiling point. Things came to a head when Betty answered the phone and spoke to a journalist who was on a fishing expedition about the mysterious owner of The Grande. Melissa was glad to remain anonymous and the rambling discourse by Betty had required some serious damage control. It took many days to call in favours with the newspapers to keep her role at the hospice a secret.

Melissa was furious. There was yelling as the recriminations flew.

'Why are you always accusing me of interfering?' cried Betty. 'You tell me nothing of your life.'

'And now we can see the reason for that!'

'You don't want me to be your mother!'

'That's right, I don't need a mother, I just want you to be my friend, but you can't seem to manage that!'

Betty had stormed out of Melissa's room.

Afterwards when Melissa left, she mused that she would have liked to have 'stormed out' too, but her simpering capitulation couldn't be described as 'storming' even by the most liberal of interpretations.

She returned to her job and the city. Back to her warm and hearty friends and her hotel suite at The Grande. She gathered the threads of her life and wove a protective cocoon around her.

Early in her time at The Grande Melissa had invested in shares in the hotel. This, along with the upgrading of her management skills made the purchase of the hotel the next logical step. And that acquisition allowed her to pursue her passion to improve the lives of AIDS sufferers. Wealth freed her and she lived well. She had a chauffeur and a personal assistant for both the clinic and the hotel.

While giving her some much needed assistance this also provided the degree of anonymity she desired with regard to the clinic. It seemed easier to allow her mother to think she was still an assistant manager.

Melissa had meant to tell Betty of her advancement, but the time never seemed right.

Melissa's reverie was interrupted by the arrival of a lumbering woman as wide as she was tall. On entering the carriage, the woman enquired loudly if she could sit in the seat next to Melissa. This request was moot as the woman addressed the question after her ample frame and belongings had taken up every available inch.

Unfortunately for Melissa the new arrival seemed determined to form a lifelong friendship and was as garrulous as she was large. Pretending to sleep did not deter the woman's efforts at conversation. With an inward groan Melissa realized this was going to be one of those 'life story' occasions.

Surrounded by calico and tapestry bags of obviously ancient lineage, the woman proceeded to share her enthusiasm about the coming event she was travelling to attend. Melissa struggled to subdue the conversation but her innate politeness forced an unwilling surrender.

Responding with diluted smiles and *hmmms* that she tried to imbue with a little distance Melissa prayed silently that the woman would soon run out of steam.

No chance. It seemed the function the woman was attending, for which she had purchased a hideous mauve hat, was equal to an invitation to Buckingham Palace.

Then, suddenly something in the tone of voice, or the content of the meandering speech had Melissa sitting bolt upright in her seat, her lethargy a thing of the past.

'I was just tellin' my Keith the other day it was high time that ungrateful girl come home to visit 'er poor mother; God only knows the woman has done enough for 'er. Given and given and given she has. And the daughter has to turn up today of all days, on the anniversary of 'er father's death. Told 'er mother she wanted to spend some time just the two of 'em. Mendin' bridges if you please— destroyin' 'em more like. Poor woman is worried out of 'er mind— that lazy girl turnin' up after just phone calls for years. Betty has asked a few of 'er close friends over so she don't have to face that girl alone ... I'm just glad to be a bit of moral support...'

Melissa thought she would suffer from whiplash after spinning her head to face her companion. The eyes she did not want to connect with a few moments ago she now scanned furtively.

It was Agnes Moorebank, dubbed 'Agnes of God' by the village children. How had she not recognized the loquacious baker's wife who lived down the street from her as a child? She looked exactly as she had when she angrily flapped her apron, and shouted at the local boys to stop eating the berries from the tree in the front yard of the house, which also served as the depot for the bakery.

If Melissa had wished her companion to be silent before she now wished with dizzying alarm that the woman would suffer a stroke— particularly the loss of language skills that often entailed. But with a sickening dread she hung off every word the old gossip said with the kind of fascination usually given to hypnotic cobras—desire to flee, but paralysed with fear.

Melissa regained her composure enough to clear her throat to offer some inane remark to hold up her end of the conversation, but it wasn't necessary. The woman was amazing. Like a ship in full sail she dipped and tacked into waters more perilous than her worst imaginings.

Melissa's life flashed before her and she wondered if she was having a near death experience. There seemed to be a strange buzzing in her head as if it was going in a direction at odds with the rest of her body.

The comfortable feeling Melissa had begun to trust over the last few months evaporated. With each word the woman spoke it became more obvious that the bonds restored between Melissa and her mother were imaginary, and Betty's lifelong habit of denial meant that her words of 'everything's fine now', 'family is all that matters' were fast losing their lustre. The reunion with her mother began to feel like an ambush.

I must be going mad, Melissa thought, I am talking circular nonsense; to myself!

Melissa let the final thread of hope slip through her trembling fingers with Agnes's next statement.

'The hide of *'er* accusin' Betty of child abuse for beatin's. Probably deserved 'em—all kids need 'em I say. Fancy showin' them teachers the bruises, Betty never forgave 'er for that, involvin' strangers in their private life ... and then to land 'erself on 'er mother after ruinin' 'er own life and job ... bullying boss! I ask you! A likely story—as if Betty didn't have enough to deal with 'er dyin' husband an' all ... I always said the girl was only after money. Well, that girl is in for one big surprise. Betty's seen a solicitor. That girl can kiss Betty's money goodbye.' The woman puffed her chest out. 'What comes round, goes round, I say.'

With a new sense of alarm Melissa realised they were nearing Mullalong Station—the small railway station that both she and Agnes were due to embark from.

Melissa quickly decided that discretion was the better part of valour. She politely said goodbye to the old biddy and wished her a great party, knowing the 'guest of honour' was going to be absent.

Alighting at the next station, she reached into her handbag for her mobile and dialled her chauffeur, Max, asking him to pick her up. Just as well she'd had the forethought to have him nearby. She settled into a quiet corner of the covered railway waiting area.

Then, with deft, determined fingers she took a sheaf of papers out of her briefcase marked 'Title Deed'.

Melissa attached a note for her personal assistant to arrange transfer of the Title of Ownership of 16 Bayside Terrace, Mullalong, from one Betty Trudale, to the Mullalong Women's Refuge Committee.

Fate steps in

Serena Lansbury hummed along with the radio as Elvis crooned out the sultry hit, 'Love me Tender'.

She told the nurses this later when she regained consciousness, as her mind struggled to come to terms with the accident that had landed her in intensive care.

She didn't remember the crash of metal, the sheering of brakes, or the thud the small dog made as it hit her car, when she careened to avoid its fluffy path in front of her Toyota Celica.

She was talking to the Pathology girl who was taking her blood when Kate arrived at 7 am for the morning shift.

Her face was flushed and her words ran into each other. Her eyes, dulled by the anaesthetic were darting around the room with unmistakable signs of panic. As Julie, the night nurse, gave the morning staff the report on Serena's condition just outside the Perspex surrounds of her cubicle, Serena's eyes met Kate's in mute distress. Her hands clutched the sheet.

Kate made a mental note to go to her first. She was showing signs of delayed shock and it was six hours since she had accepted pain relief. Julie was relaying how Serena had undergone emergency surgery the previous night following internal injuries. She had suffered two broken ribs, bruising to her spleen and required a 'left nephrectomy' - removal of her left kidney. It had been crushed by the gear stick as she was thrown sideways, when her car collided with a power pole outside the local hair salon.

'She was lucky to survive,' Julie commented as she finished giving a rundown on Serena's condition. 'Her seat belt was loose and the car is a 'write off'. She was bringing a car load of gifts back from her engagement party. She's responding and talking, but she isn't making a lot of sense. Her brother is on his way from Melbourne, he's the next of kin. He should be here soon. We need to discuss her condition when she is able and we don't want her to be alone. The brother gave strict instructions for us not to tell her the extent of her injuries until he is present.'

There was no mention of the fiancé, or when he would arrive. Kate thought it unusual to discuss the surgery with her brother. Where was the fiancé? Why wasn't he the next of kin? Apparently the brother was protective. Oh well, they would know soon enough. As she looked at the pale elfin face she saw such vulnerability that she understood why someone would want to protect her.

Serena's head snapped in Kate's direction when she entered. She mangled the sheets with both hands and was obviously in distress. She must be experiencing severe pain, but something told Kate that this wasn't the only problem Serena Lansbury was facing. The over-bright eyes, the flushed cheeks, the furtive hands all told a story. An anxious story. Serena winced as the blood pressure cuff tightened and Kate brought up the subject of pain relief.

'No, I can't have anything until I talk to Derek, I have to be clear when I see him, they won't tell me what is wrong and I have to see him.'

She seemed afraid of this brother, Derek. Kate imagined him as an overbearing man.

'I am sure your brother won't care if you're not as sharp as usual.

195

I'm sure he'd rather you out of pain,' Kate said.

'I wasn't talking about my brother, David. I was talking about my fiancé, Derek.'

She would have continued with her panicked chatter, but Kate silenced her to read her pulse, while she struggled to think of a way to have Serena accept pain relief. Her blood pressure was high and her pulse was rapid. Kate frowned. This caused another spasm of panic to flit across Serena's face. Her breathing was shallow and her voice caught on a little moan as she tried bravely to convince Kate she was handling the pain.

'Your body is under great stress and your blood pressure is higher than it should be. The pain is speeding up your pulse and making your breathing shallow. Your whole body is tense trying to cope with the pain and that will only make the pain worse.'

Serena's eyes brimmed with tears.

'If you think I should then I'll have something.'

Kate quickly had the sister sign off on an injection and gave it to Serena before she changed her mind, then sat by her bed and wrote in the notes as Serena fought the sedating effects of the narcotic. Gradually, the frown wrinkles softened and her hands were still. Her voice was sad as she murmured, 'He'll never forgive me for this.'

Kate was confused and opened her mouth to respond, but saw that Serena had drifted into a troubled sleep. Kate looked at her notes and was surprised to find that Serena was 33 and not the elfin child she'd thought. She didn't look a day over 18.

In her history, the notes said Serena had been orphaned at thirteen. Her brother had become both guardian and parent. Kate imagined a brash capable man.

There was a rustle at the curtains, as they were held back by a tall thin man in a raincoat nervously twitching at his glasses.

'Hi, I'm David, Serena's brother,' he said, his voice thick with worry.

He was not what Kate imagined at all, he seemed as timid and uncertain as his sister.

'I want to know all about her condition, this is a difficult situation,' he said.

He seemed intense and Kate soon learned why. She led him to the patient's lounge. He shrugged off the charcoal coat with measured precision and sat beside Kate. She saw the steel in his eyes and thought that reluctant he might be, but he was the hero his sister needed.

'My sister is fragile,' he said, 'it's my fault I suppose, what with us being locus parenti for all those years. Well in truth, I was the parent, and a very inexperienced one at that. I overprotected her. Now in her first year away from me she's left teaching, landed a job she mysteriously says is in the 'entertainment industry', become engaged to the bastard of the century. And nearly killed herself.'

This outburst seemed to cost him the little composure he had left, and he slumped into the chair dishevelled and distraught. 'I know,' said David with a rueful transient grin, 'it sounds very much like my sister ran away and joined the circus.'

It seemed Serena Lansbury had decided somewhat later in life to shed the shackles of her protected childhood. She came to Sydney armed with a sense of adventure, a thirst for romance and a vulnerable heart.

She fell in love with a middle-aged solicitor who had been married twice before and had been struggling with kidney disease for years. He'd been on dialysis for nearly five years. In Serena he found his perfect match. Not only as a wife, but as a kidney donor. The impact of this revelation hit Kate squarely. It shed light on Serena's fears.

'So you see what a pickle this all is,' David said, 'Serena will be devastated, she's always been so soft hearted. She'll feel she's failed. In truth, it's probably a good thing. I'd bet any money you like that Derek saw her coming. I didn't agree with her donating a kidney to him.'

He saw the jolt in Kate's eyes and responded, 'Not that it would bother me for anyone else but Derek. He's a controlling bastard. Serena is a pack of nerves around him, always trying to make him happy and make up for the 'bad hand' life gave him. I've seen the bruises, and heard all the phoney excuses. He's abusing my sister and I can't do a thing about it. She's desperate to marry him, and he won't marry her until after the transplant. Says it would be unfair to her. I don't buy it.'

'She's been asking me to phone him, but I can't get him,' said Kate.

'Well, here's his office phone number,' said David, scribbling a number. 'You should be able to get him there.' David stood rigidly while Kate phoned.

'Is this the office of Keith Clarendon? ... No, it's not about business. His fiancé is in hospital. She's had an accident, quite a bad one ... I beg your pardon, can you repeat that? ... You're who? ... His wife? ... Oh, yes, certainly ... there's been a mistake...'

Anyone but him, please God!

His every breath was a rasping struggle. He sucked air into a chest that heaved and swelled like an ancient tide on a decimated beach. He was holocaust; he was dying. The only spark left was in his sunken grey eyes.

The ambulance trolley squeaked as it rolled down the corridor of Male Medical. The old man rattled. He was propped up, in semi-recumbent position. He would never lie down again. When he spoke, his voice was a strangled whisper. The ambulance men with their big square shoulders chatted to each other; effortlessly young and full of life.

It was late in the day. We settled him into cool white sheets. We unfolded a woven cotton blanket, spreading it over his thin frame. He waved it away. The weight was too much. He was accompanied by his daughter, a tall and graceful woman with measure step and quiet control. She bent low over her father, placing her ear close to his mouth to catch his words. I shrank back; I could never do that. Please no. To be so close to a man more dead than alive; more departed than present.

I bargained with God. I was spent; beaten. '*Enough*,' I pleaded. I would do anything, take care of anyone, *just not him*, anything but that. I was too vulnerable, too human. I was clinging to myself the way the old man was clinging to life. And I feared myself more than I feared his death. But I also surely feared his death; his final journey over the River Styx. How would it affect me watching him die? I had never seen a dead body. That empty building left after the essence of humanity has departed.

God ignored me. When I left the ward that evening at the end of my shift I checked the allocation sheet for the next morning. There was his name at the top of my patient list. I railed at God, the universe and life itself. I had been given more than I could bear. I woke stiff with fear; weighed down with dread. I shuffled onto the ward with leaden rebellious feet. My heart was heavy; he was so soon to die. I would attend to him first, get this burden out of the way; over with.

He was propped up exactly as he had been the night before. Alive; still. His eyes turned slowly towards me. There was no fear in them to match mine; only calm acceptance. And intelligence, this surprised me. I thought his mind must surely have betrayed him in the same way his body had; but no. I bent to hear his words. I leaned in close to hear death's whisper. He was in the waiting room for heaven or hell, and I was trapped there with him. The vibration of his voice felt strange against my ear; so little breath, so little life. He was a shipwreck that refused to sink and leave us surviving mortals to believe in 'beauty' and 'forever'. He was a monument to the futility in us all.

The other nurses seemed far away with their laughing strides down the corridors. The murmur of daily complaint and the metallic sounds of a nurses' world barely reached me. Outside there was bundling of linen, ringing of phones, buzzing of call bells. A doctor's low rumble as he gave instructions, wheels on trolleys, aromas from the kitchen—these intruded; only a little, then receded.

I ministered to him. His name was Jack. I asked if he wanted a shower or a bed bath. I posed my questions so that a simple nod would suffice. His lips strained at the side—a smile? There was no whimpering despondency in his manner. No hasty frustration in the wave of his hands. I took my time. When he was shaved, cleaned and dressed in new flannelette pyjamas a skeletal hand beckoned me to his ear. A tear was glistening in his eye.

'Thank you,' he whispered, 'you're beautiful.'

I loved him. I hadn't wanted to be near him; now I didn't want to leave. I read to him. I told him about the world outside his door. I nursed him for five days. Five privileged beautiful days and when he died he took the inevitable piece of me with him, but he left the bountiful gift of the beauty of his spirit. When I next recognised fear in my heart, I would not shrink but accept; embrace. Forevermore I could sit with death, and not tremble. God had taken me to the edge, then freed me. He had not granted my request, but had gifted me with something more—something immeasurably precious.

We took him to the basement morgue, Sam, Estelle and I. Sam was a senior nurse; a tall blonde Canadian with a gentle nature. Estelle and I were new and had never been to the morgue. We were skittish and afraid. Sam smiled indulgently at us. All the way down to the morgue in the lift, Estelle and I talked too much; nervous chatter, filling the silence.

Sam understood. We told him that we were glad it was him with us on our first time and not one of the 'mug lair' male nurses who took every opportunity to torment new nurses with practical jokes. He grinned broadly and reassured us, telling us exactly what it was like, what we would see and experience.

We positioned Jack's body and I patted the sheet with an affectionate farewell. The water pipes in the old building rattled loudly; an exact replica of Jack's breathing. Estelle and I let out identical screams and clung to Sam.

'Well,' he said. 'This is better than anything a practical joke gets; two women in my arms screaming.'

Our screams became hesitant giggles of relief. We walked from the cold room, down the cool corridor; into the warm sunlight; arm in arm. We crossed the gardens jumping plants and walking on the forbidden grass - defying the rules. We were young; we were alive.

As I looked up, enjoying the warmth of the sun on my face, I remembered my last conversation with Jack.

'God sent you to me,' he whispered.

'No Jack, God *sent you to me.*'

The tale of the armoire

Amber stroked the buttermilk armoire reverently. It was heavy, and well built. Ornate French Provincial, and smooth as silk. Such extravagance didn't quite fit in the simple house, where it was deemed everything must serve a purpose. Aunt Bea had determined the armoire would serve as Amber's glory box.

It was Amber's anyway, or so it was rumoured, set aside by Grandma Beatty, but it had never been allowed to grace Amber's room. How she would have loved to hang her best dresses in the top section, and put her knickknacks in the drawers.

'Amber.'

Amber jumped. It was Aunt Bea, stealthy as always. Amber remembered her sister, Courtney, saying, 'We should have bought her some army boots for her last birthday so we'd know when she's coming.'

'Amber! For goodness sake! You must have heard me. I was standing right in the hall.'

'Yes, Aunt Bea.'

Aunt Bea walked into the room, her bony hands clasped together like a praying mantis. Amber shuddered.

Why does she affect me this way? Amber thought.

Aunt Bea was smiling—always a bad sign. 'You do love those

things, don't you, dear?' she said.

'Those things ... oh ... I was admiring the armoire actually.'

'Well of course. But you must love all those things I brought home. You said so.'

Amber looked at the lime green towels, not big enough to wrap a cat in. The garishly decorated casserole dishes. Why on earth would someone decorate a poxy square dish with every vegetable under the sun? Perhaps they'd done it in case you forgot the recipe. Work from left to right...

'Amber. Honestly, you're such a dreamer.' Aunt Bea's voice rose. 'I don't know how you get straight A's. It's an absolute mystery to me.' She cleared her throat. She only ever did that before a good thrashing, but Amber was eighteen and that wouldn't be on the cards, not by a long shot.

'You're leaving home tomorrow.'

Help me now. She's the Minister for Stating the Obvious.

'I guess that's why my suitcases are packed,' Amber said, emboldened by the imminent escape from her clutches.

'There's no need for sarcasm, Amber. Why, your dear mother...'

Amber folded her arms.

'Well, anyway enough of that. We need to talk.'

Amber wrapped her arms around her body. Desperately wanting to argue about her use of the word 'we', she held her tongue. Aunt Bea had her, like a cobra ready to strike or stare. Courtney claimed to have Aunt Bea's number, but it eluded Amber.

Aunt Bea was interrupted by the arrival of her poodle, Sylvia, who sat adoringly at her side while Bea stroked her rippling fur. Mesmerised by the scene, Amber wondered why Aunt Bea's affection was limited to a dog, for she certainly didn't lavish any on them. It seemed Amber was her least favourite. Her brother Damien, dismissed this as 'female nonsense', but Amber had often seen a pained look in Uncle Bert's eyes and Courtney was very forthright on the subject. Something about middle child syndrome.

'It's about your work, Amber dear...' Her voice droned on and she attempted a smile. She tilted her head. Sylvia mimicked this movement precisely and Amber thought about dogs being like their owners. They both were slender with a bearing that was obviously supposed to appear regal. The effect was undone by Sylvia's dribbling, and by the ever-present faded apron in the case of Aunt Bea.

She rustled in her apron pocket. Amber's gaze shot up. Aunt Bea had her attention now. That pocket was a place of much conjecture. All of them had joked over the contents at one time or other. It always held her large key-ring, and the key to the armoire drawer was on that ring.

Maybe I'm wrong about her intent, Amber thought. Perhaps she wants to give me a parting gift.

Aunt Bea was holding a bank book. Amber saw a slip of paper with red typeface. It looked like a withdrawal slip. Aunt Bea shifted her bony hand, and Amber saw the slim folder had her name on it. She felt dizzy. The room spun.

When did she take my bank book? I always leave it in my top drawer.
'Why?'

Amber looked her straight in the eyes, impatient for her to get to the point, but fearing the destination.

The intensity of Amber's gaze seemed to propel Aunt Bea into clarity. Her words became harder, more precise. Amber struggled to digest them, for even though she tried desperately to concentrate, shock had set in and her head was filled with a swirling fog.

Speaking of 'duty' and 'gratitude' she continued, but Amber had lost patience.

'What do you want from me?'

It was then Amber noticed that Aunt Bea was pointing at the armoire. She pushed the withdrawal slip into Amber's hands. It had been filled in with Aunt Bea's flowing script and the amount to be withdrawn was the entire balance of the account. The sum of

Amber's last six week's work as a night cleaner. Every penny she owned.

Amber's hand gripped the paper. With every fibre she wanted to crush it and throw it in Aunt Bea's face. But Aunt Bea could make her life hell. She feared home would never be home again. She had the power to withdraw even that. After all, Aunt Bea and Uncle Bert had taken them in as orphans, and Aunt Bea had never showed any delight in that 'arrangement'. Suddenly the word freedom took on a new meaning.

Aunt Bea continued, speaking of obligation and repayment. She brought things home, especially for Amber. So that's what it was about. Amber owed her for all those things. Things she'd just been staring at in distaste. Apparently they cost 'a King's ransom'.

Amber hadn't taken much notice when Aunt Bea stacked them in the armoire. It had given her some warmth to hear Aunt Bea say, 'I have bought some things for your glory box. They are for you, for your future with Michael.'

Aunt Bea was restless, 'I've only ever thought of what is best for you, Amber dear. I'm sure I made all this clear from the outset.'

Her eyes were hard, the words seemed rehearsed. Amber wanted nothing but to stop their flow. She grabbed the withdrawal slip and signed it, then pushed it back into Aunt Bea's waiting hands.

Amber slept fitfully, plagued by nightmares. She was actually glad when Damien came into her room with his heavy work boots making the timber flooring rumble. Laughing, he ruffled her hair roughly. Amber knew if she didn't respond he'd throw a glass of water over her.

Shaking all thoughts of the conversation with Aunt Bea aside she grinned and pulled him down for a bear hug.

'So Damien, Fancy having time in your busy life to come and say goodbye to your little Sis. Are you going to miss me?'

'Nah. You'll be coming home every available minute to visit

Lover Boy Michael, and torment the lot of us, so you're not really leaving home.'

'You're only saying that to get out of giving me a present.'

'Oh go on. I give you stuff all the time.'

'The last thing you gave me was a Chinese burn.'

'Well you can't say I never give you anything then.'

'I'm just glad you got out of Nasho service.'

'Yeah. World's a much safer place with me staying home.' He headed for the door. 'Can't say the same for you though, Sis. How will your patients survive?'

Amber threw her pillow at his back, then regretted it. Now she'd have to get up.

She looked over at her suitcases and felt optimism rise. She was following her dreams. Not even Aunt Bea could take that away. She would be free where it counted—in her heart.

1973 was a great year to be leaving home and heading off into the world. Australia was withdrawing troops from Vietnam. This made monumental sense to Amber, not because she was full of political savvy, but because Damien had been drafted. His number had come up.

He'd been able to defer until he finished his apprenticeship, but then he was due to enter the army. He was saved by the election of Gough Whitlam and the Labour party with their decision to abolish mandatory national service.

Amber had experienced an initial period of fear and dread about the election of the Labour party.

'We're done for now with an atheist Commie government. We'll soon fall into Godless anarchy,' Aunt Bea had prophesied.

When nothing remotely fatalistic appeared on the world horizon, and no-one was struck by lightning, Amber calmed down, thinking perhaps Aunt Bea had it wrong. So she relaxed and embraced the Labour Party, if for no other reason than the rescinding of the draft.

She and Courtney had been stiff with anxiety about Damien going to war. He appeared to have none of the qualities that would make him of any use in any army. He was shy and gentle, and although he enjoyed using the 22 shotgun to shoot aluminium cans off the back fence, the girls had grave doubts about his enthusiasm or commitment to shoot people. Besides, Aunt Bea could never get him out of bed in the morning, and if *Aunt Bea* couldn't get someone up and going, there was no Corporal or Sergeant on earth who could.

The option of him becoming a medic didn't bear thinking about either. A complete stranger had fallen off the back of his friend's motorcycle outside the house a few years previously. The young man's face had been covered in blood and he'd sported spectacular grazes on his legs.

However, he wasn't the one who needed to lie down and have a drink of water, but Damien had. The victim sat calmly in the middle of the lounge room enjoying the attention, talking ninety to the dozen.

When Amber overheard Aunt Bea calling Gough Whitlam 'a stupid man' because of his quick wit, Amber developed a great fondness for him as she had often suffered at Aunt Bea's hands for smart aleck remarks.

Later, Amber went even further, deciding he was a man of superior intelligence when Aunt Bea saw him on television and decried loudly, 'sarcasm is the lowest form of wit'. She was fond of conversing with the television, perhaps with the vain hope the person she addressed would hear and wither into silence. This character flaw of their new Prime Minister had often been thrown at Amber, so Gough's position in her affection was assured.

Amber shuffled downstairs. Courtney was up preparing her last breakfast, so she'd better show up and see what burnt offerings Courtney had ready. To Amber's surprise she'd cooked fluffy scrambled eggs in the double boiler.

'Wow, Courtney. You've outdone yourself.'

'I hope you're not going to cast aspersions on my culinary skills. Not today,' she said. 'You've no idea how hard this cooking caper is.'

Amber raised her eyebrows.

'Oh, all right! I haven't forgotten that you've made our evening meal for the last century.'

'Thrilled you noticed,' said Amber, smiling.

'Well it's your last day at home, sis. I'd do anything for you, you know.'

'I'll remind you of that one day.'

~ *~ *~

There's no place on earth like a grimy, rattling jerking train to fuel your angst, thought Amber. It's one year since I left home, and what the last day lacked in ordinariness, this past weekend supplied in spades.

It would be a story she would enjoy telling her grandchildren. When she finally got over Michael, and his unfaithfulness. She sat and looked out on the rain-soaked landscape, through the blackened windows of the diesel train as it lumbered back to the city.

The sway of the train became gentler. Amber looked at the wrought iron shelf above the cracked vinyl seat opposite that held her bulging suitcase. It contained the towels from her glory box and she smiled ruefully as she remembered Courtney's rescue mission. It had been her idea to raid the armoire containing the crockery and linen that comprised Amber's glory box.

She resumed her gaze out of the train window. She made a serious, yet fruitless attempt to divert herself watching the rapidly passing landscape. Zing went the lush green of the eucalypt and wattle trees as they passed in a verdant blur, dotted with golden yellow outside the grime-smeared window. Even the calm blue waters of the Clidemont River failed to sooth her rampant thoughts. She allowed the quiet detachment of the scenes whizzing by to lull her. Tiny ripples of crystal blue gentled the surface of the river, while Amber wished she could trade the tidal wave in her life for gentle ripples. The lobster nets were lined in meticulous rows, speaking of order, precision and the joys of ordinary life. Amber prayed for ordinary.

Solitary pylons that once supported a bridge long-gone stood deserted, but proudly elegant while the sapphire waters lapped ceaselessly at their bases. Colourful buoys bobbed cheerfully, marking safe passage for fishing vessels and pleasure boats. Tin runabouts slapped the water rhythmically, leaving frothy white curling wakes, while they mingled with larger ponderous houseboats, with carefree holiday-makers lying languorously on the sun bleached decks.

Tanned, work roughened men, their brown skin leathered by a lifetime of working in the brilliant sun moved slowly and gracefully, as they mended nets and engaged in desultory factual conversations that marked the information exchange common to men the world over.

Amber envied their purposeful movements, their contentment. All she had to do now was weather the sodding grief. At least the memory of the crazy weekend with her brother and sister as co-conspirators would cheer her up for many a day.

It had all started because Aunt Bea had conveniently "forgotten" that Amber had paid for the contents of the armoire, and in a fit of pique said she was 'donating the lot to the local Salvos.'

'I'd rather break the bloody lot and make a mosaic floor to walk on, the way Michael walked on me,' said Amber. 'Anyway, they're mine. I paid for them. And I never wanted them. They're horrid.'

'Well, missie, you won't care what I do with them in that case,' shouted Aunt Bea, slamming the door on the way to the laundry.

Courtney had hatched a foolproof plan.

'I know they're ugly Amber, but they are good quality and

someone will like them. Let's take them to Cash Converters. They are yours twice over, Aunt Bea gave them to you, then you paid for them.'

'And how will we manage that Miss Clever, with Aunt Bea presiding over the whole house in wounded silence.'

'We'll take them out the window,' said Courtney.

'Oh great Courtney! And just how are we going to smuggle the entire contents of a cupboard out of a second-storey window and ferret them off to town?'

'Ropes and pulleys.'

'Shoot me now!'

'Sh! I'm thinking,' said Courtney.

Amber could swear she heard the wheels in Courtney's head turning. And that is how they came to coerce their older brother, Damien, into side-tracking Aunt Bea in conversation, for what he claimed was 'a bloody excruciating half hour of my life I'll never get back!'

He rambled about his job at the printing press to Aunt Bea, while the two girls huddled upstairs and wrapped the crockery in the towels, bound the whole lot up in a sheet from the bed and lowered it all out the window into the rose garden below.

Damien said that act of lunacy absolutely took the cake, because he'd been forced to sit opposite Aunt Bea and watch the bulky sheet's descent past the bay window behind her.

'My heart was in my mouth!' he said.

'Don't be a sap, Damien. You've done crazier things on your good days,' said Courtney, who was fast taking on the guise of a military campaigner.

Their plans nearly went awry when Aunt Bea decided to weed the rose garden before they'd recovered the sheet full of its precious cargo. Courtney snapped into gear.

'We'll have to create a diversion. We can't let her go outside.'

'You've been watching too much telly, Courtney,' said Damien.

But Courtney was gone. She flew into the laundry where Aunt Bea was donning her gardening gear. 'The dog's dead! Ah ... sorry, Aunt Bea,' she said, 'Sylvia's been hit by a coal truck.'

'Oh my God. Those rotten trucks. My poor baby.'

The coal trucks were the bane of Aunt Bea's life because of their noisy journey past the library where she worked. The library was on a hill, thus the place where the constant grinding of gears often destroyed the silence.

This hasty statement produced the desired result, and after getting a garbled story from Courtney about how there was a champagne-coloured poodle lying on the dirt road to the bush airport, Aunt Bea rushed out the door in her gardening apron and headed to the other side of the village. But not before Courtney had sworn under her breath, raced outside to a tongue-lolling Sylvia and dragged her from her usual post at the back door, then locked her in Damien's car.

'What the hell!' said Damien. 'We can't take her blasted pooch.'

'Well, we can't leave it either,' said Courtney. 'Not now.'

'What have you done, Courtney?' asked Amber.

'Don't ask.'

The three of them carried the sheet along the path to Damien's yellow Volkswagen and stuffed it in the back seat beside a bemused tail-thumping Sylvia, who was overcome with the excitement of an outing. Damien spun the tyres in the gravel and they were off.

Sylvia set up a celebratory howl.

'How are we going to park in town with a howling dog in the car?' asked Amber.

Damien skidded to a halt. 'Out you go girl, go home,' he said to a confused Sylvia, now deprived of a cherished treat. 'Go home, you dumb mutt!'

Sylvia's desolation and abandonment was evident in her expressive twitching eyes; but she obeyed.

Courtney appointed herself as supervisor of the proceedings, declaring Amber too useless with grief to make any sense.

'Thanks very much, Courtney.'

Amber sat in the back and sorted the crockery, while clutching the seat as Damien negotiated the curves on the twisting road with his usual lead foot on the accelerator. Her mood was as furious as Damien's driving.

'It meant nothing, bloody marvellous, that is,' said Amber, repeating what Michael said about his affair. 'I wonder how Miss 'It Meant Nothing' feels about that! I hope Michael rots in hell.'

Amber carried on with this rant all the way to town; while Courtney offered Damien advice on his driving, where to park and threw in a few other miscellaneous bits for good measure.

'A bloke would end up in the nuthouse if he had to listen to anymore from either of you two,' he said.

The noise level in the car was headache-making with each talking over the top of the other. Making things worse, the road noise moaned through the back left side window that was permanently down because the manual winder for the window was broken.

The car slewed into a vacant spot in the bottom level of the council car park off the main street. The three made quite a sight carrying armloads of stuff, each of them barefoot and windblown.

'This is some plan, Courtney,' said Amber.

'It's the best I could do at short notice. Anyway, you were such a sook you were going to let Aunt Bea walk all over you.'

Cash Converters accepted most of the crockery and all the glassware. Then they stopped at the St Vincent de Paul Op Shop and deposited the remainder there.

After their return home, Courtney was confronted by a furious Aunt Bea, who listened in dismay as Courtney recounted how she'd only been relaying a message by the fat kid up the street who swore blind he'd seen a dead poodle on the road, but must have mistaken a kangaroo for a dog.

The usual argument mode ensued, with Aunt Bea declaring that kangaroos were not shaggy and the stupid kid must need glasses. Then Aunt Bea noticed the grubby sheet they'd used to carry the crockery.

'What the hell are you doing with that, Courtney?'

This brought on a lengthy ramble by Courtney explaining why one of her bed sheets was being put in the wash on a day other than wash day, when she'd showed no previous signs of any activity remotely resembling domesticity.

This dialogue so exhausted Aunt Bea that she retired to the back porch, with a medicinal sherry for her nerves, while she sanctimoniously declared she'd had 'enough Tommy rot to last the rest of her life'. She enjoyed the next hour with Sylvia sitting adoringly at her feet, oblivious to all the fuss of the humans around her.

Courtney topped off the episode by locking the now empty armoire and throwing the key into the backyard incinerator, and then brushed her hands with satisfaction.

'Let her work that out, selfish old cow!'

Love redeemed, restored

Those angry, angry words, how she regretted them. Regretted hearing them. For the words that tormented her mind were not words from her own mouth, but they seared her soul in the sharpness of the memory they brought. Dan's daughter, with his clear blue eyes and his spontaneous laugh. The daughter she would never know again.

She idly stirred her tea as she sat in the sunny courtyard they had laboured over that last summer. Laughing and throwing damp warm soil at each other, they had been children again. And in love; so much in love. In love and living in a dream with a future. Together.

Dan had been lost the first time he saw her, he told her later. The memories tinkled down from the top of her head to her toes. Melanie wriggled her feet in the soft sand of the courtyard that she and Dan had spread there. Both amateurs at construction, they had opted for sand instead of cement between the pavers of the courtyard.

The shadows of the lilly-pillies they had planted reached from the fence nearly to the back door. She should be going inside. Soon, not yet. She had slept out here on the cream wrought iron day bed for the first six weeks after Dan had been killed while filming in

East Timor. Cameraman with a soul they said at his memorial.

'It's your fault my dad is dead,' Tiffany had screamed at her on that terrible day a decade ago.

Would the wound ever heal, the pain subside? The loss of Dan was softer now, but his daughter's words were still sharp, menacing her peace of mind. Tiffany had only been fourteen, how could she blame a grief stricken teenage girl who had just lost her father?

Buttons, the marmalade cat, purred past her, brushing her leg. Waiting expectantly by the back screen door, the ancient moggy paused. It was as if he understood.

Sometimes the animal world makes more sense to me, she thought.

'Not long now Buttons, it's our anniversary, you know.'

They only had one year together. One blissful, heart bursting year. One autumn, one winter, one spring and one summer. So little time in the scheme of things. Eleven years ago today they'd had a commitment ceremony on the beach in Fiji. Neither of them needed marriage. Only this; this promise. She remembered the laughter and the sand between her toes. Dan had carried her into the ocean instead of over the threshold.

'You told me you were a mermaid and lived in the sea so this is your threshold, my darling.'

She had called him a bastard and kissed his salty lips until their laughter turned white hot.

If only Tiffany could forgive her for loving Dan. How can a teenage girl understand how love dies? How could she understand that Dan had been excluded from his family for years by a wife who no longer needed him except for his fatherhood? How could she understand the passion and heart of a man who lived life to the full and had so much to share?

These were all the things that Melanie had thought she would have time to heal in Dan's turbulent daughter. But now they were both gone from her life.

Melanie heard the side gate squeak. She had meant to fix that, but because it had been a joke between them that it gave her some warning when Dan was coming home, she had become attached to the very thing that so annoyed her before. It was a memory of Dan, a tangible reminder of their life, their love.

'Melanie.' It was a soft voice, low and sweet. Tiffany.

Melanie forgot all the words and explanations that had whirled round and round her head for years. She turned and there was a young woman so familiar but so different. Gone were the braces and the surly pout. Her smile was hesitant, wary.

Melanie's throat caught, the words trapped. They stumbled through the awkwardness, both needing, both afraid. Melanie wanted to sweep her inside where the memories of Dan were weaker. Perhaps she would be stronger there. More composed. But Tiffany stilled her anxious gestures. She reached into the carry bag that she carried and removed a gift. She handed the gift hesitantly to Melanie.

'I've had this for the last ten years,' Tiffany murmured, fighting back tears, 'I thought I'd bring it now.'

Melanie opened the cellophane and found a huge citronella candle.

'Remember how dad waged war on all the mozzies out here? I bought this for his birthday that last January.'

Melanie felt the tears prick the back of her eyes. She was deeply touched that Tiffany would give her something she had bought for Dan.

Tiffany reached into the bag again, 'And this,' she began rapidly, as if her courage would fail or the tears would overcome her. 'It's dad's last film clip, I had it copied.' And then with a tender smile, crooked with tears, she added, 'I'm sorry, I didn't understand. I thought you took him from us.' With a shuddering groan she said, 'Oh God, I'm no good at this sentimental crap.'

Melanie laughed; she was her father's daughter.

217

'Where's the Chardonnay? Still in the laundry cupboard? I never knew why you kept it there, you know. I though you must have been a closet alcoholic. But then I wanted you to be the wicked witch. Someone to blame. Anyone but dad or mum.'

The hours passed gently and when they were sitting inside by the crackling open fire, Tiffany threw a pine cone in and listened to the hiss as it flared upwards.

'I didn't *just* come to say I was sorry, you know'.

Melanie held her breath. 'Really, why then, Tiff?'

'Because he is here, well, you know, I don't know how to explain it,' she paused. 'You know, he is just *here.*'

Madame Elise-Couturier

Madame Elise de Troudeau was a couturier, a meticulous woman of punishingly high standards, a genius with silk, satins, linens and faille. She had a small but elegant boutique. It was narrow and long. In the front window were displays of her award winning designs with gorgeous fabrics draped around them.

Mme. Elise, as she was known to her clients, liked to montage diverse fabrics of similar colours. One might find a peacock satin boldly displayed beside linen of a similar colour. A flowing egg-shell silk rested beside crisp white velvet, and the palette went on to include crimson-hued microfibre, translucent aqua chiffon, interspersed with rich brocades and delicately embroidered georgette.

The ante room itself was a hypnotic mix of comfort and style. Lucinda was drawn to the decor. Katherine, Lucinda's University Fashion & Design mentor, had arranged an interview, and with quiet elegance walked briskly to the doorway, pushing aside the elegant glass door that tinkled with the sound of a small gold bell.

The windows were clear class, but the door was opaque with gold rods reinforcing it and forming frosted squares. Mme. had chosen this because the doorway was opposite the entry to the back of the shop and it softened the view to the inner rooms. Mme. Troudeau would only permit customers requiring fittings entrée back there.

The ante room was very small and dark, opulent and formal. It was a waiting room with two high-backed chairs, more commonly seen in dining rooms.

Mme. came padding into the room. Much to Lucinda's delight she wore ballet slippers. Another eccentric, how marvellous! She felt instantly at home. Mme. wore a trouser suit - a raw silk in electric blue, to stunning effect.

With a measuring tape around her neck and a wrist pin-cushion, she was a fairy godmother to nervous Lucinda.

'And who do we 'ave 'ere, Katerine? Ah, thees ees the lovely Lucinda, mais non?' purred the sophisticated vision. 'Tres bon, ma petite, enchanté,' said Mme, spinning Lucinda around as if she was auditioning, not applying for a position. 'Call me Elise, s'il vous plait.'

Lucinda was delighted. She had heard that Mme Troudeau was an exacting boss and the clothes she had seen in Katherine's wardrobe with the label, *Collectione Elise* evidenced meticulous handiwork, as well as brilliant classic lines.

Mme. Elise assumed an assessing frown.

'But you must know, ma petite, I am a tyrant, and sometimes even ... je ne sai quoi ... 'a moody cow', but we shall forgive each other often, mais non?'

And thus it was settled for Lucinda to begin her working life in the most wonderful of places. With this introduction, Lucinda was ushered into the back rooms, each separated by a curtain of embroidered organza.

'I juste deteste the plastic, do you not, aussi?' said Elise, on entering the second room.

It was the 'finishing' room. Garments in various stages of completion were hung from ornate brass coat hangers or arranged on dressmaker's mannequins. There were many wrought iron shelves lining three of the walls with baskets of laces, pearl beading and satin edging. This was where fittings were carried out and the final touches added.

The next room was the largest. It was the workroom. There was a large timber cutting table with scissors, pins, elastics, and cottons of every hue precisely lined on spools near another table that held four Bernina sewing machines, two straight stitchers and two overlockers.

Lucinda was surprised by the overlockers as she'd heard that many 'fussy' designers did not favour them. But this was a practical woman who was just as interested in making women look good walking down 'la rue', as she was in designing 'haute couture'. Not that Lucinda had ever seen anyone walking down the street in anything like Elise's 'ready to wear' in her small hometown village.

At the back of the room was a doorway into a courtyard, where Elise's husband, Francois, sat eating his morning bagel and reading the paper.

Elise introduced them in French. Francois raised warm, watchful eyes over his glasses, put down his paper and added his greeting, pressing Lucinda's small hand into both of his.

Lucinda would come to know Francois as a generous hearted man who was always ready for a discussion, a debate or 'un peu de philosophie', and in Lucinda's bright mind he found much to delight and ponder.

Katherine expressed her thanks, then claiming pressing business took leave of them. Both Elise and Francois kissed Katherine on both cheeks. Lucinda was introduced to a world of warm enthusiastic companionship where the sharing of ideas, croissants and creamy coffee was as important as the business of the day.

Lucinda had come to these two wonderful pilgrim', as they laughingly called themselves, at the time of their 'pensione'. They claimed semi-retirement. Although they said they no longer lived life at break-neck speed, it was obvious to Lucinda that these two people had always been mellow with the richness of ordinary life.

She was to learn much from both of them, and in turn, she was an unexpected bonus to their September years, when their own son was travelling the world. Lucinda, with her thoughtful calm fascination with life, was as exotic to them as they were to her.

Later, Elise would tell Lucinda of the frisson of excitement that she had felt when she had first seen Lucinda's designs and her bold, unique embroidery, the brilliant combinations of lace, thread, ribbons and fabric that so beautifully complimented her own creative style.

'So 'impressionistique'.'

Lucinda found, to her delight that although Elise was a perfectionist, she was not the tyrant she claimed to be. She thought Elise exaggerated this facet of her character. She was never to know that Elise thought of her as a bruised 'kitten', whose own tireless attention to detail and willingness to please, had endeared her to her employer from the start. Ever eager to learn, Lucinda was often called away from her work by Elise.

Early in the arrangement, Lucinda introduced Elise and Francois to Georgia and it was love at first sight for all three. Increasingly, Elise found excuses for Georgia to come on the three days Lucinda worked, and the sound of Georgia's laughter filtered from the courtyard where Francois was her willing slave and playmate.

He read her fairy stories in rumbling French and Lucinda was not surprised to find Georgia chattering in French as if it were her native tongue, crossing over into English at will. Lucinda soon became maman, Elise, grandmere, and Francois, grandpere.

And so it was that life gifted Lucinda, not only a mentor to polish and refine her, but to supply a family life for Georgia and herself.

As for her work, it counted so much more to Lucinda that someone of Elise's standing would listen with thoughtful attention to each of her ideas. Elise, in her turn, realised the value of Lucinda's vision and allowed her to add warmth to the austerity of shop. The palest terracotta tiles were laid in the front room. An antique love seat with carved legs and two matching sofa chairs were placed near a wrought iron table, where design books were casually placed for waiting clients.

Previously one to play down her French heritage, Elise was persuaded to have sepia tone prints of Parisian cafés on the walls.

However when Lucinda suggested background music, 'Edith Piaf, perhaps' Elise gave a definite, 'Mais non! No music! Not at work. Mon Dieu, do you weesh for me to 'ave always the 'mal a la tete', petite? When it is time for the relaxing, then we have the music. And we dance.'

Francois ordered and supervised the installation of large round lights in the workrooms—to give the 'illusion of skylights'. It was impossible to have skylights as the Troudeau's two-bedroom flat was above the shop connected by an iron staircase that led off the back room.

The seductive aromas of bay leaf seasoned stews, crusty warm bread, and brewed coffee wafted down into the work room.

Lucinda was home.

Anne

She holds her head high, although the shambling gait her body dictates is tortuous. Her body twists and turns, her legs making circular orbits at the knees. Her lone plastic bag of groceries sways, strangely in sync with this awkward journey. In the other hand, she holds a walking stick, that is always at a terrifying angle; seemingly useless.

Sometimes Jenny saw her sitting; waiting, but never at the usual places – the bus stop, or the taxi stand. Not on the benches outside the small shopping village. She does not sit for long.

Jenny knew her, in that way of not knowing, but of being parallel souls in this small town.

I wish I knew her name, thought Jenny. She looks like an Anne with an 'e'. I shall call her that to give her substance, identity, personhood.

Jenny remembered sitting in the same room in our small worship class at church. Noticing, but not noticing, wrapped in her own insecurities, struggling with her own fears of rejection. 'Anne' was quiet and reserved, never offering an opinion.

Not like Jenny, with her sudden words that tumbled and fell, sometimes regretted as quickly as they were said. 'My mouth has censorship issues with my head', Jenny would tell herself, while vowing to be more like her serene acquaintance who drew no interest, positive or negative.

'Why do we lose our faith?' A young man asked one morning. 'What happens?'

'Life happens,' Jenny said, then held her breath until those around nodded sagely, instead of regarding her with round-eyed shock.

But Anne held her peace; always. Dressed in flowing floral skirts with pastel knitted tops, and softly curling short hair, she was exactly who they expected her to be. But not Jenny, with her sharp hair, pencil mini-dress and stilettos.

In truth, neither of them stood out from the crowd, for there were others like Jenny, and like Anne, but Anne was appropriate for a single woman, and Jenny was not.

In an unspoken rule that would be vehemently denied, fashionable status was reserved for real estate agents and financial adviser's wives—those cashed up for designer clothing and partnered. Jenny once overheard Anne talk of making her dresses once, in a shy remark. They shared that.

Jenny was a little envious of her invisibility, knowing she could never achieve it, and in truth did not want it. But it was so safe, so secure. Anne would always fit, never to be rejected. Where Jenny would have her overnight bags shifted to a solitary room on a church camp. It was explained; delicately, in the manner these things are usually conducted. A few kind hints on how to fit in. Sit on the beach with the other women, clad in demure cardigans rather than 'draw attention' by romping in the surf with the men and children.

'Oh really?' Jenny responded, with cold eyes. 'So none of you have made the connection between beach and swimming?'

Her sharp tongue—enemy to the status quo. Enemy to herself, so they would never see her hurt, her confusion. Better to treat them to sharp words than to trust them with her heart. It distanced them, as she knew it would.

She chose the gap. But not Anne. How did her life become one stumbling journey after another? A pedestrian in a daily battle. Alone. The kind of alone that was deeper than any of Jenny's darkest self-pity, or angst. It humbled and shamed her.

Was she no better than they? As she drove past, cushioned in a lesser poverty, already sanctioned beyond their presence. Jenny had been gone for years from their fold; this church where poverty is anathema. So many lightyears before, Jenny had not gone quietly, but had chosen her isolation. When had Anne become lost? Did she still sit among them, parallel but forgotten? Still invisible?

Jenny watches Anne with a humility matching her shame.

'I have no world for her to fit into, I am alone too,' Jenny tells herself. 'She desires to belong there, where I cannot fit without losing myself.'

Jenny feels pride in Anne. In her persistence, her undemanding demeanour, her freedom from bitterness. A bitterness she surely earned.

Isobel

Isabel Bunting scanned the room, waiting for her father, Jeremy. Negligently sipping a cocktail she slid a confident smile to an older man at the end of the bar. Her eyes were hooded, smouldering. She exuded sexuality and she knew it. Carefree and young, she gloried in her youth and power over men.

'Will the day ever come when you stop responding to every flirtaceous look?' asked Debbie, leaning stiffly back on the bar stool. 'You're hooked you know, Izzie.'

'So what?' she said, sliding her finger around the champagne flute and then running it along her lips. The man at the end of bar swallowed hard.

'It's a teasing game to you, isn't it?'

'No. It isn't. I didn't ask you here to analyse or criticise me, Debbie. Anyway, I'm not a tease. I follow through.'

'And that's a good thing? You know what the other girls call you?'

'Should I care?' She turned to Debbie with fierce eyes.

'Queen Bee,' said Debbie.

'Ha. At least it's better than being a wannabee. Like them.'

'Why am I here anyway? Come and sit in the lounge area. My

back's killing me on these stools. I didn't come here to watch your man-eating routine.'

'You never used to mind.'

'I'm growing up. You should try it.'

Izzie shrugged. 'I promised to meet Daddy here.'

'And he won't find you a few metres away?'

'Of course he will, but he's counting on me to hostess his meeting with his new clients.'

'Do they know you're underage?' asked Debbie, removing a stiletto and rubbing a reddened heel.

'Why would they, I've been coming with Daddy for years. Being tall, and holding your head high will get you anywhere.'

'Of course it doesn't hurt that you're the daughter of a record label scout.'

'I don't need Daddy to get me places anymore,' snapped Izzie.

'No, I guess not. You've slept with enough of his friends and clients to make your own way in the world. And who calls their father Daddy, only English aristocrats, not Aussies.'

'If you're going to be a bitch, you can get lost,' said Izzie, turning her back on her friend. 'Anyway, you can't talk. You're a teenage mum, and you didn't get that way by being a saint.'

Debbie looked at her school friend's rigid back. 'Have it your way, Izzie. You usually do,' she said. Then picking up her clutch and peeling off her shoes, she walked resolutely to the corridor and the lifts.

Izzie didn't see her go, but she felt a warmth leave the room. A tear stung her eyes. She wiped it away angrily, then ordered another drink.

Hurry up Daddy, she thought, feeling suddenly alone.

Isobel Bunting was hardly ever alone, and she didn't like it. Never mind, Deb would come around. She always did.

Masking her face into a serene look, she walked over to the piano. As soon as she touched the keys, a husky melody filled the room. She started in the middle of Beethoven's Ninth. She played softly, losing herself in the music.

She was generally held to be cold as ice, but the music that flowed from her fingers was anything but that. There was no seduction in the music, just beauty and poignancy. Warmth enveloped her. She didn't even notice that the small talk in the secluded corner of the elite nightclub fluttered to a whisper. Dressed in a pink shot-silk strapless gown, black lace detached sleeves and a frothy evening fascinator, she looked like a courtesan of a bygone era, but the music was pure soul. It crescendoed and soared effortlessly at her touch.

Her life of being at her father's side as his equal, and her fiery relationship with her neurotic mother slipped into the velvet sounds of her relationship with the piano. Moving seamlessly into Bach she forgot all about meeting her father. She forgot everything but the moment. Her face gentled into soft angelic curves, and the touches of makeup she had skilfully applied only added to her vulnerability.

A tap on the shoulder brought her to the present. She turned, a smile covering her face.

'Daddy, finall ... but ... you're not ... Who are you?'

Izzie shrank back. He was not tall and lean like her father, but he was built like a bouncer. His stance was intimidating. The suit was tight across his huge chest. He was all male. And for some reason, he seemed displeased with her. It was hard to tell. This man would make an excellent poker player.

'I will have to ask you to leave,' he said. 'You're underage.'

Sliding elegantly to her full height, she found they were eye to steely eye, toe to unyielding toe. In that instant, Izzie knew she had never met anyone like him.

Flipping her black clutch under her arm tightly, she held his gaze. 'Do you know who I am?' she asked.

'Of course I do. I'm not accustomed to making assumptions.

You're James Bunting's infamous daughter, Isobel.'

'My father's famous,' she said, 'and you don't know what you're doing.' Her voice sounded childish and petulant.

'On the contrary, I know exactly what I'm doing. And the last time I looked 'fame' wasn't genetic, or above the law.'

'I ... how dare you ... I've been coming here forever.'

'And now you're leaving.'

For all her worldly sophistication, the best Izzie could manage was an open-mouthed stare. Where was her father? She'd never heard a bouncer talk like this. They usually spoke in monosyllables, but this large man spoke like a barrister, and was totally unfazed by her. This was all wrong. Bouncers were there to pave her way in life, not throw her out. She was furious.

'You can't be serious. Where will I go? You can't throw me out on the street.'

'You have a room here. I suggest you use it. Your orphan Annie routine won't work with me.'

'I'll have your job.'

'You're welcome to it, but I warn you – the hours are demanding and the clientele insufferable. You wouldn't cut it.'

'You...'

'Excuse me, young man. Is there a problem?'

'...Daddy, thank goodness. This mountain here is trying to throw me out.'

'Is he? We'll see about that. Do you know who I am, son?'

'I know exactly who you are, it's pity you've forgotten, Mr James Bunting of Impress Records. And I am not your son.'

'Hold on a minute ... who the hell do you think you are?'

'Not only are you forgetful, Sir, but you appear to be visually impaired. I'm wearing a name badge. Read it. And when you've done that, you may either escort your underage daughter from this club, or let her make her own way to the Penthouse suite.'

'You've gone too far ... you...'

'No, I haven't. It's well known that you stop marginally short of pimping your daughter out to clients to smooth your business path. Quite frankly, you do her a great disservice as a father. *Now*, I've gone too far, but you will find I don't care.'

'Who do you work for?' James squinted at the man's badge, cursing his pride for going without his glasses.

'I work for myself,' said the man. 'Security. Freelance. And tonight this club is my responsibility. Your daughter leaves, *now*. Unless you want the embarrassment of having the police check her ID, which I'm sure you will find most unpleasant. I have it on good authority that at least she doesn't have a fake ID, because your name and fame have facilitated her entrance to every exclusive, and seedy night spot in town.'

James Bunting forced a broad smile, and gestured for Izzie to head towards the exit. After they moved through the double doors, they both turned to stare at the man. He was casually leaning over the bar. Though only metres away his voice was a rich rumble. The barman nodded and obeyed him instantly.

Izzie spun on her elegant heels and stormed down the corridor.

The man looked at James, his face unreadable. James saluted him. Anyone passing would have thought it was a threat, but the men assessed each other, and the stranger knew respect when he saw it. Returning the gesture with a subtle movement he moved to the bar.

'Single malt whiskey, please,' he said to the barman.

'Um ... er... Sir...' stumbled the barman, looking at the security badge, '...you know I can't serve you on duty ... ah ... Stefan, is it?'

The man unpinned the name badge. Sliding it slowly across the bar, his eyes never left the barman. 'I'm not on duty. And I'm not Stefan, but when you see him, tell him to keep a better eye on his security ID. He could be sacked for 'misplacing' it. Now, where's my drink.'

The barman was confused, then seeing the intensity of the man opposite he hurried to supply the drink. The stranger smiled. Emboldened the barman asked, 'What was all that about? James Bunting is an important man. He and his daughter are often here.'

The stranger's smile vanished. He slowly sipped the drink. His eyes were fierce. The barman realised he wouldn't like to be on the wrong side of this man.

Walking to the door like a poised panther, the man turned briefly. He seemed to be considering whether or not to speak.

'She's *fifteen*,' he said.

The barman was shocked, and that was *something* in his job. He shook his head and blinked.

The stranger was gone.

Rewrite the dream

They are playing quietly, as they always do. Both building with Lego, both intense on the task. So focused that it hardly seems like play. This is serious business, this building and creating.

One has straight dark hair and a round cheerful face. He is the son of Leon, who learned some of his trade at my father's hands; perfectionists all. He is Travis, and he patiently places the Lego pieces, with an exactness that matches his playmate, my son Luke. Travis is building houses, while Luke with his blonde curls is building a spaceship. One is earthy, the other a dreamer.

As soon as Travis finishes his building he walks around it with the eye of supervisor. He sighs a satisfied 'hmm'.

'Hey Mum, what has a kid got to do to get some bickies and milk around here?' he calls to his mother Mary, in his deep gravelly voice.

'That boy will outdo Jimmy Barnes,' I remark to Mary in the kitchen as we start putting the cookies out.

'Oh Mary, me too!' calls Luke. 'My mum *never* gives me cookies, she doesn't keep them in the house. She says I can only have rubbish when we're out.'

'Thanks, a lot Brooksie,' moans Mary in mock horror. 'Now your kids wants "rubbish" at my house because you're a penny pinching miser.'

'Oh ha ha!' I say, unmoved by her indictment. 'You know I hate sugar because I was overdosed on it as a kid because Mum was an unreformed diabetic.'

'Yeah, Mum's weird,' adds Luke, glad of a comrade.

'Don't you pick on my friend,' responded Mary. 'You'll get no cookies from me.'

Luke looks momentarily confused, then seeing the bounty from Mary's cookie jar squirms into the dining room seat, eagerly waiting for his treat. The boys then discuss their 'creations', talking about what they have made and what they will do. Travis can't wait to build another house, he already has an idea. Luke looks disgusted.

'You mean you're going to pull apart what you just did to make something new?' he says in astonishment.

'Of course,' says Travis. 'That's what Lego is for!'

Luke still looks pained at the thought of dismantling his precious spaceship. I know he is thinking of his own Lego creations at home. Beautiful flying things and complicated boats that he has glued together, so no-one can ever take them apart. Dreams he doesn't want to have to remake in a life that feels precarious enough. He is still mourning his beloved Pa. He doesn't want anything in life to ever change again.

'Can we go home now please, Mum,' he says.

'No,' I say, with an edge of impatience. 'I haven't finished visiting Mary, yet.'

'Okay, I'll just sit in the car until you're ready, then.' And he does.

The years tumble and bumble and roll by. Travis has become the man of the boy he was. A meticulous builder, ready for new challenges, new dreams and beyond. He has followed his heart and his dreams, courageously moving to another country and becoming all that he can be on foreign soil, adapting and loving his new home. His gentle unchanging nature and quiet reliance draws people to him. He doesn't know why or how, that's just the way it is.

Now, here I sit at my computer, and I'm staring at a photograph of devastation, of ruin, of chaos, but of greater sadness than even that—the death of a dream. The demise of a building, by the man who as a boy, so carefully took his Lego apart to make something else. A new dream. But my heart aches because there is nothing left in this holocaust, no pieces to rebuild with. Not one plank of timber, one window or even a solitary brick.

The orange glow drags your eyes to the fire. The flames are still living, desolating the very ashes that remain. Taking the comforts of every familiar thing of a family; now huddled together in loss.

My eyes skim the page. I can't help but be drawn to the top left hand corner. The sky is clear and blue, endless and enduring. The Universe has deemed that on this terrible day, the sun shines brightly in a cloudless sky. Still reigning, unmoved, dependable.

I try to look back at the flames, why surely they are the focus of the picture, but my eyes won't heed my beckoning. They keep looking at that small corner of blue sky; showing the unmarred heavens, the steadfast ceiling of our world. I am glad that whoever took the photo caught that piece of sky, caught the eye of God, ever-watching, ever-caring, displaying His nearness.

Telling Jody and Travis that He still reigns in His heaven. There will be other dreams—He already has them, waiting, prepared and ready. Hidden now, closer than you know, better than you believed, and handmade by God for you.

A perfect plan

It was more than any man could tolerate, thought Viscount William Henry James Everdale, as he made his way down Penshurst Street. He stroked the head of his walking cane with a grim half smile of satisfaction. He would at least have his revenge.

It was so damned unfair. All of it. He had spent the last two years of his life living mainly in his aging father's house. It had been a huge sacrifice. Cutting down on his social engagements in London, missing out on Ascot and several other major events had been galling in the extreme. Not to mention his gaming adventures and calls on ladies of the night. Nevertheless he had managed to secure the hand of the brightest prize on the marriage mart.

He scowled. *'Had'* was the precise term, because when he had so generously given Victoria the chance to cry off on the engagement because of his illness, she had shocked him by doing just that. He would have bet half his inheritance that she would have demurred and declared her commitment to going through with it, for the estate and social standing, if nothing else.

'Oh William, you are a darling. I was so reluctant to cry off myself but Papa declared that I must never consider marrying for love. Oh it must be such a relief for you too, poor dear. After all, one would not wish to spend one's last days with the burden of a young wife.' She had smiled radiantly.

The Viscount was speechless. He had never been denied anything in his four and thirty years. And to be set down by a girl not long out of the school room. It was incredible. He had bowed gracefully, ground his teeth and thought of how he would explain this latest in the series of disasters that had overtaken his life.

Women. He'd never understand them. The silly chit had only to go through with the ceremony, produce an heir. The fleeting thought crossed his mind that perhaps her father, The Duke of Kensington might have heard of his flirtations on the continent. He would have been forgiven those, but his love affair with opium would not have been so readily overlooked. No, he chastened himself, that wasn't possible. He'd been so careful and everyone was convinced that he was sickening from a war injury.

For years he planned to have the satisfaction that he had outwitted his eccentric sister, Georgina by having an heir. He wouldn't have needed to worry if their forward thinking father hadn't taken the modern attitude of women owning property. It hadn't overly worried William. He'd thought he had years before settling down, but a failing liver had changed everything, and now he had to face the fact that his sister would inherit his legacy - the whole estate and all its entailments, along with an obscene amount of money. He was dying. It was the only contingency that he hadn't allowed for.

Georgina. That daft creature who had decried marriage herself, instead setting herself up in a dressmaking business. Society had been stunned at first, but when they saw the 'creations', as people were calling them, they flocked to her doorstep. Mind you, it suited him very well for her to be unmarried and with a career. But just as he settled comfortably with the thought of her remaining a spinster, thus allowing him time to produce a son, she had married a commoner. That should have pleased him, but the way society fawned over the scholar who was only a lowly solicitor was excruciating. And Irish! Ye gods, how would he hold his head up with his friends. To make matters worse, plain old Declan

O'Donnell was the son of a hotel magnate. New money.

Pain stabbed his right side, taking his breath away. He had to lean against a wall. He looked at the shopfront. An apothecary. Of course. He thought of the laudanum in his upper pocket and was filled with the familiar yearning of the addict. But he couldn't afford to dull his senses. There would be time enough after this dark day. Resisting the temptation to check his secret tiny chamber, he walked on. It was all he could do to maintain an upright gait. How he would have liked to stoop in comfort. There would be time for that later.

He caught sight of Georgina, waving joyously at him. Did she have to be so demonstrative? How she irked him. He smiled his best smile, proud of the fact that his sister had no idea of his disgust for her, and better still his nefarious plan.

She turned and a different pain shot through him. It was even worse than the former pain. Georgina was well advanced in pregnancy. And glowing. Sod's law was prevailing. It strengthened his resolve. It was bad enough that his father had claimed the right for his sister to inherit the estate if he failed to produce an heir. David George Everdale had always prided himself on being at the vanguard of change. There were half a dozen reasonable nephews who could have filled the role, but the former Viscount had dismissed this as 'tosh'.

'Oh William, how are you? You're looking so grim. Is the pain so bad,' Georgina said soothingly as she linked her arm through his, pushing the door of the faded tea house door open as she did. This very act stirred his anger further. Did she have to make a show of his lack of manliness in a public street?

'It is grabbing a little today, my dear,' he said. Her soft heart would work in his favour. He would accept her pity. This time.

'Oh darling brother, I wish I could ease things for you. You must get a nurse in to help you. I know your valet is an excellent man, but Declan knows a good many wonderful medical people.'

William grimaced. This conversation was going to be agonising. But it would be worth it.

'Do not think of me, my dearest one. I see you are to be congratulated. Let me offer you my sincerest felicitations.'

'Oh yes, we are thrilled. Declan is building a cot and painting the nursery. I have hired an assistant and taken on a partner.'

'So business is good in the dressmaking trade?'

Georgina winced. His voice was laced with sarcasm.

'Well, it's not just dressmaking, Will. But let's not have an argument. I see so little of you. I know the pain must be very hard to bear. Have you found a good surgeon?'

'Oh yes,' he said, lying quickly, 'He has promised a good outcome. I have every confidence in his services.'

'That's marvellous Will. Then maybe Victoria will understand and renew the engagement.'

William frowned. How he hated pity, especially from the lively little girl who had hung off his shirttails and never noticed his barbs or repulsion for her chattering company.

The tea house girl came to wait on their table. She was a buxom redhead. For a fleeting moment he thought he recognised her. He couldn't afford to be recognised. It had taken him some time to convince Georgina to come to this out-of-the way place to take their afternoon tea. But it afforded the necessary privacy of secluded

'I am Elise and I am pleased to wait on Madame and Monsieur, ce soir.'

'Are you French?' asked Georgina with delight.

'Ah, oui. Je suis, ah, pardonne, I am from Provence. Does Madame speak Francais?'

'Very badly,' laughed Georgina.

'We are ready to order, Elise,' said William.

'Pay him no mind, Elise. He is suffering a great deal of pain. I am lucky to be out with him today. But he tells me that he will be relieved of it soon.'

William wanted to snarl, but he was relieved that the redhead was not the girl he knew from the Willow Inn & Hostelry that was on the Stepford Road an hour out of London.

Predictably Georgina wanted Devonshire tea with clotted cream. Perfect, he thought.

'Make that for two,' he said. Tea seemed to be the only beverage that he could enjoy without reaction. Even his favourite whisky caused intolerable cramps. There was nothing in his past experience that had prepared him for liver disease and the searing pain that accompanied it. Never mind he would soon be back at the estate and could indulge in the opiate Eric had brought him.

Georgina chatted and William tried to concentrate on the flow. At least she would put his inattention down to pain, and not to preoccupation. The trays arrived and Georgina attacked her food with relish. How he hated her. He had not appetite for any of his previous treats and delicacies, but he had to try. It wouldn't do to raise any suspicion.

Part way through he said, 'Georgina darling, would you bring me a copy of The Times. It would bring me such pleasure. I promised Ernest that I would obtain a copy of his betrothal notice. He is in the country at present and I would hate to disappoint him. I will simply check the paper and then you shall have my full attention.'

'Gladly brother,' she said as she skipped towards the back of the room and rustled through the papers.

Expertly flipping open the lion's head that was the top of his cane, William tipped a measured amount of white powder into Georgina's hot chocolate. Thankfully he knew her habits - always leaving the tea until last. She wouldn't feel a thing. He could taste success.

He failed to notice the ornate mirror opposite. He also failed to notice the redhead spreading a crisp white cloth on a table - watching. Elise froze. The bastard. Thank God he hadn't recognised her. She was pleased that she had lost so much weight when she suffered from rheumatic fever. She was also grateful for the French lessons her father insisted she and her sister attend. The rest had been bravado. Thinking quickly she had invented a name - she could hardly be French and called Colleen. Now, she would need to act quickly.

'Monsieur, Je regrette to impose, but may I request that you sign the account for your repast. I hope it will not cause you too much inconvenience to walk this short distance to the book. The new owner is most insistent with these things. Je suis ... ah ... sorry, I am prone to forget my language, but a man of your stature would have learned Francais, nest pas?' Colleen concentrated on a thick accent.

'Of course.'

'Estelle will assist Monsieur.' She had a large white tablecloth over her arm and beckoned to a tiny freckled girl at the desk.

William groaned inwardly and attempted to stride quickly, but he was in great pain now and could only move slowly. Damned girl. He leant over the book.

Colleen swapped the cups, then quickly changed the tablecloth at the table nearby. 'Merci, Monsieur,' she said as he past him on her way back to desk.

After a few minutes that William used to wipe and lean his cane on the thick velvet curtaining nearby, Georgina returned happily waving the newspaper.

'You know the worst thing about this pregnancy thing is that you want to eat for two, but there just isn't enough room,' she said, leaning back. 'You haven't eaten much William. You make me look like a greedy pig.'

'Never, my dear,' he said, stroking her hand. 'I will savour my tea. Will that please your coddling nature?'

Georgina laughed and sipped her tea with evident satisfaction. William was surprised she didn't notice the sweetness of the beverage. He had added extra sugar to cover the taste of opium.

There shouldn't be much suspicion. Their mother had died of 'sugar disease' just after delivering Georgina. There wasn't much for him to gain in the eyes of society, but it gave him great satisfaction that he would leave this world with one of his cousins in the estate rather than his eccentric sister and her Irish interloper. He watched her drink with elation.

Colleen watched, partly hidden by the thick curtains. William was blinking – fighting the drowsiness. His mouth moved without sound. He looked confused, then raised his eyes. Colleen called the beefy bartender who was carrying in firewood, and whispered to him. No-one would be at all surprised to find Viscount William James Henry Everdale dead in a back street from an opium overdose.

The last thing the Viscount saw before passing out was Colleen McRae bending over Georgina, telling her to make haste to see her husband who had sent a message by carrier from his office.

Through a thickening fog William heard the maid say, 'Don't worry about monsieur. He is trés fatigué and we shall allow him to rest here, and send for his valet.'

NOOOOOOOOOO!!!!!!

Goodbye, my friend, goodbye

Elle frowned at the envelope in her letterbox. It was just addressed to 'Mrs Ella' with the street address below in unfamiliar handwriting. Who could be writing to her only knowing her first name?' Ella was puzzled. Wary of the mystery, she waited until she was inside to open it. There was a photo, a familiar face, a beloved friend and two dates underneath. A life sketch. Her hands trembled; tears began of their own accord, before her mind was fully adjusted. Denial was on her lips, but there it was; irrevocable and final—an end date for a life. The life of her friend Eva.

Eva took her in when the world had turned away. People gave no harsh rejections, just tired and retreating eyes as they closed their doors, afraid of the drama Ella's life had become, longing for the glow of their own peaceful havens. Ella was seeking a divorce, battling for custody, in need of asylum that she didn't dare petition. So her dearest friends, Arthur and Joan, with economy of words and generosity of spirit, handed her a train ticket and a name—Eva Everidge.

Ella would be met at the train. Her tiny three year old son Grady, carried an air of delight, thrilled with the prospect of travel. He asked no questions of 'where' or 'why'.

'Oh good, Mum. We will have an adventure. I like adventures.'

As soon as Ella was on the train, she sighed with a new kind of relief, unexpected and welcome. Her small son, always so intuitive of her pain, so dedicated to Mummy's worried brow, instantly discerned the change and became engrossed in the passing scenery. All around them other children harried their weary mothers or nanas with 'Look! Look!' but Grady just revelled in the tranquillity of being near a mother free from fretfulness, a state he was too familiar with. How Ella hated that her shroud of pain affected her son.

Ella saw the station up ahead. It was tiny and open-aired, more of a siding, perhaps only the length of two carriages. Grady manfully struggled with his small colourful suitcase, refusing help as they gathered their belongings. Even though Ella had relaxed, the nagging tightness of her throat refused to give up its tenacious grip.

Her fears of not finding her hostess were washed away when she saw there was only one person on the station that day. A woman was holding her straw hat onto her head firmly and scanning the train, her floral dress billowing gently in the breeze. Ella knew the woman was waiting for her. Before she even looked in Eva's eyes, she knew welcome and walked into her embrace, her soft generous body comforting her.

'You're here now,' was all Eva said, before picking up the suitcase as if it was a feather. She led Ella to a little blue Corolla and chatted brightly, as if they were old friends continuing a conversation begun the day before.

Without pity, regret or askance, Eva became a dear friend in that moment. She went about her days as if Ella and her small son had always been in them. She undertook all her chores without setting anything aside, but including the two newcomers seamlessly. Ella helped dig a pit for the contents of the dunny can, glad of the opportunity to work the tension out of her body and also help Eva. They strolled country lanes. Eva talked nonstop, while Grady dragged a stick in the dusty trails and Ella's mind wandered to yesterday's fears and tomorrow's battles.

Grady and Ella grew carefree and relaxed, wandering the gentle hills. They were miles from anywhere, in a world of stillness and green, so much green. All their stories and conversations began with "we two". They sang 'You and Me Against the World' as they lay by the pebbly creek, Grady's head resting on his mother's stomach.

'You have a sweet voice, Mummy,' Grady said, beginning to hum.

Tears pricked Ella's eyes. She'd been taken out of the school choir.

Ella had often wondered how scars were healed. In that moment the accolades of the world counted as nothing when compared to the innocent adulation of a child. Truth is their only master; their love uncomplicated.

They threw pebbles against the rocky bank of the small creek, squealing with glee when the rocks shattered, the sound echoing through the lush valley.

'We're very distant, aren't we Mummy?' said Grady. His language was not like his small friends. There was a quirky profoundness to his speech, which amused and confused his friends, and delighted the adults he met.

Eva's sister Lil lived nearby. A large woman with a heart as generous as her sister's, Lil drove a beat-up old Holden with one hand, the other gesturing to add emphasis her hearty conversations. Ella's "state of peril" became a game. Ella was "on the run".

'We'll get you a wig. What colour do you think? Better avoid red—draw too much attention, red would. Ever fancied y'self a blonde?' she questioned, eyeing Ella's black hair, squinting in contemplation.

'Oh Lil, don't be outrageous,' said Eva. 'You'll scare the girl witless.'

'Looks to me as if somebody has already done that!' thundered Lil, roaring with laughing at her own joke. 'Pale as a ghost, she is.'

'Anyway,' continued Eva, 'I've informed the police and no-one will come near.'

'Don't be wet fish, Eva. I'm just playing. I know the girl needs to feel safe...'

'Well, she is now.'

'...but she needs to know life can still go on as normal as well.'

Ella was feeling more light-hearted by the minute. No one was pretending or diminishing her situation and yet they were blissfully accepting the circumstances without question.

She stayed with Lil for a few days while Eva had to visit a sick friend in town. Lil took on the task of fattening her up and getting some 'gristle into your muscles'. She was the most physically fit woman Ella had ever met. Her movements were fast and effortless. Her obesity didn't slow her down. Ella wanted to help in any way at all.

'Think you're up for a bit of wood chopping?' asked Lil.

'Sure, Lil, I often chopped kindling and small logs as a kid.'

Ella managed to get the axe stuck on her second strike at the huge round log. Embarrassed beyond belief, she tried every trick in the book to free the axe. Thumping the axe with the other blocks of wood, then trying to gain leverage with her weight failed to move the damned axe a millimetre. Sweaty and defeated she went in to confess to Lil.

Lil gave a hearty, full throated roar of laughter. It was an irresistible laugh and Ella joined spontaneously.

'Well, that's no surprise. There's nothin' of you.' Lil went out to free the axe and Ella followed her. Lil's face was wreathed in a grin and Ella wondered if Lil been watching her puny efforts from the window.

'What kind of blasted wood is it anyway?' Ella muttered darkly. This sent Lil into another peel of laughter.

'Well, it's good to see some spirit in you, girl.'

In one effortless swing after another Lil demolished the entire wood pile as if it was butter. Ella watched in awe and carried the cut timber inside to the basket beside the open fireplace. Lil laughed all the way through, still tickled by Ella's last remark.

Ella returned to Eva's and regretted that they would have to leave this place of peace. She loved the people and the surrounding countryside with a depth of feeling I thought lost to her.

Lil's husband Joe, one of life's natural gentlemen, was a gem. He often came to help Eva with some of the trickier jobs. They razzed each other good-naturedly like brother and sister. Ella wondered if the beauty of the land bewitched everyone and made life harmonious.

At the end of one long day, when the simmering heat of the day had surrendered to the welcome chill of evening, Joe sat on the woodpile and played his trumpet. Ella was taken by surprise and transported to another world where peace reigned and joy was expected and natural. She'd never like brass instruments - hating the local brass band performances, but that night she was in the presence of a master. Added to the gift, was the fact that she was an accidental listener, a solitary audience.

Ella was in the amphitheatre of heaven. The clear pure tones of the trumpet pared back the evening stillness with a reverence that gave her goose bumps. She held her breath, never wanting the moment to end.

Ella folded the life sketch for Eva.

That time is what I will remember, she thought, along with our long letters over the years, as I say goodbye to Eva. Silently and alone, here at my own hearth, my home. Far away from the valley that nurtured me a lifetime ago.

A cold love

Carol wondered when it had come to this. How had she and her best friend, Sue, arrived at this place? Gently patting the back of Sue's head, she handed her yet another tissue from the man-sized Kleenex box.

Carol remembered that other brilliant, sun-lit day on the hillside that jutted over the sea. They had all laughed when the breeze had stiffened up, and Sue couldn't pull her veil away from her face for Dave to kiss her. Silly the things you remember. She wondered what Sue was thinking, but her jerking sobs prevented conversation. And, well, what could you say outside a crowded court when your best friend was applying for an Apprehended Violence Order? AVO sounded better, more objective, she thought as she gripped the application. Sue was even too shaken to hold the paperwork.

It would do no good to tell Sue that she and Andrew had never liked Dave. He'd been too confident, too full of bonhomie - all things that sounded positive, even wonderful. The lavish displays of romance had been so public and Dave's eyes had been on the audience, not Sue. How could you discuss those things with a woman so much in love, especially one who'd just buried her father?

Carol's only wish was to heal the pain, somehow stop that waterfall of tears. She hadn't seen her best friend cry in public since her father's funeral ten years ago. She didn't even seem to be aware of the other people crowding the bench.

At least now, they were comfortable as friends again. Dave no longer had the power to keep all Sue's friends at bay, particularly ones as observant as she and Andrew. Sue had spent hours entertaining and catering for Dave's friends, then sat alone as he went on his guy things. Three times a week to the pub, every second weekend fishing - not to mention the endless round of business events that kept him from home.

Sue sobbed relentlessly. She couldn't stop and she no longer cared. She had been on this bench before, but with her clients. As a social-worker she prided herself on her professional objectiveness, even if her soft heart agonised at home.

Her attempts to share her day with Dave had him angrily shouting, 'I've got enough problems of my own without having to listen to your whining! Jeez Sue, what does a man have to do to get peace! Get another job if you're not happy!' Of course, Dave had accepted massages for tension in his neck, along with a hundred other ministrations with merely a grunt.

Carol looked around. They didn't belong here. There was a woman swearing at her two children, landing a loud wallop on one, even though two policemen were standing nonchalantly nearby. No-one was as affected as Sue. Everyone looked like they belonged on the beach, or the shady corner of a bar.

Except for the two people opposite. An extremely well-dressed Mediterranean man had just arrived and sat next to a petite blonde woman who was dressed in a navy designer suit. The blonde was calm and still. No furtive smoking or restless flipping through pages like many of the others. Her demeanour mystified Carol. She couldn't be here for an AVO, even though this was the day set aside for them. She was far too composed. Carol dismissed the possibility she was there for a friend, the woman had been there for as long as she and Sue - over an hour.

The Mediterranean man started mumbling to himself.

God help me, this is a madhouse, Carol thought. When would this day be over?

'I don't know why I'm here?' he said.

The blonde eyed him dispassionately.

It's pretty bloody obvious, thought Carol, another Dave!

The man repeated this several times. The blonde seemed fascinated. The hint of a smile played at the corner of her mouth. There was a glint in her eye.

Oh help, thought Carol, she's not going to talk to him. Bloody hell. This could only end in trouble, surely. It was too late to sit somewhere else. They were in the corner.

'So, you don't understand?' said the woman.

This seemingly sympathetic remark had the effect of loosening the man's tongue. He seemed unconcerned that he was surrounded by other people gripped by fear, boredom, or apprehensive chain-smoking.

Carol was horrified. How would Sue cope? She'd shrunk into herself as soon as they arrived, and then had been either sobbing or wailing ever since.

'I thought we were happy. I thought we had a great marriage. Twenty years together and I never saw it coming. Why didn't I see this coming?' moaned the man.

'Well darling, that's because you are a man,' said the blonde. She now had his full attention—and that of everyone in earshot. The man focused intently on the woman.

'Well, this is how it goes. A woman gets up in the morning and thinks about the relationship. She has breakfast and thinks about the relationship. She takes the kids to school and thinks about the relationship. She has coffee with friends and thinks about the relationship. She goes to work and thinks about the relationship, and then she comes home, gets tea, thinks about the relationship. She washes the dishes, watches a little television, and she *is still thinking about the relationship*. It's what we do.'

She paused there and seemed a little chagrined to find all eyes on her. Sue had stopped crying and was also staring, open mouthed.

'But you,' the woman continued, 'get up and have breakfast and think about breakfast. You go to work and think about work. You have a few beers with your mates and think about your mates and your beer. You come home and read the newspaper and think about the newspaper. You watch TV and think about the TV program—your wife has had twenty years up on you, and working it out, and it's over sweetheart.'

The man sat staring straight ahead, silently mulling over his situation. Carol grabbed a tissue to smother a chuckle. Someone snorted with laughter. Carol turned in amazement to see that it was Sue. The newly-informed man went back to his confused reverie, still oblivious to the crowd.

'Why on earth did you do that?' giggled Sue.

'I was bored, and if people talk out loud, they should expect to have a public conversation,' answered the woman.

'Bored? How can you be bored in this place?' Sue was astonished.

'Oh that's easy; it's the fifth time I've been here. It gets boring.'

'But... but... it's AVO day...'

Carol was both shocked and thrilled to see Sue in animated conversation.

'Oh yes, that's what I'm here for. But my ex keeps adjourning things. He thinks if he puts it off enough times he'll wear me down and I'll give up. That's his game.'

'Game?'

'Yes. Well *his* game, of course. That's what controlling men do. And they're used to getting a certain reaction, so it takes a while to sink in that they can't push your buttons anymore.'

'So you've stopped loving him, *that's the secret?*'

'No. I've stopped respecting him, and I've discovered how much I need to respect someone. But even more, to be respected by them.'

'But they're so in love...' murmured Sue, clearly confused. Carol was silent, fascinated by the interchange. Sue hadn't said this much since the separation.

'Bollocks! They're in love with the concept of owning and renovating 'the ideal woman'. Then they get frustrated when their attempts to train and improve you crush you instead. The more they try, the more wounded you become. It's vicious cycle. Wounded women annoy the hell out of them. So they keep upping the ante until there's nothing of you left. Even your career and family are gone by then.'

'But how can you be so cool?' Sue asked earnestly.

'If they can get your 'number' you can get theirs. Having power over you is their button. Take that, and it's all over bar the shouting. Game over.' The woman's eyes were soft.

'How do you get to that place?'

'You have to be a sheep in wolf's clothing. Your heart doesn't change.'

Sue roared laughing. Carol was gobsmacked. Other women joined in the conversation and soon Carol was sharing the man-sized Kleenex for tears of laughter.

After Sue's case, she and Carol chatted with their solicitor outside. They'd won what they'd been told was a 'touch and go' case. The solicitor commended Sue on her dignified demeanour. The blonde walked out of the courtroom with an impassive face. She passed a tall impressive man who shot her an awestruck look. The man's hands were shaking. The woman didn't look his way. Turning to Sue, she winked.

Sue was silent again as they drove home, but it was a different kind of silence. She turned dry-eyed to Carol. 'You know what the saddest thing is?' she sighed. 'I would have stayed. I would have stayed without the beatings. No one deserves that. I was actually prepared to settle for a cold love for the rest of my life. That's the saddest thing.

A treasured moment

The sky was a pale washed out blue. One long thin cloud stretched across the whole skyline like the smoke trail left by a plane long gone. It had a sharply defined straight edge on the base and it feathered upwards like the deft gentle strokes of an artist's brush. There were other random streaks of white cloud in the sky, softening the cityscape before me. Dried leaves rustled and tickled my feet as the indulgent breeze eddied at my feet. There was no sigh of wind in the upper atmosphere where the somnolent clouds were still and airless.

It was strange to see clouds so still, insubstantial whispers, I mused as I sat stiffly on a hard bench seat outside the Camperdown Children's Hospital in Sydney, cradling my precious infant son, David in my hungry arms. A renowned surgeon would operate on him the next day, in the early morning. I remembered lying on my back in the grass as a child watching the clouds come to life and travel ponderously across the sky. 'Don't look at the sun Linda, you'll go blind,' my mother would prophesy darkly.

I shifted my position carefully on the rickety seat that was positioned outside the surgical ward where David had just been admitted. He had been transferred from King George Hospital where he had spent the previous three months following his premature birth. He would return there after the surgery. Although I had just recently been gratefully allowed my first cuddle I hadn't had him all to myself to hold and indulge my motherhood of him.

But here the nurses allowed me a few minutes to enfold him in my arms and walk with him, a luxury that was not possible in the small confines of the neonatal unit at King George where all the preemies were kept in rows of pristine incubators where the warmth and air was controlled. David hadn't felt the sun on his face, felt the caress of the wind or seen the sky and that was why I had taken him outside for a few timeless minutes. To create a memory. Mine and his.

When David was born he was 12 weeks premature and his life began with all the frailties common to preemie infants. He was on a respirator, on and off, for the first three months of his life. I was critically ill myself, having haemorrhaged soon after the delivery and I had been given blood transfusions. I had also been very ill before his birth with severe anaemia.

It was a time of crisis. In the early days his lungs haemorrhaged and he had a daily struggle to breathe. Phone calls at midnight and the early hours of the morning became expected and quick decisions were required of me about his basic survival. Like any newborn on a respirator he was monitored frequently for his blood oxygen levels due to the possibility for damage to the retina of the eye. Every day that I went in I would ask them how the blood gas levels were and they always reassured me that everything was fine.

Because I was still recovering my own health I wasn't able to drive myself in to see David so I had to rely on Randy to take me in. For him it was a bit like dragging a wet rag around and I think at times he had all the affection for me that befitted a wet rag. Sometimes he couldn't handle going in at all so although I tried to go every day it wasn't always possible.

One of the lovely men at our church who drove a taxi delivered my breast milk to the hospital as part of his daily run into the city so that David would have the best start in life that I could give him. Even though I rang often and always asked questions the information highway still had a few traffic jams.

One day I had a casual phone call from one of the nurses that I assumed was an update as it had none of the frantic nature of some of the other phone calls. 'Nothing particular'. The nurse said that when we were next visiting it would be good to catch up with the paediatrician looking after David. When we went in a couple of days later we were met by the paediatrician concerned who was quite frustrated and irate that we had taken 'so long' to come and see him. Apparently the message was supposed to be urgent. He had suffered retrolental fibroplasia, damage to the retina of his eyes due to the high levels of oxygen supplied constantly through the ever present thin plastic tubes inserted in his nostrils so assist his struggle to breath, to live. Our son was blind.

I skipped the emotions of bewildered and upset and had a little anger and frustration myself. The doctor hadn't wanted to discuss it over the phone even though we had been rung at home for so many other life threatening crises. I was shocked that my son could be sightless when we had been continually reassured. The staff were just great and the doctor was a brilliant caring professional. I was continually knocked sideways by the endless string of bad news. But the sidestepping that occurred with communicating crucial information only served to compound the pain and added insecurity to the equation. It made it hard to trust what I was told.

Cryosurgery was suggested to restore his sight. Apparently this procedure had only been performed a few times in the southern hemisphere and never on an infant. We agreed. David would be the first. He was transferred to Camperdown Children's Hospital. I saw him on the ward before his surgery and he was one of many in a row of cribs that lined what seemed like an endless wall in a ward of misery.

Even though I was a registered nurse I had never been to a place like this. Tiny bundles of helpless sobbing or howling humanity. Tired tense anxious parents pacing. Mothers with babes gathered in protective embrace or with their arms folded helplessly, empty, as they waited. And waited. For news of their children. Good news. Bad news. Infants with tubes into their arms and legs and even into their heads. Pale faces, wan cheeks, unsmiling, slumped passively in mothers' arms or backs arched bellowing loudly.

I wasn't there the next day for the news on my son. Illness overtook me. I woke up the next day with my face swollen like hippo's cheeks. I had mumps. An infectious disease, one that would prevent me seeing David for many days. My milk dried up. Another fragile bond to my son was broken.

When the phone finally rang for news of David's surgery my throat was raging, burning. My head pounding a buzzing rhythm. They told me that they'd had to resuscitate David yet again and then put him back on a respirator. I asked how long it had been before they had found him failing to breath and the nurse was distracted and vague. I asked if he had been monitored closely after the operation. I was concerned about hypoxia resulting in brain damage if he had been without oxygen for too long before being found and resuscitated.

They were reassuring but I couldn't trust what I was told any longer. They informed me that he had been returned to the same cot where I had seen him the day before. I had seen no monitoring equipment near his cot or on the wall nearby. I told the nurse that. She was anxious and flustered. She was kind and pained. She was overstretched and doing her best on a long ward with twenty sick babies.

I lost all faith in what they were telling us and requested a meeting be arranged with the paediatrician, the surgeon and a neurologist to be held on David's return to King George III to address all the issues that faced us. I didn't require promises, I desired the truth. The specialists sat down with us and discussed all the things I wanted and answered my questions. They felt the surgery had been a success and would restore most of his sight, with the need for strong prescription glasses only. Our son would see.

But they could not know; could not predict my son's precarious future. There were no pathology tests or scans or graphs to supply that picture. At least I had a fumbling tenuous grasp on the truth. And it would have to do. I calmly and gravely told them I wanted them to know I could handle the truth rationally without hysteria; that I wished to be told *any and all* relevant news over the phone in future.

They said it was hard on the staff to deliver bad news. I replied that I was his mother and I didn't live with speculation or guesswork. I lived with the truth; good, bad or otherwise; whether they told me or not.

David died five weeks after he came home. Was it harder for me to be the one who found him, lifeless? No, for my baby was home. I had nursed him in my arms for hours the night before he died. We shared an unforgettable goodbye, and for that, I was immensely grateful.

Thanks, Sherlock!

It was all becoming a bit of a nightmare really. Like when you dream you've gone to school in your pyjamas. Sara had left early enough. Parking in the city was a bitch. The council had undertaken numerous "consumer" surveys to try and ascertain why no-one frequented the shops in the main street and nearby streets. Any fool could have told them it because of parking, or more correctly, the lack of it. Not to mention, the most fastidious meter men in history. They arrived faster than a speeding bullet. They must have been fitted with radar.

Sara had an appointment with an orthopaedic specialist for an insurance company assessment. She was under no illusions. After today she would be on the skids to poverty, axed by "medical opinion". But one must obey. Surrender your weapons and go quietly, hoping to fight another day, or more likely another year.

She had her scans and X-rays, along with the letter from the insurance company stating the appointment place and time. Her appointment was with a Dr Holmes. She wasn't leaving anything to chance. Many are the traps on the way to compensation and if one detail was incorrect it was all over bar the shouting.

What had Sara in a state of confusion was that she'd arrived on the right floor, at the right time, but the name on the door wasn't the name on the appointment letter.

Oh what the heck, she thought, might as well ask whoever was in this office.

A lovely receptionist looked up and gave her a warm smile, even a little overly welcoming, truth be told. She must be in the right place, because this was all a part of the illusion. Employ ancillary staff with fabulous people skills. It will lull 'clients' aka 'malcontents' into a false sense of security. Approaching the desk Sara asked if this was the office of Dr Holmes.

'It certainly is,' said the girl brightly.

Jeez, if she tries any harder her face will crack.

'Doctor won't be long.'

Okay, Lie No. 1 out of the way.

'I was confused by the name on the door,' Sara said pointedly.

The receptionist smiled wider.

'Oh, Dr Holmes flies down from Brisbane once every two months,' she said, grinning as if she was announcing Sara had won the lottery.

Knowing the next ploy was to keep the client waiting for an indecent length of time Sara pulled out a huge book, which was a compilation of six novels; and settled in. This 'waiting' game is aimed to not only frustrate, but also discredit any claim that sitting aggravates pain levels. Sara knew they watched and recorded every detail. Why they did was a mystery because she'd lost count of the times supposed experts had the facts wrong.

She lay on the floor, using her coat as a pillow. She waited, and waited, finally feigning sleep. Then she snored. Finally a man in a white coat arrived. He was at least 150 years old and the size of Jabba the Hut. Sara took five minutes to get up, first trying this way, then the other. Leading her to his room, he was gentile to the core.

'I'm an independent specialist, you know.'

Okay, Lie No. 2 out of the way.

'You do realise that don't you? You were told?'

Oh, no, I'm not walking into that one, Sara thought. *I'm not joining this lying gig. Mum told me where liars end up. Someplace warm, and I'm not talking Barbados.* So she treated the question as rhetorical and smiled benignly. Better to be thought a fool than play their game. Being blonde always helped with that one.

Sitting opposite, he began to question Sara. This was going to take a while because Dr High and Mighty Specialist was bent on asking all the unusual questions, before even getting to the subject. Any self-respecting doctor with a busy practice would get to the point. Not Dr Holmes. He asked name, date of birth, *blah blah blah,* even though Sara could read all this information on the paper in front of him, from where she was sitting. She knew no specialist wasted time on this. They automatically assumed they had the right person when the client rose and followed them. But the point of this visit was to frustrate and waste time – Sara's.

After scribbling for a while he asked Sara to undress. There was no privacy curtain. Of course. They want to observe and comment on the client's ability to remove clothing – it just 'happens' to also discomfort and intimidate. Contrary to the criminal justice system, in Worker's Compensation you are assumed guilty until, well, until you die actually. Anyone in a wheelchair with an oxygen tank is still classified as a 'malingerer'.

He asked Sara to lie on her stomach. Yeah right, how was he going to examine her back from that position? He wasn't. He ran his hands over her torso and remarked, 'You could lose a little weight, you know. Extra weight puts stress on your back.'

This from Jabba the Hut to a size 12 woman. After this gratuitous touch up he asked Sara to stand, walk on tiptoes, touch her nose and wave her arms.

If I wasn't half-naked I would believe I'd been stopped by the booze bus, she thought. Or was auditioning for the circus.

Then, he asked her to turn around and lightly touched her lower back.

'Does that hurt?' he asked.

Hardly Sherlock, I can't feel you yet!

After the farce was over, Sara was unceremoniously dumped for "medical reasons" due to the examination of Dr Holmes. When she received the copy of his report Sara rolled on the floor laughing. In a medically careful manner, of course.

Not one fact was correct. Even her name was misspelled. Her address resembled an anagram. She had been born a decade earlier, and 10 kilos had been added to her weight. Apparently she drove a truck! She began to think he could write fiction if he ever gave up medicine. But then the rest of the letter was so poorly phrased she expected to find his address as c/- the local Dementia ward.

She had been paid for a total of three weeks.

The wrong paddock

It was a balmy spring day that followed a dismal week of rain. The children were antsy in the first activities of the morning. We could see a long day of dealing with bored and cranky children who'd spent the last week indoors ahead of us.

So Susan, the director, decided that we would take them all for a walk. They were excited about being able to go outside. There were many quiet walks in the backstreets near the preschool - the roads soon became rural and the promise of fresh air and exercise was tantalising to the staff as well. Except for Katherine, who declared she'd rather put her head in an oven than go. She'd been to a prestigious dinner with her scientist husband the previous night.

'I drank enough red wine for three day headache,' she moaned. 'It wasn't even worth the trouble. It was still the most Godawful boring night.'

Now, Katherine was a gem. There was no task she wouldn't tackle or job too menial. Her dry wit and unique take on life entertained us daily. But someone had to be on site because we had a nursery in the preschool, and there were two babies sleeping. Gabe and I worked in the nursery. We had three toddlers who would enjoy the outdoors, so we were more than happy to let Katherine stay behind.

'Put your feet up, Katherine. The babies will sleep a bit longer,' said Gabe.

'Where?' asked Katherine dryly.

We grinned. The nursery was tiny and Katherine was very tall.

Susan and Gabe knew the ropes better than I, so they did head counting and calculation of staff to child ratio. Susan declared that we were fine to go. This decision delighted everyone. The children sensed adventure. They demanded their gumboots plus a hundred other things they didn't have, along with a few things they didn't.

'Are we takin' snacks?' asked Brendon, whose life revolved around food.

Gabe moaned. Brendon wisely took that as a 'no'. He was used to being denied food. But not quite as much as he should have, because he was overweight at four.

So off we went. The children were very well behaved. That was more due to Gabe and Susan than to me. They knew about large groups of small children and motivating stragglers, whereas my single useful talent seemed to be lying on the floor getting smeared with Vegemite and paint.

This 'look' made going to the bank a bit embarrassing, but the tellers became accustomed to my appearance after a while. However, there was always another customer who gave me an incredulous look. There I was, with a business banking bag looking like a pre-schooler myself.

The children were having a wonderful time. We came across a paddock of sheep. I don't remember who it was, but I know it was someone other than me, decided that it would be great to wander among the sheep. I didn't have enough knowledge on mingling with sheep in their natural habitat to give an opinion, so I shut up.

The children were overjoyed. Gabe and I each had either a toddler or one of the younger pre-schooler in each hand. To start with.

The sheep proved to be placid and nonchalant. Except for one ewe that had 'gotten out of the wrong side of the...' well grass, I guess. She started charging the children, and she was a good aim. Not stupid either - systematically she knocked down the smallest of the children. The older children giggled to see the little ones go down like ninepins. This ewe would go well in a bowling alley.

As soon as we picked one toddler up, another went down.

'Baa!!!' we'd hear, followed by an equally loud, 'Waa!!'

This went on for a short time, which seemed like a long time. The ewe was running at what seemed the speed of light, all over the paddock. We staff ran to pick up the latest victim and comfort them. However, we couldn't pick them up as fast as the ewe could knock another one down. Which was a bit time consuming. And probably the reason we didn't seem to have a strategy for actually dealing with the sheep. Well if any of us did, you wouldn't have known.

The whole thing was becoming very worrying. This sheep had energy to burn. She appeared to be happy to spend all day at this, while we couldn't seem to rescue the tots fast enough to even think about heading out of the paddock, and danger.

Then, the ewe ran past me. Without thinking I kicked it in the belly. It went down like a tonne of bricks. It didn't move - not even a twitch.

'Quick! Get out of the field now!!' I yelled.

No one moved. 'Run!' I yelled, thinking a shorter version would do the trick.

It didn't.

'I can't believe you did that!' said Gabe.

'What?' I said.

'What about the poor sheep?' she said. Susan was looking a little gobsmacked as well.

'Who cares about the bloody sheep?' I said.

'It might be dead,' said Gabe.

'Oh well, you stay here and administer CPR while the rest of us get the kids the hell out of here,' I muttered.

'It's probably winded,' said Gabe, still holding firmly to The Rights of Outlaw Sheep.

'You live in hope,' I said, 'anyway, that's nothing. I've been winded twice. It'll survive. I did.'

'That would be you, Linda. I daren't ask how that happened.' Gabe was smirking by now and beginning to lead the children to the gate. 'I don't know how you can NOT care about the sheep, just the same.'

'I'm a vegetarian. I'm not the one who buys carved up sheep from the butcher, and has mutton stew or lamb sandwiches. But I do care about parents asking questions because their kids have been mowed down by a deranged sheep that's twice their size.'

We arrived through the gate, and all three of us burst out laughing. Some of the children joined in – some because it was funny, and others because they thought we were funny. As we looked back the ewe was scrambling to her feet. She looked fine, if a bit dazed.

'See,' I said, practising my self-righteous look. I was beginning I deserved some praise. But I wasn't about to be granted hero status.

All the way back Gabe kept repeating in a stunned voice, 'I can't believe you did that!'

I didn't have an answer. I didn't know any better than her, other than it was instinct. Which would have been fine, but it seemed it was an instinct that nobody on the face of the earth other than me would have had. I had no farm experience, but I did have an older brother who thought I was put on the earth for him to fine-tune his practical jokes. Jokes that had no practical element at all, but incorporated all the hallmarks of The Three Stooges antics.

When we arrived back at the preschool, the babies were awake and howling. A grateful Katherine handed them over to Gabe and I, as the children gathered around her with their excited versions of the sheep incident.

'Well, that puts paid to the parents not finding out,' sighed

Susan, who had all the responsibility of explaining everything that went on, and everything that didn't. Parents busy with their own lives were awfully picky about how their children spent their days at the preschool, even the ones who all the appearance of not spending five minutes with the children themselves.

Katherine howled laughing at the kids' stories. Then Gabe gave her the 'real' version of the Sheep Kicking staff member who incapacitated a hyperactive ewe.

'Oh that's priceless,' said Katherine, 'I wish I'd been there. As usual, I miss all the fun. Trust Linda. Go girlfriend!' I glowed, happy to accept any praise.

As we suspected, the first thing the children wanted to tell their parents when they came to pick them up, was the story of the head-butting sheep. Unfortunately for me, the tale wasn't restricted to the ewe's activities.

After one or two of them pointed at me and said, 'There's the lady who kicked the sheep and it lied down for a sleep,' I decided to get busy inside – away from the attention.

A mother and son passed the window where I was pretending to clean. The boy saw me. He started enthusiastically telling his mother, 'You shoulda seen it, Mummy. That lady kickded the big sheep *so hard* the others thought it was dead, and they were going to call a sheep amb'lance and operate on it. The lady was as fast as Superman. Whoosh! Bang!'

I cringed and sunk out of sight.

'Thank Goodness for that!' said the mother.

Beth's Christmas Wish

A white blanket of snow lay deep on the ground. Blistering cold winds brought sheet after sheet of swirling snowflakes. The 7.45 from Astonville was late. The clanking steam train only came twice a day.

The town had once set their clocks by its arrival, but that was before the war. The women who lived in the valley just out of town noticed its lateness first. They put their children to bed by the sound of the whistle and the trail of steam behind the ancient grinding engine.

However, they had other things to concern them. Ever since war broke out the routine of their daily lives had become unpredictable in so many ways.

The food on the table for the evening meal was no longer a matter of choice or variety. There was no longer any lingering at John Mansfield & Sons Greengrocer or George Anderson's Butchery. That was especially true at the Turner's Corner Store where the rows of Manchester and clothing racks spoke of bleak times. Business everywhere was brisk and grim.

After years of war no-one complained about their meagre rations any more. They just got on with things. How could they complain when John Mansfield & Sons had not only lost the abundance of fruit and vegetables that was their staple business but they had also lost their sons, Evan and William? John Mansfield hadn't have the heart to change the sign '& sons'. He had muttered that he would 'get around to it when this blasted war was over'.

Now the war was over, but not the waiting.

'Come away from the window, Beth,' begged her mother in a tired voice. 'You are fogging up the whole front window.'

Beth sighed and stepped back a little, eyeing the circles of cloud her breath made on the glass. Grown-ups were so tiresome, she thought. Sometimes they didn't understand anything at all. Her mother had told her a hundred times that looking out that window wouldn't make her father come home any quicker. Truth be told, none of them knew whether Peter Renshaw had even survived the war, much less when he was coming home.

Beth was too young to know that it wasn't her tireless vigil that irritated Miriam, her mother, but it was the visible hope that shone on her daughter's face that pained Miriam. A hope that mirrored her own. A hope buried deep inside a woman weary with waiting and exhausted from caring for three children. A woman with the toil-worn hands of a man.

'Beth, come and help the little ones make Christmas decorations,' said Miriam, keeping her voice cheerful.

'Yes, Besh,' begged Brian, one of the three year old twins. 'Help us get ready. Santa's coming tonight.'

'No, he's not,' began Beth angrily.

'Please Besh!' added Meg, the other twin, a dimpled child with golden curls.

Beth stopped and hung her head when she saw her mother's silent reproval and the twin's forlorn faces. Bending gently over her tiny sister, Beth brushed the curls from her forehead.

'Santa comes at midnight, but only when you're asleep,' Beth said, smiling regretfully up at her grateful mother, and sat down with the twins. She picked up a pine cone and began to paint it gold so the little ones could sprinkle it with tiny pieces of glittery material that their mother had found in the attic. Little did they know that Miriam had tearfully sat up late many nights cutting up her trousseau nightgowns to make clothes for their dolls and teddy bears. The material and ribbons left over were now being used to make ornaments for the tree.

Miriam smiled with relief. Beth was such a good child, with such a burden to carry for one so young. The twins had never seen their father. He was just a tall austere man in a uniform in a sepia photograph. But Beth had pined for her father every day of the last three and a half years.

Beth sighed loudly. She had been trying so hard to be good. At seven years of age, and the oldest, she knew she had to be brave for her mother. But she was so tired of being good, tired of being called Besh by the twins as if she were Bessie the cow and very *very* tired of hearing about Santa Claus. Santa Claus, who was supposed to bring you what you wanted for Christmas. Santa Claus who was supposed to make everything right for one day of the year. On Christmas Day when miracles happened on every street and in every home. But for the last three Christmases he had not brought Beth her wish. It was all *rubbish*, thought Beth.

Beth had even visited Santa in the local community hall when all the adults had put on happy faces and decorated the hall with tinsel and ribbons. The local choir had sounded as hearty as ever when they carolled through the town. But they hadn't fooled Beth. Why, she was *practically* grown up. She could hang out the washing, dig in the veggie patch and help bath and dress the twins. No, they couldn't fool her. She saw the pained looks in the eyes of some of the singers, those whose loved ones hadn't come home or hadn't been accounted for.

Sitting on Santa's knee had been the hardest time of all. Why this man wasn't even the real Santa! It was Mr Anderson, the butcher! How could she tell *him* her heart's desire, sitting there with his beard crooked and a pillow under his worn red coat? She had lined up with the twins and meant to escape when they asked for cars, dolls and all those things that had disappeared from Beth's dreams long ago.

But burly old George scooped her up before she could run away, and there in his strong arms she had softened, just a little. She looked out over the other children's faces in the queue. Faces shining bright with hope and she had succumbed, whispering softly, tears stinging her eyes. George bent to catch her words.

'What's that little girl? You want a doll's home? Of course, you shall have it.' George Anderson's voice boomed over the crowd as Beth leapt from his lap in humiliation. Stupid Mr Anderson. Stupid Santa and Stupid War. And Stupid Christmas.

Beth returned to her vigil at the square paned window. Miriam sighed and let her stay this time.

'The 7.45 is late again, mum,' Beth said, her eyes pleading. 'Couldn't we just go and meet it? We'd only have to stay a few minutes. *Please?*'

As she said the words Beth knew the request was hopeless. They couldn't go out every morning and night with two small children in the vain hope that this time the 7.45 carried their father home to them.

Miriam sadly shook her head, tears silently welling.

The train was very late that night. The whistle blew long after the twins had gone to bed. Beth could only go to sleep when the whistle had blown. She could hear her mother softly moving around the lounge as she drifted into dreams of yesterday.

She was sitting on her father's knee and chattering non-stop as she showed him the daisy chain she had made.

A solid stomping at the door, followed by a loud rapping, shocked her awake. That would be whiny Jim Snape she thought, silently angry with him for spoiling her dreams. He was always calling by late at night with his ugly knotted fingers sticking out of old leather gloves. He was always hungry and her mother would give him food they could little afford. Everyone said he couldn't go to war because he was sick. He didn't look sick, but he sure drank a lot of horrible smelling medicine.

Beth hid under the blankets wanting to shut out the sounds of the conversation. She could see Jim in her mind's eye, twisting his cap in his restless hands as he asked for jobs or food, or both. Why was *he* here while her father fought a war in another country? Why couldn't Jim Snape have gone to war and left her daddy home? It wasn't fair. She stifled a sob.

'Why is my angel crying?' said a voice.

That was better, she was dreaming again. She was being picked up by her father and carried to the rocking chair in the corner of her room where her favourite doll sat. She sighed, squeezing her eyes tight so that the dream would go on forever. But gentle hands were tickling her eyelashes.

She was wide awake in an instant and looked full into the crinkling eyes of her father as he gazed down at her with a bemused smile.

'*Ooooh, you're real!*' she squealed. 'But the 7.45 came hours ago. How did you get here? Have you seen the twins? They're quite big now. They can talk but they don't get my name right yet.' she said, the words tumbling out of her excited mouth.

'Oh, Daddy, have you got both your legs?' she asked, pulling up his trousers and tapping his shins.

'Ouch!' said Peter Renshaw in mock pain.

'Are those your own arms?' she added as she checked his coat sleeves and pinched his right forearm.

Peter Renshaw gave a cracking laugh as he gazed at his vibrant daughter.

'Well, at least I know *I'm* not dreaming,' he said, rubbing his arm dramatically. 'Yes, I am real, and I have my *own* arms and legs,' he chuckled. Those other wounds he would tell her about later; much later.

Beth realised her mother was standing in the doorway with something in her arms. It was huge and wrapped with brown paper.

'It's for you, angel,' her father said, handing the parcel to her.

Beth tore the paper off quickly so she could return to his lap. It was a doll's house. She looked confused.

'Don't you like it darling?' asked her father, perplexed. 'I stopped to ask Santa what you wanted. Is something wrong?'

'Silly old George Anderson,' giggled Beth. When she saw her father's astonished face she added. 'It's all right Daddy. I'm quite grown up now, you know. I know he was standing in for the *real* Santa because Santa Claus is so busy this time of year. I know Mr Anderson puts a pillow under his coat and wears a red suit and funny white beard.' Her voice rose with excitement. 'You know Daddy, this year his beard was on so crooked you could see his black moustache!'

Her father rolled his eyes. His daughter had certainly grown up. It would take some getting used to. He held her closer and relished tonight's magic. Tomorrow would be harder when he met the twins for the first time. He looked down at Beth's face glowing with radiant joy.

'So you *didn't* ask for a doll's house?'

'*Of course not!* I don't care about doll's houses. Mr Anderson must be deaf and *thought* I said I wanted a dolly's home.'

'Oh,' said her father, still confused.

'So, what *did* you say?' he asked.

'Daddy home,' said Beth slowly, with her hands spread palms up, as if it was perfectly obvious.

'What else would I wish for but you, Daddy?'

Getting my wings

The nursing care plan classified him as "resistive". Behind closed doors they referred to him as that 'belligerent old bastard'. As the registered nurse who was often on his ward, I thought of Don Winton as intelligent and misunderstood, but at least still having 'fire in the belly' for life.

He wouldn't eat with the other patients in the dining room. He said watching the 'custard dribblers' made him ill. He said that if he 'had any desire to see someone's half-digested food he would look in the garbage, not at some other old codger's tonsils.'

When the nurses said his comment was rude, I asked them why they didn't eat with the patients. They were silent.

Don was given the *appropriate medical treatment for belligerence*, which sadly to say, was to be given more of what annoyed him. He was put in a room with a dementia patient who climbed in Don's bed and rifled through his things. Don had served his country in the war, loved no one but himself and just wanted to be left alone. Good, bad or indifferent—I understood that. He was intelligent and articulate, independent and proud.

One weekend, when one of the patients departed in the usual manner of those leaving nursing homes, I decided to act. Being the RN on his ward, when the administration was away, I had a little administrative leeway that I was determined to use.

I rearranged the patients so that two dementia patients shared a room and Don was put in a private room. I wrote long, boring and comprehensive notes in the patient records. With a mixture of waffle, medical terminology and old fashioned bravado, I managed to give him the privacy and dignity he craved.

What had been done couldn't be undone after the weekend when the administration arrived back to work. The icy looks I was rewarded with made me very aware of their disdain for my championing the belligerent old bastard. I didn't care.

He smoked. Although I've never put a cigarette in my mouth, I was prepared to lay down my life for his right to smoke. Even the Sisters who smoked themselves, doled out his cigarettes with meticulous tyranny. Two at lunchtime and two at teatime.

When I was on duty, I would give him several whenever he asked for them, and often a few when he didn't. He didn't have any significant diseases impacting on him related to cigarette smoking, and one of the other patients who was not classified as 'belligerent' was allowed as many cigarettes as she liked, even though she had advanced emphysema and went outside with an oxygen tank.

I used to sit outside with Don while he smoked sometimes when I wanted to see how he was doing. He tried to take great care that no smoke came my way, and I would laugh when the wind changed and he swore as smoke swirled around me.

'That bit won't hurt me,' I said chuckling.

One day, while we were chatting, he looked me in the eye and said—'How did an angel like you get to be in a place like this?'

I shrugged. He required no answer.

I was deeply touched. Having a religious background, I had often wondered about angels and how one came to 'get one's wings'. Right then I decided I'd been gifted wings. Who was I to question the universe, if they had come from a bad man, with a bad attitude and bad habits?

Jingle Bells

♫♫ *'Jingle bells, jingle bells, jingle all the way, Oh what fun...'* ♫♫

'Will one of you blooming nurses turn off that blasted Christmas music!' says Harry. 'There's only s'posed to be twelve days of Christmas, but the way *this place* has been windin' things up, ya'd think there were twelve 'undred.'

'Somebody got out of the wrong side of the bed,' mutters Marj.

Cathy steps in to ask Harry how many eggs he wants on his toast. She has been a nurse long enough to know that Christmas isn't all joy and gladness. Especially not here, in the nursing home. This simple question is enough to side-track Harry into his daily argument that the scrambled eggs 'they serve in this place aren't real eggs—they're powdered'. He says this loudly enough so that Meg, the cook, also long accustomed to the tirades of young and old, merely rolls her eyes.

'Back in England...' says George.

'Oh 'ere 'e goes again,' mutters Harry. 'Banging on about 'Mother England'.'

'...we had a white Christmas every year. Nothing like it really. Just doesn't seem like Christmas without snow,' continues George, who holds no animosity towards Harry and politely passes him the strawberry jam. After all, it was George who found Harry swearing his head off earlier this morning when the clerk delivered yesterday's mail from the Admin office. Harry had opened a gift-wrapped parcel containing two new pair of pyjamas and was throwing them in the nearest bin.

'Not your size, Harry?' George had enquired politely, as he wheeled his chair alongside Harry.

'Hmmph,' muttered Harry as he stuffed the pyjamas and wrapping further down the bin with his walking stick.

'S'me blasted son. Hasn't spoken t'me fer twenty years, then this.' George nodded wisely.

'Have a minor stroke and some idiot *informs 'im...*' Harry raised his voice pointedly in our direction. '...next thing ya know, he thinks a bloke's ready to kick the bucket and sends pyjamas! Left his run too late, he has.'

'The nurse at the hospital phoned him, Harry, not us. You know that,' I explained.

'S'none of their blasted business. Dunno how his phone number got onta me notes.'

'It's done now, Harry. Done and dusted,' offered George.

'Too right mate. Done-in and in the dustbin.' He laughed at his own joke.

'Wonder what he would have bought if you had a *major* stroke,' murmurs George, still fascinated at the image of the striped pyjamas among the food scraps.

'Probably a satin smokin' jacket, a lawyer and a pair of flaming slippers, I'd reckon mate.'

After working many Christmas Days there's nothing new to see here. Mabel paces at the window waiting for her family even though they aren't coming until 11.30—and it is only 8.00 am. We only manage to get her to eat breakfast by telling her she'll ruin Christmas if she doesn't eat—she'll pass out from low blood sugar and end up not being able to go out with her nieces. She isn't a diabetic, but her sister Betty suffered from it and died of renal complications connected to the disease only last year.

After breakfast Marj chats with Beatrice while Ethel fusses in her purse. Harry and George move towards the front door for their early morning 'constitutional', making sure none of the confused patients escape as they leave. Harry opens the door wide enough for George's wheelchair.

Cathy, John and I exchange rueful smiles. John turns the music off, announcing he's 'had enough Christmas spirit to last another decade'. A quick flick of the cassette player and Bing Crosby singing White Christmas dies a sudden death.

'At least it's we three and Meg this year, 'I say to John. 'Last year was hell with that manic kitchen-hand having never worked in this wing and having an agency nurse who didn't know one end of the place from the other.'

'Yep, just us old hands,' John responds as he automatically picks up Emily's walking stick, while she bats her eyes at him.

'You have to stop spoiling her, John. You know she does that on purpose.'

'Oh, don't tell me. I know. She thinks she's twenty one and out on the town.' His forehead creases in a frown which still manages to show his unflappable good humour.

There's an urgent ringing of the front door alarm. I look up to see Evangeline Foster with her rather irate looking son Paul standing beside her at the double glass entrance. I throw John and Cathy a knowing glance and they look away to hide their laughter. Evangeline looks a little dishevelled and disoriented. Her son just looks cranky.

He grips her overnight bag with a white knuckled hand. Evangeline glides regally through the foyer and goes to sit beside Beatrice. She immediately starts chatting about the weather as if nothing is amiss. Evangeline was supposed to stay with her family for four days. She's only been gone overnight. I had tried to tell her son Paul, and his elegant wife Sylvia, on their infrequent visits, that Evangeline was often confused, especially at night - but they had greeted my efforts with a dismissive wave. 'Mother's fine *with us*,' Sylvia had claimed smoothly at the time, treating us to one of her 'superior looks'.

'My wife Sylvia...' Paul began.

'Top lofty, that one,' says Evangeline loudly to her seatmate. I cringe. Cathy turns the music back on to cover John's spurt of laughter. And probably whatever other confidences Evangeline will choose to share. She loves an audience.

I look outside to the darkened windows of the BMW. It appears Sylvia has more important things to do than return 'Mother'.

I calmly look Paul in the eyes—waiting. I'm enjoying this, but trying not to show it. He will baulk at any questions, but if I stand here quietly he'll feel obliged to say something by way of explanation. He's polite that way.

'*She...*' he begins again, pointing in Evangeline's direction, who is blithely ignoring her firstborn's existence, '...*she* got up during the night, drunk the sherry for Santa, ate the biscuits for the reindeers, and then opened all the children's presents. We woke up to the kids wailing, paper everywhere and her...*tipsy!*'

I hear John choking. My face wrestles to remain passive. 'Please stop Paul', I think, 'I can't hold this in much longer'. I start saying my four times tables and avoid looking at him.

'..then...*oh...you won't believe this...*' He pauses. I'm in agony. 'She packs all the toys in her suitcase and says 'I want to go home—*home—for crying out loud*', where the hell did she think she was?'

I can't speak. I dare not move a muscle. Thankfully Paul requires no response, and through his own heightened opinion of himself, assumes he sees understanding in my eyes. I deserve an Oscar. He thumps the suitcase down, rushes to his car and takes off, slewing gravel in the car park. Cathy, John and I explode at exactly the same moment.

There is a hush over the laden table—set for 13 instead of forty. The tinsel hangs crookedly. Cathy gives it a searching look, mutters 'pfft', then walks to the table. We have served the patients their Christmas dinner, and I have decided that today the staff will join them. So there we sit, at one long table, with all the trimmings and trappings of Yuletide. Bon-Bons, lollies, pudding, gifts and a colourful array of hats.

Evangeline sits with Beatrice, her hair now perfectly coiffed, although she claims to have 'an appalling headache'. Harry and George can't pull the Bon-Bons apart so they enlist John to tussle with me to break them open. Then we hand out the paper jokes and toy animals. The men read the jokes, claim they're 'a load of old rubbish', then entertain us all with their own versions of the best of the best jokes of all time. They're funny and it's infectious.

I look down the two rows. It's different from the traditional image of Christmas. There are feeding aids, special plates and walking aids. Cathy stops for a second to prevent Merv eating the serviette he's just buttered. I smile. Real Christmas comes in all sizes. Family comes in all shapes. Home...well home, can be anywhere. Anywhere at all.

One day lost

If I began at the beginning, where would I begin? It became the love story of Emily and Angelo, but I did not know it then, and neither did they.

It began in childhood, or more correctly, on the brink where the edges of childhood are blurring into that deliciously confusing world of adulthood. But, this story doesn't belong in childhood. The story where their lives began to weave together began when Emily was 14 and Angelo was 16, and it still goes on and will go on forever, still intertwined and increasing in love.

Angelo was the new boy at school. But he had confidence that no new boy ever had before, or after him. Even though he had a decidedly dorky name, no one cared. He was gorgeous. Lithe and slim with the bearing of a dancer, he had all the air of a Latin lover at just 16. And the girls sighed and wept in equal portions.

At sixteen, he was enchanted by the female sex but wary. There was a world-weary essence about him as he rolled his eyes, as if he'd seen it all before. Perhaps he had, for he was one of seven—the other six being girls. His family was Spanish and his parents were stereotypically Mediterranean. The daughters laughed and said they were straight off TV.

A single sentence never contained only one language in their home. Mario and Brigitte would roll effortlessly between the two languages without seeming to know they had crossed over. The girls were a mixture of the two worlds, but Angelo was pure Aussie male. Girls were sheilas and any Latin sensitivities he would possess, he developed later, if ever.

Angelo had never lived in Spain, spoke no Spanish and didn't give a toss about anything Spanish. He didn't play down his heritage to fit in - he was just indifferent, living in the moment. Because he didn't see the difference, he was generally affronted when approached by some breathless teenage girl who wanted him to say something in Spanish, or better still sing something (he was reputed to be 'into' music.

These overtures were met with bewilderment and a fairly terse and disappointingly Aussie response, 'Get real, I don't know any frigging Spanish.'

Any expectation that this would discourage the female species was squashed by their giggles of adoration. With black hair curling onto his forehead, generous lips, and smoky eyes, they didn't care what he said. It was when his aloofness became swaggering arrogance that Emily and Angelo became close, or at least aware of each other. It could hardly be said that they became friends, because the sparks of awareness made that possibility difficult.

Emily was far more shocked than he by the strength of their attraction. A combination of total ignorance of all things sexually related, and a romantic nature, made for a lethal cocktail on Emily's part. As for Angelo, he was playing his cards so close to his chest that Emily wondered if even *he* knew what they were. She only knew that she moved him and he moved her more than any other boy had. And with the passion of the very young she just *knew* that no one else ever would or could.

It was both a beautiful and painful awakening. For such passion so early and so young had nowhere to go but sadness and confusion. They were both so uneasy it would be a year of smouldering glances before they would again risk an encounter after a muggy spring day when they shared their first kiss. And embrace.

Even though it was the most innocent of soft embraces it shook Emily to the core with the unexpected yearning it produced. The aching tenderness of it blindsided her. Coming from a home where her father was austere and remote, and her mother dominating and cheerless, she was totally unprepared for the wave of new emotions.

Other boys had carried her school bag home, but she waved them goodbye with a cheery salute. Suddenly she was being held in the arms of someone male and strong, and she didn't want to ever move away from him.

IOU One Day—signed God

'*It had been a day of endless magic*'...bother...that was too flowery.

Emily chewed the end of her pen and lay back on the porch swing that held pride of place in the small courtyard at the back of her grandparents' house. Resting her hand on her swollen belly she groaned at the task before her.

It had seemed like such a simple idea when she sat in the counsellor's rooms trying to make some sense of the dilemma her life had become. The more pregnant she became, the less it seemed to matter that she try and recall the events that caused the miracle inside her.

Today, like so many other times, she struggled to remember the day she had lost. Not just *any* day, mind you, but the day she'd lost her virginity *and* conceived the child she was carrying. She was just so tired of trying to see this memory as so all-important when she felt such joy at the life within her. This precious miracle that was somehow uniquely hers and hers alone.

She went quite willingly to the counsellor because she had no fear, no painful longing, just a nagging gap in her mind. She realised her mother, Ethel's insistence she attend counselling was prompted by the conviction that Emily would 'see sense' and abort her unborn child. Her mother's goodwill fled when she realised Emily had no intention to terminate the pregnancy.

All the usual tools of parental blackmail were used by her mother. Strident recriminations followed by tearful begging. Loud and blustering demands to 'think of us'. Exhortation for Emily to see reason and not ruin her life (and theirs by proxy).

'Pray about it dear,' her mother said. '*Pray hard.*'

Emily had, as she knelt on the hard wooden floor of the little timber church.

'Just one day - one tiny day - is that too much to ask, God?' No revelation was forthcoming. Didn't God owe her a day?

And now, sitting in the canvas swing that had held her childhood secrets, Emily sighed. Not for lost innocence and a marred future, but with the sheer relief that she was in a place of serenity. A place where it didn't matter a jot what the world outside thought or did. There was no world outside the walled rose garden of her grandparents' home.

She smiled softly at Nana Kate's huge, tabby cat as he eyed the goldfish in the outdoor pond malevolently, if somewhat impotently.

'You're too well fed, Jasper, you're not fooling anyone with that hunting routine.'

He gazed back, and as if in agreement he jumped up on the swing and curled around her feet purring majestically.

'I'm not fooling anyone either, Jasper,' she sighed as the stroked his thick, soft fur. 'Doing assignments for school was easier than this.'

Emily put down the pen and laid her head on the tasselled pillow, then followed Jasper's example and stretched. The known to the unknown was the idea. Writing down any thoughts or memories no matter how sketchy or tentative was supposed to recreate that day in her head. A memorable day that her mind refused to remember. How ironic. She had tried desperately to remember and piece the day together. Tried and failed.

It was because of the accident that she'd lost her memory, in the first place. The doctors said it was not uncommon for people to lose a few days, weeks or even years after an accident. As accidents go, it hadn't been terribly traumatic physically. Just a mild concussion. And the *other* events of the day had assumed epic proportions compared to what seemed like a little slip of the mind at the time.

She had been riding pillion on the back of her brother's bike, when he slewed around the corner, throwing her off the bike. Paul had stepped away from the bike unharmed. He'd been wearing a helmet, whereas Emily hadn't. Not many riders, much less their pillion passengers bothered in small country towns in the Sixties.

Her brother's arrest had made her memory loss seem insignificant. That is, until her mother had taken her to the doctor for gastro, and they received the shocking revelation that Emily was 12 weeks pregnant.

Ethel was one of those women who built their egos on the skeletons left over from the gossip mill. And for the first time in her life, she was at the epicentre of not one, but two scandals.

In her worst nightmares she could not have imagined such chaos. She could not fathom why Paul had been arrested for 'speeding and negligent driving causing grievous bodily harm'. She seemed to have forgotten the many police warnings that had been directed at her son for his hooligan antics. She appeared to have no concept of Paul meeting his consequences. He'd only been letting off steam on those previous occasions with no harm done.

Of course, if she had been at the local police station she would have heard the rancour from the officers about finally 'nailing that hoon and throwing the book at him'. With many of them being fathers, the thought of Paul speeding was bad enough, but to be wearing a helmet and leave his sister without one was frankly unforgiveable.

A decision

Emily massaged her swollen belly and pondered her dilemma. It seemed to cause the whole wide world more stress and anxiety than it did her. To everyone else it was crucial she remember that lost day.

Were pregnancy hormones affecting her mind? The more time passed, the less important it seemed to remember the day that had been so completely erased from her mind, by an accident she had no control over. Maybe she was just tired of prodding a reluctant brain.

Right then, she decided it didn't matter- not how or who or why. This child was. And this child was *hers.*

And would always be hers if she found the courage to claim this miracle, this baby. She would no longer spend time trying to solve the mystery. In that moment of ownership, she discovered a different truth than she had been adjured to seek.

This child was not profane; it was sacred. Her baby was not a mistake. This child was part of her, of who she was, and the woman she was to become.

She cast aside the dreadful scenes with her mother, when she had been accused of everything from drunkenness to insanity. She knew she had not been drunk then or ever, no accident would wipe her basic soul away. How dare they accuse her of being anything other than what she had always been?

And even though she retained no shred of memory, she knew in her heart that she had not been raped or abused. She had no explanations to give to her family and she would give them none, even though her mother tirelessly reminded her that she owed them that at least.

She couldn't owe them what she didn't have. She would give them the truth, nothing more. Nothing less.

She tore the page into satisfying little strips and began to write quickly and concisely all of the plans and the people she would need in her life with her child and their future.

The first step would be to tell her grandparents of her decision - and then her parents.

Emily had no illusions that she could depend on bringing this child into her parent's home. Thank God for Nana and Grandy.

The pen fell from her hand as she remembered Grandy's shining eyes when she walked through their door.

'She'll be OK,' he said, arms outstretched.

There had been a wealth of understanding in his eyes. And something more—trust. He trusted her - her actions as well as her decisions, and he would move heaven and earth to stand by her side.

Telling her grandparents she had chosen to keep her baby had been relatively easy compared to the nuclear fallout of telling her parents, or more precisely the fallout of telling her mother, Ethel. It was then Emily realised just how large a stake her mother had invested in Emily giving her baby up for adoption. She wasn't sure which was worse, the tears or the anger, the proclamations of love or the accusations, as Ethel swerved mercilessly between the two.

When Ethel delivered the ultimatum that it was abortion or adoption, it had never occurred to her that her studious, submissive daughter would do anything other than comply with one or the other.

It was inconceivable that she, Ethel, would have to face the shame of not only a pregnant daughter, but one who lived with her paternal grandparents. Thank God Leonard's parents lived three hours away. She'd be able to invent reasons for Emily's absence until she came to her senses. As she surely would.

Aiming at a show of solidarity Ethel had insisted the whole family visit to sort out the problem. Even Paul, who normally found a way around his mother, had been beaten into submission by the sheer weight of her determination.

Ethel was running out of patience.

They had been discussing things for four hours she had and

gained no leeway. She hadn't come to sit here on the patio of her husband's parents, politely pretending to enjoy afternoon tea, to be thwarted at every turn.

'Of course I don't my only daughter on the street with no roof over her head and no food in her stomach,' she said.

The superior attitude that accompanied this protestation suggested otherwise.

'I am ready to welcome my daughter back to my care and the hearth of home,' Ethel added.

This speech faltered a little when Paul said they hadn't a hearth because they were peasants.

'I got myself into this mess; I'll find a way out - without giving up my child,' said Emily.

This calm statement only served to provoke Ethel.

'A great many more people will be required to get you out of this mess, than the one who got you into it. A great number of people who didn't choose this particular mess, and who have offered solutions that haven't been listened to, much less heeded.' Ethel drew breath.

Emily chose that moment to retort, 'A great number of people called Ethel?'

'You can all go to hell!' yelled Ethel.

It was a moment of fine hysteria, and what the statement lacked in theological standing, it made up for in its ability to end the painful interchange.

Everyone knew that when Ethel consigned anyone to hell, it was over. Turning her back on Emily and her in-laws, Ethel grabbed her handbag.

Then, Paul, who had just been released from his two month sentence in the local jail, was offered the privilege of driving Ethel and Leonard home.

'Paul, dear, you've paid your debt to society. You need to get back in the saddle and hold your head high,' said Ethel, if only to emphasise the point that she was no longer talking to the others.

Paul found this casting of him in the light of Restored and Reformed much to his liking, and took leave of everyone with a newly superior nod of the head.

Nobody corrected Ethel's parting statement, but there was little surprise in that, nobody ever corrected Ethel. She barrelled forward with the certain conviction beating in her large bosom that saying her piece would bring everyone around. It was only a matter of time before the family would be restored to its original form and everyone would admit she had been right, and wonder why they hadn't listened sooner.

Ethel ran this scenario around her head a few times and liked it more and more. The others thought it strange to see a small triumphant smile play on her lips as Paul careened out the driveway, throwing gravel and nearly unseating Leonard, who'd been relegated to the back seat.

Emily and her grandparents went back into house where they sank wordlessly into the comforting depths of the faded lounge with the cabbage roses. Grandy in the recliner, Nana Jessie in the rocker, and Emily in the love seat, her feet up.

How simply and effortlessly they each found their favourite place, Emily thought, as she looked at the beloved and worn faces of the two people who had 'gone to bat' for her. How different was this place, this home? It was as if the seats were just like the 'soul' of the house—a special place for everyone where you were a perfect fit.

Her murky future seemed clearer and brighter. This was reality, this was home. She could close her eyes and see a tiny, bright new person running with arms outstretched.

Her dreams were not over, they were just beginning. She hadn't destroyed her life simply by creating another, and she would move heaven and earth to make sure her child, this child of grace, would never feel it was a mistake. Grace, that was a lovely name—maybe if she had a girl she would call her Grace.

Grandy looked around the room at his two favourite women and smiled at the likeness between them. Feisty and feminine. Cool-headed with logic, and warmth combined with love. Women of grace.

It seemed strange (no, not strange - just new) to think of Emily as a woman, but she was. For all the fuss and bother about a child having a child, Emily would be 18 in a week, and he had no doubt that she was more than capable of raising this child.

Why if that bossy, sour-mouthed Ethel could raise a gem like Emily, anyone could see that even on her own Emily had more than a fighting chance. He wasn't a gambling man, but he'd lay odds on Emily doing it, and doing it well. And she would add that special way she had of savouring every moment and 'extracting the best'.

A chuckle escaped from deep down in his chest at the thought of Ethel having to bow to the one person who'd ever defied her—her daughter.

He might be wicked, but he had enjoyed that day of reckoning. He wasn't going to miss this adventure for the world, and he thanked the gods for the good fortune that had landed his incredible granddaughter in his lap for another few rounds with life.

Nana Jessie leaned back in the faded rocker and finally allowed herself to take a long slow breath. She had watched her husband of over four decades knot and unknot his rheumatic hands. She relaxed as soon as he rested them on the arms of the recliner. As she watched the slight ripples of sleep twitch across his brown, lined face she marvelled again at her good fortune in life. She would choose this moment in life to be happy.

As she gently rocked and watched the other two she smiled a slow, indulgent smile. Let Ethel with her unerring compass for the negative, cover the dark side of the situation - heaven only knew she was up for the task. But Jessie would not travel down that road.

Contrary to what Ethel said, Jessie knew exactly what she was getting herself into by taking in this warm and witty girl, who already loved and adored her - a love that was returned. This was *her* chance too, and she would make sure it was Emily's.

Today had been a proud day for Jessie—to see Emily claim her place in the world as a woman. She had bristled in anger at the inference that Emily would 'fail and come crawling home'.

Emily had already shown maturity beyond her years. While many of her peers were chasing boys and partying, Emily was often wrapped up in her room with a book. This 'child' knew how to be a woman.

Everyone talked about how much Emily had to offer the world and how those hopes were blighted.

Ethel had made much of the notion that Emily's childhood was over, but Jessie mourned that Emily's childhood had been over before it began.

She remembered a little girl sitting alone. A little girl with a joyous smile that would light up anyone's world, and a giggle that was as outrageous as it was spontaneous.

A Goodbye

Tiny, shining tears slipped silently down each cheek. Tears that were unbidden and unchecked. More genuine than any of the surrounding finery that celebrated the passing of a life. The perfect scrolls of printed words on parchment. The perfect wreaths, vibrant with life and discordant with the soil they rested on.

Emily clutched her bouquet of wildflowers and dandelions that she'd brought as a tribute to the love she barely knew—the man she had adored, and better still *admired.*

There was a world of difference between her simple flowers and the divine display before her. This same distance had existed in her relationship to the man she now mourned as poignantly as anyone ever mourned a lost love. A distance marked by mismatched timing, separation, and the misunderstood gestures of love's first awakening.

She remembered love's first kiss. A tender mingling to speak of hope and promise. The kiss she experienced was full of tremulous anticipation and breathless delight. Angelo had added desire—damn him. How she hated him for crystallising desire and bringing the painful emotion of yearning.

And how she loved him. In that poignant moment she'd known heaven and hell. She had been introduced to the most difficult emotion she would ever deal with—Hope. One joyous moment away from heartbreak or happiness. She had not known which then, but she knew now.

Wise beyond her years, she had known that she had come close to something wonderful. And *this* she could take away with her today. This she could claim. This gift of admiration, this respect.

For just a small parcel of time she had bathed in the sunlight of his awe of her. For a moment she had danced with the gods, she had walked with angels. She had that memory, that small piece of him, the best man she'd ever known.

She smiled softly as she dropped the last of the flowers on the new earth of Angelo's grave. They were only petals now, having been twisted and torn in her hands. The wrenching of her hands had been the only outward sign of her grief.

Her calm warmth and gentle touch to the other mourners belied the emotions that swam wildly in her heart. Had she been playing a part to feign composure on such a day as this? No, the world would not give her permission to mourn this man, this love because he had never belonged to her.

It hadn't been difficult to follow his career as he rose to fame as a celebrated cellist. Although he rarely graced the society pages, he had been referred to as a personable man, if somewhat solitary. They had crossed paths on occasion. Emily had been shocked to relive the same feelings, their power undiminished, his eyes still seeking.

And now, with everyone gone, she gave herself permission to mourn the man who had never known that he was loved by her.

As she turned away from the grave, she glanced briefly up into the clear blue sky and wondered if he looked down on her now and understood. Was there anyone there with him? In her imagination she saw him turn to a faceless, cosmic companion and say, in his quiet soft, way—'She loved me best of all didn't she.'

She adjusted the snappy little black hat that added simple elegance to the basic black dress she wore. It shaded her from the relentless sun and the prying eyes of others. She wouldn't wear the dress again and she'd surprised herself by wearing it at all. In fact, she had never worn all black to a funeral before. In a kind of rebellious gesture to the bleakness of death she always wore something dark, with a splash of colour in defiance of that final sentence.

But today she'd added no touch of colour. There was no defiance today, for death had won, utterly and completely. Not only was Angelo gone, but he would never know her love.

Angelo.

She repeated his name soft and low into the gentle breeze that was beginning to pick up the fallen leaves and swirl them up from this earth and take them to another place.

Angelo, where are you going? Are you an angel now?

She turned away. Whispered on the breeze she thought she heard, 'What fools these mortals be.'

I return and you find me

And this is where he found her. Among the weeping willows with their delicate narrow leaves trailing gently in the creek. In the frivolous flower-strewn dress Grace had chosen for her that morning resplendent with promise.

There had been a quality about today since waking at dawn. The creek was moving as if it too knew of change and promise. The recent rains had made the old creek hurry and worry the eroding banks. The cement weir under the bridge once again had a fine misty waterfall flowing into the once muddy surge.

Grace had fretted over her this morning, child becoming mother, daughter gentling the nurturer—completing the cycle of love and life. Emily had resisted half-heartedly and then acquiesced to her determined daughter. She wore the dress.

At first she thought she was dreaming.

He was just the way she last remembered him. Unruly curls falling into his cloudy sensuous eyes. Lithe body stretched casually into faded, torn blue denims. He was resting against the old paper bark tree with both hands in his pockets.

'This creek is disgusting, muddy horrible thing,' she said.

The words shot out unbidden and unrehearsed. She bit her tongue. What would he think of her? But he was laughing, a full throated joyous sound.

'That's what you said on that day too.'

'What day?'

'The day God owes you.'

Emily sucked in her breath too quickly for a response.

'Yes, I am here to give you back that day.'

Oh God, now he is answering my thoughts.

He came and sat down beside her, cross-legged. A hidden memory sparked. He splayed his large hands on the checked blanket as if to show her some smooth secret blueprint.

She dared not breathe.

His large brown eyes speared hers and held them captive. He held her heart in the palm of his hand.

She breathed. 'It was here wasn't it?'

'Yes.'

'I should have known.'

'You have always known.'

'I have one day?'

'One day.'

'And then?'

His gentle eyes bid her silent, and she obeyed. He reached out one strong brown arm and encircled her, swinging her around to rest against his chest. A kookaburra laughed. The creek sang. A cricket burred. Emily melted into yesterday.

~ ~ ~

She was seventeen. In the frothy party dress she felt out of place at the creek. Throwing her strappy sandals on the ground she swore. She was too angry to cry. Why had her mother insisted she go with her brother to the party with his friends? It was bad enough having to tolerate their leers and winks at home.

Emily had dawdled and fiddled, hoping he would leave without her, but he'd called out, 'Come on sis, hurry up.'

The party had been a disaster, or the beginning had. She hadn't stayed for long. The party went on without her. After being trapped twice against the kitchen fridge by Paul's mate, Keith, with the wandering hands, who was making a precarious start on the banned alcohol, she bolted.

She would have to return. As much as she wanted to phone her parents to come and get her, she didn't want to get her brother into trouble. It was bad enough that she would have to go home on the back of his motorbike, trying to avoid burning her leg on the exhaust, while holding her floating white dress.

They would both be in trouble for that. Their parents thought the bike was safely in the shed, and that they were being driven home.

Cross and hot, she climbed down the embankment to the fort in the eucalypts where she intended to hide until the party was over.

She could still hear the raucous male voices intermingled with girlish giggles floating through the cool afternoon air.

And there she found Angelo swimming in the creek with his dark curls plastered down his smiling brown face.

'This creek is a disgusting, muddy horrible thing.'

'You cannot say that from your high horse, river nymph,' He was laughing at her.

She laughed.

'You didn't mind it the last time we were here.'

She blushed. He remembered. It had been where they'd shared their first kiss.

'So, if I'm a river nymph, are you Neptune, ruler of the deep?

'Why don't you come in here and find out.'

And it was a simple as that. Two young hearts leaving childhood, unready for the world, but prepared for love. She stripped to her bra and pants and bombed him with an outrageous shriek.

'And what brings you here, fair maiden?'

'I have escaped a fire-breathing boy with arms like an octopus.'

Angelo was immediately still in the water and leashed his arm around her like an avenging archangel.

'What happened? Tell me.

With a defiant tilt of her chin Emily began to form the words, but was stopped by his sweet hot mouth on hers. With the kiss of the cool water to guide them, their passion ignited slowly and tenderly.

'I have waited to do this a very long time,' he breathed against her slick, smooth forehead. 'But you ignored me. I watched you.'

'You withdrew from me.' She was plaintive now.

'We were children warming ourselves by the heat of an adult fire.'

They became playful. They were still. He told her of his latest composition, and talked of the master cellist he would study under for a year in Spain. He would be gone in a few weeks. She spoke of fashion design, clothing made from silken threads and nubbly wools. Her art spun into dreams, her dreams into art. They spoke of everything; except his leaving.

He showed her the hidden place under the burgeoning waterfall and found the secret places of her body and soul. They sat side by side under the waterfall in a world of their own, holding hands. With cement at their cool young backs they were cocooned with only the roaring sheet of the water in front of them.

No sounds entered their world that they did not choose or invite.

No words were said. No promises made.

They made love later, when breathless and chilled, they lay in the tree house.

'Angelo.'

'Emily.'

Twilight turned to night. She slept. Under the watchful eyes of her first lover. In his arms.

And when she left, he leant against the paper bark with his hands in the pockets of his torn blue jeans, his eyes a secret. She stopped at the edge of the clearing, turned and said, 'You never said goodbye.'

'You never said hello.'

~ ~ ~

'Angelo.'

Her heart was light as a cloud. Like a cloud shredded and scattered over the sky. How could she experience fullness and emptiness at the same time? All the questions she ever wanted to ask, he answered, with his seeking brown eyes, as he held both her hands in his and promised to watch over her and his daughter.

She closed her eyes and leant back into his arms once more. She wrapped her own slim pale arms around his strong brown ones and clasped both their hands together in front of her, their fingers intertwined. Everything was still. She felt lightness. Her breath and all the air around swept upward, drawn to another place.

She thought him gone.

'You never said goodbye,' she whispered to the wind, in sweet remembrance of that time long gone.

The only sound she heard was the scuttling of the leaves as they spiralled upwards, whirling rhythmically around the paperbark trees. She opened her eyes to bring back something familiar to her scattered mind. She looked for her old friend the creek. She saw it all - far, far below - a woman asleep against the paperbark with that same quiet smile Angelo said she wore. She saw herself, with the gentle breeze now stirring her long wild hair, as it fell over their entwined hands. She could still feel his arms around her, way up high among the whispering clouds.

'You never said goodbye.'

'I came to say hello.'

Where do you begin a sad story?

Where do you begin a sad story? At the beginning or the end? Perhaps the middle.

My mother, Elsie Brooks, died in my arms on Monday, August 3, 2009. At the end of a life lived on her own terms. I'm often cynical and question everything, but her leaving gave all the appearance that she had chosen the time, the place and the person—me, the wriggling sprite, the joyous chatterer of nonsense, but always the daughter with the open heart.

The nursing home rang to say they had sent her to hospital with renal failure, pulmonary oedema and a failing heart. Only minutes later a doctor phoned from the Emergency Department of Wyong Hospital to ask what measures should be taken. I felt the sense of something I had always known deep down inside, that I would be the one to walk that tough road. The choice was to have her put on machines: respirator, dialysis; to prolong a miserable life.

I told them her stated wishes that she did not want to be on machines, but to be comfortable. She had been in severe pain from a fractured spine for months.

A year before she'd undergone open heart surgery and been close to death.

Not long after she celebrated her 90th birthday and wanted a small gathering to say thank you to her friends.

'Good grief Mum, that's not a birthday,' I protested.

'I don't want a fuss, mind you,' she said. 'I just want to thank my friends for a lifetime of love and support.

'Okay,' I faltered, swallowing hard, wondering where she was going with this. 'How many?'

'Oh, just half a dozen or so,' she said with a vague wave of her hand.

'Okay.'

I started to organize tea and scones for a morning tea. Because she was frail, I didn't want to risk a lengthy gathering. I worded the invitations for her. My brother Peter's wife is a gifted scrapbook crafter, as are both her daughters and they were going to hand make the invitations. I sat and wrote a few names down and told her to give me the final names so that I could email them. I came back two days later and asked for the list.

'Oh that,' she said nonchalantly. 'I posted it. Modern nonsense - that computer caper.' When I asked my sister-in-law for the list I nearly fainted. The wily old bird had sixty names. To make matters worse, she told me she had casually mentioned the event to a few others.

'How many?' I squealed.

'Just the odd few,' she said.

'Who were they?'

'Don't exactly remember.'

'Are they coming to the party? Did you invite them?'

'Not precisely,' she said vaguely.

'Mum!'

'Don't give me that look! A person can't leave certain people out.'

'*Really!* Did you put it on the church notice board? The newspaper perhaps? Television advertisement? Leaflet delivery?'

She offered me the disdainful look she reserved for when she felt I didn't deserve an answer. She simply handed me her purse.

'It's my money.'

I was organizing her wake. Regal and gracious, she loved it. I couldn't speak articulately to any of the guests, for even though she would never have admitted her intent, I alone knew.

Nearly a year later after the heart surgery when we were chatting she said, 'I wanted to go when I had the operation, but when I saw how hard you tried to save me and cried for me, I couldn't leave you. Did you bring my salad sandwich?'

She often did that, said something of great moment and then went straight to the shopping list or the latest visit from a friend. My heart melted, she had stayed for me. I felt a little shame at my selfish love. We had become compatriots, friends. I became her primary carer, along with my oldest son and his wife. All my nonsense became interesting, my quick mind a blessing. She no longer tried to follow my twists and turns. She had many hospital visits. When I walked through the door to visit her she would introduce me to the staff.

'This is my daughter Linda. She is a registered nurse and she will take over now.' She delivered this speech in a tone that said she felt I was competent for anything, possibly brain surgery if necessary. Then she would rest back into the pillows and ignore the conversation. If pressed by the doctors she would fix them with a fierce gaze and repeat what she'd just said, adding, 'All this medical nonsense is over my head. It's my daughter's 'department'.'

She began to love our visits to her GP. He had grown up in our street, and he and I were on a first name basis after years of working as colleagues. Once when I wanted him to do something for her, I made an obvious ploy at buttering him up.

'You know I'm fond of you, don't you Richard?' He gave me a suspicious look and a twinkling eye.

'*Really* Linda?'

'Yes! You were the only boy in our street who didn't try to run me over with his pushbike.'

'I'm beginning to wish I had!'

When we were leaving his office Mum said, 'He enjoys us.'

I thought of the trust she was placing in me.

'You've never really seen me as a good nurse before have you Mum? Even though you saw me nurse Dad?' She gave me a scornful look as she gave the walking frame a jaunty sweep into the curve, while we turned the corner to leave the surgery.

'Ha! Well, you never nursed *me* before.' She gave an imperious look, as if I was dense not to see the perfectly obvious. It was all the explanation she saw necessary. My heart was warmed by her trust and I was amused by her straightforward logic.

My oldest son and his wife became pregnant. She was thrilled and determined to stay on and meet her latest great grandchild. They told her the baby's name, Victoria. Although in the latter months she confused us all with each other, she never forgot Victoria and awaited her arrival with eager anticipation.

Mum's hopes were not to be.

When I arrived at the Emergency Department on that bleak day in August, I was taken to the Resuscitation room. The young nurse attending her told me Mum was terribly confused.

Mum opened her eyes, pointed at me and said, 'Lin.' Then she looked at the nurse and pointed at me again, pulling at the heart monitor cords with all her strength to remove them, until she had freed them and placed them on the over-bed table.

'That's not confusion. That's eloquence,' I responded.

I thought back to the many times she had said, 'This is my daughter Linda, she is a registered nurse' ... and I knew that Mum was fully aware of her state, she was just too weak for the whole speech. She didn't feel the need to say anymore. I had arrived and she was 'my department'.

Her lungs were filling with fluid and it was difficult for her to speak. She was wracked with pain and murmuring soft mewling moans. I phoned my brother and we both knew putting her on machines was wrong and against her wishes. We consented to 'comfort measures'. The staff allowed me to stay in the room while I phoned him and his wife, because her eyes were constantly seeking me wherever I moved in the room. I didn't want her to be alone. Once when I had asked her what she wanted she had simply said, 'I don't want to be alone.' So I had told her I would move heaven and earth to be with her.

After a difficult conversation with my brother, where Mum recognized my sister-in-law's voice I sat down beside her, cradling her arm, stroking her hand.

Then, she looked up towards the ceiling, smiled and waved.

She turned to me, her eyebrows furrowed in a question.

'Yes, Mum,' I said, aware and yet not knowing, putting all my heart into a smile of reassurance.

'Yes,' she repeated peacefully. 'Yes.'

Several times her eyes returned to mine.

She mentioned my son's name with the same questioning look. 'Yes, Mum.'

She whispered his wife's name; another question.

'Yes, Mum.'

'Yes. Yes.'

They gave her some slow release morphine for the pain, and arranged the ambulance to take her back to the palliative care room at the nursing home. As the ambulance men transferred her, she gave them a sharp look. I remembered her telling me the year before that they were 'as rough as hessian underpants', and I smiled.

I was waiting back at the nursing home when they brought her out of the ambulance. She took a long look towards the clear blue sky, drinking it in, then breathed a calm deep breath. When we arrived in the palliative care room she looked serene; the groaning breathing had eased. She looked deep into my eyes, lifted her left arm, curved her right arm towards me, reaching for my embrace. I held her, kissing her neck. I looked into her face. She closed her eyes.

Her heart failed and mine constricted, tight with the agony she would no longer feel. One last lingering sigh and she was gone from me. After decades of nursing and comforting others, the sister standing beside me held me and stilled my wrenching sobs.

I stayed with her while they washed and dressed her, ordering the nurse to take back the black cardigan and bring a pink one to dress her in—it had always been her favourite colour. Then I sat beside her—alone with death. I cried, I talked and drank cups of tea.

'Don't be bossy in heaven Mum. Don't tell people to take off their shoes before they come in the door, because heaven doesn't care. Heaven doesn't care about a lot of things you cared about. And you were wrong all your life - because you were not 'an ugly old thing' or a 'silk purse out of a sow's ear'. You are beautiful now, and always were.'

There wasn't much more to say, because we had forgiven and been forgiven. Been lost and found. In the manner of our jigsaw puzzling games on holidays, we had carefully put the pieces back into place as we had talked and listened many times, understanding each other and life.

How can I accuse and acquit in the same moment? Grace, love and an intimate knowledge of my own human frailties, flaws and mistakes. Her hard-worn hands had laboured for me; toiled and fought battles, some necessary, some not.

She was a child of her generation where walls were built to protect children from seeing the pain of life, the reality, but also the authenticity of themselves, as parents and human beings. The generation who thought they were doing right by us by 'letting alone' some subjects. I thought of the Berlin Wall and how its tumbling descent had brought jubilation. I felt privileged that I had witnessed both of my parents tear down that wall as they faced death. I thought of how my brother and I had hated those walls and walked into parenthood with open emotions, hearts and minds, leaving nothing unsaid, undone along the way. I knew when I walked through that palliative care door to leave my mother; I would have to go on with my life, so I stayed with her until I was ready.

'You never needed any Berlin Walls, Mum. I love you,' were my last words to her.

The night before the funeral I spent the entire night throwing up and trying to convince the family it was a virus. Two wards at Wyong hospital had been isolated due to gastric flu.

At the funeral I held the hand of my beloved cousin, his sweetheart wife on my other side.

The funeral, like every other area of her life, was planned to her wishes. She didn't want accolades or a life sketch. I often went to funerals with her over the years and had a lifetime of hints and instructions.

'Don't let them do *that* at my funeral,' she would intone severely.

'Shush Mum! It's a funeral. You're talking too loud, remember you're deaf.'

She would ignore me completely, looking ahead with imperious indifference.

The Pastor who conducted the service was a lifelong family friend who had been given the status of 'honorary Stockdale'. He spoke of this—he was brother, father and friend to Mum. As I sat clutching one of her handkerchiefs, I was about to plunge into grief and despair when the sound system playing her favourite hymn, 'Be Still My Soul', faded and rattled, grew loud, then soft, then loud again. Dad had been the sound technician at their church. In my mind, I could see her face frowning and knew what she would have said.

'That wouldn't have happened if Max was here.'

As the pastor filed past the family with his condolences I asked him when he was going to adopt me after such fine words of family. He looked terrified and laughed.

'You'd talk in the coffin.'

He visited us the next morning. I bounded up to him.

'Hi Dad,' I said with a welcoming smile.

'Get away from me. I've been hurling all night.'

Now, I proudly wear her wedding ring, the ring of trust between the flawed and wonderful people who were my parents.

Mum used to tie a piece of string around my finger to make me remember things when I went on childhood errands.

'Now that will help you to remember,' she would pronounce confidently.

I would return with the piece of string intact, but without the thing she desired.

'What is wrong with you? I put a piece of string on your finger!'

'The piece of string forgot too.'

But I will never forget what that ring means.

'Don't ever stop living when you grieve for me,' she had often said.

I will go on.

The story is told in an ancient book; of justice that reigns from a kingdom afar, where a judge sits in judgment, no jury, no bar. If in that high court I am called to witness, I will come for the defence and not as accuser. But, as the story goes, there is One who was crippled, beaten and defeated, who will stand in her place, no punishment, no crime.

Author

The rich texture of Linda's life is reflected in her writing, which is both joyful and poignant. With her own brand of raw humour and courage, Linda's writing engages the reader.

Linda was drawn to nursing. She watched and listened to the rich fabric of the lives of others. Fascinated by their stories from the ordinary to the extraordinary, she brings this love of people to the page. Linda spent many years as a registered nurse working in aged care facilities, as a community nurse and in child care. As a career, nursing was Linda's first love and this book is a fine example of that passion.

Linda was born and raised a small country town on the east coast of Australia, near Lake Macquarie. Her friends tell her she should be a stand-up comedienne, which is a good way to terrify Linda; she would rather write and paint.

Linda writes regularly for the local Gazette, and gives author talks to support groups for the Autism spectrum. She is a passionate advocate for Asperger's and disability rights.

A Curious & Inelegant Childhood was Linda's first published book. She uploaded many of her warm and humorous stories to 'The Making of Modern Australia' website, run by the ABC, where they regularly ended up in the Highest Rated section.

Her story *A Dangerous Time* was chosen by the producers as one of a few *Featured Stories*. Her stories also landed on top of the pile with readers and she caught the eye of a publisher.

Other titles by the author:

Nonfiction:
A Curious & Inelegant Childhood

Adult fiction:
Behind Whispering Hands
The Unprize
Scarlett doesn't live here anymore
Under the Bracken Fern

Children's books:
A Tabby Never Forgets
An Angels Tears
Beth's Christmas Wish
Callan the Chameleon (Asperger's Syndrome)
Dusty Bunny's Very Important Job
Ethereal Land
Izzy & Pudding the Cat
I want a monkey!
Madam Iris Bigglesworth
The Frog that Hiccupped
Who Stole Christmas?

Publisher of the anthologies:
We are Australian
The Great Australian Shed
Waltzing Matilda

www.ingramcontent.com/pod-product-compliance
Lightning Source LLC
Chambersburg PA
CBHW061920130726
47908CB00016B/523